Guilty For You

A.M. McCoy

Contents

Copyright	V
Chapter 1 – Delilah	1
Chapter 2 – Delilah	9
Chapter 3 – Delilah	19
Chapter 4 – Delilah	31
Chapter 5 – Delilah	45
Chapter 6 – Delilah	63
Chapter 7 – Delilah	73
Chapter 8 – Delilah	81
Chapter 9 – Delilah	93
Chapter 10 – Delilah	101
Chapter 11 – Delilah	113
Chapter 12 – Delilah	129
Chapter 13 – Delilah	137
Chapter 14 – Delilah	143
Chapter 15 – Delilah	151
Chapter 16 – Delilah	157
Chapter 17 – Delilah	169

Chapter 18 – Delilah ... 175

Chapter 19 – Delilah ... 183

Chapter 20 – Delilah ... 193

Chapter 21 – Delilah ... 207

Chapter 22 – Delilah ... 217

Chapter 23 – Delilah ... 223

Chapter 24 – Delilah ... 235

Chapter 25 – Delilah ... 243

Chapter 26 – Delilah ... 255

Chapter 27 – Fox ... 261

Chapter 28 – Fox ... 271

Chapter 29 – Delilah ... 277

Chapter 30 – Fox ... 285

Chapter 31 – Delilah ... 289

Chapter 32 – Fox ... 297

Chapter 33 – Delilah ... 307

Chapter 34 – Fox ... 313

Chapter 35 – Fox ... 319

Chapter 36 – Delilah ... 329

Chapter 37 – Delilah ... 341

Chapter 38 – Fox ... 353

Epilogue – Delilah ... 359

Epilogue – Fox ... 367

Other Books ... 371

COPYRIGHT

Chapter 1 – Delilah

Present

I closed the linen closet door with more force than necessary, but it was better than screaming at the infuriatingly needy woman in bed eight. In the six hours that she'd been in the ER, she had requested three different meals because the options given by the hospital cafeteria were not up to her standards, an almond milk mocha latte with cold foam, a private room because the little boy on the other side of the curtain cried too much, and every pain killer known to man.

For her broken toe.

Had to love rural Emergency Rooms on Saturdays.

To get my silent revenge on the patient from hell, I moved the sick little boy who cried too much for her liking to a private room down the hall so he wouldn't have to deal with anyone else like her while we treated him for his food poisoning. It was the least I could do to make up for her unacceptable behavior toward the sweet little baby.

I enjoyed the outraged look on her face when she realized he was getting the private room, not her.

"Delilah." Dr. Franklin called from the nurse's desk, "Can I see for you a minute?" He nodded curtly toward the brightly lit on-call room, then pushed through the door, leaving me no choice but to follow.

"Shit," I whispered, the word catching in my throat as I watched Winnie's suggestive eyebrow dance and a low, throaty snicker rumble in her chest. "Shut up." I flicked my best friend's ear as I walked past her. I felt like a kid again on my way to the principal's office.

"What's up, Doc?" I asked lightly, betraying the anxiety pulsing through my body.

Dr. Oliver Franklin leaned against the counter with his long legs stretched out in front of him, and crossed at the ankle as he stirred a cup of coffee with a straw. He was in his mid-thirties and attractive in a golden boy next-door kind of way, with perfectly combed blonde hair and bright blue eyes.

The exact opposite of my type.

"I want to check in with you. Make sure you're all right, because you seem frazzled today." My time in the Belden Community Hospital ER spanned a few years, and among the on-call physicians I worked with, Dr. Oliver was the one with whom I paired up with most. While we were friendly, we weren't friends.

I was too jaded and cynical; I didn't make friends easily anymore.

He never stopped trying, though. While that was commendable, given that I wasn't ever a ray of sunshine, it was a lost cause.

"I'm good. Bed eight is just testing my patience today." I said, swiping my bangs back from my face to look at the clock over his shoulder. "I should get back to her actually, it's been ten minutes since the last time she rang her call bell. She's probably going through withdraws without my lovely disposition."

He smirked and sipped his coffee, "Yeah, she's been a real pain in the ass today." He sighed, "And I only do a third of what you do."

"The sooner ortho gets down here to give her the second opinion she's requesting, the better for everyone involved." I smiled and took a step backward towards the door.

He leaned up off the counter, "Before you go," he cleared his throat and set his coffee down. "There's something else I wanted to ask you."

Fuck.

Don't do it, Oliver.

Please don't do it.

I was already cringing internally as he smiled his pretty boy smile at me that no doubt made these small-town girls melt for him. Because any girl would be lucky to have Oliver Franklin smile at them like he was me, but I wasn't interested in his smiles. I wasn't the type of girl that could let pretty boy smiles like his affect me anymore.

He went on, bold and brave, and I had to give him some credit for that, knowing I was less than approachable on a good day, and today wasn't even close to a good day. "Do you want to grab a bite to eat some night? Maybe grab a beer or something over at Cherry's."

"Uh-," I bit my lip and tried to get my words right to let him down gently, seeing as how he was my boss after all. "I appreciate-,"

He cut me off, holding his hand up, "Don't say no." He smiled again and took a couple of steps forward, "You never go out, you never meet up with the group or anything. You just work." He laughed when I rolled my eyes good heartedly, "You deserve to take a break from life and have some fun."

"I can't." Interrupting him, "I appreciate the offer, I do, I'm just not at a spot to go out and have fun right now." I took a step back towards the door and smiled to lessen the refusal, "I appreciate it, though."

He nodded with his little smirk still in place. "I hear you. I'll let you off the hook this time, but I'm going to try again someday. Because this sleepy little town doesn't get fresh faces very often, and we *never* get pretty ones like yours." He winked. "But we can table it for now."

"Okay, Casanova." I smirked back and then walked out before he could say anything else embarrassing.

Winnie looked over the top of her computer screen with mischief in her eyes as I walked back to my desk. "Not a word." I hissed at her.

She snorted and wagged her eyebrows at me again, "Told you he wanted to make pretty little babies with you."

I looked at the clock again and mentally counted the minutes until my shift was over.

"Mama!" Penelope screamed as I walked in the back door of our rental house a few hours later.

"Oof." I grunted and caught her midair off the chair she'd been standing on at the counter.

My four-year-old was almost as tall as I was, and it was getting harder to carry her every day. "I missed you, Mama." She said and clung to my neck.

"I missed you too, June Bug." I said and kissed her head before setting her back down on the chair at the counter. She had more nicknames than I had room for in my memory, but somehow I added to the list regularly. Penelope June was her full name, but she was called an array of Penny, Juney, PJ, June Bug, or my baby sister's favorite, PB&J. "What are you doing?"

"We're making you cookies to take to work tonight." She said proudly.

My sister, Madeline, walked back into the room with a bag of chocolate chips in her hands and a bright smile on her face. "Hey, Sis."

"Hi." I nodded to the bowl of batter on the counter, "My favorite. What did I do to earn those?"

She shrugged her shoulders, "Just thought you could use the pick me up between jobs."

"I appreciate it." I flashed her a grin. "I'm going to go shower off the hospital."

"I just finished a load of laundry, so I don't know how much hot water you'll have." She grimaced, and I shrugged my shoulders.

"I don't even hate the cold showers anymore, to be honest." Kissing PJ on the head again, I headed for the stairs. "I'll make dinner when I get out."

"Good! Because I was drawing blanks on a menu for the night." Maddie joked. She was never good at cooking. Baking yes, cooking no.

Dragging my aching body up the creaky stairs, I went to my small bedroom and fought the urge to just strip down and crawl under the covers and forgo a shower all together.

And I probably would have if I didn't have to be at Cherry's in a few hours.

Which meant I only had a few hours with my baby girl before she went to bed, and I was determined to make the most of it.

Even if I didn't have an ounce of energy left inside of me.

I'd fake it for her.

Just like I had for the last four years.

Because that was my role as a single mom.

So instead of crawling in bed and losing myself to the sorrow like I wanted to, I made dinner and played three games of Candy Land with PJ and Maddie before bedtime at eight. And by eight thirty I was walking into Cherry's for my Saturday night bartending shift. I made good money as a nurse in the ER, especially with overtime basically always available.

But two weekend night shifts at Cherry's gave me almost the same amount of money in tips alone. So, I forced my tired body to put on the revealing clothes that helped my endeavor and poured beer for another six to eight hours after a grueling ER shift.

I'd face the weekend throngs at the bar, a chaotic crush of bodies and booming music, even if it felt like it was draining the life out of me.

"Hey, babe." Lora, my partner bartender, called as I threw my bag behind the bar. "Busy place already."

"Yay." I droned on and she winked, popping open a Redbull and handing it to me before tossing one in upside down into a fishbowl drink she was making. "Thanks."

"Anytime." She winked and turned to give her drink to the server, waiting.

I clocked in and pounded the energy drink and then restocked my station and got to work.

The music was loud.

The smoke was thick.

And the men were on their game, throwing pickup lines and big tips every time I turned around, flashing them a seductive smile and a glimpse of my tits over the top of my tight tank.

What a great Saturday night.

Because this was what I lived for, if I was honest.

Pretty boy smiles and clean-cut faces didn't do it for me.

Gnarled whiskey smiles and three-day-old stubble on faces that were scarred and rough were the only things to get my blood pumping.

Thanks to *him*.

In his own way, his roughness had ruined me for anyone soft. I never stood a chance of finding a good, gentle man to keep me warm at night because the only things I craved were calloused hands and rough kisses.

Rough, like my fucking life had been since the day I met him, too.

Because Paxton St. Claire was never gentle. Not in the way he seduced me. Or the way he loved me. Nor the way he destroyed me.

He ruined my chances of ever being in a healthy relationship as an adult because I had been just a kid in a relationship with a fucked-up man that left me with a baby and a headstone to love. He turned his back on me and walked away forever.

So, I got my high on dangerous encounters with men that should scare me. I lived on the edge a few nights a week before crawling into bed next to my perfect little baby girl that the rough man had given me, pretending I was normal and nice, like everyone thought I was.

Chapter 2 – Delilah

Past

"Whatcha doing?" Blaine asked as he flopped down on my bed next to me. He reeked like skunky weed and day-old booze, and I turned my nose up at him. Even if he was my brother and best friend, I had limits to my love, and his smell was one of them.

"God, you stink. You know that, right?" I curled my lip and pulled my pillow out from underneath his head.

"I don't smell any worse than Fox does, but you still swoon over him every time he comes around." He challenged with a smirk, grabbing my pillow back and fluffing it under his head.

"Wrong." I replied, "He never smells like body odor like you do."

He snorted, "But you don't deny swooning over him."

"Whatever." I felt the flush crawl up my cheeks at how he trapped me. "Do you even know what swooning means?"

He looked over at me as I sat crossed legged next to him, "You got it bad for him, huh?"

"No." I said instantly and rolled my eyes at him. "He's just nice to me."

"Fox isn't nice to anyone. That's literally how he got his name. He sneaks into little hen houses like this one and eats defenseless girls like you for dinner."

I rolled my eyes at him again, reached into my bedside drawer and grabbed the taser he got me after break-ins started happening more often around our house. "I'm not defenseless."

"Hmm." He hummed and laid his head back down on the pillow.

"Where have you been?" I asked him, "You haven't been home in three days."

"Around." He shrugged his shoulders and let his eyes close.

"You're going to get yourself killed running *around* like that, Blaine." I said for the millionth time since he started hanging out with a rough crowd a few years ago. He dropped out of school in his senior year and got a job at a motorcycle garage across town. And then he'd gotten dragged into the MC's drama and problems and it worried me every single time he rode off on his bike.

"Hmm." He said again, and I huffed, "Only the good die young, Delilah, you know that."

"You are good." I reminded him, "Or at least you used to be."

"You're good, D. Maddie is good." He said with his eyes closed, "I'm just trying to make sure you two stay good. If I can do that, then I can die a happy man, whenever that happens."

Running my fingers through his dirty blonde hair, he groaned, always a sucker for a good head scratch. "I need you, Blaine." I whispered, "It's hard keeping Maddie on the straight and narrow on my own."

Our dad dipped on us when we were kids, and mom died two years ago in a car accident on her way home from the hospital. She had worked a double shift in the ER and fell asleep behind the wheel on her way home. The firefighters said she died on impact, but it didn't help ease the pain in my chest every time I remembered opening the front door at three am to the police officers there to inform her three teenage kids that she was never coming home.

Blaine had been saddled with raising a sixteen and fourteen-year-old because we didn't have anyone else that cared to help out.

And I loved him for it.

But the last year or so, he'd been around even less than normal, and I hated how the distance felt more than just physical between us anymore.

"If anyone has a prayer of keeping her straight, it's you D. Not me." He said and yawned, with his eyes closed as I continued to play with his hair.

"Yeah." I said sadly, feeling the weight of the task pushing my shoulders down further.

He was asleep within a few minutes, and I went back to studying for my anatomy test the next day. Maddie was at her friend's house for the night, so it was quiet in the house as I tried to memorize the different veins and arteries in the arms of a human by looking at pictures of my dissected cat in the lab at school.

Nursing school was weird.

I was so engrossed in the red and blue blood ways that when a figure in my doorway finally caught my attention; I jumped and covered my mouth to keep from screaming in surprise.

Fox.

Blaine's best friend stood in my bedroom doorway with his shoulder leaning against the frame and his arms crossed over his wide chest like he didn't have a care in the world.

His dark hair was long and shaggy, hanging around his shoulders tonight to match the dark stubble on his jaw. He had cleaned up since work at the motorcycle garage, and he wore his signature white tee and dark wash blue jeans over his motorcycle boots.

And my god, did he look yummy in it.

"Hey." I whispered when my tongue finally unstuck itself from the roof of my mouth.

"Hey." He said back quietly. His hazel eyes flicked to my brother, who laid on his stomach with his boots hanging off the end of my bed, snoring into my pillow, then back to me.

I looked down at my brother and then up at him, "Are you here to steal him away from me again?" I asked.

He raised his eyebrow at me and leaned up off the doorframe to walk across my room and lower himself down in the chair next to my side of the bed. I scanned around my room for anything embarrassing lying out that he might see, as he kicked his long legs out and crossed his ankles. He was so close I could smell him.

But he didn't stink like Blaine did.

He smelled like his aftershave and mechanical grease.

It was intoxicating.

"You think I take him from you?" He asked quietly.

"You think you don't?" I challenged him.

Which was nuts, because Blaine was right. Fox wasn't a nice guy.

He was one of those guys who usually stayed quiet at the edge of the crowd until needed; then he moved with such speed and grace that you never saw him coming until it was too late.

He was one of the enforcers of the MC that Blaine and he were in, and he was scary as fuck because of it.

But not to me.

Or at least I tried to pretend he wasn't.

"I think Blainey's a big boy who makes his own decisions." He said, watching me closely.

The oversized graphic tee, a hand-me-down from Blaine's high school days, and the ridiculously short cheerleading shorts left me feeling exposed and frumpy; the worn cotton felt uncomfortable against my skin. I needed to be fully clothed and stunning to feel adequate around Fox.

"Either way, we need him here."

"Why?" He lobbed back.

"Because." I sighed, "There are..." I threw my hand up in frustration and then sighed, "Never mind. You wouldn't understand."

"Why wouldn't I understand?"

"Because you don't have anyone to take care of like us, and you're not a girl yourself. So, you just don't get it."

"Try me." He contested, running his thumb back and forth over his bottom lip. I doubted he meant anything by it, but it made me want to taste the flesh he rubbed and made it hard to focus.

"Why do you care?" I threw back with a shake of my head. "I'll just wake him up so you two can be on your way." Fox reacted quicker than me; before my hand reached my brother, he seized my arm and pulled it back.

His fingers were hot wrapped around my wrist and his face was right in front of mine as he leaned over the bed. "Tell me why you need him here with you, Delilah."

He didn't pull back, his face stayed only inches from mine, his warm breath ghosting my skin, and his mesmerizing green eyes held me captive. I'd never been this close to him before.

I licked my lips and swallowed, and his eyes darted down to my lips before snapping back up.

"Because we get hassled when he's gone." I whispered.

Fox's jaw clenched, making the muscles in his cheeks pop and roll under the skin. "By whom?" His voice was menacing and low, and I shivered. He cocked his head to the side and moved my arm back to my lap, sliding his palm over the sensitive skin of my inner wrist. "Who, Delilah?"

"The neighbors." I nodded my head towards my window, looking over the backyard and to the house behind ours.

"JJ." There was a strange, almost hypnotic glow in his eyes; I felt powerless to deny him anything he asked for. "What does he do?"

"He just hassles me."

"When?" He snapped, "How, Delilah?"

My brother stirred next to me and popped his head up, glaring sleepily at his best friend and me as we faced off with his hand still on me. "What the fuck's going on?"

"JJ's been harassing your sisters when you're not here." Fox bit out, "Did you know that?"

"What?" Blaine snapped, sitting up and scrubbing his hand over his face. "What do you mean? What are you doing here, man?"

Fox didn't look at my brother, he never pulled his eyes from mine or backed up, "Tell me what he does to you." He asked again.

I swallowed, aware of Blaine's eyes on us and how my arm still burned from Fox's touch. "He bangs on the doors and throws things at the windows. Calls out obscenities, all night sometimes."

"Why didn't you tell me that?" Blaine cursed, standing up and pacing the room.

"Because you're—." I paused and shook my head, hating the accusation that burned the back of my throat.

"Because I'm not around." He finished for me, and Fox let go of my arm and leaned back a bit.

"Blaine." I started and stopped, not sure what to even say, because he was right.

"I'll take care of it." My brother said, nodding to Fox. "Let's go."

"What?" I cried, unfolding my legs, and standing up as Fox rose and followed Blaine out of my room. "No," I panicked.

JJ and his crew next door were bad news. Unaligned with any local club or gang, they faced no rules or consequences. They had no leader to keep them in line. Instead, they wreaked havoc on everyone because they could.

For some time, they had been harassing Fox and Blaine's MC, the Rust Hawks. Which meant that a storm was brewing under the surface, just waiting for a spark to ignite the fight. And I had just given that to Blaine.

"Please, Blaine." I followed them down the hallway and the stairs. Fox was between me, and my brother and I clawed at his arm to get around him. "Don't do anything Blaine!"

Fox spun around as Blaine flew out the front door and pressed me back into the wall. "Stay. Here."

"Please don't." I begged, pushing against his muscular body to no avail. "Please." I begged. "He'll get hurt!" I cried.

I knew my brother did illegal things with his MC and I'd seen him fight a dozen or more times, so I knew he could hold his own. But JJ's crew was bigger than just him and Fox.

"I got him." Fox said, pushing me back against the wall again as I fought him. "Delilah!" He yelled, pressing his large body against mine until I had no choice but to be still against him. "I promise you; I've got his back. Nothing bad will happen to him."

"Paxton, let's go!" Blaine yelled from outside as he started up his motorcycle.

"Paxton?" I asked, but he shook me off.

"Stay inside." He said and his eyes flicked from my eyes to my lips as I bit my bottom one and sucked it into my mouth to stop myself from yelling at him like I wanted to.

"Fox." I groaned, tightening my hands in his shirt against his stomach, "Please don't go," I begged, "Just get him and come back inside and just let it go."

His nostrils flared, and he swallowed, "No one harasses you, D. Not on your brother's watch. And sure, as fuck not on mine." He growled and then backed up and walked out the front door without a backwards glance.

I sagged into the wall before my panic forced my feet to move, running for the front door and watching as Fox threw his leg over his large motorcycle and looked at me, "Inside, D." He yelled over the roar of his loud pipes. "Now!" He pointed at the house, and I backed up into the doorway.

Blaine nodded at me and then took off, with Fox roaring down the street behind him.

"Fuck!" I screamed and then went back inside and locked the door behind me.

Hours later, I woke up, sensing a noise or something had disturbed me, but I couldn't remember what it was. I laid there still as a statue and listened for it again, and then I heard it.

Breathing.

Not mine.

I bolted upright in my bed and gasped when I saw a shadowy figure sitting in the chair next to my bed.

"Shh, D." Fox's deep voice rumbled through the darkness, and I gasped for breath in alarm.

"What are you doing here?" I hissed and looked over at the clock on my end table. *Four am.* "Where's Blaine?" I ripped my blanket off and threw my legs out of bed in a panic. If Fox was here, that meant that Blaine wasn't.

"Shh," he said, leaning forward to put his hands on my arms and push me back into bed. "He's passed out on the couch downstairs."

I took a deep breath and stared at him in confusion. "He's okay?" I asked finally.

"Perfect as a peach." He smirked and I could see his white teeth in the darkness as he leaned back into the chair.

I swallowed and ran my hand through my long hair, pushing it out of my face. "What are you doing up here, then?" I asked.

"Fuck if I know." He sighed, running his hand over his jaw and then paused. "You should get back in bed." He replied, leaning forward to pick the blanket up off the floor before holding it out for me. "Cover up."

"Why?" I took the blanket from his hand and shivered when our fingers touched.

"D." He groaned, "Cover up." He was close enough now that I could see his eyes through the darkness and noticed he was staring at my chest.

When I looked down, I saw that my sleep tank had shifted, and most of my right breast was visible to the intriguing man.

"Oh." My nipples were painfully erect and clearly visible through the thin material as I pulled the strap of my sleep shirt back up. In a rush of shame, I grabbed the thin cotton blanket and pulled it over my chest, hoping to disappear.

Fox sighed and scrubbed his hand over his face again, "Go back to sleep." He yawned, "Everyone is safe for the night."

"And what about you, *Paxton*?" I asked, as he leaned back in the chair with a glare, "Aren't you tired?"

"Hmm." He hummed, and I watched as his eyelids closed and he laid his head back. "Don't ever call me Paxton again, D. My name is Fox."

"Blaine called you that."

"Only because it pisses me off." He said with his eyes still closed, "And I don't want you to piss me off."

I sat there and watched him for a few minutes as he silently fell asleep in my chair, wondering why on earth he'd want to sleep in my room, bunched up in my chair instead of at his own place in his bed.

But I'd be lying if I said it didn't give me a sense of security knowing a giant, intense, powerful man was sleeping a few feet away after the fear I'd felt at night lately.

I quietly laid on my side facing him and pulled the blanket up over my body as I watched him sleep. Before long, a peaceful slumber pulled me under as well.

Chapter 3 – Delilah

Present

I laid on the couch with my little girl tucked in against my side, watching TV after another hectic work week. I had to go to Cherry's in a couple of hours, and the idea of leaving PJ was gutting me for some reason.

My sister, Maddie, came downstairs with a yawn and a stretch before flopping down on the other end of the couch.

"How was class?" I asked her. She did online classes for her business degree, and it worked out splendidly for us because she could stay at home with PJ while I went to work. It saved me the cost of childcare, which was astronomical, and it saved her the cost of rent, so she didn't have to work and could focus on her studies.

"Boring, but good." She said, picking up PJ's feet to put on her lap so she had more room.

Our house lacked a lot of things, and big comfortable furniture was one of them. That shit was expensive and providing for three people on my income alone was hard, so we dealt with what we had.

"Grades still good?" I asked her and she rolled her eyes.

"Yes, Mother."

Penelope snickered, "Mama, are you staying home tonight?" She turned and looked up at me.

"No," I pushed her long dark hair back from her face, "I have to work tonight, but I'll be home when you wake up."

"Okay," She sighed and laid her head back down on my lap.

"You know," Maddie started, "I could take your weekend shifts, so you could stay home."

"No." I grunted, shifting my daughter from my lap so I could get up and walk away from the conversation.

But my baby sister followed me into the kitchen when I stopped to make a cup of coffee. "I can handle sixteen hours a week, Delilah. Let me shoulder some of the burden."

"No." I cut her off, "The deal was you'd stay home and focus on your studies, and I'd take care of the bills."

"But you're dying here." She propped her hip against the counter and crossed her arms. "You're skinny and tired all the time, and you hardly even eat anymore." She sighed, "All you do is work and take care of Penelope and me, and I appreciate it. I get it, Delilah, but don't you want more for yourself?"

"Like what?"

"I don't know," She threw her hands in the air, "Love. Friendship with someone beside me. Literally anything outside of these walls."

I rolled my eyes and blew on my coffee, "I don't have time for any of that."

"That's my point!" She protested, "If I took Friday and Saturday night work from you, you could go out and have fun."

"And who's going to watch P?" I snapped, annoyed by the same conversation we'd been having for years. "You'd be at work, and I'd still be here at home."

"You could find someone and incorporate him into your life here at home."

"Agh," I cringed, hating how that idea made me feel. "I'm not interested in bringing anyone into our lives. That's not up for discussion."

"It's been five years, D."

"I know how long it's been." I shuddered hearing it out loud. "It's my vagina, after all."

She pursed her lips and sighed again. "I just want you to be happy."

Forcing a smile to my lips, I leaned over and kissed her cheek. "I think I've lost too much to truly ever be happy again, Maddie." For the first time in five years, I admitted my greatest fear. "I think this is all I am anymore. And I'd appreciate it if you'd refrain from pointing out where I'm lacking."

"I didn't mean to make it sound bad." She cringed.

I snorted and opened the fridge to figure out what to make for dinner, "Yes you did. But that's okay, just don't do it again."

"Mama," Penelope interrupted our conversation by moseying into the kitchen, "I'm hungry."

I smiled at my sweet baby with her dark hair and sea glass green eyes, "I'm on it, Toots."

"Good." She said and climbed up in a chair at the table, "Because Aunt Maddie can't cook, and she always burns the freezer pizza when you're not home."

"Hey!" My baby sister objected, "I do not."

My daughter rolled her eyes at her and smirked at me knowingly.

Those two were all I needed.

"Hey, big tits," A gruff voice called from behind me, "Get me another Bud."

I fought the urge to tell him to fuck off as I rang out another tab at the computer and schooled my face before turning around.

"If you ask nicely, I'll think about it." I smirked and leaned over the bar top to pick up his glass.

"Please," he looked directly at my tits that I laid on the wood for him to admire. "Can I have another Bud?" He was one of my usual customers, but I'd be damned if I could remember his name. All I knew was he drank no less than a dozen drafts every time he came in and tipped twenty-five bucks ahead of time each night. So, he could call me whatever he wanted as long as he paid his cash up front.

"Yes, you may." I smiled sweetly at him and pulled another draft for him. "Didn't your mama ever teach you that you get further with honey than vinegar?" I asked him.

"Hmm." He snorted with his friends and tilted his head to look down at my ass. "You got enough honey for both of us, baby."

"Nah," I grimaced, "I'm all whiskey at this point in my life. The only thing I attract anymore is crotchety old men like you." I winked at him and moved down the bar to another customer as they roared with laughter. I could almost hear the big tips cha-ching in the tip jar from their drunk asses.

"Hey," Lora said, sliding up next to me. "Taz is here."

I froze, punching in the order I'd been doing and looked at her, "With his whole crew?"

"Mmh-hmm." She nodded and grabbed a liquor bottle off the shelf. "Just a heads up."

"Thanks." I groaned and got back to what I was doing.

Avoiding the crew for as long as I could, I let my other customers keep me busy enough to ignore them. But Taz always gravitated towards my end of the bar when I was working, and his crew was big enough to push out anyone that had been sitting there until I had no choice but to acknowledge them.

"Fellas." I said with a sweet smile while wiping down the bar top, "What can I get ya?"

"Well, you can start by going out for a smoke with me on your next five-minute break." Taz said, looking at me up and down as he licked his lips.

In terms of scum bags, he was alright to look at. He was tall and in somewhat good shape with a good head of hair and nice teeth. He was near my age, a bit older if I had to guess. But that was where his good features ended. He was the ringleader of a small time MC that had just moved to the area and from what I could tell from the locals' chatter, they weren't welcome.

But that didn't stop them.

They were the bad penny crowd, just like JJ's crew had been back home. They didn't belong, but they were just big enough to push their weight around to cause trouble.

There was already an MC in the area, The Black Eagles, who were notoriously private and lethal. No one even dared to talk about them, for fear that The Eagles would appear out of thin air and retaliate if it was negative in any way.

So, I knew Taz and his crew, The Riders, were living on borrowed time. And I didn't want to be anywhere near him when the shit hit the fan.

I moved to the sleepy town of Belden, Oklahoma, a couple of years ago when I graduated from nursing school, because it was in the middle of five different states and yet near absolutely nothing at the same time. They were recruiting hard for new nurses at the ER and their sign-on bonus was big for a baby nurse, making it the perfect location for a new start.

And because it was as far away from Central California that I could get on the money I had at the time.

I didn't have an end destination in mind when I packed up my entire life with my teeny, little baby and younger sister who just graduated from high school, but Belden was going to have to do for a while longer, until Maddie decided what she wanted to do after she finished college. I was going to keep my nose clean and my ass intact in the meantime. Which meant I needed to get Taz off it.

"If I use my five-minute break on you, what am I going to do with the three minutes left over once you're done?" I retorted to his offer with a smirk as I pulled drafts for the group. It wasn't the first time he'd outwardly offered to fuck me against the building on my break.

Like it was a romantic gesture or something.

Jeers and snide comments flowed from the men surrounding him, alongside other offers, and crude looks. But I was immune to it all.

Nothing hit its mark anymore when they aimed it at me.

I was numb to life.

"Come on outside with me, baby, and I'll show you just how good I can make it for you." Taz tried again, and I shook my head.

"Thanks, but I'm going to pass, big guy." I tried keeping it fun and light, because I knew guys like Taz didn't take rejection well. "Though I hear big red is looking for a date tonight." I nodded behind the crowd to the over six-foot-tall woman named after her fire engine red hair who would willingly let a man like Taz take her home for the night.

Hell, she'd let him ride her in the parking lot if he asked right. But I wasn't going to deflate his ego by telling him that.

Taz looked over his shoulder at her and flicked his tongue over his lip, "I'll pass on that." He grinned, showing off his one gold tooth, "I'll wait for you to come to your senses." He looked me up and down, "Something tells me you'll be worth it."

I shook my head and looked down at the bar, "Cut your losses while you're ahead. I'm a nun."

He laughed, as did his crew, "I can't wait to see what's under your robes, sister." He joked.

"A dump truck's under there, look at that thing." One of his guys threw, and they all laughed as they all looked down at my ass again as I walked away.

"Is it closing time yet?" I asked Lora on my way to the kitchen for a break.

"Only five more hours." She smirked with a wink, and I flipped her off.

It was going to be a long fucking night.

"Have a good night, Delilah." Bones, the bouncer at Cherry's said as I walked out to my car six hours later.

"Night! See ya next week!" I called, clicking the unlock button on my car door to turn my headlights on to light the way.

My car was in the back of the lot, thanks to how busy it was when I got to work earlier, and I scanned the mostly empty pavement as I neared my run-down Toyota SUV.

"Hey." A man called from the darkness to my right, and I leaped a foot into the air, swinging my arm wide and striking the surprise guest in the cheek out of fear. "Fuck." He grunted.

"Taz?" I asked, recognizing the voice as he grunted again, holding his jaw. I clicked the flashlight on my key ring, pointing it in his eyes to double check before scanning it over the parking lot between us and my car to check for more of his crew. It was empty. "The fuck are you doing?" I snapped at him.

I slid my hand into my purse and wrapped my fingers around the can of mace I carried every day, even though I never thought about using it.

Even though he'd been mostly harmless before; I didn't trust Taz.

"I was just making sure you got to your car safe, girl." He said, rocking his jaw back and forth a few times. "Damn, you hit like a dude."

I shook my head and started walking towards my car again, "I'll take that as a compliment."

He followed after me and my eyes rolled so far, I saw the back of my skull. "Ain't you going to offer to kiss it all better for me, at least?" He asked as he fell into step next to me. His heavy boots stomped across the pavement ominously.

"Something tells me you'll be alright." I countered, keeping my pace.

"Hey, wait up," He put his hand on my arm and pulled me around to face him. "What's the big hurry?"

"Taz," I sighed, "We've been over this." I said firmly but nicely.

Fragile egos were so fucking annoying.

"I'm not asking for a blowjob in the back seat of your car." He said with a smirk. We both knew he wasn't *asking* for anything. He was trying to force it.

"I have to go," I ignored the comment, trying for safer ground. "It's been a long day and an even longer night."

"Why don't you let me give you a ride home, then?" He tried again, "You ever been on the back of a bike before?" He said with a wink, "I bet it will wake you right up."

Memories assaulted me of a time so long ago and threatened to pull me under into a nightmare of heartache and mistakes.

"Look, Taz—," I started, but then suddenly, lights flicked on from three different sides of the parking lot seconds before rumbling motorcycle engines came to life.

Taz looked around us as the bikes closed in on all sides and I could tell by the look on his face that they weren't his men. Panic threatened to claw its way out of my throat on a scream as I clutched the mace tighter and backed up towards my car.

Five motorcycles pulled across the parking lot from the shadows and parked around my car in a half circle of menace. When the engines cut off and the lights lowered, I made out the patch on the front of one rider.

Black Eagles.

Double fuck.

I watched as three of the riders got off their bikes while two others stayed on, watching us both closely.

The president of the club, a man I only knew of as Houston, walked around the front of his bike and smirked at Taz before looking at me. "Where are your little buddies, Tazzy?"

The man was terrifying. He was almost seven feet tall and had a beard long enough to reach his belly button and death in his eyes. "Just out for a night of fun." Taz responded, "Nothing more."

"Fun huh?" Houston asked, looking at me again. "What do you say, darling? Are you looking for some fun?"

"I just tend bar here." I said flatly. "I don't associate with him; I'm on my way home."

Houston smirked again, "Yeah, I could kind of tell by the right hook you gave him that you weren't down with him or his crew." He adjusted his gloves again, and I recognized them as the kind with armored knuckles in them. Which meant if he swung on someone, they'd do some real damage.

Blaine used to wear those kinds of gloves.

Pain radiated in my chest, battling the fear as the president looked me up and down again.

"I think you should get on home, Sweetheart." Houston said with a nod to my car, "Dark parking lot like this ain't safe for a pretty little thing like you at this hour."

Giving Taz a half-second glance, I nodded back, knowing he wouldn't be let off easily. I all but ran to my car and threw myself inside, locking the doors behind me and started up my car.

Backing up into the grass because of the bikes around me, I then pulled around them.

As the two bikers who had been on their bikes dismounted, I watched them circle around behind Taz and Houston as they talked.

The guy was about to lose a few teeth if I had to guess.

As I drove around the bikes, one rider was looking directly at me through my window. He was tall, just like Houston, and wide as the day was long, with shoulders better suited for an ox. His dark hair, tied up in a topknot, gave him the fierce appearance of a Viking king ready for battle. Black jeans and a white tee peeked from under his black vest, while a skull-jawed face mask enhanced his menacing expression.

But what made my skin prickle and the hair on the back of my neck stand up was the way his hazel eyes glowed in my headlights as he stared at me, ignoring the little gathering going on around him.

Familiarity tried to burn its way into my gut from the color of his eyes, but I refused to allow it. Because the green eyes that his reminded me of belonged to a man who was locked away in a California state prison serving a life sentence.

There was no way he was out, staring at me through the darkness.

Yet, that small part of my brain tried to tell me the mysterious biker in front of me was Fox St. Claire.

But it couldn't be.

Because the last time I laid eyes on him, I walked away and left him sitting in a courtroom after he got a life sentence for murder.

And I never looked back, even though he reached into my chest and pulled out my still beating heart and laid it on the table in front of him before I left.

Holding it hostage.

Holding me hostage.

For now, and forever.

Chapter 4 – Delilah

Past

"Maddie! If you don't call me back in the next five minutes, I'm going to call Blaine and have him come get you!" I screamed into the phone and then hung up.

My little sister was being a real pain in my ass. I didn't have any authority over her to make her follow my rules, and she knew it.

She told me she was staying at her best friend, Stella's house for the night, since it was Friday. But when I had stopped at the grocery store on my way home from my six-hour lab, Stella had been at the checkout ahead of me with her boyfriend.

I made small talk with them and asked what they were up to for the weekend, and Stella said they were heading out to her family camp with her parents for the next two days.

I smiled and told them to have a good time, while seething with anger inside the whole time.

As soon as I was in my car, I called my sister's phone, and she sent me to voicemail.

It was almost eight pm. If she wasn't at Stella's, then she was more than likely getting herself into trouble somewhere. Which had been her favorite activity as of late.

"Ugh!" I screamed in the silence of my car and then started driving around town, looking for her. She was supposed to be the good one, the one I didn't have to worry about because I worried about Blaine enough for the both of them.

I drove around for an hour, calling her over and over until I couldn't take it anymore and turned my car towards the clubhouse where my brother always hung out at.

He had told me never to go there, given the highly illegal and dangerous things I knew that went on inside. But I didn't have a fucking choice.

The parking lot was packed with cars and bikes, and the building vibrated with the beat of the music, loud enough to be heard from outside. With a sigh, I pulled out my phone again, punching in Blaine's number then Maddie's, the cold metal a stark contrast to my clammy hands; both calls went straight to voicemail.

There was no choice left, but to get out of my car and search for my brother amongst the outlaws. Pulling my hair out of the ponytail it'd been in all day, I fluffed it to look better. My worn-out jeans, faded Nirvana tee, and scuffed boots felt comfortable and familiar so at the very least, I would fit in at the motorcycle club party. I wanted to just blend in and find my brother and get the fuck out.

People hung out all over the outside of the building, smoking, drinking, and partying. Men in leather vests and women in less clothes than I wore to the swimming pool partied as I walked past toward the door. Some of them looked at me, some of them ignored my presence completely, and I didn't know which I liked better.

"Hey, baby, you want to go for a ride?" A man twice my age called out and grabbed his crotch as I walked by. I quickened my pace and all but ran inside to get away from him. His mocking laughs chased me, and I changed my mind.

I wanted them to all ignore my presence.

The clubhouse was smoky, dimly lit, and smelled like stale beer and weed. Which was exactly how Blaine had smelled since joining. I coughed into my hand as my eyes watered from the haze.

I would never find him in a crowd like that, and I didn't even know if he was there. I couldn't pick his bike out of the dozens of them outside because they all looked the same to me.

Black, chrome, heavy and loud. I had no business getting near one to know his from the others, so I knew I had to find him personally.

But if he wasn't around, I didn't know where else to look. He was so private since joining the club, just telling me he was going out, but never where or when he'd be back. I didn't know where he hung out apart from here and work.

"Hey, baby," A large hand slapped my ass, and I yelped, turning away from the pain. A man with a bald head and a missing front tooth laughed at me, "Come on over here sweet thing, I want to take a closer look at you." He grabbed for me, and I backed up quickly to avoid his touch, but bumped into another person walking behind me.

"Watch it, cunt." A man sneered at me as he walked with a woman tucked under his arm. Neither of them even looked conscious enough to be walking upright.

"I'm sorry!" I said quickly, sidestepping and trying to avoid any more collisions.

"Hey, big tits." The bald man yelled again, drawing attention from more men around him. "Get back here, baby." He demanded and got up off his stool as I tried to walk away.

"I'm sorry," I said, holding my hands up, "I'm looking for someone." I said, trying to avoid him at all costs, but the crowd seemed to grow thicker, blocking my exit.

"Well, get back over here and I'll help you." He licked his lips and looked at my tits as he talked, and I shuddered.

Fuck finding Maddie or Blaine.

Fuck them both, they weren't worth this.

"I'm just going to go." I grimaced, "Sorry for bothering your—," I looked around, "party."

Rough hands from behind shoved me towards the bald man and I bounced off his chest as his arms wrapped around me tight, "Party's just getting started sweet tits." He said and then kissed me with his foul-smelling mouth as he pawed my ass and groped me. I shoved against him with all my might, but couldn't get away from him. I clenched my teeth and lips closed so hard to keep him from putting his tongue in my mouth despite his best efforts, but the smell of him still assaulted my senses like I could actually taste him.

"Get off me!" I screamed when he finally released me enough to take a breath. I flailed in his arms, desperate to get away and get the fuck back to my car.

"Let her go!" A deep voice roared over the jeer and laughter before the big man's body was thrown across the room. I stumbled into my freedom and fell to my ass as a giant stepped in front of me, facing off against the crowd. "Nobody fucking touches her! Understood?"

I looked up and noticed the tattoos on his right hand fisted at his side above my head.

"Fox." I breathed in a whimper.

"I don't see a cut on her, boy!" A man said threateningly, "She's fair game, you know the rules."

"She doesn't need a cut." Fox growled, widening his stance. "She belongs to me. And nobody fucking touches what's mine."

I watched in horror, afraid of what was going to happen, but the men just grumbled about hot heads and young kids before dispersing.

Fox turned and glared down at me with angry eyes, and I recoiled away from him, scooting back on my hands and ass in fear. He squatted down in front of me and held his hands up, "Get the fuck out of here, Delilah, right now."

My face burned with embarrassment from his scolding and anger burned in my chest from the entire situation. I was burned out on life and the whole night was the cherry on top of my mental health decline. He grabbed onto my upper arms and lifted me up as I swatted at him to get his hands off me, "Don't touch me." I turned and started shoving my way through the crowd.

Being polite didn't do me any favors before, maybe if I acted like the raging bitch I wanted to be, they'd get the fuck out of my way.

Grumbles and curses followed me as I made it to the door and slammed my way through it. I stomped across the parking lot and heard Fox's heavy boots follow me to my car, which just angered me even more.

"I'm leaving, don't worry!" I snapped at him as I got to my car, "Go back on inside to that—" I threw my hands up in disbelief, "*fun time* you and Blaine insist on having every night." He had his hands on his hips as he silently watched me throw my fit. "Like there's no such thing as responsibilities or expectation hanging over you both. Meanwhile, I'm trying to keep our heads all afloat by keeping Maddie in school and out of trouble that she has no business getting into while taking care of all the household things like paying the bills and making sure there's food in the cupboards to feed her with, out of the piddly money left from Mom's life insurance." I rambled, "Oh yeah, and on top of all of that, I'm trying to finish school so I can go work my fucking life away in the same hospital that killed my mom so I can provide the same dismal life she did." Throwing my hands up in the air, "But maybe I should just give up and run drugs and steal shit like you all do because I failed my exam today thanks to JJ and his dip shits next door throwing rocks at the house all last night because Blaine, once again, wasn't home to run them off!" I turned and kicked my car tire over and over as the frustration burned into an inferno. "But the one time I actually need to find my long-lost brother and get help from him—." I paused and turned back on Fox, "The one time I actually try to ask for help, I get assaulted inside the place he loves more than us anymore!" I cried. "So don't you worry, I'll take my pathetic-self home now so you don't have to be embarrassed to be around me in public. Sorry to interrupt your evening!" I screamed.

I fumbled with my car keys and then threw my door open and got in my car, slamming it behind me. But when I went to start my car, I realized that in the short time I was inside, a dozen more bikers showed up and parked right in front of me.

Blocking me in.

I slammed my fists down on my steering wheel and screamed into the worn leather before laying my head down against it in defeat.

My blood was pumping through my body so fast I felt like I was going to have a heart attack as all my fears and stress bubbled over. I tried to calm my erratic heart rate, except it wasn't listening to reason as my car door opened and Fox kneeled down next to me. Tears poured out of my eyes and dropped onto the top of my thighs, but I refused to look up.

He reached forward and swept my hair back out of my face and looked at me. "Talk to me." He whispered with the gentleness I remembered from the night he slept in my room. I hadn't seen him since he woke up that next morning and left. I'd pretended to be asleep when he got up, and on his way out he stopped next to my bed, brushed my hair over my ear and looked at me for a while before walking out.

That was weeks ago, and I hated to admit that his absence since then felt personal. He was always around before that, coming and going with Blaine at all hours. After that night, he stayed away.

Still, here he was, pushing my hair back over my ear again with that softness that belied the dominating strength lying in his hands.

Strength I'd seen tonight when he shoved that man off me and when he prepared to fight them all to keep me safe.

Before he said I was his.

I knew better than to let his words affect me. Because I belonged to no one. Other than my relationship with Blaine and Maddie, I was utterly alone in the world. And even they abandoned me for better things.

"Delilah," He tried again, reaching forward to wipe away a tear that ran down my cheek. "Why are you here?"

"It doesn't matter." I whispered and took a deep breath. "Blaine isn't here, is he?"

"No." He rested his forearms on the tops of his knees, "He's on a job, he won't be back until morning."

"Okay." I swiped at my tears and looked out the windshield at the bikes in my way. "I'll walk home, and he can bring my car home whenever. I don't even care anymore."

He was still kneeling in my way as I reached for my backpack on the front seat of my car and tried to stand. "You're not walking home." He said firmly before rising and holding his hand out to help me out. "Come on."

I looked at his hand, and then at him in question and decided to just let the fuck go for once and let him pull me up. His hand was so warm on mine, just like that night when he held onto my arm when I tried to wake Blaine up for him.

My skin pebbled from the contact, and I shivered. "Have you ridden before?" He asked, then pulled me around the many bikes to where he was parked by the retaining wall at the edge of the lot.

"Motorcycle?" I asked in disbelief, and he nodded, "No."

He smiled, and I was mesmerized by the sight of it on his dark face. "Well, there's only two rules to it, really." He said as he grabbed his jacket out of the pack on the side of it. He took my backpack from my arm and set it on the ground before wrapping his large leather jacket around my shoulders and then zipped it up. "Rule number one, lean with my body, not the bike."

"Huh?" I asked in total confusion. The scent of him was surrounding me from the worn leather of his jacket.

"And two," He continued, "Hold on to me. Tight." He stressed the last word as he grabbed onto the front of the jacket I was wearing and pulled my body tight to the front of his. "Got it?" He asked, looking down at me sternly.

"No. I don't *got* it." My eyebrows crinkled together over my eyes, and I shook my head, "I just screamed at you for five minutes straight. Like, I'm pretty sure I just had a psychotic break in the middle of the parking lot." I shook my head again, "And now you're offering to give me a ride home?"

"I'm not offering, D, I'm taking you home, no question about it." He said, releasing his hold on the jacket and I stumbled backwards a step. He picked my backpack up and slid my arms into it before buckling the front clip over my chest and I sucked in a quick breath as the back of his hands brushed over my breasts. Even over the thick fabric of his jacket, it felt powerful. "Now," he said, reaching up and tying his long hair into a bun on the back of his head. "What was rule number one?"

"Huh?" I asked stupidly, I wasn't confused anymore; I still was in shock. The temper tantrum I'd thrown had really frazzled my usually calm and levelheaded brain.

"Rule one, D, tell me what it was."

"Lean with you."

"Good girl." He smirked at me, and I bit my lip to hide the smile I wanted to give back. "And rule two?"

"Uh, hold on to you."

"How tight?" He raised a dark eyebrow at me.

"Tight."

"Like I'm a bull at a rodeo and you're trying to stay on for your full eight seconds. Got it?"

I swallowed audibly, "Yep."

Fox smirked again. "Tie your hair up, or it'll be a nest of tangles by the time I get you home." He said, and I instantly did as he said, tossing it into a bun on the top of my head. He threw his leg over his bike and folded down the pegs behind his legs, starting the bike up.

"Get on toots." He yelled over the roar of his pipes and held his hand out, but I froze. He smiled and shook his head, grabbing my hand and pulling me forward. "Right foot on the peg and throw your leg over." And then he hauled me forward so hard I had no choice but to throw my leg over his bike or I would have fallen on my face.

I clutched at his leather vest as he reached down and lifted both of my feet onto the pegs, and then put his leather gloves on.

Why was that sexy?

I took a couple of calming deep breaths as he adjusted himself to ride and then he looked over his shoulder at me, "Tight, D." He grabbed my hands and wrapped them both around his waist. I clutched at the soft fabric of his tee as my chest plastered against the warm leather on his back. "Here too," He grabbed my knees and pressed them tight to his thighs, "I'm a bull remember. Squeeze me tight with your thighs."

I nodded my head again and then he flicked his kick stand up and gave it throttle, pulling us out of the parking lot and onto the street. "Shit." I gasped, tightening my arms and legs around him as he weaved in and out of traffic at breakneck speeds.

Okay, not breakneck exactly. But sitting on the back of a Harley, clinging to this man, it felt like Lightyears passed us with the blur of headlights from oncoming traffic. As I dared to look past his broad shoulder, I saw what lay ahead: large, indistinct shapes that made me gasp as he skillfully weaved around them.

So, I tucked my head back down behind his back and burrowed in against his warmth. He took a deep breath and then rested his elbow on my knee and ran his hand up and down my calf. "You doing alright back there?" He asked over his shoulder as he slowed down for a red light. I wanted to roll my thighs and rub my clit against the vibrating leather underneath of me. His touch was sending shivers of pleasure up my spine and he was only touching my calf, through my jeans and his glove. Yet it burned like a brand.

"Yeah." I squeaked and nodded my head in case he didn't hear me over the pipes. His touch was intoxicating.

"You cold?" He asked, and I shook my head no. I was on fire. Electricity burned through my body like I was living for the first time in my entire life thanks to the high. He took his hand off my calf and ran the inside of his bare arm over my fingers where I fisted his shirt. "You're freezing."

Sure, my fingers were cold from the breeze, but I didn't feel it. I was too exhilarated.

The light turned green, and he took off again and when traffic opened up and he cruised down the mostly empty highway, he tapped my hand and I released it from my death grip on his shirt, "Under." He said over his shoulder and then lifted his shirt up and tucked my bare hand against his stomach.

Jesus, Mary and Joseph.

I closed my eyes and shuddered at the electricity that burned up my fingertips as I laid my hand flat against his hard, ribbed abdomen. He lifted my other hand from his shirt and tucked it under as well, leaving my hands nice and warm against his bare skin with the barrier of his shirt against the wind. I tried not to notice the way his skin was covered with a smattering of coarse hair from his belly button down towards his belt. Because if I noticed it, I'd imagine what he looked like without his shirt on and then I'd imagine what he looked like without anything on, kind of like I'd been doing on repeat for months. Now was not the time to get all worked up.

"Better?" He asked.

"Much." I answered honestly, and I felt him chuckle, his abs constricted under my hands.

"Hang on tight, D. We're going to go fast now."

"This isn't fast?" I cried and then screeched giddily as he opened the throttle and tore it off into the darkness ahead. "Oh, my god!" I screamed and tightened my arms and legs around him even more.

"Good girl." He said, and I could hear the smile in his voice. He drove across town to my neighborhood and all too soon my carefree motorcycle ride was over and as soon as his engine turned off, my problems came back to the forefront of my mind.

I loosened my grip and slid my hands free of his skin and then off of him completely before slipping off the back of his bike. He stayed on the bike, and I took that as he wasn't going to offer to come in and check under my bed for monsters.

Or offer to come in and be the monster in my bed.

So, I shucked my backpack off and then unzipped his jacket and handed it to him.

"Thanks for the ride." I said, sliding my hands into my back pockets as I tried to seem cool and unphased by the ride, even though it had been the most fun I'd had in—years.

"Maddie home?" He asked, looking at the dark house.

"No." I sighed and kicked my toe into the dirt. "She's off being a rebellious teenager somewhere."

"Is that why you came to the clubhouse?" Fox asked, leaning his elbow on his knee.

"Yeah," I said, "I was hoping Blaine could find her and kick some sense into her for me."

He chuckled and shook his head, "He's the last person to be giving that kind of speech."

"Yeah, maybe." I shrugged, "But I'm tired of doing it so—."

"So don't." He said easily. "Just let her learn her mistakes for herself."

I rolled my eyes and walked backwards towards the house. "Easier said than done when you know someone isn't meeting their potential. I only gripe at her because I want more for her than I have. I don't want her to screw up her chance to get out of this life."

"What's so wrong with what you have?" He asked cynically.

I scoffed, "School and *what*?"

He shrugged his shoulders, "Freedom. To be whoever you want to be."

"Right," I said, shaking my head. "Thanks for the ride home."

"Anytime, D." He watched me closely. I knew he was biting back an argument on the topic, and part of me wanted to fight him on it. I wanted to see the passion burn in his green eyes when we argued. Just like that night in the house when he pressed me against the wall on his way out with Blaine to find JJ. I wanted to see that burning inside of him, because it lit something inside of me.

Having taken a few steps toward my house, I heard him kick down his kickstand and get off his bike. I looked over my shoulder at him as he stalked towards me up the walkway and turned to face him. "What are you doing?"

He cut me off when he fisted my hair bun and tilted my head back to look up at him. "Giving you a taste of freedom." He lowered his lips to mine and kissed me. It started out gentle and seductive, like a dance of two lovers slowly moving together. I slid my hands against the flat of his stomach and gripped his shirt, pulling myself closer to him.

He growled against my mouth and the vibration tickled my lips. He tilted his head and kissed me deeper, persuading my lips to open so he could taste me with his tongue.

"Fox." I purred in his arms, and he deepened it even more. His arms were strong around me, caging me in as I clung to him, trying desperately to get even closer to him.

When I thought I was going to pass out from the pure adrenaline running through my body, he pulled back and pressed his forehead against mine. He panted and licked my lips one last time before pulling back and pushing his thumb under my chin to hold me still. "Don't shy away from freedom, Delilah." He gently kissed my lips once more. "You deserve to embrace it and let everyone else worry about themselves."

He pulled away, walked back to his motorcycle, and climbed on without another word as I stood in utter shock. I lifted my fingertips to my lips, expecting them to feel different since the taste of him still seared them.

He watched me and then nodded towards the front door, instructing me to go inside before he left.

I dutifully turned and walked away before I could say something stupid to him.

Like want to come inside and help me be carefree for the night?

Fox was not the kind of man I needed to get wrapped up with. He was too dangerous and mysterious. Even if his kisses were downright magical.

It wasn't like he was interested, anyway. Not in someone like me when there were several women in bikini sized outfits back at the clubhouse; no doubt, ready to throw themselves at him. He was hands down the sexiest man in the world.

And never meant to be mine.

I might as well get on board with that before I let myself hope for a second.

I was meant to be alone in life and even Fox St. Claire wasn't going to change that.

Chapter 5 – Delilah

"Hey."

I gasped and turned to the voice that surprised me on my way out of my front door. "Fox." I pressed my hand to my heart and tried to bring it back down to a normal rhythm. "You scared the shit out of me." He wore his usual dark jeans, white tee, and black vest. He had his shaggy brown hair pushed back off his face and wore mirrored aviators.

He was so fucking sexy. I bit my lip as I remembered the way his lips felt on mine when he kissed me the other night in almost the same spot we were standing in now.

"Sorry." He said sheepishly with a dark smirk. "I'm waiting on Blaine."

My gaze shifted from him to the house, then to my watch; "At eight am?" I asked and rolled my eyes. "Good luck. He wasn't moving when I went by his room."

"Pain in my ass." He cursed, tossing his cigarette butt to the ground and crushing it.

I snorted and nodded, "You're telling me."

"He didn't give you too much trouble for finding your car at the club, did he?" He asked, falling in step next to me on my way to my car.

"Eh," I shrugged, "Something like that."

"Sorry." He sighed, "I wanted to get it home for you before he got back, but I got tied up." I tried not to wonder what exactly had tied him up. Or who.

"Don't worry about it. It's not your responsibility." I opened my car door and tossed my backpack in the seat. "You made sure I got home safe, that's more important than saving me from an ass chewing."

"Hmm." He hummed and put his hands in his pockets. "Was it safe, though?"

I squinted up at him, "What do you mean?"

"I kissed you." He said, looking over his shoulder towards the front door. "I shouldn't have done that."

Embarrassment coursed through my veins as I dropped his gaze and looked down at my car door between us. "Why not?" I asked, cringing at how pathetic I was for even bothering. The man clearly regretted it, and I was stupid enough to ask him why.

Like I needed another blow to my self-esteem.

"C'mon, D." He sighed and ran his hand over the back of his neck.

"Right." I said and closed my eyes, "Got it."

I turned to slide into my car, but his hand gripped my upper arm and pulled me back. "Don't be like that." He said, turning me to face him. "Please."

"It's fine. You regret it. I get it. I wasn't ready for this conversation so early this morning. That's all."

"I don't regret kissing you, Delilah." He said firmly, and I looked back up at him. "I regret that I tainted you like that."

"Tainted? What the hell does that mean?"

"You're good." He sighed, loosening his hold on my arm, and letting his fingers slide down the skin before dropping away completely. Goosebumps grew in his wake. "Pure."

"Pure?" I hissed the word like it tasted bad, "Seriously? I'm not a nun."

"No," He stepped forward, and I backed up against my car frame and bent my head back farther to look up at him at his impossible height. "But you deserve better than to let me touch you like I did. I don't deserve such gifts."

I shook my head and stared at him. "Then why are you crowding me in?" Challenging him was not my brightest move. I had no idea where I got the strength to be so bold, but something about Fox made me feel like even if I rattled his cage, I was still safe because it was him.

He swallowed, and I watched my tongue slide out to lick my lips in the mirrored reflection of his glasses. He slid his arm over my car door and put his hand on the frame next to my back, leaning down until he was looking directly at me. "Because I can't stop thinking about how fucking good you felt wrapped around me on my bike." He licked his lips and bit the bottom one gently before letting it pop, "Or the sounds of delight you made when I opened the throttle up and let it rattle between your thighs." My chest rose and fell in pants, but I held my ground while the giant man tested my strength with his sexy words. "Or how damn sweet your lips tasted and how erotic the moan was that you gave me when I kissed you goodnight."

"Fox." I said with a groan and tilted my head, hardly able to stand up on my own two legs from the insane amount of need coursing through my body from his words. He wasn't even touching me, and I was mush.

"Run away, D." He said, leaning forward until I could feel his breath on my lips. "Get in your car, go to college, and get far, far away from this place and men like me. Just like you said you were going to do."

"And if I don't want to get away from you?" I asked, reaching up and pushing his sunglasses onto his head so I could see his green eyes that captivated me every time he looked my way. "If you're the one thing that makes me think I could stomach to stick around here."

He tilted his head, and his nostrils flared as his green eyes dropped to my lips. "I'll destroy you."

"You won't hurt me, Fox." I shook my head, "I know you won't."

"You don't know me at all."

I swallowed and leaned back against my car again, creating space between us. "If you really believe that, then go." I nodded towards the front of the house as anger burned in my gut. "Because I don't think you do. I think you're just trying to make me be the one to turn you away so you can put the blame on me later for not giving it a shot." He grunted, and it sounded animalistic in the small space between us. "When you work through the hangups in your head and decide to give into the desire that we're both feeling here," I leaned forward and kissed his lips in a sweet soft peck, "You know where to find me." I whispered, and then lowered myself into my car and started the engine.

He stayed frozen in place for a few more seconds before stepping back and slamming my door shut as I put the car into reverse and backed out of my driveway, all while he stared at me.

"Holy fuck." I whispered to myself as I rolled down the street, leaving him in my rearview.

Hook, line, and sinker.

I lay on my side facing the wall, trying desperately to go to sleep, but it kept evading me.

Noises from outside the house had kept me on edge all day as JJ and his buddies partied early in the afternoon and then into the night. They drank all day long, and I knew it was going to be a long night of torment as soon as the sky turned dark.

They stood along the fence line between our houses, yelling obscenities at our windows and making crude gestures every time I dared to get near one.

And it didn't help that I was once again home alone.

Which they knew, of course.

Further amping up their antics.

"C'mon baby." I heard someone yell, "Give us a show!"

"Ugh." I groaned and rolled over again, pulling the blankets up over my head.

Hours passed like that until the loud roar of their bikes showed they were finally going off to sleep it off somewhere else, and I finally felt my body relax into the bed.

My bedside clock said one o'clock, and I'd been up since four in the morning to study for my anatomy final. It was officially Saturday morning—day one of summer break—and I was determined to sleep in and ignore all responsibilities for the next forty-eight hours.

It was only fair, considering Maddie and Blaine had bailed on me again.

And if I was asleep, maybe I could pretend that Fox hadn't ghosted me since our little tug of war in my driveway last week.

I knew he was battling with some inner demon about us, because I knew he wanted me too. That much was clear every time he was around me.

I just had to have faith that he'd figure it out before too long.

I smiled to myself and sighed; snuggling deeper into my bed as sleep pulled me under. Sometime later, a creak of a floorboard on the stairs in the hallway vibrated right through me and my eyes flew open.

I forced myself to lie still as I listened for another sound to indicate it wasn't just the old house creaking by itself. A second later, I heard another one.

Closer to my open bedroom door.

Oh my god.

Panic filled my body as I heard a third one and then I turned to peek over my shoulder as a dark shadow filled my doorway.

"No!" I screamed and flailed, trying to get out of my bed. My blankets and sheets tangled around my legs as I fell onto the floor on my hands and knees. I flung myself across the floor towards the window, intent on throwing myself out of it rather than daring to stay inside to fight off the large intruder.

"Stop." A deep voice demanded as the man crossed my room in two quick steps and grabbed my arms as I threw the window open. "Are you insane?"

I screamed again, hitting him with closed fists that did nothing but bounce back off him. "Let me go!"

"Delilah." He grunted when my knee connected with his thigh, "It's Fox. Stop it damnit." His words slugged their way through my brain in slow motion as I continued to fight him. "Fuck." He grunted and then wrapped his hands around both of my wrists and pushed me backwards onto my bed, following me down with his body. "D, it's me."

He pinned my arms above my head and used his legs to immobilize mine. I had no choice but to stare up at him until my panic made way for reason.

"Fox?" I whispered in shock. "Oh, my god." I sagged back into my bed and nearly wept from the relief pulsating through me.

"Who the fuck else would it be?"

"I don't know!" I hissed, "JJ or a serial killer!"

He smirked and the soft glow of my alarm clock lit up his perfect white teeth. "Nope, just a big bad wolf."

I sagged into the bed, "Hmm." I sighed and flexed my arms that he still pinned, but I couldn't move against his strength. His body was so big and hot on top of mine and the adrenaline that had been filling my veins turned into lava as arousal sparked inside of me. "Are you going to let me go? What are you doing in my house, anyway?"

"I hadn't planned on pinning you down, but now that I have you here." His voice dropped an octave more, and it rumbled against my skin where he was pressed against me. His eyes scanned my face and then lowered to my chest, and he sighed, letting his smirk fall into something more sinister. Almost like a snarl. "This fucking tank top, D." He groaned, and I looked down at my chest.

I wore the same sleep top I had on the last time he made a surprise appearance in my bedroom, and it had gotten twisted and tangled between us in my fight. I could see the darkness of my bare nipples through the dim lighting, and they pebbled as he continued to stare down at them.

My hips flexed under his body on their own and I panted from our fight and the desire trying to take over.

I had never felt a man cover every inch of me like this before, and it was intoxicating.

Especially because it was Fox.

And I wanted nothing more than to strip down and offer myself to him like a meal to a starving man.

He was all I thought about anymore.

Every fantasy starred the dark and mysterious man that had given me my first motorcycle ride and real first kiss. I laid in bed every single night, sometimes as soon as I got home from class and played with myself imagining what it'd feel like to be consumed by him like this. Now I was getting it in real life.

But he acted like our kiss had never happened, and then challenged me to run away from him a few days later. So, I'd thrown the ball back in his court and told him he knew where to find me when he was ready to act on the desire we both felt.

A few days ago, with nothing but radio silence from him, I got a ride home with a friend from class; a male friend. I hadn't planned it, but Fox had been in the driveway working on my brother's bike with him when we pulled in. The darkness that heated his face when I got out of my friend's car was enough to melt the rubber on the black top.

But still, he said nothing to me.

He just stared a hole into my chest and then turned around and ignored me.

Which pissed me off.

"Stop moving." He growled when my hips rose again, and I froze under him. I didn't realize I moved again, but then I felt something twitch against my inner thigh.

He scrunched his eyes shut, and I watched him with fascination as he tried to control himself.

I didn't know much about sex or men, but I knew he was aroused.

So, I flexed my hips again.

"D." He hissed as his eyes popped back open. "Don't."

I did it again, this time I slid one leg out from under his and I twisted it around the back of his knee. "Then get off of me." I challenged, and the green in his eyes ignited into a full inferno. "You don't want me, so get off me."

But he didn't move.

I tightened my leg around his, not even knowing what I was hoping to achieve. But I knew that the way his hard body pressed against mine every time I moved sent shivers of pleasure into my clit and I wanted more. "You said I was free to be anyone I wanted to be." I whispered, and his eyes fell to my lips as my chest rose and fell in fast pants. "And I told you I want to be free with you. And then you show up here in the middle of the night and act like you don't want me. Make up your mind, Fox." I groaned, tilting my hips again and riding him from underneath brazenly. "I'm getting bored with the emotional whip lash and my body is getting needy enough to find someone else if you won't give in."

He growled and pushed his thigh between mine and kicked my other leg wide around his hips. I instantly brought it up around the back of his legs and pulled him in tighter to me. "Be careful, little girl." He spoke. "I'm not one of the little teenage boys you're used to playing with."

And he was right.

He was older than me, almost twenty-five.

"I'm not afraid." I licked my lips and tightened my ankles around his ass, "Are you?"

"What do you think?" He rolled his hips against me, rubbing himself up my clit and I moaned, pressing my head back against the bed. "Does it feel like I'm afraid, baby?"

"Again." I panted.

He smirked at me and rocked against me again and again until I was writhing underneath him, begging him for more. "Good girl." He said before leaning down and nudging my face to the side until his lips pressed against my ear. "You haven't even kissed me yet tonight, and you're already humping my cock."

"Fuck." I murmured and bit my lip to stop from begging him to fuck me like I wanted. I had no business begging a man like Fox St. Claire for sex.

He'd ruin me without even trying.

"Where's Maddie?" He asked, flicking his tongue against my earlobe as he raised my pinned wrists above my head to hold in one of his hands.

"Friend's house." I grunted when his hand skated over my bare breast. "Staying the night."

"Good." He growled.

"Where's Blaine?"

"On a job. He won't be back until tomorrow." He leaned back to stare down at me. "Tell me to leave you alone, D."

"No." I shook my head. "I want this."

"I'm no good for you." He said and lowered his face to my chest, kissing his way down to my nipple before blowing on it. "Tell me to leave." He flicked his tongue across it and then swirled it around. "Believe me, you don't want this."

"What if I do want it?" I asked, pushing my breasts up higher towards his face, desperate for more. "What will you do to me?"

He looked up at me and bared his teeth as he nipped my flesh before sucking my entire nipple into his mouth drawing a long line of moans and curses from my lips. "If you don't come to your senses in the next ten seconds. I'm going to strip you down and fuck you so hard the entire neighborhood will hear your screams."

"Please." I groaned as he shifted and took my other nipple in his mouth. "I want you."

"I won't share you." He growled and kissed his way back up my chest until he hovered directly over my lips. "The first time I fuck you, is the last time you let someone new into your body. It'll be mine after that."

"Yes." I moaned, rubbing myself against his groin again, "Fuck me. Please, for the love of god, fuck me."

I lost my damn mind.

And it was his fault.

His possessive nature and sweet gestures had sucked me in until I couldn't think about anyone but him. Then he showed up at my house, when he knew I was alone and ready for him. He baited me into this.

And I walked into it with open fucking arms.

I wanted to be consumed by him. I needed it.

"Say it. Say you're mine."

"I'm yours!" I yelled. "I'm yours Fox."

"That's my girl." He cooed and in a split second he let go of my wrists and grabbed the front of my shirt, ripping it off me in one quick pull.

"Yes." I gasped and fisted my fingers into his long hair, pulling on it as he once again dropped to my breasts. "Just like that." I groaned when he sucked on my nipple again as he pushed his fingertips into the top of my sleep shorts.

I held my breath and raised my hips as his rough fingers slid against my bare skin. "No panties baby?" He quipped with a smirk and then leaned back on his heels. "Let's see this pretty pussy, D." He hooked his fingers into the band of my shorts and pulled them down my legs and then tossed them to the floor. My knees stayed shut as I laid there in front of him, even though I knew the darkness hid most of me.

It was still the first time a man had seen me like that.

Even if he didn't know that. I was sure as hell not going to tell him and ruin the moment.

"Show me." He rumbled and slid his hands to the insides of my knees before pushing them apart. I laid there in abject horror as his eyes skimmed down my naked body and locked onto my wet, naked pussy. His nostrils flared in the glowing light, and he licked his bottom lip before slowly letting his eyes rise to mine again. "So, fucking pretty."

I whined and covered my face with the back of my arm as he kissed his way down the inside of my thigh until he hovered directly above my swollen clit. "Fox." I pleaded, but couldn't say the words out loud.

"I know, baby." He hummed, and I felt every breath against my flesh, "Let me take care of you."

My back bowed up off the bed as he laid his mouth flat on my pussy, sucking my clit into his mouth before running the tip of his tongue from my ass to the top and back again. "Oh, fuck." I groaned, threading my fingers through his hair. He pushed his tongue into me and moaned and vibrated his lips deep into my soul. "Yes."

"Tell me what you like." He instructed me as he pushed my thighs wide again when I tried to tighten them around his ears. "What feels good for you?"

"All of it." I panted, "Everything you do."

He chuckled and pushed one finger into me, "Do you like it when I suck on your clit?" He asked, doing just that and I gasped and nodded my head furiously as I looked down my body. "And finger your tight pussy?" He twisted his single finger inside of me, stretching me out. Again, I nodded quickly. "And tongue your ass?" He asked before dropping his tongue over my tight puckered ass again, pushing on it until the muscles gave way to his invasion.

"Fox!" I screamed and felt every single muscle in my body snap under the tension of his touch. "More!" I gasped as my orgasm peaked. He spat on my ass and rubbed one finger over it as his other twisted and curled inside of my pussy and his mouth sucked on my clit. "Yes! Yes! Yes!" I moaned on repeat as he drew my orgasm out of me for what felt like ages until I was twitching and convulsing under him.

He crawled up my body, slowly kissing his way across my stomach and up to my breasts, stopping to nibble on each sensitive nipple before laying his weight back into the space between my jelly thighs.

His rough jeans and smooth worn leather vest contrasted against my bare skin, reminding me that he was completely dressed while I was exposed.

"How was that?" He purred, nestling his face in against my neck before pulling back to look down at me.

"Hmm." I said with a satisfied grin on my face. "Better than I thought it'd be, to be honest." I admitted with a smirk.

"Is that so?" He asked, "Did you think I'd be bad in bed?"

"I didn't think about you much at all," I lied, and he bit my neck, making me giggle at being caught. "But what little bit I did, I imagined you as a brute type of partner. Just throwing yourself around for your own pleasure and to be damned with anyone else's."

"Brute?" He asked, leaning down to bite my collar bone. "Don't lie and say you haven't laid in this very bed and played with this sweet, sweet pussy every single night since I kissed you. Imagining this exact situation."

I opened my eyes to stare at him. "Were you watching me?" I joked frankly.

He smirked and licked his lips again in that way that made my pussy drip. "No, I was too busy stroking my cock until I blew load after load of come trying to get over the maddeningly sexy little sister of my best friend that smells like heaven and tastes like sin." He said and then leaned down to consume my lips. His words were dirty, and his lips were delicious. I moaned into his mouth, wrapping my arms around his neck to hang on to him as he kissed me passionately. "But I think I'm done trying to fight you off me. I'm only a man after all, I can't say no to someone so insistent forever."

"Get out." I pouted, and he sucked my bottom lip into his mouth again and kissed me deeper. "Do you always eat a girl out before you kiss her hello?" I asked when he finally pulled back to let us catch our breath.

"I never eat pussy, D." He shook his head, "I haven't in years, yet with you-," He smirked, "I craved tasting you like it was my last meal on death row."

"God." I moaned and rolled my hips under him. "I need more."

He leaned back on his heels again and stared down at me. He shucked off his black leather cut and then his tee and I watched, panting with need as his tight abs and strong pecs came into view.

Gah, he was just as sexy as I knew he'd be when I touched him under his shirt on his bike. That happy trail that had teased me that night mocked me again as I craved to know where it led. He popped the button of his jeans open, and I bit my lip and spread my thighs invitingly, praying he didn't back out on me.

His eyes dropped to my pussy as he shoved his jeans and briefs down before standing up to kick them and his boots off.

"Jeeze, it's so thick." I cursed as his cock swung heavily between his legs. At my praise, it jumped and jerked like it was happy to be appreciated.

But in reality, I feared it.

It was going to rip me open.

And it was going to hurt. He took a condom out of his pocket and rolled it onto his length with slow precision while I watched, and I felt myself getting even wetter from his show.

He slowly climbed back into my bed and laid his weight down between my open thighs as he pushed my hair back off my face. "Last chance to back out."

"No way." I answered instantly. "I want you."

"You shouldn't." He lobbed back. "I'm no good for you."

"I'm not looking for prince charming." I answered honestly. "I'm looking for a bad boy on a motorcycle to help me feel carefree and happy for once." He stared down at me with those thoughtful green eyes. "I want to remember what it feels like to be happy."

He swallowed and looked down at me intently before adjusting himself to lay the thick head of his cock against my entrance. "You sure you want to lose your virginity to a man like me?" He asked, pushing the head of his cock in just the slightest bit, stretching me out. "I'm not gentle or nice."

"How?" I gasped and arched my back to accommodate his size as embarrassment burned my cheeks. "I didn't tell you-."

"Your pussy is too fucking tight to have been used before, D." He groaned and pulled back to let the head of his cock pop out before slowly pushing it back in. "It strangled my finger, trying to suck it in and keep it forever. I can only imagine how it's going to feel milking my cock for the first time."

"Fuck." I hissed, "Please, please fuck me." I wrapped my legs around his waist again and pulled him deeper until he met the resistance we both now knew was there and he paused. Sweat lined his upper lip like the act of restraining himself was strenuous.

"Beg me baby." He growled, "Just like that, use your pretty lips to beg for my cock."

His dirty talk was so hot, my pussy gushed around the head of his cock, and he growled deep in his chest, pushing forward into it like he couldn't control himself.

I locked eyes on his and stared deep into his soul and begged him, "Please fuck me, Fox, I need you so bad. I want you to claim me as yours."

He clenched his jaw, and his nostrils flared as he pulled the head of his cock back out. "Hang on tight." He surged forward, burying his thickness inside of me with one brutal thrust, "Because I'm branding this pussy as mine for life."

I cried out at the invasion and dug my nails into his shoulders and neck as he savagely fucked me into the bed. He didn't pause when he was deep inside to give me time to adjust or try to take it easy on me. He fucked me like a man possessed, spreading his knees wide and pounding into me again and again as the pain faded and pleasure quickly took its place. It wasn't gone completely, but there was an edge to the pain that made me crave more. I wanted to know what it would feel like to orgasm with him inside of me.

"Yes, just like that." I mewed, biting his shoulder as he grunted in my ear. "Fuck yes!"

"Take my cock, Delilah, take is so deep you feel it in your heart." He hooked one of my knees over his arm and opened me up further for him. "This is the best pussy I've ever had." He groaned, tossing his head back as he rolled his hips and rubbed my clit with his pubic bone. "So fucking good."

"I'm-." I panted in his arms, "You're making me come." I gasped as he continued to pinch my clit between our bodies and hump me through my second orgasm. "Yes."

"My name, D." He growled into my ear, "Scream my fucking name."

"Fox!" I screamed, completely uncaring about who heard. "Please, don't stop."

"That's my good girl." He bit my neck and sucked it deep into his mouth, marking me. "Mine."

"Yours." My eyes rolled as he slammed into me again, "I'm yours."

"Damn fucking right you are." He hissed and then his hips jerked madly, "Milk me baby, take my fucking come."

"Jesus," I groaned and felt his cock twitch deep inside of me as his eyelids fluttered closed and his mouth hung open as he orgasmed into the condom between us. For a split second, I ached to know what it felt like to feel the warmth of his come without the barrier.

"Best. Pussy. Ever." He groaned before collapsing on top of me and then rolled us over until I laid sprawled out on top of him.

I snorted and buried my face in his neck as his hands roamed over my spine and ass leisurely. I wasn't sure what happened after life changing sex with a man like Fox St. Claire.

But I was ready to give him whatever he wanted.

What I ended up with was his giant, sexy, hot body wrapped around mine the rest of the night until the late morning sun shined through my window. Three times in total, he slid into my body and claimed me as his.

As I laid there on my side with him wrapped against my back and his hand covering my heart between my breasts, I knew I'd never be the same as I was when I crawled into bed the night before.

Because he was right.

I'd never belong to anyone else after something so potent and powerful passed between us.

I was his.

But I knew he'd never be mine, because men like Fox St. Claire never truly belonged to anyone.

And it was going to hurt like hell when it all came crashing down around us.

Chapter 6 – Delilah

Present

I drove home on edge after the run in with the Black Eagles in Cherry's parking lot. My fingers hurt from how tight I gripped the steering wheel the whole way to my shitty run-down rental home.

When I got home, I made sure every single door and window were locked before I crawled into bed with Penelope.

She was too old for me to sleep next to her, especially because she was in a tiny twin size bed. But at that moment, I needed to wrap my arms around her and smell her sweet floral kids' shampoo and just let her presence on earth calm me.

I had a lot of regrets and grief over how my life had turned out, even though I was still in my early twenties. But one thing I'd never regret was my sweet daughter.

She was too pure and innocent of the evils of this world for me to hold her conception against her.

And after the night I had, I selfishly let her innocence and sweetness lull me into peace and relaxation a mere hour before my alarm went off to go to the ER.

I needed to ground myself before I went to the hospital for another soul sucking shift.

Sunday mornings were usually relatively quiet in the Belden Community Hospital ER, most of the wild and crazy Saturday night visitors were taken care of and either released or admitted by my seven am start time.

But when I walked in after a wild and crazy Saturday night of my own, the chaos inside assaulted me.

"What on this green earth happened last night?" I asked in a huff as I threw my things into my locker.

Winnie, my partner RN was tying her hair up in a bun next to me at her locker.

"I heard there was a brawl somewhere. A bunch of bikers came in about four am and it's been chaos ever since."

"Bikers?" I snapped my head in her direction, "Who? Which MC?"

She glared at me and then rolled her eyes, "I don't know, the Sons of Anarchy kind with the black vests and scary faces. I only saw one that was hot, like Jax Teller, though." She shrugged, "More Opie-esque, actually. You know; the tall, dark, and dangerous kind that would put some bullets in the back of a federal agent's head in a car for killing his wife. Not quite as charming as Jax, but still just as hot."

"Ladies, let's get out there and lend a hand." Marjorie, the charge nurse called on her way through. "Looks like it's going to be a busy day."

I didn't shy away from chaos, I thrived in it because it made the day pass faster, so I quickly got all my gear on and ran out after her and instantly got dragged into the thick of the bedlam.

Winnie was right, a brawl broke out.

From the looks of the patches, the Black Eagles put a hurting on a rival MC. But it wasn't Taz's Riders from what I could tell.

In fact, I didn't see any rival patches at all as I went from room to room with Dr. Franklin stitching gashes and the occasional stab wound. From the good mood of the bikers, I knew the Black Eagles had won.

I worked tirelessly, mending and discharging the dozens of bikers so our regular patients would stop commenting on the smell of weed and booze from the dirty men sharing their rooms.

When would people learn that the ones complaining never got the better treatment? It just made us like their counterparts even more.

"Hey, Delilah," Winnie called from her desk with the phone tucked under her shoulder. "Can you take bed seventeen for me? I'm on hold with stupid cardio. Again." She groaned.

"Yeah," I took the paper chart from her and tossed down the four I discharged in the last hour that still needed filing. "What's the chief complaint?" I asked, looking over my shoulder at bed seventeen's private exam room behind me. The curtain was drawn across the glass wall so I couldn't see who the patient was.

"Uh," She scratched her head, "I don't know, laceration or broken rib or something. Biker from the fight." She said and then rose in her seat excitedly, "The hot one." She winked. "Opie's twin."

"Gee thanks." I droned. "I hope he lives up to your Redwood fantasies." I called out and then walked across the hall and pulled the curtain back as I looked down at the chart in my hands. "Hi, I'm Delilah, I'm taking over for Winnie as your nurse Mr...." My eyes finally landed on his name, and I gasped before looking up at my patient for the first time. "St. Claire." I whispered.

Fox St. Claire laid back on the gurney, dwarfing it and making it look tiny under his giant body. His green eyes, burning with intensity, fixed on me; I felt as if I would burst into flames. He'd aged in the last five years; he was almost thirty now, and the time had been unfairly kind to the man.

He looked delectable.

His dark hair was long and wild in normal Fox fashion and, to add to it, a dark beard covered his jaw, hiding the scar I knew ran from his earlobe to his chin.

He wore jeans and boots with a black and white plaid flannel under his motorcycle vest, and it was unfair how damn good he looked.

"What are you doing here?" I whispered, when I finally got my tongue unstuck from the roof of my mouth. "How-?"

"Hey D." He said with his deep caramel voice that I used to fall asleep listening to so long ago. "You're a hard woman to track down."

"Get out." I cried, falling back a step in complete shock from his presence. "Now." I stumbled over the trash can in the corner, sending it flying across the floor with a loud crash.

"I need stitches." He said, sitting up and it was then that I noticed the gash on the other side of his head taped shut.

"Go to the vet then." I snarled as pain and anger burned in my gut. "We don't tend to animals here." I snapped, ripping the curtain open and pointing to the door again, "Get out, Fox!"

"What's going on in here?" Dr. Franklin asked as he walked into the room to investigate my outburst. "D, are you okay?" He put his hand on my shoulder, and I watched as Fox's eyes zeroed in on the touch, before I shrugged the overly affectionate man off me. Now was not the time for Oliver's familiarity.

"I want him out." I snarled, never taking my eyes off Fox as he swung his long legs over the edge of the bed to put his boots on the floor. "Get him out of here!"

"What happened?" Oliver tried again. "Sir, please sit back down." He said, holding his hand up as Fox stood up off the bed.

God, the man was big.

Over six and a half feet tall and he had put on about a hundred pounds of muscle since the last time I'd seen him.

"I want him out, I refuse to care for this son of a bitch." I hissed, shaking off Oliver's touch as he once again put his hand on my arm. "Stop touching me damnit!" I all but screamed.

"Touch her again, and I'll put you on your ass, Doc." Fox growled, and I hated the shiver that ran up my spine from his threat.

"Now wait, just a second." Oliver tried again, looking between the two of us. "What's going on?"

"Find someone else to stitch this animal up," I groaned, holding my hands up, "I'll stab him in the eye if I get close to him."

"You know you've never followed through with your threats, D." Fox threw from across the room, and I glared at him.

"Fucking try me, Fox." I turned and burned right back out of the room. Winnie stood up at her desk as I charged towards her, with the phone receiver still stuck under her ear. "If I go back in that room, I'll go to jail." I threw his chart back down at her. "Take care of him yourself." I stormed back down the hall towards the break room and yelled over my shoulder. "And he's not like Opie. He's that snake Jimmy from Ireland!"

Two hours passed with me throwing my hissy fit before Oliver cornered me in the linen closet. He shut the door behind him and stood against it with his arms crossed over his chest. I glared at him from the corner of my eye and then sighed. "I'm sorry." I droned on, "For yelling at you."

"Apology accepted." He said evenly, "But you need to tell me what that man did to you to get you so worked up."

Using my elbow, I shut the cabinet while carrying a stack of gowns. "I don't, really." I shrugged. "It's personal."

"You threatened to stab him in the eye, Delilah," He tried again, "And then he threatened to kick my ass for touching you."

I tilted my head to the side and shrugged, "Is he still here?"

"Yes." He uncrossed his arms and leaned up off the door, "I need to go in, numb him and suture his head laceration. CT came back clear."

"That's a shame. A lobotomy might have been his saving grace." I hummed, and then raised my eyebrows at him when he didn't offer anything else, "I'm not helping you."

"Yes, you are." He replied instantly, anticipating my response before I gave it. "Everyone else is swamped still. You're the only one who has finished charting and is now restocking."

"So, I get punished for being efficient?" I hissed, clutching the gowns tighter. "That's not fair."

"I didn't say it was fair." He quirked one eyebrow at me. "But it's where we're at right now, so come on." He opened the door and nodded for me to follow him. "I need to numb him and then you can clean him up before I suture it."

"Ugh!" I groaned and walked out in front of him, tossing the pile of gowns into an aide's hands as we walked down the hall towards the room I somehow managed to avoid until now.

Every time I sat down at my desk to chart, I could feel his eyes on me from where he lay on the bed. My skin burned with his glances like it used to do from his touches.

"Mr. St. Claire." Oliver announced our arrival, "We're extremely short staffed at the moment thanks to the little pow wow you and your boys had last night. So, I need Delilah to assist me in your suturing to get you out of here and on your way. I won't hesitate to have you thrown out of my ER at the first sign of disrespect or rudeness coming her way, do you understand?"

Fox glared at the young doctor before looking back over at me. His green eyes stoked the fire that had been smoldering in my belly for years. "I used to be the one that demanded respect for you, D."

My spine prickled with resentment, "Now look at us."

"Hmm." He hummed.

I readied the supplies that Oliver needed to numb Fox's head in silence as he instructed him about the procedure and then obtained his consent.

My brain was swirling like I'd landed in some alternate universe as my body worked on autopilot.

"Damn." Fox hissed, and I looked up to see Oliver jamming the needle in his skull a little more aggressively than necessary.

"Alright, I'll be back in about ten minutes after that's numbed up, and then we can get you out of here. Delilah's going to clean your wound up for me and I'll be back."

"Thanks Doc." Fox said, but he stared at me.

I washed up and put gloves on in silence because I knew if I started talking to the son of a bitch, I'd say far more than I wanted to. So, I tried to bite my tongue tight enough to stay silent.

"You look good." He said after a long stretch of silence, and my anger boiled anew.

"Don't." I snapped, pulling the tray over to the bedside and pushing his face away from me so I could see the wound.

Fuck patient care and bedside manner.

This man deserved nothing from me.

"A bit too skinny." He shrugged his shoulders and grunted as I poured antiseptic into the wound. "And a whole lot more tired than you should be. But I guess that's expected when you frolic around with bikers in dark parking lots until three am. You still look damn good, nonetheless."

It was him last night.

"Fuck you." I hissed and slapped a gauze onto the gash. "I was working until three, then I was trying to leave to go home, and he stopped me. We weren't frolicking."

"Taz is bad news, D." He turned his head to face me, pushing against my attempt to hold it down. "Houston isn't going to let him play around on his turf for long. And you're going to get hurt in the crossfire."

"Thanks for your concern." I deadpanned, "Turn your head so I can do my job."

He didn't move though, he just stared at me. "D, please." He whispered and closed his eyes like saying the word was painful for him. "I don't want you to get hurt."

"Why?" I taunted, not even trying to pretend to work on him. I just stood there and glared at him, hating the way he smelled so fucking good up this close. "Because you're the only one who can hurt me?"

"I-." He started, but I cut him off.

"How are you here right now?"

"I got out."

"How? The judge sentenced you to life without parole." My eyes burned with the unshed tears that were trying to fall at the memory of how it felt to hear the judge say those words and how conflicted my teenage self was in that moment.

He swallowed and my eyes fell to watch the way the muscles in his neck worked. Memories of how the skin right above his jugular tasted assaulted me, and I forced myself to step back.

"I was cleared."

"That doesn't make any sense." I groaned, "You pled guilty." I pushed my hair back with my arm. "You sat there, and you said the word guilty. I read your statement. Word for word, describing what you did."

"I know." He clenched his jaw. "Give me a chance to explain everything to you."

"No." I shook my head and stepped back again, "I can't-."

"Don't." He said, wrapping his hand around my wrist and pulling me forward, erasing the two steps away that I took. "Please, don't walk away from me again." He closed his eyes and took a deep breath. "It almost killed me to watch you walk away from me that last day in the courthouse, not knowing if I'd ever see you again. Please don't do it again."

I hated how conflicted he always made me feel.

Since the day I met Fox when I was eighteen, I knew I shouldn't feel anything remotely gentle toward the dangerous man. Yet he was the only one to ever show me genuine kindness outside of my family. He was tender with me; always.

But I knew he wasn't gentle with anyone else.

That was how my brother ended up in a grave next to my mother.

"No." I frowned down at him. "Don't you dare blame me for that."

"Give me a chance to explain, D." His face was so close to mine, the urge to lean forward, melt into his touch and kiss him with five years of pent-up heartache nearly consumed me.

But then I remembered how that heartache felt five years ago.

I couldn't go backwards.

Not with Fox.

"Alright, let's get you stitched up and on your way, Mr. St. Claire." Oliver interrupted from the doorway, pulling the curtain closed behind him.

I stepped back and gave the space to the doctor to do his job. "Good-bye Fox." I whispered and threw my gloves in the trash on my way back out.

I didn't care that Oliver liked to have a nurse by his side while suturing to hand him his tools.

I didn't care that for any other patient, I'd stand there and offer to hold their hand as a needle pierced their skin repeatedly.

I didn't care that my ethics were being bent because of how much pain Fox had inflicted on me in the past.

I just needed to get away.

"You're up." I ordered Winnie as I took her charts off her desk and threw them down on mine. "He was your patient to begin with."

She watched me and then got out of her chair. "Fine, but you're telling me all the nitty-gritty details about the obvious sexual tension burning between you two when I'm done."

"Not on your life." I whispered as she walked away.

Chapter 7 – Delilah

Past

I heard the creaky floorboard outside of my bedroom door and smiled to myself in the dark. I didn't fear the ominous sound of motorcycle boots gently walking across the floor or the soft click of my bedroom door anymore.

Because it was never a monster coming to hurt me like I used to fear.

It was Fox.

I pretended to be asleep as I listened to him take off his clothes before he pulled back the blankets and slid his giant warm body against my back. "You can't fool me, trouble." He purred into my ear as his warmth instantly lit an inferno inside of my own naked body. His arm encircled my waist before moving up my chest to cradle my exposed breast. He slept with his hand nestled there almost every night for weeks now, and I felt incredibly empty and lonely without him nearby.

"In my defense," I yawned and stretched like a lazy kitten, "I was sleeping before you stomped your way upstairs and woke me up."

He pinched my nipple, rolling it between his fingers as I moaned and pushed my breast into his hand. "Liar." He growled and slid his other arm under my waist before pushing his hand between my legs. His impossibly long fingers slid through my wetness without any guidance, like a well-rehearsed move. "You're wet for me, which means you weren't sleeping while you waited for me."

I chuckled and lifted my leg back over his hip, opening myself to his talented fingers. "You're right, I played with myself when I couldn't fall asleep without you wrapped around me."

He flipped me over onto my back and pushed my legs wide before settling between them. His hard cock rubbed against my belly when I wrapped my legs around his narrow hips and locked my ankles together.

"Mine." I purred, and he smirked at me in the darkness.

"Did you make yourself come without me?" He asked, rocking his hips until his hard cock slid through my wetness, stroking my swollen clit.

"Mmh." I moaned, and threaded my fingers into his hair, pushing it back to see his face. "Yes."

"Minx." He growled, leaning down to bite my neck. "I told you, no orgasms without me."

"You're late." I challenged, "Two hours late." Rocking my hips, I rubbed myself against him needily. "I was horny and desperate to come, and you have no one to blame but yourself."

"How is it my fault?" He asked, nibbling against my neck and ear.

"You've turned me into a nympho." I giggled when he smiled against my neck.

"You were always a nympho baby." He said and flipped us until he landed on his back with me straddling him. "I just finally gave you a cock worth begging for."

"God." I moaned and palmed my aching breasts. "I need you."

"I thought you already came." He teased, "I think I'm going to fuck your ass and blow my load into you without letting you come. As punishment for playing with your pretty pussy without me."

"Will it help lessen the sting if I tell you I was thinking of you the entire time I did it?" I moaned seductively and leaned forward to kiss his neck and earlobe.

"Tell me everything and I'll decide." His large hands wrapped around my waist, and he rubbed me up and down on his cock, teasing us both.

"Hmm." I pondered, "I came upstairs, crawled into bed naked and ran my fingers down to my pussy. I was so soaked already; I moaned the second I touched my clit."

"Fuck." He groaned and tightened his grip on my waist.

I moved to the other side of his neck and bit the skin directly under his ear and moaned into it just how he liked. "Then I pushed two fingers into my dripping pussy and fucked it just like you do when you're inside of me." I moaned again when he spanked my ass before gripping the cheek and shaking it. He was on edge, and I reveled in the fact that I did that to him. "I couldn't quite get to that spot that you do, so I spread my legs so far, it hurt. But I got it." I rolled my hips in a figure eight across his cock. "It felt so fucking good, baby." I moaned breathlessly. "It was almost like you were here with me."

"You don't need me anymore, then." He growled, lifting my hips to press the head of his cock against my opening. "You don't need my cock or my fingers if you can do it yourself." He tormented me and pushed the thick mushroom head into me, making us both moan.

"I need you, baby." I sighed, lifting and pressing my hands against his hard chest. "I need you so fucking much it hurts." Pushing down, I took him deeper inside of me, fighting against the resistance my body put up every time thanks to his size. I rocked side to side to loosen up, and he thrust harder, burying himself deep inside me. "Yes, just like that." I threw my head back and pushed my breasts forward between my arms as he pulled out and pushed back in roughly.

"Nothing and no one else will ever fuck you as good as I do." He groaned, using his tight grip above my waist to hold me still while he pumped into me. "You need me."

"Yes." I agreed, leaning down when he opened his mouth for one of my nipples. He was such a tits man, and it drove us both crazy when he sucked on them like that. "You feel so good inside of me, Fox."

"Only you." He panted, pushing me down onto his cock. "It's never felt so good with anyone else before." He threw his head back into the pillows, "Only you, Delilah."

"I'm coming." I dug my nails into his pecks and squealed through my clenched teeth as my orgasm tightened my pussy around his cock, squeezing him to death as he filled me in ways I never imagined possible.

"Good girl." He slammed into me repeatedly and reached down to rub my clit with his thumb. "Milk my cock, kitten." His dirty talk was always so good, and he knew it got to me. "Fuck, you're going to make me blow." He groaned and slammed deeper before flipping me on my back and pulling his cock out. He crawled up my body and stroked himself, erupting onto my chest and stomach as he tilted his head back and roared with his orgasm.

I watched him with rapture as he came unglued above me.

I did that.

And it was so empowering to watch, every single time without fail.

"Tell me something important." I said as I picked a seed off my cheeseburger bun and tossed it onto the ground. I sat on top of a picnic table with Fox next to me as we looked over the city below and ate takeout cheeseburgers from my favorite diner.

"You're the most beautiful woman I've ever seen before." He said, looking at me out of the corner of his eye, "Even when you have mustard smeared on your lip." He smirked and I rolled my eyes.

I lifted my hand to wipe my mouth, but he caught it and pulled it back before leaning forward to lick away the mess and kiss me.

"Not what I meant." I whispered against his lips, and he smiled.

"I know." He leaned back and took another bite of his burger. "How about you tell me something important and I'll return it."

I groaned and glared at him, but ended up smiling as he shrugged his shoulders and smirked. He always looked so young and carefree when it was just the two of us like this. He had this totally different personality when he was around Blaine or the other guys from the club, and I couldn't decide which one I liked more.

To be fair, the rough, tough, and dangerous biker was the first side of him I ever met, and it had called to me instantly. As time went on, he gentled himself for me and became a sort of knight in shining armor for me.

A charming prince on a Harley, if you will.

I mulled over what I wanted to tell him and decided to give him something deep.

"I want to mean something to someone someday." He looked at me and scowled, like he didn't like that answer. "I mean," I paused and chewed another bite of food, "Like I want to do something with my life that impacts someone along the way where they can look back and say, *that was the moment my life changed for the better*." I shrugged and took a deep breath, "I just don't want to die someday knowing I never made a ripple in the ocean for someone else."

He watched me silently, and I was afraid I'd somehow offended him until he smiled and leaned over to kiss me. "You will." He said against my lips, "You'll fill the entire ocean with meaning for someone else someday. I just know it."

I smiled and leaned my head on his shoulder, "Your turn."

He sighed and laid his cheek against the top of my head and looked back out over the lit-up city below. He was quiet for so long, I thought he was going to ignore his turn, but he finally said, "I want to get out of the MC life and have a family someday."

I leaned back to look up at him with surprise. "A family?"

"Yeah." He nodded, watching me closely. "A wife, kids, a dog or two. Stability and peace." He shrugged. "Everything I never had." He tapped the end of my nose with his finger. "Does that surprise you?"

"Very much so." I answered honestly, and then elaborated, "You're usually so stern and serious, I didn't think kids were the kind of thing you'd long for." I smiled gently, "But it makes perfect sense."

"Why?"

"Because if I actually sit back and imagine you with a wife and kids, I know without a doubt you'll be the best father and husband ever." He watched me without blinking, like he really considered what I said with weight behind it. "You're the most protective and thoughtful person I've ever met, Fox. Both of those qualities will make a great foundation for a family man someday."

"What about you?" He asked.

I rose my eyebrows at him, "What about me?"

"Do those make good qualities in the man that you'd want to marry and have kids with?"

I swallowed quickly in shock and felt my face brighten up with a blush. "Are you asking if I'd want that with you someday?"

"Yes." He answered without hesitation, and I could tell how strongly he felt about it in that one word.

I didn't hesitate to respond, because I already knew the answer. "Yes." I nodded my head, "I think I'd like that very much."

"Good." He said with a smirk before leaning over to kiss me gently. "Because I want that with you so fucking bad." He growled, and I moaned against his lips like a needy bitch.

He could make me come with words alone, I just knew it.

"Are you sure?" I asked, digging for confirmation and reassurance. "It's only been a few weeks and you've been a single man for a while."

Picking me up, he sat me on his lap so that I straddled him. He lifted my hand and put it on his chest over his beating heart, "I know it right here." Lifting my hand and kissing my fingertips. "I've never met someone like you before, Delilah. I know you're young and doing your own thing right now, and I respect that. I plan to wait and not get in the way of it. But I just want you to know my intentions are to someday have it all with you."

"I'm not young," I whispered, "and I'm not doing my own thing." I slid my fingers around the back of his neck and pressed my forehead to his, "I want this." I said firmly, "I want you. Now."

He groaned and wrapped his arms around me tighter, "I'm yours." He kissed me, soaking up every moan and hiss I gave him as he teased me. "Every single part of me is yours. I love you, Delilah Beckett."

"God," I cried and tightened my hold on his neck, "I love you, too."

"Mine." He hissed and stood up off the picnic table with me in his arms.

"Where are we going?" I asked with a squeal of laughter as he marched us off towards the woods.

"To find a tree strong enough that won't break against your back while I fuck your brains out."

I tipped my head back, laughing loudly at his caveman tendencies, "Who said romance was dead?"

Chapter 8 – Delilah

Present

I walked to my car after my shift, looking over my shoulder and around every corner, expecting to see Fox waiting for me to finish the conversation he tried to start earlier in the ER. But I couldn't be a part of it.

I ran my hand over the center of my chest to ease the ache of longing and anxiety that had built throughout the entire day since his green eyes bore into mine.

So many nights I spent with him lying on his side facing me, staring at me with those mystical green eyes, thinking how I'd never tire of seeing them like that. Then reality hit, and my happy ending was taken from me before I even realized I wanted it.

I drove through Belden to my side of town and parked around the back of my house, hiding my car behind the back porch like a criminal on the run.

What a fucked-up turn of events my life had taken.

My car was easy to pick out of a crowd, with the mismatched front bumper and ding in the back hatch from its days before it was mine. I wasn't going to take the chance of Fox finding me at home and stopping by.

I didn't know why I cared to think he'd try to find me after all this time, given what he did all those years ago to betray me. But that small broken part of my heart that still beat for the sweet, gentle biker that cared for me so tenderly when he was the worst kind of monster towards everyone else, wouldn't stop hoping for a reunion.

Like some fucked up episode of Jerry Springer where the disfunction ran rampant through a family and everyone ignored the red flags.

That tiny part of my heart still wanted it, anyway.

But I couldn't give into that part. Because the rest of my heart, brain, conscience and pride wouldn't let me even think about it for long.

I opened the back screen door and shut the inside door behind me, turning the dead bolt and then closed the lace curtain closed over it after peering out to make sure no one followed me into the driveway.

"Uh, hey, Sis." Maddie said from the kitchen table where she sat with her laptop and textbooks sprawled out.

"Fuck!" I screamed and clutched at my chest, "You scared the shit out of me." I panted and sagged against the wall as I glared at her. "What are you doing lurking like that?"

"Lurking?" She squinted her eyes at me and closed her computer, "You're the one looking over your shoulder and dead bolting a door we hardly remember to even close at night. What's with you?"

I pushed off the wall and kicked my shoes off onto the rack by the door and took my bags off my shoulders, looking around the corner towards the living room. "Where's P?"

"Upstairs, having screen time." She rested her forearms on the table, "Tell me what's going on."

I sighed and busied myself with putting my lunch dishes in the sink before refilling my water bottles and placing them in the fridge for tomorrow. When I had no other tasks to busy my hands, I turned and leaned on the counter behind me and faced her.

"I ran into someone. Last night and today." I said and watched her closely. "I didn't know it was him last night until I saw him again today and now, I'm—" I sighed, "Freaking out."

"Who?" She asked.

"Fox St. Claire." I whispered his name like he was Beetlejuice and was going to appear out of thin air if I said it too loudly.

"Are you fucking kidding me!" She yelled and stood up from the table.

"Shh!" I rushed forward and put my hand over her mouth, "Keep it down or P will come down and I'm not ready to face her right now."

"He's here?" She swatted my hand away, "In Belden? Why? How? Did you talk to him?"

"I don't know why he's here." I said and ran my fingers through my tangled locks. "He was at Cherry's last night with the Black Eagle crew, but I didn't know it was him; he had a mask on, and it was dark. But his eyes-." I groaned, "His fucking eyes." I rubbed my temples with my fingertips and started pacing. "And then there was some sort of brawl after I left between the Eagles and another crew. The ER was full of patches today and he was there and he just—said, *Hey*." I threw my hands up exasperatedly, "Like nothing fucking happened!"

"Oh, my god." She cried and then looked at me. "Oh my god, Delilah,"

"I know!" I cringed.

"What if he came to do to you what he did to Blaine?" She rambled, "Or Penelope?" She gasped as panic gripped her.

"Stop." I cursed and swung around with my finger pointed directly at her, "Don't you dare say another word about her like that or I'll lose my fucking mind." I cried, "Believe me, I've already imagined every single scenario possible about why and how the fuck the man who's supposed to be serving a life sentence is now breathing the same fucking air as us five years later, thousands of miles away from home."

She grabbed her phone off the table and her thumbs swooshed over the screen rapidly. "Hang on."

"What are you doing?"

She held her finger up to me and put her phone to her ear as I groaned and paced around the small kitchen as my mind circled itself into a frenzy. "Detective Dailey, please." She said politely and watched me as I swung back around.

Detective Dailey was the man that put Fox behind bars five years ago. God, she was smart to think to call him. And I was the one spiraling into a panic attack while she was being smart.

How the fuck did we switch roles?

She groaned and rolled her eyes and whispered to me, "Voicemail." Before putting on her best phone operator voice and leaving a message. "Detective Dailey, it's Maddie Beckett. I'm calling about Fox St. Claire. My sister, Delilah, said that he's here, in our new town. We have so many questions about that, please call me back as soon as possible. Thank you." She hung up and slammed her phone down on the table. "Was he mean to you?"

"No," I shook my head helplessly, "He was—Fox." I sighed, "The Fox from before, when he was kind and gentle and protective." I cried out, "Everything I ever wanted."

"What are we going to do?" She asked.

I shrugged my shoulders and shook my head hopelessly, "I don't know." I whispered as tears pooled in my eyes. Her face crumbled as she raced across the space and wrapped her arms around me, holding onto me as I fell to pieces for the first time since the birth of my daughter. "I'm scared, Maddie."

"I know." She whispered, squeezing me tighter, "We'll figure it out, I promise."

"He can never find out." I pulled back to look at her, "He'll lose his mind if he knows the truth." I shook my head, "He'll kill me, Maddie, out of spite and anger, he'll kill me with his own bare hands, I know it."

"Shh." She pulled me back against her chest, "He'll never know. I promise."

She held me for a long time as I fought to compose myself. I knew I couldn't break down like that, because I had to be strong for her and Penelope, but it didn't stop the overwhelming urge to crawl into a hole and hide. They always looked at me for guidance and strength so, I couldn't fail them now. Not when this was all my fault to begin with.

They needed me.

I just had to figure out how to get the fuck out of Belden with Fox St. Claire, never knowing where I went.

It was the only way to protect what was left of my family.

I'd die to protect them.

And if Fox ever found out the truth behind my secrets, there was a real chance I'd get a one-way ticket to the cemetery.

Four days went by uneventfully since seeing Fox in the ER at my shift. It was Thursday, and I was off work from the hospital today and tomorrow and didn't work at Cherry's until tomorrow night.

I walked around the small grocery store in the center of Belden with my tiny paper list and threw as many of the items possible into the cart as quickly as possible while I was free for a few hours. Penelope was at school; she went for half days to the elementary school for Pre-K and absolutely loved it.

But I'd be lying if I said I hadn't considered pulling her all together until we moved.

Because Maddie and I had sat down Sunday night after Penelope went to bed and laid out a plan. We needed to move. Quickly. As far away from here as we could manage. I applied to a million different

RN positions all over the western United States and now just waited to hear back on one. Any of them would do, as long as it started asap and was far away.

"Oops, I'm sorry," An older lady said as we collided at the end of the aisle. "I was distracted looking at the meats."

"No, I'm sorry." I said, pulling away from her cart with mine, "I was rushing around." I smiled at her, and she passed as I turned down the empty aisle.

It was the last aisle at the end of the store. Just one more sweep and I was done. I could check out and get back home.

Leaning down to grab a loaf of Maddie's special bread, a shadow slid over my feet as I tossed it in the cart. I swallowed quickly before I stood back up and turned my face to follow the person casting the darkness on me.

Fox.

He stood a foot away, and he was close enough to tower over me, blocking the bright fluorescent light from above.

"Hey, D." He said in his deep rumbly voice. I gulped at the torment of emotions colliding inside of me. His hair was pulled up in a bun on top of his head and his beard was trimmed short to his jaw; I hated that I ached to feel it against the sensitive skin of my neck. I hated him, but my body still responded to him like nothing had happened at all.

He wore a black bomber jacket and black tee over dark wash jeans, looking normal and casual, like he wasn't capable of murdering someone with his bare hands.

But I knew better.

"What do you want?" I asked breathlessly.

"I told you the other day." He crossed his arms over his chest, "To explain myself."

"Did you follow me here?" I shook my head, "Never mind, I don't want to hear it." I closed my eyes. "Five years ago, I asked you to explain yourself. I *begged*." I opened them back up and looked at him. "And you refused. You don't get another chance now."

"You don't understand." He argued and then sighed, "And that's my fault, because you're right, I wouldn't tell you the truth back then. That was to protect you."

"Protect me?" I hissed, "You murdered my brother! And then laid in my bed and held me for days afterwards while I disintegrated into pieces!" I backed up, knocking into my cart as I felt the stupid tears of betrayal burning in my eyes. "You pretended to be just as distraught as me. You pretended it hurt you while you comforted me and promised to make it right. You swore to me you'd make the person who killed him pay." I swung the cart around to put it between us, "And the whole damn time you were responsible for my pain to begin with."

"I wasn't." He said and then clenched his teeth and glared at me. "Please, let's get out of here and go talk somewhere."

"How did you find me?" I ignored him, "I left the only home I ever had and ran because of the pain you left in your wake and then you show up here. A free fucking man."

"I didn't know you were here." He said, uncrossing his arms, "I looked for you when I got out. I searched high and low, actually. But no one would tell me anything, they just said you took off with Maddie in the middle of the night and never came back." His face scrunched up like that had hurt him, which didn't make any sense. "I never thought I'd see you again, and then there you were. The other night in that parking lot with that fucking scumbag."

"I told you; I wasn't with him!" I hissed, hating the way I felt the need to defend myself to him. He had no idea how alone I'd been for the last five years and the fact that he thought I'd give someone like Taz the time of day hurt.

"I know." He sighed, "I saw the way you clobbered him when he snuck up on you."

"Then why did you say it like that?" I sneered in anger.

"Because I'm a jealous man where you're concerned, Delilah. But I believe that we are both here, thousands of miles from home, for a fucking reason. Some greater power is at work to bring us back together, baby." He said plainly and my heart stopped beating completely.

"You have no claim on me, Fox." I pushed my cart directly into his thighs, "I'm not yours! You made sure of that when you killed the only man that ever truly loved me." I pushed around him, "Now leave me the fuck alone, I never want to see you again."

I walked away from him and listened for the heavy fall of his boots to chase after me, but there was only silence.

Which both relieved me and made me angry at the same time. I hated the fucking tug of war going on inside of me. I should hate that man with every single ounce of my being.

The sad reality was that even when he pled guilty in the crowded courtroom to killing my very own flesh and blood, I still ached for him.

"I'm not going anywhere, D." He called out from the other end of the aisle as I walked away. "Because *I'm* the only man that ever truly loved you, and I still do."

The icy box that held my frozen heart cracked a little as those words penetrated my brain. I refused to turn around and face him. Instead, I ran to the counter, paid for my groceries and made a hasty exit to my car.

I circled the town three times to make sure I wasn't being followed before I went home and parked behind the house again before running inside.

When I put the groceries away angrily, Maddie came down from her room and watched me. "Did something happen?"

"Yeah." I growled and then closed my eyes and laid my forehead against the cool fridge door. "Fox happened."

"Explain, because then I have some news."

I looked at her and sighed. "He cornered me at the grocery store, demanding that I let him explain. And then he said—." I faded off, shaking my head. "It doesn't matter. What's your news?"

"No, finish what you were going to say." She leaned against the door frame.

I turned and looked at her and crossed my arms over my chest, hugging myself like it could keep me from falling apart again. "He said he still loved me." I cringed as I said the words out loud. "He must think I'm a fucking moron to believe that." I said, but that small fucking part inside of me was bigger than it was the other day and I hated that.

I hated him.

I had to.

I owed it to Blaine to hate him.

"Actually—" Maddie groaned from the doorway, "I think you should have a seat."

"Why?" I scowled at her as alarm tingled up my spine.

"Detective Dailey called me back finally. He said he wasn't in that department anymore and was looking into how Fox was free before getting back to me and that it took some time to sort through the paperwork on it."

"What are you saying?"

She sighed and pulled me into a chair at the table and sat down across from me, holding my hand in hers. "Detective Dailey said that two years ago, someone turned in fresh evidence to the police, clearing Fox of the charges."

"I don't understand." I whispered, fighting back the nausea that rolled through me.

"There was DNA on Blaine's body that they ran through the system during his autopsy, but they couldn't find a match. And then, when they brought Fox in for questioning, he admitted to killing him.

So, they never ran the DNA against his to prove it, they didn't need to."

"Maddie—." I swallowed and shook my head.

"Hang in there, D, it's a wild ride." She said and squeezed my hand. "But an anonymous source turned a video into the police two years ago." She licked her lips, "It was a video of Blaine's murder."

"No." I backed up in my seat and dropped her hand, knowing what she was about to say.

"It wasn't Fox." She said with tears in her eyes.

"No." I repeated as every single heartache that I'd held onto with every fiber of my being swirled around us.

"It was a man named Jason Harter." She said, shaking her head like the puzzle confused her at this point. "Once they had the video, they tried to get a sample of his DNA to prove it, but they couldn't, because—. She paused.

"What?" I gasped, "Just fucking say it."

"He was already dead."

"No." I shook my head and stood up to pace. "That doesn't make any sense."

"Someone killed him in prison, babe." Maddie said, standing up and following me. "He went to jail on a robbery charge after he killed Blaine. And he was *murdered* behind bars. The file said it was gang retaliation or something."

"I don't understand." I cried spinning on her, "Why did Fox admit to it then if it wasn't him?"

"I don't know." She shook her head, "I wish I did, he wasn't in the video at all, Detective Dailey said." She pursed her lips, "He didn't do it though. I don't know why he lied, but he didn't betray you or me. He didn't destroy our family, someone else did."

"He *did* destroy us!" I gasped, "Penelope." I scrubbed my hands over my face in agony. My brain exploded as a migraine hit full force from the turmoil. "I need," I paused, "I need a minute."

"Why don't you go upstairs and lay down?" She said gently, "I'll pick up Penny from school and take her to the park for a while and give you some time to let this all process."

"Thanks." I nodded to her absently, because she was right. An hour wasn't enough time for me to get myself together to pick up Penelope from school.

I walked up the squeaky stairs on autopilot into my room and shut the door behind me as the tears fell from my eyes like rivers. I never cried.

Never.

Yet in the last few days I'd cried so much I didn't even recognize myself.

I stripped out of my clothes and drew the dark curtains shut and crawled under my covers, burying myself away from the world as I gave life to the burning ache in my chest that I'd dulled for years.

Fox didn't kill Blaine.

He didn't murder him.

And he was free.

And he said he still loved me.

But euphoria couldn't burn inside of me because guilt and fear took up too much space already.

Because when I thought the man I loved murdered my brother, I did something I couldn't take back.

I ran away to hide from it.

If Fox found out the truth, he'd never forgive me.

Chapter 9 – Delilah

Past

"Did you know Delilah and Fox are fucking like rabbits every single night that you're not home?" Maddie said in the middle of a bite of noodles like she asked what we were doing after dinner.

I froze as I twirled my fork in the spaghetti I made for dinner as my ears burned with embarrassment. "Maddie." I hissed before sneaking a glance at Blaine in the seat next to me.

He finished chewing, but glared at me in silence.

"What?" Maddie shrugged her shoulders, "It's not like he even *tries* to sneak in at all hours of the night. And it's not like you ever try to be quiet while he bounces your headboard off the wall."

"Jesus Christ Maddie, shut your mouth." Blaine ordered her, and she sank in her chair. "Is it true?" He asked me, and I straightened my shoulders under his gaze.

"We're dating."

His nostrils flared, and he scraped his fork across his plate as he scooped up another bite. "Fox doesn't date, D. He fucks. Everyone."

"Are you saying he's fucking someone else right now?" I argued, and he quirked a brow.

"Probably."

"Shut up." I snapped, hating how he chose to be an ass instead of my brother. "He isn't. I know he's not."

"When did it start?" He asked angrily, opening and clenching his fist on the table.

"A few weeks ago."

He pursed his lips, "About the time I took his role as head enforcer." He scoffed, "Sounds about right."

"What's that supposed to mean?" I pushed my plate away and glared at him.

"I'm just saying it doesn't surprise me that he starts giving it to my little sister right after I take his job."

"Fuck you." I hissed and stood up, taking my half-eaten meal to the trash and throwing it away.

"Oh, come on!" He shoved his chair back and toppled it over as he chased after me. "You think he actually wants you for you? You're eighteen!"

"I'll be nineteen in a few weeks. And you're twenty-one!" I yelled back, "You're not much older than me, Blaine! Stop treating me like a child."

"But he's twenty-five!" He threw it at me. "What could you possibly get out of being his toy, D?"

"I'm not his toy!" I rounded on him, "I'm his girlfriend."

"Then why hasn't he mentioned you to me or the other guys?" He questioned, "Why hasn't he brought you to any of the parties or get togethers at the club?" He voiced the concerns I'd managed to ignore.

"Because he doesn't want me around the club after my last unpleasant experience there. And I don't want to be there, one time was enough for me." I said meekly, deflating a bit, in uncertainty. "It's dangerous."

"Not with him. Or with me at your side." He challenged. "Admit it, D. He shows up here only when I'm not around, uses you and moves on before the morning light. That doesn't sound like a relationship."

"Whatever." I pushed past him and walked back through the house. "Your opinion doesn't matter to me."

"You don't get it." He stomped after me, "He's using you."

"He's your best friend; do you really think so poorly of him? You're the one that brought him around."

He whitened a bit at that. "He's no good for you."

"Says who?" I cried, "You? You're exactly like him!"

"And I'm a scumbag on a good fucking day, D. We both know we haven't had a good day in years!"

"Don't say that." I sighed, standing at the bottom of the stairs.

"Don't let him use you. You deserve better." He said gently, lowering his voice like I did. "He's not good enough for you."

"He makes me happy."

"It won't last." He sighed, "He doesn't stick with one girl for long. Not in the four years I've known him."

"It doesn't mean he won't settle down with me."

"Yes, it does." He shook his head and scrubbed his hand over his face. "That's exactly what that means. Fox will never be the come home at night to the white picket fence home kind of man. And that's the kind of man that you deserve, not someone like us."

"You don't know that." I said, but even I could feel the doubt in my voice.

"Yes, I do." He tried one more time.

Tears filled my eyes, and I hated how he made me feel like he was right when ten minutes ago I was blissfully content with the status of my relationship with Fox. "I need some fresh air." I said, grabbing my keys off the hook and walking out the front door.

He followed me. "Where are you going?" He put his hands in his front pockets as he stood on the porch.

"I don't know." I shook my head in defeat. "What does it matter? It's not like you or Maddie will notice my absence, even if I'm not here. Neither of you give a flying fuck about me, and you haven't for months now, so go do what you do every night and so will I."

I got in my car and tore off out of the driveway, leaving a fresh strip of rubber on the concrete.

He was wrong.

He had to be.

I drove around aimlessly for hours with my windows down and the music blaring loudly. I needed to clear my head and get away from Blaine's disapproving glare or I was going to give in and let his doubts give life to my own.

Because he was right, in a way.

Fox wasn't the settling down kind.

Right now.

But Fox said that was what he wanted. He wanted to get out of the MC thing and have a wife and kids someday. He said that, and he said he wanted those things with me.

And that he loved me.

I just had to trust in him, and I'd be fine.

People changed. I knew they did.

My phone rang for the millionth time in the center console, and I groaned, looking down expecting to see Maddie or Blaine's number again. They had called basically nonstop since I left.

But this time, Fox's name popped up. I hesitated, knowing he'd hear the emotion in my voice if I picked up, but I didn't want him worrying about me if I didn't.

"Hello." I said, turning my music down and rolling my windows up.

"Where are you?" His voice was deep and commanding, I shivered as it ran down my spine.

"Driving around. Why?"

"Where, Delilah?" He snapped and then sighed.

"What's wrong?"

"Blaine just stopped by the club, screaming at me for—." He groaned, and I imagined him walking around with his hand, tousling up his hair over and over. "He said you took off, upset and that he hasn't been able to reach you for hours."

"I'm fine, I just wanted to clear my head."

"Where are you?" He asked again, "Why didn't you call me?"

"I don't know, Fox. I guess I just wanted some space."

"Space." He whispered, sounding pained by it. "From me?"

"No." I shook my head and hit my fist against my steering wheel. I was so exhausted from the emotional turmoil, and I needed to go back home and go to bed, but I didn't want to face my brother just yet.

Not after what he said to me.

And not after what I said back to him.

"Let me make this better for you, baby." He said softly, and I groaned, wanting to give in to the comfort he offered.

"Okay."

"Go home, and I'll meet you there." He said quickly, like he was excited I was letting him in.

"Do you think that's best? With him so mad?"

"I don't care what he wants, you're a grown ass woman, and he's not your daddy." He grumbled, "He's going to have to get used to the idea of us together, because I'm not fucking going anywhere unless you tell me you don't want me. And even then, I'm probably not going to just give the fuck up on you. I love you."

"I love you too." I sighed and laid my head against the headrest. "Okay, I'll be home in about an hour."

"I'll meet you there." He hung up the phone, and I tried to ignore how angry he sounded when he talked about Blaine.

I hated that I may have been the cause of a rift between them, they'd been friends for years, but I wouldn't lie and say Fox wasn't worth a little disturbance to our everyday life.

When I got home an hour later, Fox wasn't there. But Maddie was.

She flew at me the second I walked in the door and wrapped her arms around my neck. "I'm sorry." She whispered and sighed as I hugged her back.

"I know." I replied heavily. "He deserved to know, just not like that."

"I know." She pulled back, "I'm jealous, that's all."

My brows crinkled on my forehead as I looked at her in confusion, "Of what?"

"You." She said meekly, "That's why I blew you in like that."

"What could you possibly be jealous of me about?" I wondered. "You go out and live your life every single day without a care in the world and I'm the little old lady left behind to make sure everything gets done around here for you and Blaine to have a nice place to land. All while busting my ass in nursing school." My bitterness seeped out the second I opened my mouth, and it left my mouth sour.

She sighed and deflated even more, "I'm jealous that you can just go on with your life and make something of yourself. I feel like since mom died, I'm on a hamster wheel that I can't get off, but I can't get it to go anywhere and I'm just circling the fucking thing day in and day out with no direction or destination in mind." She sniffed, "I just want to have a purpose, and you have one. School, then becoming a nurse, and now you have Fox and-," She groaned, "He's the most delicious man on the face of this earth, and the man fucking adores you. So, I'm jealous."

I smirked at her description and pulled her with me up the stairs towards our rooms, "I'm sorry that you're struggling, here I've been the one jealous of you for being able to be so carefree, I didn't realize it was because you were frustrated."

"Do you think Blaine will come around to the idea of you and Fox together?"

"Yes." I answered honestly, "They're best friends for a reason, after all. I just think he needs to see how Fox is when he's with me for him to understand it's not a fling. It's serious."

"Do you love him?" She asked, leaning her shoulder on her bedroom door as I opened my own down the hall.

"With literally every single thing inside of me." I answered truthfully.

"I think you're going to get your happily ever after." She smiled, "And I'll just have to learn how to keep my jealous green monster hidden when you do."

I laughed and shook my head, "You'll get yours too someday, babe."

"Does Fox have a sexy younger brother you haven't told me about?" She smirked.

"No." I laughed, "Only child."

"Damnit." She thumped her fist into her hand and then pointed like she had a lightbulb over her head, "I got it!" She cheered, "Sister wives."

"Get fucked." I groaned, "No way are you ever getting Fox in bed."

"Oh, come on! You make it sound so good, though."

"It is," I smirked and walked into my room, "The man has many talents indeed."

"Bitch." She joked as I shut my door.

I smiled and felt lighter as I got into pajamas and cleaned my face and brushed my teeth. I waited for him a little longer before giving into the exhaustion inside of me and crawled into bed. He'd get here when he could, I knew that. And I knew he'd make his way to me, and everything would be okay again.

Everything was okay when Fox held me in his arms.

Chapter 10 – Delilah

Past

*B*ang. Bang. Bang.

I woke up with fear already burning through my chest as I sat up out of bed.

Bang. Bang. Bang.

My bedroom door opened, and Maddie ran in with fear in her eyes. "Who is it?" She hissed at me.

"I don't know." I looked at the clock on my end table. Four am.

Fox wasn't here, even though he told me six hours ago he'd meet me here.

But he didn't knock.

Ever.

Bang. Bang. Bang.

"Rawlings County Sherriff's Department. Open up, please." A loud voice boomed from the front porch outside of my window.

"What the fuck?" I whispered and leaped from bed to look out my bedroom window.

Sure enough, two police cruisers were parked along the curb.

I grabbed a pair of jeans off the top of my basket and slid a hoodie over the sleep tank I wore and pushed Maddie behind me. "Stay up here."

"No way." She whispered, "Do you think Blaine got arrested?"

"I hope not." I grumbled, "I'm out of bail money this week."

I made my way downstairs, still on edge, and turned on the porch light, illuminating two police officers on the porch, and opened the front door. Maddie tucked in behind me as the men looked down at us. "Good evening miss, I'm looking for Delilah Beckett."

"I'm Delilah." I said softly, "What can I do for you?"

The first officer, a younger man, looked at me with a bit of a puzzled look on his face and then looked behind him to his partner, an older man. The older officer nodded with a bit of a shrug and the younger officer faced me again.

"I'm sorry miss," He said, removing his hat, "But I'm afraid I'm here to inform you that your brother, Blaine Beckett, was killed this evening."

"What—?" I asked and grabbed for the door frame to support me as my knees became weak. Maddie's nails dug their way down my arm as she stumbled backward from the news. "What did you say?" I asked again, louder; surely I misunderstood him.

"I'm sorry miss," the officer said again, "Someone found your brother outside the Corner Stop gas station a few hours ago. Someone fatally stabbed him."

"No." I hissed and fell to my knees. The jolt of the wood floor made my teeth clash together. I felt like I was going to pass out.

The officer said more, but I heard nothing past the blood roaring in my ears. Maddie's screams turned blood curdling as she clung to me, but I couldn't offer her comfort.

Every mean and unjust thing I'd said to Blaine before I left resurfaced, and my stomach revolted. I shucked Maddie off me, ran onto the porch and fell to my knees on the edge, throwing up in the bushes with violent heaves.

The officers circled slowly, everything moved in a weird slow motion around me. They asked if they could call anyone for us, a parent or a relative maybe, but I just shook my head.

We had no one that lived close, my mom's sister lived in Kansas, and she hadn't been to California since my mom's funeral.

It was just me and Maddie now.

We were all alone.

I finally got myself up off my knees and grabbed my phone off the table where I laid it when we came downstairs and blindly dialed my number one emergency contact.

Blaine.

They made a mistake. He wasn't dead.

It was a mistake.

Ring.

Ring.

Ring.

Ring.

"Hey, it's Blaine, leave a message."

"No!" I sobbed.

I pulled the phone away and did it again.

Ring.

Ring.

Ring.

Ring.

"Hey, it's Blaine, leave a message."

"It's not true." I pleaded into the voicemail, "Say it's not true, please."

It felt like my heart was being torn from my chest, while an elephant sat down on it, squeezing the air right out of my lungs. The phone clattered to the floor, and I covered my face in agony. I didn't know how to exist in the world without my mom *and* Blaine. How was I expected to pick the pieces up and move forward anymore?

"Delilah," Maddie cried, stumbling across the floor to me. "What do we do?"

I stared at her with my mouth open, "I don't know."

"Call Fox." She whispered, picking my phone up and handing it to me. "He'll know what to do." She insisted, "He'll know what we need to do."

I blindly dialed his number and put the phone to my ear as the police officers lingered in the doorway. I didn't know what their protocol was, but it felt like they were standing there in case one of us lost our actual minds.

But they couldn't help us.

"Baby, I'm coming. I'm sorry I got tied up with something." Fox's tired voice filled my ears, and I covered my mouth to stifle the sob that escaped. "Delilah?" He asked, more alert, "What is it?"

I shook my head and cried harder, something about hearing his voice tore down any last piece of strength I had, and I sank to the floor sobbing for what I'd lost.

"Talk to me, baby." I heard noise in the background, like he was outside.

"Blaine." I croaked and choked on my breath. Maddie sobbed next to me, clinging to my hand so hard it felt like it would fall off, but it grounded me just enough to get it out.

"What about him?" I could hear the fear in his voice.

"He's-," My voice broke, "He's dead."

"No," His own voice cracked, "No he's not. No, don't say that. Why would you say that, D?"

"The cops. They're here. He was murdered."

"I'm coming. Where are you?" He screamed Blaine's name as he lost control. "No! Are you home?"

"Yeah, please hurry Fox. I need you. Please." I begged him to save me from my heartache.

"I'm coming, baby, stay with me. I'm coming." I heard the roar of his motorcycle, and then it was just wind and his screams as he drove through the night to get to me.

I didn't pay attention to how long it took him to get to me, but in what felt like seconds, he was at my door, thundering up the steps and shoving his way in past the cops to get to me.

"Come here." He slid across the floor and wrapped his strong arms around my shaking shoulders as I wept. He kissed my forehead and held me tight before grabbing Maddie and pulling her into the embrace as well. She clung to us both, so scared and unsure at only sixteen.

And Fox held us up, his strength alone kept us from disintegrating into the floorboards with our tears. "I don't know what to do." I gasped and wrapped my arms around his neck.

"Don't worry about it right now. I've got you." He kissed my hair and rubbed his hands up and down my back before turning his attention to the police. "What happened?"

The young cop stepped inside, "Mr. Beckett was stabbed outside the Corner Stop a few hours ago."

"Did he get to the hospital?" Fox asked.

"No, he passed away in the parking lot before the ambulance could get to him."

"The Corner Stop?" He shook his head, "That makes no sense, he was supposed to be here, hours ago."

"We have some questions about Blaine's whereabouts this evening if you have any information that could help us find out who did this?"

"Wait," I unburied my face from Fox's neck, "You don't know who murdered my brother?"

"No," The officer said, "He was found lying in the parking lot by another customer, and there are no security cameras on that part of it. We don't know how long he was there before he was found."

"He died alone?" I cried, aching even harder. "He didn't have anyone to even hold his hand?"

"I'm sorry, Miss." The officer said in response.

"Oh god." I sobbed, and Fox tightened his hold on me.

"I need to call Aunt Suzie," Maddie said, pulling out of Fox's embrace. "I feel like we need a parent here."

I nodded at her as she got up and walked to her bedroom in a trance, but the hits kept coming.

"Delilah," The older officer said, stepping into the house, "I'm sorry to darken this evening for you even more, but we need you to come down to the coroner's office to identify him."

"What?" I shook my head wildly, "You don't know it's him?" How the fuck was this happening?

"We do, his fingerprints were run electronically at the scene, but we need a physical ID made before we can release him to the funeral home after the autopsy."

"No," I shuddered and looked at Fox, "I can't."

He tried to soothe me and pushed my hair back, "I know baby." He hummed and turned back to the cop, "I'll do it."

"I'm sorry, but it must be next of kin. It won't be until tomorrow or the next day, so you have some time to come to terms with it."

"Son of a bitch." Fox cursed and hugged me tighter.

"But back to Blaine's whereabouts tonight," The officer said, "If we could start there it could help us find who did this."

"Come on, baby, let's help them find he son of a bitch that did this." Fox said and helped me stand up off the floor and got me into a chair at the table before taking the seat next to mine as the cops pulled up the others.

Last night Blaine sat in the very chair I did and ate the dinner I made before our argument.

"Okay," The officer said and pulled out a notepad. "Let's start with you, Delilah, when was the last time you saw your brother."

I swallowed and forced down the bile that once again tried to burn my throat. "I left here about seven. He was on the porch when I left."

"Do you know where he went after that?"

I shook my head, "I was mad at him, so I left to get some fresh air, and I didn't come back until after eleven."

"You were mad at him? Why?" The officer stared at me, and I hated the way this part of the conversation was going to sound.

"Because we got into an argument."

"What about?"

"Does that fucking matter?" Fox bit in.

"Yes, it does," The cop said firmly. "It helps paint the whole picture."

"We fought over my relationship with Fox." I swallowed, "Blaine didn't know about it until tonight."

The officer looked at Fox and then back at me. "Then what happened?"

I shrugged and sighed, "I came home and went to bed, my sister Maddie was the only one home when I got back, and we were here all night."

He nodded and looked back at Fox. "Did you see Blaine this evening?"

"He came to the clubhouse around ten. Was only there for ten, maybe twenty minutes and then left."

The office wrote that down, and I felt a prickle of apprehension in my gut.

"What happened when you saw him?"

"We argued. We shoved each other around a little and then he left."

The older cop leaned forward, "Anyone else around when you two got into a shoving match?"

"Half the club." Fox snapped back. "Same half saw him leave."

"Where were you for the rest of the night?"

I bit my tongue and forced my face to stay impassive as the questions took a turn towards Fox because he had been MIA all evening and I didn't know why.

"At the club and on club business." Fox gave veiled truths, and I could tell the cops were persecuting him in their brains, which tore me to shreds.

"They're best friends." I added, "In case you're stupid enough to think that Fox had anything to do with this."

Fox squeezed my hand in my lap and kissed my forehead. "Shh."

"We're just doing our job, Miss." The younger cop said and wrote down the information. "Did either of you talk to him after the last time you saw him?"

"No." Fox said instantly.

"He called me a bunch, but I-." My voice cracked and tears pooled in my eyes again, "I ignored them because I was mad."

"When was the last time he called?"

I pulled up my call log and scanned through my missed calls.

Twenty-seven times he tried calling me and he left four voicemails.

"Ten thirty." I said, eyeing the voicemail icon, knowing I'd never hear the voice on the other end in person ever again.

"Thank you." He said and closed his book.

"Do either of you know of anyone that would want Blaine dead?"

"No." I whispered, shaking my head and Fox agreed silently.

"A detective from the Homicide Department will be in touch tomorrow for more questions, and they'll be able to set up a time for you to come down and take care of the identification." They both stood up, but I couldn't rise to walk them out.

Fox did in my place, shutting the door behind them and then returning to my side.

"Let's get you in bed." He said gently.

"No," I shook my head and kept my feet planted on the floor and turned to him. "Where were you?"

He clenched his jaw, and his nostrils flared slightly, but he remained silent.

"You said you were going to meet me here, but you didn't show." I whispered.

"Club shit came up."

"Not good enough Fox." I shook my head, "I deserve a real answer."

His brows dropped over his face, "What are you trying to say, D?"

"You've never stood me up before."

"Shit happens all the time, this was unavoidable."

"Did you see Blaine after I talked to you?"

"What the fuck?" He roared and backed up like I slapped him. I stood up from my chair and forced my spine to stay strong. "Do you think I fucking killed him?" He snapped.

"I think you had an argument with him and didn't show up when you said you would. When I clearly needed you!"

"I showed up now!" He yelled, "I didn't kill your brother!"

"Delilah?" Maddie said meekly from the bottom of the stairs as we stood in a tense standoff.

I knew he didn't kill Blaine, deep inside of me, but the pain hurt so bad I couldn't think straight.

No one said anything else as we stared at each other. Fox paced back and forth, running his hands through his hair with his chest rising and falling rapidly as tears spilled over my cheeks.

"Make this make sense for me, Fox." I whispered.

"I can't." He turned on me, "I wish I could, D, but I don't know what happened." Roars of motorcycles outside rattled the windows of the house as headlights lit up the front yard. Fox turned and looked out at the lights as his men walked up the front steps. "But I plan to get to the bottom of it," He turned back to me. "I promise you I'll make this right. Even if you don't believe me."

I didn't have a chance to reply as he opened the front door and a dozen men from the Rust Hawks MC walked into my dining room with somber looks on their faces. Fox shook hands with them and then came to stand by my side as the President, Colt put his large hand on my shoulder and looked at me with empathy.

"I can't imagine what you're feeling right now, but I want you to know that we're here for you through this."

"That won't bring Blaine back to me." I said and shrugged his hand off me. "Tell me that you'll find the son of a bitch that murdered my brother, and then I'll be interested in talking to you. But if you can't do that, then leave."

I didn't recognize the anger inside of me or the bravery to address such a scary man so forwardly, but I wasn't the same girl I had been before tonight had happened either.

Colt nodded his head solemnly, "We'll find him; and when we do, he'll pay for it in blood."

"Good." I said, feeling strength and exhaustion trying to battle each other inside of me.

Colt turned to Fox, "Cops been by?"

"They were here when I got here, they informed D."

"What they say?"

Fox clenched his jaw and looked at me. "Go upstairs baby, I'll be up in a few." He kissed my forehead again, and I let his touch comfort me even as the police officer's doubts replayed in my head.

I wanted to fight him; I wanted to say fuck that, this was my house. But I was bone weary, and I knew Maddie didn't need to hear the specifics they were about to discuss. I was naïve to a lot of what happened inside of the illegal MC, but not of everything.

I knew if Colt said they'd make someone pay in blood, that meant they'd kill him.

An eye for an eye.

I walked out of the room and took Maddie's hand, pulling her upstairs and into my room.

"What are they going to do?" She whispered as their voices faded to murmurs through the floor.

"I don't know." I answered truthfully. I turned the lights off in my room and took my jeans off and pulled my sweatpants on before climbing into bed. "I can't think about that right now. Come here." After pulling back the blankets, she quickly climbed in next to me, and I wrapped my arms around her as she sniffled and shook, losing control of her emotions again. "I'm going to take care of you, Maddie. I promise you that."

"If I had kept my mouth shut at dinner, you wouldn't have fought and he would still be here." She cried.

"Shh," I smoothed her hair back as my own tears and guilt washed over me anew. "It's not your fault. Whoever did this made the decision regardless of what we did." I sighed, "I just know he didn't deserve it, and I don't know how to move forward now."

"Me either." She tightened her arms around me. "Aunt Suzie will be here tomorrow; she'll know what to do."

"Yeah," I said, knowing that my mom's sister would have some sort of guidance for us, even if she'd never dealt with murder on her ranch in Kansas. But she was older and wise, and heaven help us, she was our only hope.

Because I didn't know how to even put one foot in front of the other and traverse this terrible situation on my own.

Maddie fell asleep in my arms and rolled over away from me after a while, curled in a ball. I heard the motorcycles leave and soon after that my bedroom door opened, and I looked over at Fox as he walked in.

His face was somber, and he looked older than he had just yesterday when I saw him last.

"She asleep?" He whispered as he toed his boots off.

"Yeah," I replied and scooted over towards her to give him room in my queen size bed.

"I'll sleep in the chair." He said, not meeting my eye in the darkened room, but I could feel the hurt and pain radiating off him.

"Please." I said as my voice cracked, "I'm sorry." I wiped away tears that fell over the bridge of my nose as I held my hand out to him, "I know you didn't do it, Fox."

He clenched his jaw and stared at the wall with his hands on his hips, refusing to face me. "My whole life people have doubted me and made me the bad guy in their own story." He whispered. "But you—." He turned and looked at me and I could see the unshed tears in his eyes as I sat up in bed, "You're the only person in this world that has ever known me here." He thumped his fist over his chest and worked his jaw opened and closed. "If you doubt me, about this, I can't—." He shook his head, "I won't survive it."

"I don't." I cried, swiping away the tears, "I'm sorry, I'm just upset and lost and feel like my entire world is exploding around me and I don't know what to grab onto to anchor me anymore."

"Me, Delilah." He hissed, kneeling next to the bed, and grabbing both of my hands to squeeze against his lips where he kissed them. "You grab onto me and let me hold you steady while the world swirls and torments around us. I'm your anchor, baby; I'll hold you down and keep you afloat in the same fucking moment, because that's what you do for me. Every second of every day, you're my saving grace." He sighed, "Let me be yours."

"I know." I cried, scooting forward, and wrapping my arms and legs around him, "I'm sorry." I whispered repeatedly into his neck. "You lost your best friend tonight too, I'm sorry."

"Shh," he said and sighed. "Just get some sleep, baby. We'll worry about everything else later."

"Lay with me, please." I begged, "I need you."

"I'm right here." He slid in next to me and I clung to him like a life raft in the ocean. He tightened his hold on me and clung back just as fiercely.

We were two broken souls holding onto each other for dear fucking life.

Chapter 11 – Delilah

Present

I walked downstairs like a zombie a few hours later after my shock induced nap and forced myself to smile at my baby girl as she flung herself off the end of the couch into my arms. With burning eyes and a tight squeeze, I cursed the tears.

I would not fucking cry in front of Penelope.

"Hey, honey." I kissed her temple. "How was school?"

"Good!" She cheered and jumped from my arms to climb over the arm of the couch and jump onto a pillow on the floor again, one of her favorite games. "We learned songs for Halloween. Want to hear one?" She asked.

"Of course," I said, sitting down in the chair and pulling my legs up under me to listen to my sweet baby girl.

"Five little pumpkins were sitting on a gate..." She sang with merriment as I watched her intently. She held her fingers up and counted down the song and amazed me with her knowledge.

She was so smart; and she was my entire reason for existence. Without her, I'd be nothing.

When she was all done singing, I clapped my hands, and she took a big elaborate bow in the center of the living room. Maddie walked in with a cup of tea and handed it to me as Penelope slid into another song about scarecrows excitedly.

Maddie sat on the arm of the chair and offered her silent support to me. That was what she had done since Blaine's murder.

In a way, the tragedy was what she needed to climb out of the trouble making hole she'd fallen into in high school. I was glad for another positive to come from such a dark time.

The first one was my daughter.

"Mama, can we watch a movie in your room after bath time?"

"Hmm." I said and tapped my chin, "Depends, do I get to pick or do you?"

She rolled her eyes and leaped from the couch onto the pillow again, "Me. Duh," She pushed her dark hair back out of her eyes and panted from exertion.

I smiled at her and pretended to be offended. "What? I pick good movies."

"No, you don't," She giggled, "Yours are boring and you always fall asleep, anyway."

It was my turn to roll my eyes at her as I got out of the chair to start dinner, "Fine, but I get to pick the snack."

"Deal!" She screeched as she Peter Pan'd herself across the room and landed in a fit of giggles.

Regardless of what was going on in my life, I had to keep it together for her. She deserved so much more than the hand she was dealt because of my own recklessness.

So, I put every ounce of love I had into her favorite dinner and even whipped up a chocolate cake from a box in the pantry and held back the winces as she licked the beaters, coating her pretty face and hair in the sweet mess.

After dinner, I let her help me frost it with her favorite peanut butter frosting, then threw her in the bath to clean up the gigantic mess she made, eating it all just as quickly as I put it on.

When I settled into bed next to her with a plate of sugary sweet comfort food and a movie about superhero dogs, I let myself relax and embrace the relief of her presence.

I was going to make sure everything turned out okay; I had no other choice.

After I put her in her own bed and walked downstairs, Maddie sat at the kitchen table with a cup of tea in her hands. She wanted to talk, I could tell. Judging by the look on her face, it felt ominous. "I think I should take P to visit with Aunt Suzie for a week."

"What?" I gasped in shock. Pain instantly skyrocketed into my chest at the thought of going that long without my baby. "No." I shook my head, "Absolutely not."

"How long do you think it's going to take before Fox shows up on the doorstep, D?" She asked gently, "And when he does, what's he going to say when a beautiful little girl with his eyes answers the door that he doesn't know exists?"

"I can't go that long without her, Maddie." I cried, shaking my head.

"She'll be fine, I promise. Suzie is only a three-hour drive away, and she's been begging for us to visit, but we haven't because of your work schedule. I think this is the perfect opportunity for you to have some time to handle this whole thing." She tilted her head to the side, "You have to tell him the truth, D."

"I know that." I hissed.

"I think it'd be the perfect situation to have time to reacquaint yourself with Fox and tell him without the pressure of him finding out on his own. Because we both know that wouldn't go over well."

Defeated, I collapsed into the chair opposite her; she was right. I had to tell him, and every day that passed just made it even more pressing.

"I don't know how to survive without her for that long." I said honestly, "Or without you, for that matter."

"I know, babe." She patted my hand reassuringly. "But it's going to work out for the better in the long run. I just know it." She sighed, "I already talked to Suzie, and she's expecting us tomorrow night. I told her we'd come after dinner tomorrow before you go to Cherry's for the night. You'll be gone all night and day Saturday and Sunday, so it'll be like getting through those first two days alone without even realizing it."

"Maddie." I shook my head, "Not tomorrow. Maybe next week."

"No, Delilah." She said firmly, "It must be tomorrow. Every second that passes just makes this whole situation worse. We'll go tomorrow and she can have a fun break at Aunt Suzie's ranch. I can still do my schoolwork wherever, and you can enjoy some peace and quiet. Relax a little too. Take some time for you because we both know you never do that."

"I don't know."

"It will be fine. I promise you."

"I'll miss you both so much." I said sadly, and she nodded knowingly.

"I know, but I think it's for the best."

"Maybe." I said, staring off into the distance. "Make sure she has the best time of her life, Maddie." I sniffled as tears started pooling, "God knows she deserves it."

"Mom, can we eat cake for dinner tonight?" Penelope asked me on the way home from school the next afternoon.

"Uh—." I paused and then shrugged my shoulders, "Why not."

"Yes!" She hissed, pumping her fist in the air and I smiled at her in the review mirror.

I slept through the entire night last night, something I hadn't done in years. And I tried to pretend that it had nothing to do with a certain level of peace settling in my troubled heart from finding out that Fox didn't kill my brother.

Regardless of its cause, it had left me in a good mood, and I was feeling generous to her ridiculous ploys.

Maybe it was stupid, it probably was, but it made me feel less guilty for longing for him still.

The fear assaulted me the second I let myself feel that relief, though, knowing I'd hidden a big secret from him for five years. And he was going to be pissed when he found out.

Regardless of my motive behind it, Maddie was right. I was in a hole, and every day that passed now that I had knowledge of his innocence, I dug myself deeper into it as I kept my own secrets.

I just didn't want to admit the wrong I'd done based solely off the wrongs I'd thought had been done to me. Only there was no avoiding it any longer, for when we got back from school, Maddie had both of their suitcases by the door.

Penelope eyed them curiously as she tossed her backpack in the closet, "Mama, are we going somewhere?" She asked.

I took a deep breath and put on my best brave face. "You and Aunt Maddie are going on a special vacation!" I said excitedly, "Do you want to know where?"

"Yes!" Penny jumped up and down eagerly.

"You're going to see Aunt Suzie on her ranch in Kansas. You get to stay there and help her with her horses and goats and chickens and all the other fun animals I'm sure she's collected since we talked to her last."

"Do I get to ride on a horse?" She clasped her hands together under her chin like she was begging for it.

"I'm sure she has all of it set up for you, baby." I ran my hand over her hair, "You're going to have a great time. And Aunt Maddie will be with you the whole time, doesn't that sound like so much fun?"

She tilted her head to the side and dropped her hands. "You're not going?"

I shook my head but smiled, "No, I must stay home and work. But I promise you'll have so much fun even without me. You can call me every day and we can video chat and everything. You won't miss me a bit, I swear."

She hesitated, chewing on her little bottom lip as Maddie walked into the room. "We're going to have so much fun, Juney Bug, Aunt Suzie said she bought a whole bushel of carrots so you could feed her horses."

"That sounds fun." She said hesitantly. "If you're sure." She asked, looking up at me.

"I'm sure baby." Holding her tight, I lingered much longer than necessary. "I miss you already, but you'll be back before you know it. I promise."

"Okay, Mama." She said and then jumped down to check over her suitcase in excitement. I sat back and watched her, letting her joy fill my aching heart with anything other than despair. Being away from her for a whole week while also facing down the painful conversations I was going to have to have with Fox were both daunting tasks.

Persuading myself to put my big girl panties on and do it, as I had with everything else in life.

I made dinner, grilled cheeses to go with the cake I promised her, and we ate in the living room around the TV like we didn't have a care in the world. When it was all done, she jumped into the back seat of Maddie's car and waved out the window as they pulled away down the street.

I wanted nothing more than to call in sick from my shift and lay in bed sobbing for my little girl and all the wrongs that were done to her without her knowledge, but I forced myself to go to work anyway.

I had to stay busy and figure out a way to tell Fox of my deception because if I didn't have a plan in place, I'd fuck it up.

When I parked in my spot along the edge of Cherry's full parking lot, I scanned the pavement for trouble like I'd been doing for years.

And found it leaning against his motorcycle seat, smoking a cigarette.

Taz.

Or at least it was Taz's bike, but the man leaning against it wasn't very recognizable with two swollen black eyes and some scrapes over his nose and lips.

I put my hand in my purse, gripping my mace and got out of my car to walk in the back kitchen door of the bar.

"Hey, Delilah." He said as I approached, looking me up and down. "Fancy meeting you here." He grinned and grimaced as his lips pulled.

"You look like shit." I said honestly, walking past him to the safety of the building. Except he reached out so quickly I didn't see it until his hand snaked around my elbow and pulled me to a rough stop in front of him.

"And I wonder who I have to blame for that." He sneered into my face, and I saw the pure rage in his eyes behind the bruises and broken blood vessels.

"I had nothing to do with it." I shook my arm, trying to dislodge his hand, but he had an iron grip and I whined when it felt like he was trying to snap my bones.

"Right." He scoffed and shook me a couple of times, "You really expect me to believe you had nothing to do with the Eagles showing up here and dancing on my face?"

"I don't run with the Eagles." I spit out and shoved against his chest. He reeked like body odor, and I wanted to gag from being so close. "I don't run with you either, so let me go."

"Fuck that." He hissed and pushed me against the car parked next to his bike, slamming my back against the mirror so hard that it snapped and hung off the door uselessly. "You've been wanting my dick since the moment you stepped foot in this town. Then suddenly you set me up, like a fucking bitch."

"I didn't ask you to wait for me after my shift Taz, you did that all on your own. I didn't have anything to do with it."

"Bullshit." He spat and pulled me off the car, only to slam me against it again. "The big guy with the mask said you were his. And here you were, running around flirting with me and every other dick in the bar for tips like you didn't belong to someone already."

"I don't." Shoving at him, trying to dislodge him again, but the way he had me pinned made my mace inaccessible. I couldn't even get my hand out of my purse. "Get the fuck off of me, Taz!" I yelled and kicked, but it was useless with my back bent over the rounded door of the car. He had leverage over me, and I was on the short end of the stick of karma.

"Fuck you, bitch." He cursed and landed a fist to my side, sucking the air out of my lungs so fast I didn't have a chance to take a breath first. I gasped and doubled over against him in agony as stars danced around the edge of my vision. A car pulled into the lot and their headlights scanned over us as they parked on the other side. He leaned against my ear while I desperately fought to move air into my lungs and hissed, "This ain't over, Delilah. I'll be seeing you around and when I do, you better have that pussy good and wet for me. I'm taking my cut of it."

With that, he shoved me to the ground before landing a kick to my side. I cried in agony as my lungs protested the lack of oxygen and tried to crawl to my feet as he threw his leg over his motorcycle and took off. I sat there on my hands and knees, working air in and out painfully when Lori ran up the walk.

"Holy shit, D. Are you okay?" She crouched next to me, running her hands through my hair to push it back from my face. "D!" She yelled, and I nodded, still unable to talk. "Let's get you inside."

She helped me stand up and threw my arm over her shoulders to walk us into the kitchen door of the building. I fell into the closest chair, and she ran to get me some water. When she came back, Bones, the front door bouncer, was on her heels and they both stared at me with concern in their eyes.

"Talk to me, tell me what happened." He spoke.

I shook my head and took the water from Lori's hands, sipping it slowly. "Nothing."

"Bullshit." He hissed. "I saw Taz ride out of here like a bat out of hell and then Lori comes screaming that you're hurt. Tell me the truth, did he touch you?"

"He thinks I set him up with the Eagles." I said, taking another small sip of the water. My right side burned with each breath, and I was confident at least one rib was bruised if not cracked. I tenderly probed the spot and hissed on contact.

Definitely cracked.

"You're talking about the beat down he got last weekend out back?"

I nodded. "They pulled up while I was walking to my car after work, he was harassing me and they told me to get lost and then," I shrugged, "I guess settled some beef with him. But he blames me."

"You don't run with the Eagles," Lori droned on, "You avoid bikers like the plague even."

"Well," I groaned and stood up, "There's one rider," I lifted my arm up to see how far I could go before I wanted to throw up from the pain, "With the Eagles, we have—history." She raised her eyebrows and Bones scowled, "I didn't even know he was with them now, but he was part of the beef settling group last weekend and I guess he said something to Taz about me. That's what got him started on it."

"Men," Lori groaned and put her hands on her hips, "There's no way you can work tonight." She sighed and tried to figure out what to do.

"Yes, I can." I countered, "I'll be slow for a while, but I got this." I grabbed my purse from the ground where she'd set it down and smiled my best fake and cheery grin at her. "Even my slow body is better than no body backing you up behind the bar tonight and you know it."

"Ugh," She groaned and flipped her hands up in the air because she knew I was right. She turned on Bones and pointed at him, "She gets an escort to and from the building from now on and Taz doesn't get in."

"Duh." He grumbled at her and eyed me closely, "You going to be alright?"

"I'll rally." I sighed and pushed my hair back. "I always do."

"Hey, baby, can I get four shots south of the border and four more heavy on the walker?" A man called over the loud noise of the bar to me as I cashed someone out.

"Yeah," I yelled back, not even bothering to turn around. The place was packed and I was exhausted. The ridiculous amount of Tylenol I'd chewed earlier was finally kicking in, and I could breathe a little easier.

I worked at the ER in the morning, so I was just going to get through the night and get a Xray then. Not that anything could be done about it, but at least then I'd be sure my broken rib wasn't displaced and poking around at my organs like a pitchfork.

I gave my customer back his change and started making the shots the new guy ordered and looked up as I did, trying to be a little personable. The tips were better when you smiled.

As soon as I did, my eyes locked on a pair of glowing green ones sitting next to the man that had ordered the shots, who turned out to be Houston, President of the Black Eagles.

In fact, in the time that I was turned around, my entire section of the bar had flipped and was now littered with Eagle riders.

Fuck.

"Hey." Fox said as I tried to roll with it to not let him know how he affected me. I knew I was going to have to face him soon, I just didn't know it was going to happen tonight. And after everything that happened with Taz, I was not on my game.

"What are you doing here?" I asked, pouring tequila in the glasses.

"We wanted a drink." He shrugged, nodding to his comrades, who watched with fascination. "Figured we'd come here."

"You had a dozen other options." I pointed out the obvious.

"None of them have you, though." He said, staring directly at me.

I froze and spilled expensive top shelf liquor over the rim of the glass and cursed, shaking it off as I tried to focus on the task at hand. After turning to grab another bottle, I looked at him in the mirror as Houston nudged him with a smirk on his face.

I turned back around and finished off the shots and placed them on the bar top in front of the President. As I reached for the last one, I grimaced slightly, noticing Fox's gaze fix on it.

"Seventy even." I said and took Houston's card, "Want to keep this open or just this round?"

"Open, baby, we're going to be here for a while if my man Fox has anything to say about it." He smirked again and nudged Fox before handing him a shot and passing out the rest of them. I put his info into the computer and walked away to help other customers, putting much needed distance between us.

However, every move I made, I could feel Fox's eyes, watching me, studying me and my actions. It was exactly what he used to do when he started coming around with Blaine when we were younger. Silently watching was his game.

Back then, it warmed me and sent fuzzy feelings of excitement through my body every time I caught his stare. And now it did the same damn thing, which confused me and left me on edge.

"You've got a lot of fucking nerve showing up here tonight." Lori snapped as she came out of the kitchen and I whipped around to see her pointing her finger at Houston, before turning her ire on the group of bikers surrounding him, "Which one of you fuckers threw Delilah's name in the mix while you beat the fuck out of Taz last week, huh?" She snapped and I pulled her back.

"Enough." I hissed. "Don't do that."

"I did." Fox said firmly, looking between the two of us, "Why?"

"Don't." I said to Lori and turned to Fox, "Drop it." I shoved Lori and hissed in pain, holding my side, but she didn't give me the break I desperately needed. She had no idea what she was going to start if she told him what had happened.

"He attacked her!" She yelled over the music, pointing directly at him, "Because of you!"

"What the fuck is she talking about?" Fox turned his attention to me, standing up and leaning over the bar.

Houston scowled and watched me intently, too.

"Nothing." I shook my head, "Just drop it Fox."

"Fuck that, D. Tell me or so help me god I'm going to lose my fucking mind."

I cringed at the look of pure menace in his eyes and remembered every nightmare I'd had in the last five years where he stood over me, looking at me exactly like that right before he killed me with his bare hands. Just like he did to Blaine.

Only, he didn't actually kill Blaine.

But that didn't help the fear blooming in my stomach at the current time.

I shook my head again and backed up. Instead, he turned his attention to Lori, "You answer me then, damnit." He growled, "You started this shit, now finish it."

"He broke her ribs in the parking lot a couple of hours ago. Punched and kicked her with his fucking boot like a dog! Blamed her for setting him up last week when you boys showed up." She held her head high as mine sagged in defeat. "He probably would have raped her right there if I hadn't pulled up. Because you spit her name in some caveman act of dominance while you beat him up." She huffed.

"He touched you?" Fox sneered. "Why didn't you tell me?"

"What good would it have done?" I implored, trying to get him to see reason.

He ran his teeth over his bottom lip and stared at me before tapping his fist on the bar top. "I told you when you were eighteen years old that nobody fucks with you on my watch." He raised his eyebrows, and I could read his intent clear as day.

"And then you let me believe that you murdered my brother and went to jail on a life sentence." I snapped back at him, ignoring the curious glares from his biker friends and Lori, "And in the process, you abandoned me to figure life out on my own! You haven't been around for five fucking years Fox; I've handled myself that whole time in ways you would never understand. You don't get to just swoop in now all of a sudden and expect me to go back to the way things were."

"No one touches you!" He hissed, leaning over the bar top. "Stay here. I'll pick you up at closing." He pointed his finger at me. "Don't push me on this either, D. Stay the fuck here and I'll take care of it."

"Fox, just drop it," I tried tiredly, "You'll just make it worse."

"No." He shook his head, "Belden isn't like it was back home, babe. There's an order to how shit gets done and handled. He fucked up."

"He's right." Houston said, standing up and adjusting his cut. "Whether or not you're Fox's girl, doesn't matter, no one is going to touch you because of something I ordered." He nodded, "My apologies for your ribs; I'll be making sure it's taken care of." He tapped his knuckles on the bar top, "Let's ride boys."

And with that, he walked away with the group of bikers following him. Fox looked at me intensely one last time before nodding his head to me. "Stay here and I'll pick you up."

I watched in horror as he walked out the front door with the rest of the Black Eagle MC and turned to Lori, "What the fuck!" I snapped.

She shrugged her shoulders and collected their empty glasses, "I won't apologize if it means you finally have someone to look after you."

I didn't respond, because it was irrelevant.

Because Fox's anger and dedication to me cracked another piece of the icebox in my chest and I felt my heart take a beat for the first time in years. And then he walked out the front door with it firmly in his large hands.

I hated how it felt to stand there yet again, and hope he returned with it.

Chapter 12 – Delilah

Past

"You need to eat." Fox whispered from next to me. "Just take a bite."

"I can't." As he lifted the grilled cheese, I pushed his hand away. "I'll throw it right back up."

He clenched his jaw and put it back on the end table next to my bed. "I need you to try, Delilah. You haven't eaten a bite of food in two days."

"I can't." I moaned, fighting to keep my eyes open. "Just hold me."

"We have to get up, we have to go to the coroner's office in an hour." I stilled and panic filled my nerves. "Relax, I'll be with you the whole time."

"I don't want to see him like that, Fox." I cried; with tears I thought had long dried up. "I don't want to remember him that way."

"I know, baby, but if you don't do it, they'll make Maddie."

I trembled, the cold air seeming to seep into my bones as I imagined my innocent baby sister in the stark, sterile morgue, identifying our brother's still form, a burden I had failed to bear.

"No." I sniffed and forced myself to sit up in my bed. I hadn't gotten out of it for two days. Responsibility hung over my head, and I couldn't ignore it. Not if it would negatively affect my baby sister. "Fine, let's just get it over with."

Fox slid his hands over my hair and looked at me with such tenderness, "Let's get you in the shower and then we'll go."

He picked me up and carried me into the bathroom, gently undressed me and then himself and stood in the small shower with me, holding me up as the weight of the world tried to push me down.

"I love you, Delilah Faith Beckett." He whispered as he shampooed my hair and rinsed it out. He whispered it continually as the steam and the scents mixed in my senses and blocked out everything else.

All that remained was Fox.

Mine.

He was my strength and my rock. I clung to him, and he didn't let me down. He held firm and strong and was everything I ever imagined one could want in a time of need like mine.

"I love you, Fox." I laid my forehead against his wet chest and kissed his skin. "I wouldn't survive this without you." I looked up at him and he stared down at me with such tenderness. "I won't survive anything without you. You're it for me."

"Me too, baby." He growled, leaning down to kiss me slowly. I wrapped my arms around his neck, and he lifted me up and pinned me against the wall. "I can't breathe anymore when you aren't around." He sighed, "It's like you're the lifeline I never had until now, and I don't know how I managed to make it this far in life without you before now."

"I know." I sighed and relaxed into his touch, "I never want to be without you."

"Never." He growled intensely, "I'm not going anywhere, D. Ever."

My hands felt clammy as I ran them up and down my jeans to wipe them off. Fox stood by my side, with his hand on my back, offering me his support silently.

Rawlings County Medical Examiner's Office.

The sign was decorated nicely. I wondered who bothered to design a sign for a place that represented so much pain and loss.

"Let's go." Fox said, gently urging me forward as he opened the front door. The air was cold, and I shivered in apprehension. "Hi, Delilah Beckett is here." Fox said to the receptionist, and she told us to have a seat and they'd be right with us.

My mind raced and my heart felt like it was going to beat out of my chest as we waited, but when the doors opened and a middle-aged man in scrubs called us back, I thought it would stop beating completely.

"Come on, baby," Fox said into my ear, "As soon as it's done, we're gone."

I was silent, I had no words.

The man led us down a hallway to a door where two detectives that were working on my brother's case waited for us.

"Ms. Beckett." The man said, "We're going to go inside, I'll pull down the sheet covering his body to reveal his face and then you just have to let us know if it's your brother or not. Then you can leave."

I nodded on autopilot and grabbed onto the front of Fox's flannel shirt as he hugged me tighter to his side. The door opened and the cold air rushed out, swirling around me like the hands of fate that had tried to strangle me for years now.

A single table lay in the center of the room, and it was obvious a body lay underneath the sheet. It was like a scene out of CSI or something, but my heart broke knowing my brother was lying there, all alone, and cold. He died, alone and cold, with no one there to hold his hand or offer him comfort in his final moments.

For the last two days, every time I closed my eyes, I saw his horrified face, staring up at the dark nighttime sky as he gasped, struggling to breathe as his organs bled out internally. The cruel theft of him from our lives was a constant ache, and every time I allowed myself a single moment of forgetfulness, I'd be overwhelmed by the image of his fear and loneliness.

Almost as if I tortured myself with his pain, it would absolve my guilt for what happened.

The man stood on the other side of the bed as I neared it, and the detectives stood at the end as Fox and I took our place.

"Okay, I'm going to lower the sheet now." The man said and Fox tightened his hold around me.

My heartbeat roared in my ears and my knees felt like they disappeared beneath me as an out-of-body experience took over my mind.

The first thing I saw was the dirty blonde hair that he loved for me to play with and the sharp eyebrows that, even when his face was relaxed, made him look intense. His perfect nose with a slight curve in the bridge of it from when I punched him and broke it after he jumped out from behind my bedroom door at me in the dark when we were kids, was next. And then his day-old stubble that he thought made him look rough and tough, but in reality, it made him look old.

Life had made him look far older than he was.

His perfect face was untouched by the violence he encountered, and for that, I was thankful. I stared down at him and ached for his skin to be pink and full of life instead of the odd gray it was now.

Tears burned in my eyes, but I forced them back because I didn't want to lose this image of him to the blurriness they brought. I wanted to memorize every perfect part of him and store it away inside of me for the long days ahead without him.

It didn't seem possible to imagine walking around on this earth without him existing on it with me. But I knew it was, because that was the same sense of doubt that I felt when I stood at my mom's funeral years ago.

Still, here I was, still alive and managing every day without her.

Just like I would without Blaine.

"It's him." I whispered and reached out, sliding my palm over his hair one last time. "It's Blaine."

I had known it would be, but that didn't keep a small part of my soul from hoping there had been some terrible mistake.

"Thank you." The examiner said and covered his face with the sheet again as I took a shuddered breath.

One of the detectives cleared his throat and closed his notepad, "Mr. St. Claire, we still need you to come down to the station for those questions."

I looked at him and then at Fox in confusion. "Questions about what?"

"Don't worry about it." Fox replied, kissing my temple and nodding to the cop. "I'll get D home and then come down."

"Good." The detective said, "Because if we have to come find you, we won't ask the next time." His threat was there, and I shivered from the menace behind it.

"Let's go." Fox steered me from the room and out into the warm California sunshine, and then into the passenger seat of my car.

When he got behind the wheel and drove us away, I turned to him, "Tell me the truth."

He looked over at me out of the corner of his eye, "I told you the truth."

"No," I sighed, "What do the cops want?"

"To ask about my fight with Blaine."

"Why?"

"I don't know," He shrugged, "Trying to make me the bad guy I guess."

"That's not fair." I turned back in my seat and crossed my arms over my chest, "The real murderer is out there somewhere and they're wasting their time harassing you."

"I know, babe." He grabbed my hand and placed it on his thigh, squeezing it. "But I'll play their game, so they get off my ass and go back to investigating real leads."

"I just don't like it." I pouted.

When we got inside my house, Maddie, Aunt Suzie and Colt sat in the living room. It unnerved me to have the President of the MC inside of my home and so close to my sister, but if I was honest, he'd been nothing but comforting and supportive over the last few days.

So, I had to give the guy a break.

"Was it him?" Maddie asked quietly, and hope shined in her eyes behind the puffiness from crying nonstop. I nodded and looked away from her pain. "Damnit." She whispered, "I was hoping they were wrong.

"Me too." I sighed and watched as a look passed between Colt and Fox.

Fox nodded and Colt cleared his throat, "I'm sorry, D." He said, "I'll let the boys know." He walked around the furniture and headed out the front door, patting Fox on the shoulder once on his way out.

"I have to go out." Fox said to Aunt Suzie, "Can you look after them?"

"Of course," She said with a bit of annoyance, like him even asking was ridiculous.

He kissed me gently, pausing to take a deep breath against my lips. "I'll be back as soon as I can." The way he said it sounded ominous. "I love you."

"I love you, too." I said and grabbed the front of his shirt as he pulled away, "Come back to me, Fox." The instruction ached in my throat, like if I didn't say it out loud, he might not do it.

The look on his face was unreadable, and he just leaned forward and kissed my forehead "You're my only reason to walk this earth, D. I'll always come back to you." He whispered before walking away from me.

I watched him go, with a feeling in my gut that things would never be the same between us ever again.

This darkness was going to hang over us for the rest of forever, if it didn't manage to tear us apart first.

I could feel it deep in my bones.

Chapter 13 – Delilah

Present

"Are you ready to go, D?" Bones asked at the back door of Cherry's after closing.

"Yeah." I nodded and picked up my bag as I scrolled through the pictures that Maddie had sent me of Penelope frolicking through the barn at Aunt Suzie's ranch mere minutes after they arrived. I smiled at the pictures of my baby and then pocketed my phone before following Bones out.

Apprehension pricked my skin like I was jolted with electricity as soon as we walked down the hallway towards the back door.

"Do you think he's out there?" Lori asked, walking up next to me.

"Who? Taz?" I asked.

"No dummy, *Fox*." She sang his voice and winked at me. I rolled my eyes and tried to ignore her as Bones opened the door, letting the cool nighttime air in.

"Doubtful." I said and took a deep breath of fresh air.

No sooner had the words left my mouth, though, I saw a dark figure sitting on a motorcycle next to my car, and I paused.

However, I'd recognize his shadow anywhere. So many nights it lurked in my bedroom and brought with it comfort and pleasure.

I'd never admit it, but seeing Fox waiting for me instead of Taz brought those same two feelings to the surface. And another crack to the icebox, because he cared enough to follow through.

"Want me to kick his ass?" Bones asked as Lori stopped at her own car, tossing out a good night as we kept going.

"No." I shook my head and patted his beefy arm. "I appreciate the offer, though."

"Hmm." He grunted and nodded to Fox as he stood up off his motorcycle. "Have a good night, D. See you tomorrow."

"Night, Bones." I nodded and watched him walk off as Fox's eyes bore into the side of my face. "You didn't have to come back." I said, turning to face him.

"I told you I would." He answered easily and raised an eyebrow at me, like he dared me to challenge him. "We didn't find Taz yet, but the club is still looking for him."

I didn't have it in me to ask what exactly was going to happen to the man when they found him, because I was tired beyond reason. "Thanks." I unlocked my car door, "I got it from here."

"You look dead on your feet, let me give you a ride home." He said, putting his hand on the frame of my door to stop me from opening it any further.

"No." I shook my head, "I have to work in a few hours at the ER, I got it."

"Why are you working yourself to death, D?" He asked, with a pinched brow. "Surely you make enough at the ER to survive."

I scoffed and rolled my eyes, "You don't have a clue what it costs to provide."

"Then tell me." He argued and pushed my door shut, and I sagged against the back door in defeat.

"I can't, Fox." I sighed, "I'm so fucking tired, I just want to go home."

"Let me take you." He stepped closer and his manly scent engulfed me, and I lost myself in the memory of how good he smelled when he held me close. "Come on, D, let me take care of you."

"It's too late for that." I shook my head, "I can't."

"You can." He said and reached up slowly before placing his hand on my cheek and slid it around the back of my neck. It was the first time he touched me in five years, and I melted into it. I tilted my head back to look up at him and tried to ignore the way electricity burned on my skin where he touched me. "I didn't kill Blaine." His face was in shadow, but I could feel the intensity of it as he stared down at me. Time had changed him, but it wasn't in a bad way. He was more mature and filled in, like a grown man where a young man had been before.

But I knew that time behind bars must have had something to do with that, too.

"I know." I closed my eyes and pretended for just a minute that this was okay. That letting him touch me was alright. I leaned against his big hand, and he supported the weight of my head instantly, cradling it gently. His thumb ran over the side of my cheek like he was aching to touch me everywhere. "But either way, too much time has passed. Too many things can't be undone."

"I want you." He growled, taking another step and closing the last bit of space between us as his torso pressed against my breasts, "I love you, Delilah, and I know you still love me. Because if you didn't, you would have told me to get lost by now."

"I *did* tell you to get lost." I opened my eyes in a rage, finding his smirk waiting for me.

"I know, baby." He took a deep breath, and I instantly reached up to push my hands against his hard abs as they touched my chest, "But we both know you don't mean it." He leaned down until his lips were right above mine, "Give me another chance. Let me make up for the last five years."

I moaned, hating how badly I wanted to give into him. "Why did you plead guilty?" I whispered. "Before I give you anything from me after all this time, I deserve the truth, Fox. The whole fucking truth."

"I know you do." He sighed, and I could taste nicotine and whiskey on his breath, "Not tonight though. You're too tired for it all tonight. Call off sick tomorrow and let me take care of you."

Reality took hold, dissolving the magical moment between us as I shook my head. "I can't." I pressed against his stomach until he stepped back reluctantly. "I didn't get that option five years ago, and it doesn't just get to magically become an option now."

"I can support you." He tried again, "I have money. More than enough for us to get that fresh start we dreamed of, baby." I ached to give into his lofty words. "We can have everything we want together. We can set Maddie up too; I know she's important to you, she's important to me too. Just give me a chance to do what's right."

I shook my head and opened my car door again, and winced in pain. "I have to go and get some sleep, or I'll be dangerous for my patients tomorrow."

"What time is your shift?" He asked.

"Seven to three."

"Jesus fuck, D, that's four hours away."

"Hence why I need to get home, Fox."

"Let me drive you, please. We'll take your car, and I'll walk back; I don't care."

"No." I said and slid in the front seat. "I have to go, but thanks for offering."

"I'm not letting you go this time." He said loudly, and I shut my door, pretending that I didn't hear him. "I'm fighting for us." He yelled.

I backed out of my spot and drove home, trying to tell myself the single motorcycle headlight following me out of the parking lot should be alarming.

But all I felt was comfort.

Like a sturdy set of arms wrapping around me from behind and cradling me against his powerful body all night long.

Something I dreamed of for half a decade.

Maybe there was hope in having it again after all.

When I pulled into my driveway, he parked across the street and watched me go inside as he lit a cigarette and leaned over his tank.

He was going to sit there until I went to work in a few hours, I just knew it.

Because deep down, I knew that was who Fox was.

A protector.

A champion.

Mine.

Chapter 14 – Delilah

Past

"Where have you been?" I hissed into the dimly lit room when Fox slipped into bed next to me. It was four am and Blaine's funeral was only a few hours away.

He had left to go to the club yesterday afternoon, and I had gotten only radio silence until now.

"I was trying to make good on my promise to find Blaine's killer." He said, turning me to my side to face him and then wrapped his arms and legs around me. He took a deep breath and let it out slowly, like he was breathing freely for the first time in hours.

The argument I'd been ready to have with him about abandoning me in my time of need faded away as I saw his needs instead.

He needed this.

He needed me.

And I wasn't going to deny him that when he'd been by my side for the last week.

I leaned forward and kissed his chin, then his neck and lifted my head so I could reach his ear where I nibbled and licked the lobe of it. "What are you doing?" He asked and tightened his arms around my waist.

"Loving you." I said before pushing him onto his back and sliding over on top of him. We were both naked, as per our usual sleep routine, but we hadn't had sex in a week.

I had been too distraught, but tonight I needed to see to his wants and desires as much as my own. Because the more I kissed him, the more the fire in my belly flamed to life.

And god it felt good to feel alive again.

"We don't have to. I'm sorry I was gone all day."

"I want you," I purred, rubbing my breasts across his chest as I kissed his lips gently. "If you don't want to, just say so."

His hands tangled in my hair, and he held me still against his face. "Does that feel like I don't want to?" He asked and flexed his hips, rubbing his rock-hard erection against my inner thigh. I shimmied onto his lap fully and tucked his cock between us.

"Then sit back and let me love you without so many interruptions." I smiled and licked his lips. His fingers tightened in my hair before sliding free and I took that as permission to continue my worship of him.

I kissed down his neck, nibbling and sucking on the skin just how I knew he liked and then down his wide chest, stopping to flick my tongue across both of his nipples. He groaned and tucked one arm up behind his head as he ran the pad of his thumb over my bottom lip. "I love you." He whispered in awe.

"I love *you*." I kissed his stomach, lingering on each defined ab on my way down. The happy trail that I loved tickled my nose as I ran my tongue down one side of the deep V that made my mouth water.

He sighed and watched me closely as I picked up his heavy cock where it laid against his stomach and laid gentle wet kisses against the crown and the underside. He loved blow jobs, as much as the next guy I was sure, but he really loved slow sensual ones with lots of tongue action.

So, I gave him what he craved. I swirled my tongue over the head and flicked the slit, tasting his pre cum before rubbing it against my lips. "You taste so good." I purred and pushed his thighs wide so I could lie down between them.

"You're so fucking sexy when you look at me like that." He growled lowly. My Aunt was downstairs sleeping in my mom's old room and if she hadn't been here, we would both be loud like normal. But tonight, I'd be slow and quiet, taking my time and drawing it out.

I sucked him into my mouth and got him nice and wet before sliding both of my hands up and down his shaft as I sucked the tip. He groaned and looked up at the ceiling as his hips flexed, making his needs known.

I removed my hands and pushed my head down to take his cock deep into my mouth, where it pushed against the back of my throat and made me gag.

Which made him groan again because he loved making me gag. So, I did it again, but pushed deeper until his cock was in my throat when I gagged, tightening around him.

"Fuck." He grunted, burying his fingers in my hair, "Again." He hissed, flexing his hips, and pushing my mouth down on his cock. "Yes."

I popped back off him and twisted my hands around his cock, swirling them over the head of him before opening my mouth and letting him push me back down. My lips brushed against the short hair that covered his balls, and I gagged again, tightening around him as he flexed his hips, pushing it deeper still before pulling me off him.

"You like that, baby?" I asked him seductively as I twisted my hands up and down him.

"You know I fucking do." He growled quietly. "No one has ever sucked my cock like you do."

"I've never sucked cock as well as I do for you." I smirked and groaned when he pushed my head back down for my cheekiness. Before him, I'd never given a blow job, and he knew that, and now it was one of my favorite things to do for my man when I wanted his pleasures.

"Up." He commanded, pulling me up his body until his wet cock laid between us again. He pulled my knees tight around his hips and flexed them, so his cock rubbed through my wetness and up my clit.

"Yes." I threw my head back, pushing my hands flat on his chest and rolling my hips up and down his length.

"Good girl." He grabbed my hips, and we rode in sync with each other. "You feel so good, Delilah." He groaned, "So wet."

"I need you." I whispered, leaning forward and he fisted his cock, holding it up for me to lower myself onto. "Yes." I rolled my hips, so I could get all of him inside of me. "So deep."

"Take it all." He ordered, lifting his hips until his balls pressed against my ass, "Good girl." I kept grinding my hips back and forth, keeping his dick deep while rubbing my clit on his pubic bone. "Just like that."

"God, you feel so good." I moaned, sitting up tall to grab my breasts as he watched. While grinding back and forth on his cock, I pinched and rolled my nipples as he stared like a starving man. "I didn't realize how much I missed this until right now."

"I missed it." He groaned, covering my hands with his as he took over, stimulating my nipples. "I missed you."

"I'm right here now, baby." Placing my hands flat on his chest, I arched my back, lifting my ass off his lap, and he immediately rose to fill me up once more. "Yes, Fox." I spread my legs wide and took him deep as he fucked up into me.

"You take me so perfectly." He let go of my tits and anchored his hands around my waist for leverage as he went harder. "You were made for me."

"Yes." I hissed, tipping my head back as he pushed me towards an orgasm. "I'm coming baby." I whispered, and he grunted as I started tightening down on him. Falling onto his chest, he wrapped both arms around my back and held me tight to him before biting the top of my shoulder as he started coming. He filled me up with come and I moaned at how erotic it was for me to feel him lose it inside of me.

He fisted my hair and pulled my lips down to his and kissed me in a slow, sensual dance. There was no rush, or demand for more, just this.

Just us.

"I love you." He whispered after a minute and I laid my forehead against his, sighing as my body relaxed fully against him.

"I love you, Paxton." I whispered back, using his first name because something inside of me didn't think using his road name was adequate for what had just passed between us.

They lowered the casket into the ground, and people stepped forward to grab a handful of dirt and throw it into the hole alongside the flowers. But I didn't move.

I was frozen in time as the entire thing brought with it the finality to Blaine's life.

He was gone.

Buried in the ground, never to be seen again.

It didn't feel real, yet as Maddie squeezed my hand and Fox kissed my temple, the weight of it all was almost enough to push me down into the dirt alongside my brother.

"Delilah." Colt stopped in front of me in his black leather vest and dark sunglasses as the people who weren't a part of our family, or the club, filed away from the site to their waiting cars. "Anything you need, you come to me." He said firmly, but I couldn't bring myself to look up at him. "You and Maddie are forever a part of our family, and we'll take care of you." He said, reaching up to put his hand on Maddie's shoulder. She thanked him and then gave him a hug while I was frozen.

"Let's go." Fox said against my hairline as he gently pulled me away from the barren earth next to my mom's headstone. "Let's get you home."

"We're having a get together at the club tonight, for Blaine." Colt said as we walked away, "D, I think you should come."

"Why?" I finally asked, clearing my throat against the scratchy dryness that had settled since the last time I spoke before the ceremony started. "Why would I want to come there?"

Colt looked from me to Fox and then to Maddie, giving her a small smile that she returned. "Because whether you like it or not, we're your family now. And Blaine would want to make sure that you're safe and watched over."

"No, he wouldn't." I shook my head angrily. "My brother never wanted the darkness of the club to touch me or Maddie." I looked at my sister and glared at the way he still had his hand on her shoulder. I grabbed her and pulled her away from him. "He didn't want that life for us, he said so repeatedly. So no, I won't be coming to the club to celebrate his life by doing the one thing he fought to keep us away from."

I turned and walked away with Maddie's hand tight in mine and heard Fox politely apologize to the President, explaining that I was upset and not thinking clearly, but I couldn't care what they thought of me.

I was numb inside to anything except my pain.

"He means well." Maddie whispered as we walked towards my car.

"I don't care." I answered truthfully. "It's too little, too late."

"I know." She sighed and took her black cardigan off and tossed it into the car, "But it's better than nothing. I'm going to choose to allow anyone that wants to give a damn about us to do it. Because the sad reality is, we don't have anyone else. So, if the big guy wants to watch out for us and invite us to his clubhouse to have a couple of beers and remember Blaine where he was happiest, I'm going to do that." Anger bristled under her tone and disappointment flashed on her face as she climbed into the back seat.

Fuck.

She was right. I knew she was.

But I didn't know how to just move on and let the weird changes to our life take place.

"Hey." Fox said, walking up behind me and resting his hand on my back, turning me to face him. "Take it easy on him, will you?"

"Why?"

"Because he means well."

"So I've heard," I snapped and then sighed, looking over my shoulder to where Maddie glared at me through the window. "Let's just go home and I'll think about it."

"Okay." He nodded and walked around the front of the car. When he got to his side, he looked at me over the roof and rested his arms on the metal and stared at me. "For what it's worth, there might be a time that I'm not around and you're going to need someone to look after you." He swallowed as I glared at him in confusion, "Colt is trustworthy D. He may be your only ally someday, so you'd do well not to burn the bridge before you find yourself needing it."

With that, he got in the car and slammed the door behind him and started up the engine.

I pondered that cryptic scolding in complete confusion until I had no choice but to get in the car and face the disappointment coming from both my sister and my boyfriend.

As we drove through the cemetery, the trees outside the window seemed to fly by while I tried to process the anger and pain building in my heart to let it go. I just didn't know how.

I didn't know how to move on and act like everything was okay.

Frankly, I didn't fucking want to. I didn't want to feel better; I didn't want to heal and move on because I didn't want to ever forget the way my life had been with Blaine inside of it.

So, I was going to curse, and scream, and shake my fists at the sky when the weight of it overwhelmed me. Because I wasn't ready to say goodbye.

I never would be.

Chapter 15 – Delilah

Past

We buried my brother six days ago.

Six days into a long line of days without him ahead.

"What are you thinking about?" Fox asked where he laid back on the blanket next to me.

He surprised me at lunchtime, showing up with a picnic packed and whisked me away to the hills.

I looked over at him and took a deep breath. He looked amazing in his black jeans and white tee, both tight and form fitting. His shaggy dark hair was tucked behind his ear and his stubble had grown out into a short beard.

Subtle changes had started happening to him in the last few days. I wanted to bring it up and ask him about it, but I was also afraid of the answers he'd give me.

He had been gone more often, leaving me alone for longer periods of time. Just like the night before Blaine's funeral when he didn't come to my bed until four am. Last night he didn't come home at all. I tried to be patient and understanding, giving him grace and time to figure out his life without his best friend. But in the span of a week, I'd lost my brother, and now I was losing my boyfriend.

He was quieter too, choosing to simply watch me over conversing. It was almost like he was trying to memorize me and simply forgot to speak while he did it.

"You." I replied bravely and picked at a stray blade of grass along the edge of the blanket.

He looked away and stared back out over the hillside, "Don't waste your time giving me the luxury of being on your mind."

There it was again.

Another subtle change to him he maybe thought I wouldn't pick up on, but it was impossible to ignore, paired with so many other ones.

I looked back down at the grass and kept my mouth shut, afraid if I vocalized my fears out loud, he'd confirm them.

"I think you should go spend some time at your aunt's house with Maddie." He said after a while. "I think maybe we should—," He paused, "Take a break for a second."

I whipped my head around to look at him as my heart rate picked up in my chest. But he just kept staring out over the hillside like he hadn't just told me he wanted me to go away. I looked back out over the grass as my heart ached in my chest.

Every single night since the first time we slept together, he came to my room and held me all night long after making sweet love to me.

Except last night.

Now he was telling me to go across the continental US to my aunt's house for a few weeks because he wanted to take a break. Maddie was going for three weeks to get away from it all before school started again, and I didn't blame her. That didn't mean that I wanted to go, though.

"Delilah." Fox said my name, but I could hardly hear it over the echo of my brother's voice swirling around inside of my head.

"He shows up here only when I'm not around, uses you and moves on before the morning light. That doesn't sound like a relationship."

"It won't last. He doesn't stick with one girl for long. Not in the four years I've known him."

"Fox will never be the come home at night to the white picket fence home kind of man. And that's the kind of man that you deserve, not someone like us."

My brother's warning from the night he died flashed through my mind like a breaking news banner on the bottom of the TV.

I should have seen it coming, but I didn't want to believe that Fox could use me like that. I wanted all his whispered secrets and longings to be true. I wanted the part that he didn't show to anyone else to be real.

"Delilah." He said again, more firmly, and I looked over at him. My mouth hung open, and I closed it before rapidly blinking to clear the thoughts racing through my head. "Did you hear me?"

"I want to go home." I whispered and stood up off the blanket, brushing grass and dirt from my jeans as I slid my sneakers back on.

"Just like that?" He sat up and watched me. "I want to talk to you about this. Help you understand it."

"Please take me home." I said, picking up the wrappers from the takeout lunch he brought for us, tossing them back into the grocery bag.

"Stop." He put his hands over mine as I hurried to pick it all up. "Wait, just a second, D."

"Take me home." I snapped and then bit my tongue to keep from saying anything else.

He sighed and watched me as I stared at the ground. "No. Not until we talk about this."

"Fine." I said and stood up, "I'll make my own way back home."

I walked away from him towards the dirt parking lot where a few other cars lingered. "Damnit, D!" He yelled from behind me, and I heard his heavy boots running to catch up with me seconds before his hand wrapped around my arm and pulled me to a stop. "Would you just take a second and think about it? I think it's best."

"He was right!" I screamed directly into his face. It was the second time I yelled at him, the only other time was that night at the clubhouse before he gave me a ride home on his bike.

The night that started it all.

While today was the day that ended it just as quickly.

"Who was right?" He asked quietly, like he was taken aback by it all.

"My brother." I ripped my arm out of his hand and put a few feet of space between us. "He said you wouldn't stick around for long." I swallowed down the bile that rose in my throat as pain shot through my heart. "He said you weren't the kind of man to come home to the white picket fence life, and he was right even though you told me that was what you wanted." I closed my eyes and wrapped my arms around my stomach, trying to ward off the pain and nausea. "And I yelled at him and told him *he* was wrong. I walked out the front door in anger and it was the last time I ever saw him." He stared at me in horror as I unraveled. "And here we are, two weeks later, and he was fucking right." I hissed in pain.

"I just—." He started and stopped, like he wanted to explain and make it all better, but decided not to. "I'm not." He breathed, looking out over my head to the hillside. "I'm not a settling down kind of guy. I need variety, I guess."

I nodded and felt the tears that had been pooling in my lashes spill over onto my cheeks. "Got it." I was numb, and distraught at the same time.

"I'm sorry." He said gently, swallowing down his own emotions.

"Don't be." I laughed bitterly, "Because deep down we both know you're not."

Turning, I walked away from him. I pulled up the ride share app on my phone and ordered a car to meet me at the pull off down the hill. I needed to use the time to walk and calm down or I'd get into a stranger's car and have a breakdown in the middle of nowhere.

He told me the first time we had sex that if I let him have me, I was his forever.

But he lied.

I kept waiting to hear his motorcycle start up and imagined that he would chase me down and tell me he was sorry and that he was wrong. That he didn't want to break up, maybe he even needed me as badly as I needed him.

But he never came.

He let me walk away.

"Where's Fox?" Maddie asked the next morning as she grabbed her duffle bag off the floor, "I never heard him come in last night."

I shook my head, swallowing down the scream I wanted to set free. "Club stuff." I shrugged, "You know how it goes."

She smiled sadly, "Are you sure you're okay with this?" She looked over her shoulder to where Aunt Suzie's rental car was idling in the driveway, waiting to take them to the airport to go to Kansas.

If she knew something was up with me, she wouldn't go. And that wasn't fair to her because she needed to get away from all the sadness and grief within these four walls. "I'm fine," I smiled at her, mustering up the strength to make it look real. "I'll miss you, but it's only three weeks. I want you to go, have fun, and take a break."

"If you're sure." She said as Aunt Suzie beeped her horn, "Coming!" She yelled at the front door and turned back to me.

I walked forward and grabbed my baby sister in my arms and hugged her like it was the last time I was going to see her.

Because one thing I'd learned in the last few years was that people walked out that front door; but they rarely came back.

"I love you. Have a great time." I whispered into her hair and looked up at the ceiling to ward off the tears.

"I love you, too." She whispered, pulling back to smile, "I'll call you all the time and send you pictures."

"I can't wait." As she ran down the path and jumped into the car, I said goodbye from the screen door. I waved and waited until they were down the street and out of sight before I stepped back and shut the heavy oak door, letting the ominous thud of it rattle my bones.

Turning the deadbolt, I sank to my knees on the worn-out hard-wood floor, releasing all my pain into the world. I screamed until my voice broke and faded, ruining my nails by digging them into the floor, then collapsed and sobbed until the daylight faded into darkness and came back again.

I was alone.

I had no one.

It was a heartbreak too strong to overcome.

Chapter 16 – Delilah

Present

A noise blared in the back of my skull, trying to pull me out of the slumber I finally found what felt like only minutes ago. I opened one eye and forced myself to look around my dark room and realized the noise was my alarm clock.

"Fuck." I groaned. Work.

I reached over to grab my phone and hissed as my ribs burned. Then it all came flooding back into my brain.

Taz and his kick to my side.

This ain't over Delilah. *I'll be seeing you around and when I do, you better have that pussy good and wet for me. I'm taking my cut of it.*

His words echoed in my brain on repeat for a long time after I crawled into bed last night. During my shift, I had been able to push it into the back of my head because I knew I was safe there with Bones and Lori looking out for me. But once I got home to my empty house, fear took place of my loneliness.

At one point, I looked outside and saw Fox sitting against his bike, watching the house like a noble guard.

My heart ached to give into the desire to call him inside and let him comfort me. I wanted to allow myself comfort for the first time in years.

But I didn't.

Instead, I laid in the dark and battled fear and loneliness in silence. Just like every other day of my life.

I rolled out of bed and held my arm around my waist for support and walked to the window, dragging the curtain back to look out front.

And there he was.

Fox walked back and forth along the sidewalk next to his bike with his head down and his hands in jeans pockets. His hair was loose and swaying in the breeze as he paced. It was longer than it was when we were together; I ran my fingers up and down the smooth curtains and imagined they traced the strands of his hair like they used to instead.

Talk to him.

Let him in.

Find out the answers you need.

Tell him the truth.

Heal.

My conscience spoke through the silence to me, begging me to do the right thing.

However, I looked around my bedroom and saw all the signs of Penelope's existence—her clothes strewn across the chair, her books piled on the nightstand, the faint scent of her shampoo still lingering in the air. It was like that throughout my entire house, and I knew he'd notice the second he walked in the door. I couldn't do that until I had time to talk to him.

So, I forced myself to get ready for work. I walked out the kitchen door, the slam echoing in the quiet morning, to my car, and quickly threw my bags and travel coffee cup inside.

And then I took the second cup I prepared and walked down the driveway to where Fox sat on the curb watching me silently as I approached.

"You didn't have to stay all night." I said and held out the cup to him. He looked from the cup, then to me and back before rising to his feet and taking it. His hand covered mine when he did, on purpose I was sure, and my skin burned from his touch.

"It was three hours." He said in response before taking the lid off the cup and looking inside.

"I didn't poison it." I said defensively. "I'm all out of arsenic until I go grocery shopping again."

He smirked at me and then put the lid back on, "I wouldn't be able to blame you if you did." He took a sip of it and groaned, letting his eyelids flutter closed before looking directly at me. "You always could make the best cup of coffee." He looked exhausted, just like me.

I fought the urge to smile and looked down at my feet to hide the way my muscles twitched at his compliment.

"Go home, Fox." I sighed, "I'll be safe at work."

"Can I drive you?" He questioned.

"No." I shook my head, kicking the dirt. "Go home."

"You are my home." He countered, and I closed my eyes to the desire I knew I'd see if I looked up at him. "When can we talk? We *need* to talk about this."

"I know." I swallowed and looked down the street as a car passed by. "I'm off tomorrow."

"What about tonight?"

"I work at Cherry's."

"No!" He shook his head and took a step forward, "Damnit, D, that's too much. You can't possibly survive on such little sleep! And with your ribs busted, please." He reached out and put his hand around the back of my neck. "Please, you have to take care of yourself."

"I'm trying to Fox." I shook my head and backed up, making him drop his hand, "I have to pay the bills for my household and that means I have to work stupid hours."

"I hate this!" He roared, pacing away from me. "Let me fix this."

"I have to go, or I'll be late." I backed up a step, "Please go home, Fox."

He shook his head, and his shoulders deflated, "I already told you; you are my home."

I pursed my lips to keep from arguing with him and stepped off the curb. "I have to go." Reluctantly, I returned to my car, started the engine, and reversed out of the driveway, despite how badly I wanted to stay.

As I drove by, Fox's gaze—filled with a desperate plea—met mine. The sound of his bike's engine revving filled the air as he sped after me, his shadow clinging to my car until the sanctuary of the hospital employee parking lot. He parked along the curb and silently let me walk past him into the ER, and lifted the travel mug for another sip. "I'll be here when you get out." He called to me as I walked in, and I smiled to myself at how fucking relieved I was to hear that.

"Go home." Oliver groaned at me four hours later. "Seriously, D, I appreciate your dedication and loyalty to the cause but go the hell home and get some rest and come back on Tuesday refreshed and better."

I tried ignoring him as I fought with an IV machine that was getting the better of me. "I'm fine."

"You have three cracked ribs." He droned on, "I ordered the films, remember? And don't try to lie and say you slipped in the shower or something, because I know what I'm looking at." He snapped and I looked over my shoulder at him in surprise.

"I think that's the first time you've ever raised your voice at me."

He put his hands on his hips under his lab coat and gave me a curt nod, "I don't like doing it, Delilah, so don't make me tell you twice. Go home."

"I can't leave the floor short staffed like that."

"We're fine." He rolled his eyes and huffed, "I mean it, as your supervisor, go the fuck home."

My hands fell to my side as we stared at each other. He was right, though I'd never tell him that. I was useless.

I couldn't physically care for my patients because of the pain. And I couldn't even chart my backlog because I was so tired, I fell asleep twice already when I stopped moving long enough to try.

"Fine." I sighed, "But I want it written that you made me do it."

"Done." He said and smiled, proud of himself for getting his way. "I'll see you on Tuesday. Fill the script I gave you for pain and swelling." He pointed at me with authority.

"Sure thing, Dad." I droned as I walked by him. When I got to my desk, a pharmacy bag sat on my keyboard and I paused, looking over at Winnie.

"You weren't going to fill it, so I had pharmacy drop it off on their rounds." She said with a shrug of her shoulders.

"Thank you." I answered, "I'm being sent home."

"I'm glad he listened to me and forced you to go." She smartass'd.

"Thanks." I said and grabbed my things. "See you Tuesday."

"Don't rush it, D. Come back when you're feeling better." She smiled gently and I could see the sympathy in her eyes and hated it.

I hated being pitied for what I couldn't control. Neither of them knew what happened to me, just that someone had obviously broken my ribs. It was too messy to tell either of them the full truth.

I grabbed my things, shoving the prescription bag into my purse and walked out to my car. I was so incredibly bone weary that the idea of even driving home was daunting, but I wanted to get in bed so badly I was willing to suffer a bit longer. As I walked across the parking lot, I noticed two men on motorcycles sitting in the spot that Fox had been earlier. My step faltered when their gazes landed on me. One of the men was tall like Fox but even wider and the other was small, but had tattoos on every single inch of visible skin.

The small one nudged his cohort, and they both watched me approach as anxiety rose in my spine.

"Delilah Beckett?" The big one asked, standing up and adjusting his cut, revealing the patch over his left chest.

Black Eagles.

Relief poured through me even as apprehension continued to burn in my gut. "Who's asking?"

I paused on the sidewalk, ten feet away from them. If I had to make a run for it, I needed every bit of a head start I could get.

"Fox is the one asking. I'm Tony, this is Hammer." The small one nodded to his friend. "Houston put us on watch while Fox took a break."

"Watch for what?"

Tony shrugged, "To make sure no one fucks with you."

I lifted my head up and down like I followed that train of thought, "You mean Taz and his crew?"

"Or anyone in general, but yes, mainly Taz."

"You haven't found him yet, huh?" I asked, taking a couple of steps towards my car parked a few rows past where they sat.

"Not yet," Hammer grunted, "But we will."

"Okay." I said, "I'm headed home for the day so you can go back to whatever club business you got pulled off of for babysitting duty."

"We go where you go." Tony replied like it was obvious.

I wasn't going to stand in the parking lot and argue with a couple of strangers when I didn't have the energy to even stand. So, I just turned and walked away to my car.

Only when I approached it, I realized something wasn't quite right about it.

I paused and tilted my head, trying to figure out what was off, and then realized what it was.

Both of my tires were flat.

I walked around to the other side and both of them were flat as well.

"What the hell?" I whispered, walking up to one, and running my hands over the rubber, feeling the slow leak still letting air out and found a slash the size of a quarter in it. "No." I cursed and quickly felt over the other three, finding three identical slashes.

"Everything okay?" Tony asked, walking up behind me as I laid my forehead against the corner panel where I crouched next to my front tire. "Shit." He hissed and whistled loudly, whipping his hand around in a circle in the air.

Hammer's bike roared to life and was parked behind me in an instant as Tony took his phone out and dialed someone.

I lowered myself to my ass right there on the hot blacktop and dropped my head onto my knees in defeat.

Fucking Taz.

I didn't have the money to replace four fucking tires at once right now. I could either eat for the next two weeks until I got paid, or I could buy tires. I couldn't do both.

Reaching into my purse, I grabbed the bottle of painkillers Oliver prescribed and took two with some water; I couldn't take it anymore.

The pain of the day was overwhelming, and I was ready to escape it any way I could; if peace couldn't be found, I would seek oblivion.

After a while of listening to Hammer and Tony whisper a few feet away from me, more bikes pulled into the lot. I could feel the haze of the strong medication kicking in, and I couldn't even bother to lift my head at their approach.

I didn't care anymore.

I didn't have any fight left in me.

"What the fuck happened?" Fox's deep voice rumbled as my skin prickled with awareness.

"We never saw anyone over here, she found it when she walked out here." Tony mumbled, no doubt balking at the furiousness in Fox's tone.

"It's not their fault." I said, finally picking my head up off my lap. "It's not their job to watch my back."

"No," Fox snapped, "It's mine." He stood in a tight white tee and light blue distressed jeans, and I let my eyes rove over his cut body in the tight fabric.

And then I laughed.

Like *actually* laughed; I tilted my head back to the bright sunlight and laughed for what felt like the first time in forever. I laughed so hard I snorted and then laughed again before I had enough sense to cover my mouth to stem the flow of the mirth as the giant scary bikers all stared at me like I'd lost my mind.

Anyone with half a brain wouldn't be laughing in Fox's face when he looked downright feral. But I was effectively high, thanks to the strong ass meds and decided to laugh in the face of danger.

I was Simba, and Fox was the hyenas.

He glared down at me with his fists on his hips and I giggled at him.

"Are you drunk?" He snapped at me, "I thought you were working until three."

I shrugged my shoulders and held my hands up. "I dunno."

"I'm guessing it's the pills she took about fifteen minutes ago when I called you."

"Pills?" Fox crouched down in front of me, and my head fell back as I tried to look up at him, but I nearly toppled over backwards. "Fuck, D." He grunted and caught me. He took the pills out of my purse and groaned before putting them back in. "How bad are the ribs?" I held up three fingers at him and shrugged. "Three fucking broken ribs because of me." He hung his head in frustration and then stood up, turning back to his men.

"What you want us to do, Boss?" Tony asked.

"Find the piece of shit scum bag that put his hands on my girl so I can take him fucking out for it." Fox growled and everyone stepped back a step further.

"Hey." I said, scowling and snapping my fingers at him until he looked back down at me. "Be nice."

He glared at me, and Hammer snorted into his hand and turned away before Fox could see the grin on his face.

"Get out of here and find him." Fox repeated and everyone fled from the parking lot, hot on the job of finding Taz.

"What are you going to do with me?" I asked from under my eyelashes as I sat on the ground like a toddler.

He crouched back down in front of me and pushed my bangs behind my ear. The pills took away my inhibitions because the moan I wanted to stop, fell free as I leaned into his touch.

I knew I was being a sloppy drunk, but I didn't care.

"Can you ride on the back of my motorcycle?" He asked.

I focused on his face right in front of mine and raised my eyebrows. "There are only two rules to it, right?"

He smiled at me, and I smiled back, saying fuck it to the urge to hide it from him.

"What are the rules, D?" He asked, sliding his hands under my arms, and lifting me to my feet.

"Hmm." I hummed as he took my work bag and wrapped his arm around my waist. "Sway with the lines on the road, not the bike."

"D." He growled, tightening his hold on my hips as I snorted.

"Lean with you, not the bike." I droned dramatically.

"Good girl." He said, and I leaned into him, desperate for another praise. "And rule number two?"

"Ride you like a bull." I said before he even finished talking and he groaned, pulling us to a stop, backing me up against the side of my car. "Careful, baby." He warned and leaned his hand against the roof before lowering himself down to look at me. "Try again."

Desire burned through every single cell of my body, and I leaned forward against his wide chest, "Stay on for all eight seconds." I purred, proud of myself for not forgetting my words as the medicine relaxed me even more.

"Fuck this." He said and then his lips were on mine, strong and dominant and all Fox.

I moaned into his mouth, opening my lips instantly and letting him push his tongue in against mine. He kissed like a hurricane and always had. He was never gentle or reserved when he kissed me like this, and I ached for more of him. Five years was too long to go without his touch. Any touch.

"More." I begged, gripping his shirt in my hands. "I need more."

"You need to sleep." He growled against my lips. "Tell me rule number two to riding with me baby, and I'll take you to bed."

"Only if you promise to come to bed with me." I mewed and in any other circumstance I would have literally kicked myself for sounding so pathetic, but I didn't have it in me to fight what I wanted.

And I wanted Fox wrapped around me while I slept.

Just like the old days.

"D."

I rolled my eyes until I saw my brain and then sighed. "Hold on tight. Like you're a bull and I'm trying to stay on for the full eight seconds." I whispered against his lips. "Now take me somewhere so I can sleep." I leaned forward and kissed his perfect fucking lips and bit the bottom one before pulling away. "Or I'm sleeping in my car and never speaking to you again."

He leaned up off me and pulled me towards his bike. "You're sure you can stay on?" He glared at me.

"Eight seconds baby." I smiled again and snorted at my own joke as he shook his head. But in the time that he'd been back in my life, I hadn't seen a single flicker of the man from before the bad shit came between us. Yet standing here, next to him, as he threw his leg over his bike and smiled back at me when I climbed on gently, he was back.

My Fox was here, front and center. The one that no one else ever got to see; he was here.

And I didn't realize how much I had missed him until right that very second.

Chapter 17 – Delilah

Present

I slid my hands under the front of Fox's shirt, regardless that it was seventy degrees out and I had no excuse to touch him like I was. I didn't need one.

Because he was mine.

I laid my palms flat on his stomach and reveled in the way his muscles twitched under them. I pressed my cheek against the warm leather of his cut and held on, letting my body flow with his as my eyes closed. The hum of the engine and the steady thumping of Fox's heart against my ear through his back calmed me.

I wanted more of that calm in my life.

He ran his palm over my knee and down my calf to my ankle and hooked his fingers there, holding me as he leaned back against me further.

Just like old times.

Only a few minutes into the ride, he turned off the main road and skirted through an upscale neighborhood until he got to a paved driveway leading back between tall trees, obscuring the house.

"Wrong neighborhood, Dum Dum." I joked. "I couldn't afford this place with a year of paychecks."

He grunted but drove down the long drive, and a beautiful house came into view at the end. A white colonial stood on a large green grass yard with a three-car garage wrapped around the side of the house. As we neared it, one of the garage bays opened, and Fox pulled the bike directly inside and turned it off.

The door closed behind us as I remained seated, looking around in confusion.

"Jump off, baby." He said, tapping my knee and I slid off the bike.

"Where are we?" I asked as he grabbed my bag from the saddlebag and took my hand in his.

"You said to take you somewhere you can sleep." He replied, pulling me through a door and into a stylish kitchen.

"Fox," I dug my heels in as I got more confused. "Stop. Whose house is this?"

He sighed and licked his lips, "Mine."

My mouth hung open as I looked around the space again and then back at him. "I don't understand."

He didn't come from money. When we were together five years ago, he lived in a studio apartment in a rougher neighborhood than I did. It didn't add up.

"I know, but it will make sense after we talk when we wake up from a long fucking nap." He said, "I'll explain everything then." He kissed my forehead and pulled me along with him, "Come on."

My feet followed him as he walked through a giant open living room with three different couches and a massive TV the size of an entire wall in my small rental. "When I said take me somewhere to sleep, I meant my house."

"I know you did," He opened a door off the living room and then shut it behind us, "But there was no way you were going to stay conscious long enough to ride all the way back across town to your place. Mine was closer."

"Yours is in the wrong tax bracket." I said sarcastically, and he glared at me with a smirk. "I can't sleep here." We were in his bedroom; I could smell him in the air like a sensual kiss and I ached to take a deep breath but I refrained.

Barely.

"Why not?"

"I don't have any of my stuff here."

"What do you need?" He asked as I eyed the king size bed across the room with pillowy white blankets that were all ruffled and flung back. Dark shades hung on the windows muting the bright sunlight from outside and a small part, okay a large part, inside of me ached to sleep here. It looked like he was interrupted from bed and hadn't had time to make it up, and I wondered if the sheets were still warm from his body.

"Uh—." I shook my head, looking away from the bed that beckoned me, "I need sleep clothes, and shower stuff."

"I have clothes you can wear if you insist, though I'd rather you just sleep naked next to me like you used to," He said as he walked over to the bench at the end of the bed and sat down. He leaned over and unzipped his boots and took them off, placing them under the bench in a well-rehearsed move. "And I have shower stuff you can use." He stood back up and yawned, stretching his arms high over his head until his tee lifted and showed off the delicious V at his belt that I used to drool over when he was mine.

He is mine.

Was.

Fuck.

"D." He purred my name and held his hand out for me to come near, "I'm dead on my feet, too. I was an hour into a dead sleep when Tony called me about your car, so come over here, climb into bed with me and let's sleep for a while."

"Sleep." I eyed the bed speculatively even as my feet started carrying me closer to him.

"Sleep." He repeated, "And then we can go from there."

"Hmm." I replied, and he lifted my purse off over my head and set it on the bench.

"Can you lift your arms up?" He asked as he gripped the bottom of my scrub top. I slowly raised my arms up and he pulled my top up over my head, leaving me standing before him in a white tank top and black bra above scrub pants. "Sit." He said, kneeling in front of me.

I fell onto the bench, simply because the sexy man was on his knees for me, and I had nothing better to do but see what he intended. He slid both of my sneakers off, tucking them perfectly in line with his boots under the bed, and took both socks off my feet, slipping them into my sneakers.

My fingers danced up to his cheek, and I slid my palm over his beard. He leaned into it and looked at me, "Why am I still so affected by you?" I whispered thoughtfully, "I hate you."

"You love me." He replied without hesitation.

"I do." I responded. He knew I did. "But I don't want to."

"You will." He turned his cheek and kissed my palm. "Give me time, baby, and you won't regret it anymore."

He pulled me to stand in front of him as he still kneeled, and he slowly lifted the hem of my tank top and pressed the gentlest of kisses against my stomach. His eyes were on mine the entire time, but my breath caught in my throat when I felt the softness of his lips against my stretch marks.

"Pants." I whispered. He slid his fingers into the waistband of my scrubs and pushed them down over my wide hips, and I shimmied to help with the process. They fell to my ankles, and I stepped out of them. I reached up and undid the clasp at the front of my bra and then took it off through the armholes of my tank. "What?" I shrugged, "You know I can't sleep in a bra."

He smirked and stood up, keeping his eyes locked on my hard nipples through my shirt. "You're not going to hear me complain, baby."

"Which side is mine?" I asked him, no longer able to deny that his bed was calling my name and I would be a fool to deny it. He nodded to the side furthest from the door and I turned away from him, smirking at his protective nature before sliding into the cool, soft sheets. "Oh god." I sighed heavily as the softness ate me up.

Fox walked around to his side of the bed, and I turned on my side to face him. He reached up behind his head and lifted the collar of his shirt over his head, taking it off. He folded it and laid it on a chair next to the bed and then popped the button on his jeans.

"You'd better have some underwear on under those jeans." I said, as my eyes stayed glued to his impressive body.

Because Jesus, Mary, and Joseph he was sexy. He had added tattoos over the years to his shoulders and arms, and the dark happy trail that had run down the center of his abs five years ago now spread out over his chest as well in a deliciously mature man kind of way.

"Keep staring at me like that and I'm going to fuck you straight into this mattress before I let you sleep." He growled, reaching down to palm the erection that was growing in his jeans.

I smiled and then shrugged, trying to act nonchalantly. "I'd probably sleep through it."

"Bullshit." He cursed and hooked his thumbs into his waistband and pushed.

Everything.

Down.

"Fox." I growled as he stood naked in front of me for the first time in five years with a hard on that deserved to be sculpted by Michelangelo. He was so thick. I could remember how it felt to feel every single inch slide into me. My pussy throbbed as I laid there, watching it bob and jerk under my attention.

He picked up his pants and folded them, adding them to the pile next to his bed and then undid the tie in his hair, letting his long dark hair fall around his face. It was longer than before, dancing below his shoulders, and I longed to run my fingers through it. He smiled at me and crawled in. "Roll over or I'm going to crawl between those sexy thick thighs and rut into you like an animal during breeding season."

"Mmh. I think that's the most romantic thing you've ever said to me." I smiled sleepily and dutifully turned over on my side, because as much as I ached to be fucked by Fox, I wasn't ready for that mind trip.

I needed sleep if I had a hope and a prayer of getting through my shift at Cherry's tonight.

As soon as I was settled on my side facing away from Fox, he slid his giant hot body up against my back and gently laid his heavy arm over my hip, careful of my ribs. He flexed his hips and pushed his erection against my ass until it slid between our bodies to lie heavily against me like a weighted reminder of what I could have if I wanted it.

"Go to sleep, D." He hummed and leaned in to kiss the sensitive skin behind my ear. "I love you."

I didn't reply, I didn't have to because we both knew I loved him too. With so much uncertainty between us, I was just proud to admit it.

It took me absolutely no time at all to fall asleep with his scent and warmth surrounding me, just like old times.

If only I could go back in time and memorize moments like this before they were tainted with deceit and betrayal.

Chapter 18 – Delilah

Present

My stomach grumbled so loudly it woke me up from the deepest sleep I had ever been in. The haze of confusion and disorientation gave way as I opened one eye to gauge what time of day it was.

The sun was going down and there was a warm red glow coming in around the curtain on the window next to my bed. I closed my eyes, content to go back to sleep until my alarm went off for work and snuggled back down under the blankets that were keeping me so warm. But my blanket suddenly came to life and tightened around me, squeezing me like a monster from Penelope's nightmares, and my eyes flew open.

The window I'd admired the sunset through wasn't mine.

Where the fuck was I?

I lifted the blanket and looked down at my tank top and panties, relieved that those were still on at least. The arm that wrapped around my waist was attached to a hand wedged between my bare breasts underneath of my tank top.

"What the fuck?" I groaned and tried to shake it off and get out of bed.

"What?" A sleepy baritone voice asked from behind me seconds before the arm tightened around me even more and pulled me back against the hottest body I'd ever felt before.

And it was naked.

I looked over my shoulder and shuddered when Fox lifted his head from the pillow with a mane of sexy tousled dark hair fluffed up in every direction and a scowl. "What's wrong?"

"What's wrong?" I gasped and shucked him off harder, this time he let me go. My ribs screamed as I flailed my way out of his bed, where I stood looking around in confusion. "This is not my house."

"It probably will be one day soon." He said and rolled over onto his back, tucking both hands under his head. The blankets laid alarmingly close to revealing everything below the waist to my traitorous eyes, so I looked away.

"Stop it, that's not funny, Fox." I ran my fingers through my hair and gasped at the pain in my side, "Damnit." I sat down on the bench at the end of the bed out of pure necessity because the more I moved, the more the room spun. Memories of him showing up at work when my car was vandalized flooded back. The way I had joked and laughed at him thanks to the lack of sleep and heavy pain killers. Then the sexy ride on his motorcycle to his giant lavish house

"Hey." His voice dropped all humor, and his concerned, caring side shone through. "Is it your side?" He leaned to the end of the bed and put his hand on my shoulder to turn me towards him. I went, simply because it hurt too much to breathe suddenly, let alone fight him. Tears swam over my eyes and his face blurred as I looked at him. "Hey." He said again, leaping from the bed when he saw my tears. He crouched, naked and wonderful, at my feet and put his hands on each side of my face, swiping his thumbs across my cheeks, "Don't cry, baby."

"It hurts." I whispered, hating how weak I felt unexpectedly. "And I'm so tired." I sagged against his hand as he cupped the back of my neck.

"I know you are." He leaned up on his knees, so we were face to face. "But you're done carrying the burden on your shoulders alone anymore, Delilah." He stared at me intently. "You were never meant to do it all on your own, and now that we've found each other again, you won't. I'm going to take care of you."

"I don't know how to let you. I've done it on my own for so long." Shaking my head, I whispered my biggest fears out loud. "What if I can't just let you in again?"

"I'm not expecting you to just do anything, baby. I'm going to earn it. Every. Fucking. Ounce. Of. It." He said, leaning forward to press his forehead against mine and I dug my nails into his forearms and sagged against him. "I love you, D."

I nodded and took a shuddering breath, "I'm sorry I went all crazy on you just now," I said, "It took way too long for my memories of this morning to catch up to me."

He chuckled, "Good to know you don't hit the hard stuff enough to be good at black outs."

I scoffed, "I don't even drink that much. I have no life."

"Good." He said and stood up while making sure I was still supported. I was quickly reminded that he was naked when I was face to face with his semi-hard cock. I raised one eyebrow at him as I tore my eyes away from it to look him in the eye. "Sorry, it misses you and has a mind of his own." He said with a shrug and helped me stand.

"What time is it?" I looked around for a clock. "I have to get ready for work soon."

"No." He said without hesitation. "No more Cherry's."

"I have to work."

"No!" He repeated, "The ER is one thing, but Cherry's isn't up for argument. I'll stand at the door and scare every single customer off before they can even think of walking in that place and hitting on you or acting like a disrespectful cunt towards you. No." He shook his head. I raised my eyebrows in silent wonder, and he glared at me.

"Let's table that discussion for another day, because I think my ribs are hurting enough to warrant a night off, anyway." I said pointedly when he started to object. "And then we can talk about the millions of other things we need to discuss and go back to that one in the end, if it's even important at that point."

He clenched his teeth and pursed his lips, but finally sighed and nodded in agreement. "Let's get showered and then I'll feed you and we can talk."

"Let's get showered?" I dug my heels in when he lifted my hand and started walking towards the ensuite.

He winked at me and gave me a one-sided smirk, "I want to wash your hair for you, like I used to."

I scoffed as he pulled me forward again, "I don't want to get naked with you."

"Why not?" He sounded offended.

"Because" I tsked my teeth, "My body isn't what it used to be, and I don't want you to see it."

He paused in the doorway and looked at me, "Seriously?"

"Yeah." I answered honestly and deflated a little at how insecure I was at that moment. I hadn't meant to vocalize my lack of confidence to him, but it had just come out, because it was the truth.

He sighed and walked us into the bathroom further and I dropped his gaze to look around.

My fucking god.

The bathroom was as lavish as the kitchen was, with white tile on the walls and dark wood floors. A shower covered one entire wall of it with a tile accent wall up to about my shoulders and then a glass panel to the ceiling. A double vanity took up another wall with a backlit mirror that every makeup enthusiast would dream of owning.

But what caught my attention and kept it was the giant soaker tub laid under a frosted window. The thing could fit three of me in it, and it was deep enough that both my tits and my knees would be under water.

At. The. Same. Time.

"Like what you see?" Fox asked as he walked back to me from turning on the shower. I looked over and two waterfall showerheads poured steamy water down and I groaned at how good it would feel to shower under them compared to the Walmart brand plastic shower head I had at home. It only had two settings, trickle or trickle with a single errant jet stream spraying you in the face. And you never got to pick which stream would pick that day to go all hulk mode.

"Something like that." I said, "But it doesn't change what I said."

"Your body has changed in five years, Delilah. So what?" He slid his fingers into my hair. "Do you think I need to see you naked to notice that? Your breasts are larger," he looked down to my bare chest under my thin tank top and my nipples traitorously pebbled from his gaze alone. "In a fucking good way." He growled, "And your hips are wider," He slid his hands over my hips and pulled me closer to him. "I don't need to see you naked to imagine how you'll look on your hands and knees with those in my hands while I pull you back onto my cock."

"Fox." I groaned, squeezing my thighs together as arousal coursed through me.

"You matured in the years we've been apart, and your body did, too." He kissed my forehead, "And I love every single inch of it now as much as I did the tiny teenybopper body you used to have."

"You don't get it." I whispered, remembering how my body changed with childbearing and wondering if he'd relate the changes to that.

"You're right; I don't." He said gently, "I'm a man who doesn't have to deal with society judgments and trends relating to my body every single day like you do. But I am a man who is deeply infatuated with you and your body, however different it may be. Even more than that, I'm in love with you." He tapped his finger on my chest over my racing heart. "I see nothing else."

Warmth and affection burned inside of me at his words. He was saying and doing everything right, and I couldn't resist him anymore. I leaned up on my toes and pulled his face down to mine, kissing him. I took him by surprise, his lips were stiff against mine for a moment before his entire body reacted to me. He growled, deep down in his chest, and slid one hand around the back of my neck with the other around my hip and pressed me into the door. I clung to him, letting down every wall and safety net that I'd put up since seeing him again and let him feel exactly what was going through my body.

He lifted me with his arm around my hips and pinned me to the door, still in his naked glory as the humidity in the room built.

"Tell me you're mine." He growled, biting my lips, and squeezing my ass in his big hands. "Tell me this means you'll give me another chance."

"We haven't talked." I panted, knocking my head back against the wall as I tried to think. "I don't know the complete story." I gasped when he bit my neck and moaned and rocked against him in his arms. "You don't know my story."

"Nothing you say or have done in the last five years will make me love you any less." He said automatically. "I mean it, Delilah."

"You don't know." I recoiled, grabbing a handful of his hair to pull his head back from my neck so I could think. "You don't know that, Fox. We need to talk first." I said seriously, trying to express with my eyes how grave this situation was.

He paused, taking a few deep breaths, and nodded. "You're right." He sighed and let me slide down his body. "Take a shower, I'll leave some clothes for you on the counter and then we can have dinner and talk." He leaned in and kissed my lips in a gentle peck. "God, even after five years, you still drive me wild, D."

I watched in silence as he walked out of the bathroom and shut the door behind him as I slumped into the wall.

Jesus fucking Madonna.

I just kissed Fox St. Claire.

Actually, I attacked him and sucked his face off.

But he kissed me back and said everything right.

I just hoped we felt the same way after we told each other the truths we'd hidden for so long.

Chapter 19 – Delilah

Past

I made it six days on my own until I couldn't ignore the signs anymore. I had laid in bed all six of those days, fielding calls from Maddie and texts from friends asking to visit or get together. But I was too tired to even move.

Fox's betrayal cut me too deep, leaving me bleeding out on the floor with no way to stop it.

He didn't call. He didn't text. He didn't stop by. I never heard the rumble of his motorcycle coming down the street to even drive by and check on the house.

He was gone, like he had never been more than a figment of my imagination.

Here today, gone tomorrow.

But on day six of my solitude, the nausea started. I had gotten sick a few times since finding out that Blaine had died, but it had been controllable. Until suddenly, I couldn't even lay down without throwing up.

Day seven and eight were the same and by the time day nine rolled around, I could hardly walk to the bathroom anymore.

So, I did what any teenage girl who realized she was late for her period and was constantly throwing up in between long bouts of fatigue would do; I ordered a pack of twelve pregnancy tests on the internet with a bunch of ice cream pints from the pharmacy and chicken noodle soup from the diner down the street and had it all delivered to my front door.

I took my loot to the kitchen and opened the pregnancy tests there, unfolding the elaborate and extensive instructions as my stomach rolled once again.

This time, I was pretty sure the nausea wasn't from potential morning sickness, and more likely caused by the anxiety of staring down the barrel of a loaded gun.

I couldn't be pregnant.

I was only—twelve days late for my period.

Stress did that sometimes, and god knew I was stressed.

And the nausea, it could be a stomach bug from hell or something.

"Just fucking do it." I groaned out loud and forced myself into the bathroom. After peeing on the stick, I did another one just to double-check and placed both on the counter while I cleaned up. I paced back and forth in front of the bathroom door for the recommended three minutes and it somehow felt like years.

I didn't even realize I was crying until I turned off the alarm on my phone and struggled to see the buttons.

Because deep down, I already knew the answer, and it devastated me.

I walked into the bathroom and looked at myself in the mirror, forcing a deep calming breath in before I flipped the two tests over at the same time.

Pregnant.

Times two.

I bought the digital ones, because there was no way I was going to leave it up to the famous 'is that a line' bullshit.

But as my hands shook on the vanity and more tears swam in my eyes, there was no doubting the results.

I was pregnant with Fox's baby.

And he didn't want me.

I'd stupidly let him stop wearing condoms early on because I was on the pill, and I trusted him.

I trusted him to take care of me if something like this happened. He had said he wanted a wife and kids one day, but threw me out with the trash the next.

"What am I going to do?" I sobbed, covering my mouth and sliding to the floor once again, as every decision I'd ever made in my life weighed me down like it had been the last few weeks. I cried on and on for what felt like hours until my legs and back ached from being on the floor.

I couldn't just stay on the floor forever, though, as enticing as it was. So, I wiped away the tears that had run dry on my cheeks and forced myself to get up and eat. I didn't want to; I wanted to just waste away to nothing and let fate take its hold of me. During my pity party on the bathroom floor, I imagined what my life was going to look like, alone and pregnant and then alone and as a single mom.

Underneath all the fear and regret and despair, there was a tiny bit of happiness or excitement or—maybe *hope* when I imagined what the little baby inside of me was going to look like or act like. Whether it would be a girl or a boy. If they'd be tall like Fox or short like me.

I knew that until I decided what to do about my situation; I needed to take care of myself and the little one. It was the only responsible choice to make, and I was always responsible.

Unless you count the time I fell in love with a biker who didn't love me back enough to stay.

I eyed the soup and the ice cream and decided to be responsible, once again, and chose the soup. But in the back of my head, I knew I'd eat the soup first and then finish off all the pints of ice cream. Simply because I deserved a little indulgence.

I'd probably throw it all back up anyway, so what would it hurt?

To escape my bed for a bit after over a week of staying there, I took my soup to the couch, turned on the TV to silence the quiet, and forced myself to stay up.

I had to do this right.

I had to be an adult and make decisions that no longer affected just me. And I was sure that was the scariest part. I didn't know how to be a mom. Hell, I didn't know how to be a dad, I never had one of those.

And chances were my baby wouldn't either. But I had to try.

The longer I sat on the couch, sipping on my soup and letting a million possible outcomes race through my head in a kaleidoscope of fear and hope, there was one thing I knew for certain.

I had to at least tell Fox.

What he did with the information was up to him, but the moral compass in me pointed to telling him. Because if someday my little baby asked me why their daddy wasn't a part of their life, I wanted to be able to tell them honestly that I tried my best for them. That was the least they would always deserve from me.

A shuddering breath hitched in my throat as I picked up my phone; my palms were sweating, my heart pounding. I scrolled over Fox's name that I hadn't deleted because I knew it by heart anyway, so why pretend, and then pressed call.

The phone rang repeatedly before his automated voicemail picked up after I put it to my ear.

Forcing myself to take a deep breath, I tried to ignore how much anger I felt when he didn't even bother to answer the phone when I called but pushed on. Responsibilities and all.

"Hi." I said and then cleared my throat; it was scratchy and hoarse from crying earlier. "I uh—I need to talk to you about something. I know you don't want to be together; I get that. That's not what I'm calling about." Sighing after rambling like an idiot, I wrapped it up. "Please, just call me back. I need to talk to you, Fox." I hung up and took a deep breath again.

I was proud of myself for making that call, because he didn't deserve it from me, but my baby did.

The last spoonful of soup was gone, and I was already reaching for a cool, creamy pint of ice cream in the freezer. The pangs of starvation were intense after several days without food, but the nausea had lessened, allowing me to proceed. As I popped the top off the pint, I dialed my GYN's number and took a bite of the creamy chocolate and peanut butter concoction.

Within a few minutes, I had my first OB appointment booked for the following week and a sense of accomplishment as I ticked the task off my mental to do list.

Maybe I *could* do this. Maybe I'd figure out a way to manage and make it work, with or without Fox in my life.

Because deep down, I knew he would not be a part of this chapter in my life.

Acid, bitter and burning tried to ruin my meal the more I accepted my face.

Three more bites into the ice cream the nausea set back in, and five minutes later I sent it all back up into the toilet, soup included. The chill of the bathroom tile seeped into my body as I sat against the wall, desperately scrolling through morning sickness tips on my phone. I needed to feed the baby and myself if I had any hope of going back to school in a few weeks for my last year so I could graduate with my RN degree.

I didn't know how I was going to go to school, pregnant and then as a new mom. But I was going to figure it out. That's what my life had become, just a series of events that I had to figure out.

A loud knocking on my front door startled my google search, and I put my hand over my chest as my heart raced. Was it Fox?

Would he just show up after my call? Was that all it would have taken to get him here? Doubtful.

I listened for more and then dreaded that it was JJ or his asshat friends from out back, getting braver and walking onto our front porch. They had to have noticed that Fox wasn't around; the whole town knew Blaine was dead.

They knew I was alone.

Again.

It had been quiet on their side of the fence for the last week or so, and I had stupidly thought that maybe they were giving me a break because my brother died. But I should have known better than that.

"Delilah," A voice called out from the front door, "It's Detective Dailey."

"Oh, fuck." I got to my feet quickly, peeking in the mirror to make sure I didn't have any throw up on my face or shirt and then all but ran to the front door.

Detective Dailey was the man trying to find my brother's killer. Maybe he had news.

I opened the front door, swallowing down the nausea from moving so fast, and looked at the man and his partner on the porch. "Sorry, I was in the bathroom." I rushed on and the detective nodded at me.

"Can we come in?" He asked, and I stepped back, holding the door open as the two men walked into the dining room.

It was the first time I'd ever met with them alone, actually; it was the first time I had ever been alone with strangers in my home before. Maddie or Fox had always been around. Before that, no one came by for me, always Blaine as he was the oldest.

"What can I do for you?" I asked, running my hands down the front of my sweatshirt as they took seats at the table and indicated for me to sit as well.

Dailey had a brown file in his hands and laid it down on the glossy tabletop, and stared at me closely.

"We have made some progress in relation to your brother's case."

"Really?" I leaned forward hopefully. "What do you have?"

"We got a confession from the man responsible for Blaine's murder." Dailey said. Something about the way he said it left me on edge.

"That's a good thing—right?" I looked between the two men; his partner was always quiet when we met, but I was waiting for some clarification, and I'd take it from either of them at this point.

"It is, but it's left us with some more questions, actually." Dailey opened the file and took a pen out of his pocket. "When was the last time you saw or spoke to Paxton St. Claire?" He said and my ears rang loudly in my head.

"Paxton?" I wondered, "You mean, Fox?" No one used his real first name. But apparently the cops did.

"Correct." Dailey responded, offering nothing else.

"We broke up. Almost two weeks ago, so then." I replied, trying to keep the emotions off my face that those words wanted to bring up.

"You broke up?" He asked cynically, "Who ended the relationship?"

"Why?" I rested my forearms on the table and leveled him with a serious stare. "What does that have to do with anything?"

Dailey squinted his eyes at me and set his pen down, "Paxton St. Claire is who killed your brother."

My heart lurched violently, a terrifying sensation that stole the blood from my head and left me weak-kneed and gasping. "What?" I whispered, horrified, "What did you just say?" I gripped the edge of the table as my entire world spun in my head.

"He gave a sworn statement five days ago to his involvement."

"No," I shook my head and grabbed my forehead, "That's not right, he wouldn't kill Blaine, they were best friends." Tears streamed down my cheeks as the two men watched me closely. "I don't understand."

Detective Daily grabbed a paper out of the file and held it up as he read from it. "This is his signed statement about the incident." He cleared his throat and started reading. "I, Paxton Paul St. Claire met up with Blaine Peter Beckett at the Corner Stop gas station on East

Ave at approximately twelve forty-five, on Tuesday July Eleventh, Two Thousand Seventeen. We argued about my relationship with his sister, Delilah Beckett, in the northeast corner of the store in the parking lot, and started fighting. He got the upper hand on me and pinned me to the ground, hitting my sides and my stomach with closed fists. I pulled my five-inch pocketknife from my pocket and stabbed him four times in the back as he sat on top of me. He rolled off me onto the ground, I sat up and stabbed him five more times in the stomach and chest. He was alive and asking me for help when I walked away. I got on my bike and rode out of the southwest entrance towards Holly Ave at approximately one am." Dailey paused and set the paper down.

I stared at him in horror as the scene played out in vivid gore in my brain. I visualized them fighting and Fox taking a knife from his pocket and stabbing Blaine viciously in the back and again as he laid there defenselessly. Then I imagined the look on Fox's face as he stared down at my brother and walked away from him, knowing he would die alone in the dark.

I covered my mouth with my hand and cried as the men watched me. "It can't be true."

"Who ended your relationship with Fox, Ms. Beckett?" Dailey asked again, and I glared at him.

"Fox did." I sneered. "He told me he wasn't the kind of man to settle down and that he wanted to take a break."

"And you haven't spoken to him since?" Dailey asked again.

"I called him today for the first time since we split, but he didn't answer." I said angrily, and the detective scrutinized me.

"Why did you call him?"

"It doesn't matter, he didn't answer."

"It matters, Ms. Beckett; we need to know if you had any involvement in the murder. Either in the planning or suggestion of it, or in the execution of it."

"Oh, my god." I covered my face with my hands as more anger and grief settled in my chest. "You think I had something to do with it?"

"Well, we did." Dailey said, "To be honest. But if you and Fox are no longer together, then our motive for your involvement is no longer relevant."

I stared at him and sneered, "I didn't ask him to kill my brother, and I sure as fuck didn't know he was going to do it."

"We know, Delilah." The second detective spoke up from across from me. "We just need to ask the questions to do our due diligence." He stood up and buttoned his suit jacket in a show of finality to the discussion. "We'll leave you be." They walked around me towards the front door as I sat there in shock.

"What happens now?" I called out, not even bothering to look over my shoulder at them.

Dailey answered, "He pleaded guilty before the judge and will be sentenced in a few weeks."

"How long?" I asked desperately, "How long will he rot for what he did?"

Dailey sighed, "My guess is he'll go away for twenty-five. But it will depend on what the DA requests. But he won't be a bother for you anymore."

"Thank you." I said automatically and listened to them let themselves out. I sat on the hard wooden chair and put my hand over my flat stomach where my little baby was growing. They were never going to know their father, because I was never going to let a man like Fox St. Claire darken them with his evilness.

It was on me to raise and protect them from all the bad things I'd seen in my years.

That meant I needed to graduate and get the fuck out of California and as far away from him as possible so that when he did get out, whenever that was, he could never find us.

Chapter 20 – Delilah

Past

My bravado of being a rockstar single mom lasted about another week. Then Maddie came home from visiting Aunt Suzie and I realized how hard it was going to be to provide for not only myself as a full-time student, but for Maddie and my baby.

I didn't tell Maddie about Fox's arrest or that he murdered our brother. I knew I should, but I couldn't stomach the blame she would put on me for it.

Not when I was barely surviving as it was.

Eating was impossible. Sleep was all I could manage.

Well, sleep and cry.

My heart was destroyed, and my mind was clearly warped because even though Fox killed my brother, I still longed for him like I had before discovering the truth. And that obliterated my soul with shame.

He was the father to my baby, but I couldn't ever tell anyone besides Maddie that. How would they look at me if they knew the truth?

"Hey, you in there?" Maddie asked as she sat across from me at the same table the detectives had ruined my life at, eating a bowl of cereal.

"Yeah," I shook my head and took a small sip of my tea, "I'm good." I hated tea with passion. But it was literally the only thing that stayed down these days, and even then, it was a gamble.

"I have to go to school today to pick up my supply list," She eyed me, "I will try to use what I can from last year, but—" She faded off and a blush crawled up her cheeks.

"We'll get you what you need." I said firmly, even as I did math in my head.

"How?" She asked gently, and I hated that she even had to worry about it.

"I've got some saved." I shrugged and stood up, because I knew she'd see the lie on my face.

"Really?" She followed me and I had to bite back the groan that tried to escape. "How did I not know that?"

"Because I kept it quiet, so Blaine didn't come up with some hair-brained excuse to use it." I lied.

She smirked and shrugged, "He did have a tendency to blow through money, didn't he?"

"He did." I smiled back even as more of my heart cracked under pressure. "Don't worry about school supplies. We can go tomorrow morning if you want. I've got an appointment this afternoon."

"An appointment?" She squinted her eyes slightly, "What for?"

"School physical." I gave her the rehearsed answer I'd planned and poured the rest of my tea down the drain and rinsed it out.

"Oh, okay." She rinsed out her cereal bowl and wrapped her arms around me, leaning her head on my shoulder. "I'm happy to be home, even if Kansas was great. I needed to come home and be with you."

Self-conscious of the slight bulge of my lower stomach against her, I wrapped my arms around her and hugged her back. I didn't have a baby bump, but I'd lost so much weight already from being so sick that my uterus literally just pushed out of my body. "I'm glad you're home too Mad, I missed you."

She pulled back and kissed my cheek, "I'm going to head out and get that done. I'll see you later."

She turned, collected her purse and keys, and walked out the front door as I slumped against the counter.

I needed to tell her.

Or she was going to find out on her own, and that would destroy her.

Though, before I could do that, I needed to get ready to go for my first OB appointment. I'd face all the other stuff another time.

Right now, I had to focus on me, on my baby. I had no other choice.

"There's the little heart," My doctor said as she waved the ultrasound wand over my stomach and highlighted the small blinking organ on the screen. "Let's take a listen." Seconds later, the sweet melodic beating of my baby's heart filled the room, and I fell so in love with it my own heart wept.

And so did I.

My doctor was one of the sweetest people I'd ever met, and she took everything I told her in the initial part of my appointment in stride.

It wasn't every day a new patient came in, pregnant by a man that murdered her brother and was now facing twenty-five years in jail.

She gave me nausea meds to help combat the morning sickness and set me up for another appointment in a few weeks. I left with the small black and white photos of my baby to treasure until I could see it again, and that same annoying hope burning in the back of my brain.

The entire way home, I continued to imagine everything my little baby would accomplish in their life and how I would work my hardest to give them everything I had never had. Suddenly the idea of working my ass off in a busy ER so I could afford to pay for sports and Christmas presents and everything else kids wanted didn't crush my soul so much. I would do it gladly, to ensure that they were happy.

But all those optimistic thoughts swirled down the drain when I pulled in my driveway and saw the President of the Rusty Hawks MC sitting on his Harley, talking to my sister.

I shoved the evidence of my appointment into my purse and ripped off the tape from the inside of my arm, where they drew my blood and scrambled out of my car.

"What are you doing here?" I snapped at Colt and stood between him and Maddie like I could physically shield her from the news I was trying to hide from her.

Colt put his hands up in front of him. "Just stopping by for a chat, D." He shook his head, "I meant no harm."

"Go inside, Maddie." I hissed and gave her a gentle shove towards the front door.

"No." She said, and I looked at her for the first time. Her eyes were wide as she looked between the two of us. "Something is going on, and I want to know what it is."

"Please, Mad," I sighed, closing my eyes as the weight of the world rested on my shoulders. "Please, just go inside."

"No!" She hissed and put her hands on her hips. "Tell me what's going on."

"You should tell her, D." Colt said with a level of concern, "You can't hold it all together on your own."

"Stop." I barked at him and flung my hands out at my sides. "I want you to leave."

He'd stopped by a dozen times since I got the news of Fox's arrest two weeks ago, but I ignored him every time, refusing to acknowledge his presence on my porch until he left. Sometimes he left a note, asking me to call him, other times he'd leave cash taped to the door. But I just mailed it back to him, I didn't want anything from the club.

He pursed his lips together and adjusted himself on his bike. "I came here to get you. We need to go somewhere."

"No." I shook my head, not even caring where he wanted to take me. "No, Colt."

"Yes, Delilah." He argued. "You're going to tell Maddie the truth, and then you're going to come with me to see Fox."

My blood ran cold as the man inserted himself into my business, forcing my hand.

"What's the truth?" Maddie asked, "And where is Fox?" She grabbed my arm and flipped me around. "What is going on?"

I looked into my baby sister's innocent eyes and hated how I knew they'd change when I told her what really happened. "Maddie, please." I closed my eyes to block out my own pain. I felt a wave of nausea cross over me and I pressed the back of my hand to my mouth to fight it off.

"D!" Maddie snapped angrily.

"Fox killed Blaine." I said in a whisper and opened my eyes as the last of the words left my lips. "He was arrested, and he pled guilty to the charge."

"What?" She asked with wide eyes and her mouth open. She took a step back like the news tried to blow her over physically. "That doesn't—." She shook her head and swallowed, clenching her jaw hard. "They were best friends."

"I know." I cried, swiping angrily at the tears that fell over my lashes. Pregnancy hormones were a bitch on a good day, and today was the worst day. "I didn't believe it either, until I heard Fox's statement, detailing it." Flinching, I then shuddered as the mental images violated my brain again. "I'm sorry." I whispered.

"You." She hissed and took another step away from me. "This is because you were fucking him!"

"Maddie." Colt snapped, stepping off his bike, but I held my hand up to stop him. She needed to get this off her chest. I had to be the adult and let her be the child.

Which meant I had to let her hurt me.

She continued. "This is because you came between them!" She looked so angry, I couldn't remember another time I saw that much anger in her eyes, especially aimed my way. "You just couldn't leave him alone, could you!" She pointed at me, "This is your fault. And you didn't even tell me! You hid it from me because you knew I'd hate you for it."

"Yes." I agreed, speaking of the guilt that had weighed me down since I learned that Blaine was dead to begin with. "I'm sorry, Maddie, I didn't know it was going to happen. I didn't know."

"Bullshit!" She screamed and tears fell down her face. "I have to get out of here." She turned around and ran inside. Seconds later, she came back with her car keys and her backpack.

"Where are you going?" I chased after her as she ran to the street where she parked, "Please stop!"

"Fuck you!" She screamed, never turning around to look at me. "Stay away from me."

"Please, Maddie," I begged, grabbing her arm before she slid into the car. "You're all I have. We only have each other now."

"Wrong!" She screamed in my face. "You took everything from me with your selfishness, and now you're dead to me."

"No." I whispered in horror.

"I never want to see you again, Delilah, I swear to god if I ever have to look at your guilty face again, I'll strangle you with my own two hands."

She shoved me backwards, and I fell onto my ass on the rough pavement as she got in her car and tore off down the road. I pulled my legs toward me in the last second before she ran them over, not even caring about inflicting bodily harm on me.

She was done with me.

She didn't care about me.

I was alone.

And pregnant.

And alone, so fucking alone.

"Come here," Colt said gently as he slid his hands under my elbows and pulled me up to stand, "Let's get out of the street before you get hit."

"Don't touch me." I whispered, but I didn't have conviction behind it.

"It's not your fault." He said firmly, but I didn't look up at him. "There are circumstances to it, Delilah."

"What does that mean?" I finally looked up, and he stared down at me with something on his face that I couldn't read.

"I can't explain more. But I need you to come with me to see Fox."

"No." I shook my head and pulled my arms from Colt's hands. "I don't want to see him."

"You need to."

"Why?" I hissed angrily, "Why do I have to see him?"

"Because I think you might get some peace from it."

"I don't want peace." I cried, feeling my shoulders sag in defeat again, "I want my family back!"

"I know." He said sadly, "I know you do, D."

Four hours later, I sat in a visitation room inside of the Rawlings County Jail with Colt at my side. I'd been searched, questioned and judged from the second I walked through the door, and it made me feel sick.

Like I was the bad guy.

And I guess, visiting a bad guy kind of made me one.

My knee bounced rapidly underneath the table as the cold AC made my skin pebble up with goosebumps. "I shouldn't be here." I whispered for the millionth time since walking in.

Colt put his hand on my knee, making it stop, and patted it somewhat affectionately. I didn't want to like him. I didn't want to lean on him like my brother had, because he had failed Blaine. And if push came to shove, he would fail me too, because he didn't owe me a fucking thing.

"Remember, everything discussed and done in these rooms is recorded. He could catch charges for more if it's spoken about in here. You and I aren't immune, either."

"Charges?" I rolled my eyes, "Like anything I have on him could be worse than what he already admitted to."

A loud buzzing noise sounded from outside the solid steel door, and I jumped in surprise. I watched in silent horror as it opened, and three guards led Fox in. His hair was shaved down to a short buzz cut, and it made him look even angrier and more menacing. He wore a bright orange jumpsuit with his wrists and ankles shackled to a heavy chain around his waist. He had to shuffle his feet to walk, and I hated how incapacitated it made him look.

Tears burned in my eyes and nose from the pure weight of seeing him again after I swore I'd never lay eyes on him again.

He stared at me the entire time he walked across the room in the painful shuffle. His hazel eyes looked dull and washed out in the fluorescent lights, his skin was flat and gray. I hated everything about it.

Even if I knew he deserved this and more.

I hated it.

I ached to get him out of here.

That realization was a gut punch, a painful confirmation that, despite my efforts, my loyalty to my brother remained questionable, a fact that haunted me. Not even in the grave was I faithful to my own blood as I stared his killer down with my own eyes.

"Prez." Fox nodded to Colt as he gently sat down on the metal stool attached to his side of the table. The guards arraigned his chains aggressively and one grunted, "No touching, no swearing, and no acting out. Got it St. Claire?"

"Got it, boss." Fox said back as he watched me openly. I tried to read the look in his eyes but couldn't see past the mask he wore.

When the guards left the room, Colt leaned forward on the table, "How are you doing, kid?"

"Fine." Fox said gruffly, but I could hear the negation of that in his voice. He was not okay. I wanted to know why I cared in the first place, but also, I wanted to know what was happening behind the cinderblock walls that had him on edge.

"Maddie got back to town today." Colt said, looking at me over his shoulder where I sat hunched over. "D, didn't tell her until right before we came. She bolted."

Fox looked back over at me, "Why didn't you tell her?"

I licked my lips and felt my nostrils quiver as emotions threatened to boil over inside of me and make me snap. "That's the first thing you have to say to me?" I hissed.

He swallowed and sat up taller, "You're right. I'm sorry." He licked his lips and sighed, "You're losing weight." He let his eyes fall down my torso, "A lot of weight."

"Fuck you." I whispered.

He finally showed the first ounce of emotion as my words hit their mark, but only for a fraction of a second before he turned away to look at Colt again. "I told you there was no point."

"I saw how you were together. Before." Colt nodded and sighed like he wanted to say something more. "I'm just trying to save even a small bit of that. Make it last, ya know?"

"What does that mean?" I looked over at the hulking man next to me. "Make what last?"

Colt rolled his shoulders and leaned back on his stool. "Your love for each other."

"For fuck's sake." I cursed and stood up, "I can't be here."

Colt grabbed my arm and pulled me back down onto the stool. "You agreed to twenty minutes." He said pointedly, "I didn't take you for the kind to go back on your word."

"And I didn't take you for a hopeless romantic." I snapped, crossing my arms over my chest and glowering at him.

He smirked and winked at me. "I am when I see two people meant to be together."

"He murdered my brother!" I yelled, like he needed to be reminded of the fact, as if the environment around us could have let him forget.

"Enough." Fox snapped from where he sat, and he leaned forward over the table when I finally faced him. "I'm sorry." He said evenly, and I paused, letting those words wash over me. "I wish I could take it back and go back to when we first met. I would have told your brother about us from the start. I would have earned his trust with your heart before I took it. But I didn't." He sighed, "I got caught up in my feelings for you and then it all went south."

"Why did you tell me on the cliff that you didn't want me?" I asked, straightening my spine and forcing bravado into it I didn't know I possessed. I needed answers, and Colt was right. The only way I was going to get those was to speak to Fox face to face.

"Because I was trying to get you as far away from the fallout of this as possible." He swallowed and the muscles in his neck flexed, reminding me of the way they did it when he laughed with me. "I knew I was running out of time, and I didn't want them to come looking at you when they busted me."

"They did anyway!" I hissed through my teeth, "They sat at my fucking table and accused me of being involved in his murder, Fox!"

"I'm sorry." He said quietly.

"Hey." Colt put his hand on my knee again and patted it, "Calm down or they'll kick us out before we're ready to go."

I glared at him and then looked off towards the wall like a pouting child, buying time until he would let me leave. I felt Fox's eyes on me like a caress and my skin ignited with longing. It had been so long since I felt his touch.

"Why did you leave him there to die alone?" I whispered to the wall, before looking at him out of the corner of my eye. "I know you. And that's the only part that makes little sense to me."

"Don't think too hard on it, D." Fox said dismissively.

"I want answers." I turned my attention back to him fully, "You owe me that. You made me love you, and then you took Blaine from me and left me to take care of—." I clamped my jaw shut, preventing my secret from being revealed.

I went back and forth the entire drive to the jail whether I was going to tell him I was pregnant or not. And I still hadn't come to a conclusion before he walked into the visitation room.

"Take care of what?" He asked, squinting his eyes slightly at me.

"Maddie." I lied. "She blames me for all of this, and I can't fault her. Because if I'd have just left you alone and told you to fuck off the first time you slept in my room overnight, none of this would have happened. I never would have fallen for you and felt this agonizing regret and grief that you left in your wake." I pounded my fist over my heart, "It hurts so fucking bad."

Fox's nostrils flared as his eyes rounded. "None of this is your fault. My fight with Blaine was a mistake that got out of hand." He shook his head, but for the first time, I saw through his facade.

He was lying.

I couldn't tell if he was lying about it being my fault or if he was lying about his fight with Blaine. Either way, it felt—wrong. "You're lying about something." I squinted at him.

"I need you to go on with your life, D. Thrive and be successful like I know you will be. I need you to forget about me and move on."

"I don't care what you want or need, Fox." I whispered and wiped away the tears that fell over my cheeks. "Why did you lie to me when I found out about his death? Why come over and lay in my bed and hold me. You were so angry with me when I let the detectives' words fill my head with doubts about you right away and I thought that was genuine hurt. Was it just guilt?"

He licked his lips and looked away from me to Colt. "Take care of her. All my savings and possessions, sell them all and take care of her."

"Fuck you!" I hissed, even as Colt nodded. "Answer me, Fox!"

"The club has her and Maddie for life." Colt said, as they both ignored me in an intense stare off. Something was being said between them silently and it was driving me mad to know I was on the outside of it all.

"Tell me!" I banged my fist on the table angrily. "You owe me that!" I yelled.

The steel door opened, and the three guards walked in. "Visit is over St. Claire." The gruff one said and unhooked the chains from the table, and they pulled him to his feet.

"No!" I cried, climbing to my feet.

"Delilah." Colt hissed, as one guard shoved me back down into my seat so hard my teeth chattered together.

"Don't fucking touch her." Fox snarled at the man, lunging forward like he was going to do something to him, even with his hands and feet chained together. "Fucking Pig."

One of the guards punched Fox in the stomach so hard that I heard the air hissing out of his lungs as he doubled over and turned red, unable to move any breath into his chest.

"Stop." I whispered in shock. "No, I'm sorry!" I pleaded.

"Calm down, kid." Colt put his arm over my shoulders, pulling me in against his side and away from the guard, who looked all too willing to show Fox he could do whatever he wanted. "Keep your head on straight, don't forget the point of it all."

There was a veiled message behind his words, but I couldn't decipher it as the guards dragged Fox backwards by his elbows. "I love you, D. I always will. I'm sorry." He hissed and stared at me the whole time with his wild eyes and angry face and what little bit of my heart that was still intact broke.

I sat frozen in place as my eyes jumped back and forth around the room as we heard Fox yelling and screaming down the hallway, thuds and grunts followed, and I knew the guards were beating him for his outburst.

"No." I whispered in horror covering my ears to stop the assault from permanently marking itself on my eardrums. But it was too late, I'd replay Fox's screams for the rest of my life. "Please make it stop."

Colt turned my face to him and forced me to look at him. "That feeling you have right now, right here." He tapped his finger over my sternum, "Remember it." He instructed me. "Remember how much you love that kid right now, because even under the pain and grief and confusion, you know you do. You don't get a choice with a soulmate, and you two are fucking destined to be together." He shook me gently by my upper arms when I stared at him in shock, unspeaking. "Remember that feeling D. Because someday, someday sooner than you think, you're going to have to let that feeling back into your heart. And if you don't, you'll miss out on all that is destined to be."

"I don't understand."

"Promise me." He demanded, "Promise me you'll remember how much you love him and how much it hurt to see him treated that way just now."

"I can't—." I shook my head.

"Promise me, Delilah! For Blaine, because believe me, he'll want you to remember that."

"I promise." Whispering, so confused and in utter shock. "I promise." Because whether or not I wanted to, I would always remember the pain radiating through my chest as I watched those guards haul him away from me.

Colt was right.

Fox St. Claire was my soulmate, but what he did was unforgiveable, and I was never going to get my happy ending with him.

And that meant I was going to be alone for the rest of my life.

Except for our baby.

The only piece of him I'd ever have, would be in our child.

Chapter 21 – Delilah

Past

Sentencing day.

I was seventeen weeks pregnant, almost halfway through. And my bump was getting harder and harder to hide. I had lost so much weight at the beginning of my pregnancy that when I started showing; it popped out so much easier than it would have had if I had more meat on my bones.

Maddie still didn't know. She moved in with her friend Stella after she found out the truth about Blaine's murder. It destroyed me to come home one day and find all her belongings—gone.

I had sunk to my knees in the center of her empty room and sobbed for hours at how utterly empty I was inside.

First mom, then Blaine and Fox, and now Maddie. The only one I had left was my itty-bitty baby inside of me.

My daughter.

I ended up hospitalized twice during the first sixteen weeks of my pregnancy because of morning sickness. They had upgraded it to hyperemesis gravidarum, *extreme* morning sickness. Like adding the word extreme to the front of it would somehow make things better. There wasn't anything to stop it from happening, but they did prescribe me stronger medication to help with the nausea.

Twice I got so dehydrated and run down, my doctor made me stay at the hospital in the maternity ward for the night to get fluids and electrolytes to perk me back up while they monitored the baby. They were worried about the stress on my body and my baby girl would put me into pre-term labor. And she wouldn't survive if she was born that early.

There was something that broke inside of my soul as I walked in and out of the hospital each time for appointments and longer stays, alone with no one to care how hard I was struggling. I maintained my rigorous school schedule, spending twelve-hour shifts at the hospital for clinical training in between classes and labs, on top of taking a part-time job in the gift shop in the lobby to help pay for some of the bills piling up without Blaine's income. I ended up taking out student loans bigger than the tuition costs so I could afford to keep paying taxes on our home and rub enough pennies together to eat and keep the electricity on.

All the while, life kept moving on around me.

But I felt empty and desolate other than those few times I managed to muster up enough excitement about my baby girl's future.

She was going to have so much more than I did.

It was a promise I made to her every single night when I crawled my tired body into bed and ran my hand over my bump and talked to her.

She was going to thrive if it was the very last thing I ever did. She'd never know hardships or struggle.

I'd bear it all on my shoulders for her.

The first step of that plan was forcing myself to be strong and show up at Fox's sentencing court date to find out how long he'd sit behind bars for what he did.

Because like Colt said, someday he'd get out, and I needed to know when that would be so I could figure out what that meant for me and our daughter.

I hadn't seen him since the guards dragged him from the visitation room that day, even if I ached to go and see him again. But I knew I wouldn't be able to stand to look at myself in the mirror if I selfishly went to visit the man that murdered my own flesh and blood. Even if his own flesh and blood grew every single day inside of my belly.

"Hey." A soft voice called from the front door as I stirred a cup of tea in the kitchen.

I quickly wrapped my oversized sweater around my waist as Maddie walked through the doorway. "Hi." I whispered in shock. It was the first time she'd been back in months. "How are you?"

"I'm okay." She said gently as she put her hands in the back pockets of her jeans, "I thought maybe we could ride together today." She shrugged one shoulder, "I thought maybe I could hold your hand through it." I didn't know how she knew about the sentencing, but if I had to guess, I'd put money on Colt.

I licked my lips and looked down at my cup to keep from sobbing at her olive branch, "Yeah," I croaked through my emotions and then cleared my throat, "I'd like that."

She smiled softly and took a deep breath, "I owe you an apology first though." She said and walked further into the kitchen. "I left because I was angry that you kept something so important from me, and then after more and more time passed, I didn't know how to come back. How to say sorry."

I shook my head and grabbed both of her hands in mine, "You don't owe me an apology Maddie, you had every right to blame me for everything. It's all my fault."

"No, no, it's not." She pulled my hands towards her like she was going to pull me into a hug.

"Wait." I said and stepped back. My chest shook with anxiety and my palms were clammy. "In the name of honesty and transparency, I want to tell you something right now. Before any more time passes."

"What is it?" She asked cautiously and wrapped her arms around her waist in uncertainty.

I slowly opened my sweater from around my stomach and let her see the swelling baby bump under my white T-shirt.

Her eyes dropped to it instantly and her mouth opened in a big O as her eyes widened, too. "Oh, my God." She whispered and looked back up at me. "Oh, my God, D."

"I know." I said, and then wrapped my sweater closed over it and looked away. "I just wanted you to know, in case that changed how you felt about reconciling with me."

"Oh, my God." She cried and flung herself at me. "I'm sorry!" She said, wrapping her arms tight around my neck, "You've been alone through all of this because I left you." Her small shoulders shook as I wrapped my arms around her waist and clung to her. It was the first hug I'd gotten since she got back from Aunt Suzie's Ranch months ago. I didn't realize until just that moment how desperately I missed human touch. "I'm so sorry."

"No." I said, running my hand over her hair, "You were dealing with your own grief and pain, it's not your responsibility to support me through mine."

She pulled back and glared at me angrily, "That's exactly what my responsibility is, Delilah! Because if the roles were reversed and you found out I was pregnant, you would have stayed by my side and held my hand through the entire thing. But I abandoned you."

Tears slid down my cheeks as she validated all my feelings without me even having to say them, and I just pulled her close again. She tightened her arms around me and took a deep breath. "You're here now. That's all that matters. I love you so much, Maddie, and I've missed you so much."

"I miss you, too." She cried. "Can I come home?"

"Yes!" I gasped and pulled back to hold her face in my hands. "Of course, you can!"

We made our way into the living room and sat down on the couch, and I told her everything. Every single ounce of information, from how Fox broke up with me on the cliff's edge, to finding out I was pregnant and my visit from Detective Dailey to tell me that Fox was the one who had killed Blaine. I told her about my visit with Fox at Colt's persistence and the veiled warnings he gave me before we left. I told her how sick I'd been, and how I had laid alone in the hospital afraid that my body wasn't strong enough to carry my baby to term. Then I told her how she was going to be an aunt to a little girl, how I didn't tell Fox about the baby and that today's outcome would determine what path I took tomorrow and the day after that and so on.

She promised to be by my side every step of the way, regardless of the outcome.

I hated that I weighed down my little sister with all my darkness, but I would have been lying if I said it didn't feel good having someone at my side again. It all felt survivable with a hand holding mine.

Hours later, we walked into the courthouse hand in hand to face the terrible situation together. I changed into a flowing top and baggy jacket to hide my bump even more, but I felt like everyone could tell, regardless.

When we got to the doors of the courtroom, Maddie paused with her hand on the knob and turned to me. "Are you ready, babe?" She asked, and I nodded silently.

She pulled the door open, and we walked in. The side behind the defendant's desk was packed with Rusty Hawk riders and other bikers I didn't recognize. At first, I felt anger that those men were choosing to sit behind Fox, giving him their support when Blaine was a rider and friend to them as well.

But then that other part of me was glad that there were people still in his corner.

"Delilah." Colt said, standing up and gaining the attention of everyone in the room. He walked down the aisle and stopped in front of my sister and me. I instinctively clutched at her hand and my jacket to hide my belly. "You haven't returned any of my calls."

"I don't think there's anything left to say." I said with practiced grace.

"I promised Fox I'd take care of you." He said firmly, and I wanted to wilt under the pressure of it. "I sold off the things he asked me to and put all the money in an account in your name." He tried to hand me a slip of paper, but I wouldn't take it.

"I won't take his guilt money, Colt."

"It ain't guilt money girl. It's his way of trying to take care of you, even from the inside." He lowered his voice and stepped closer, "Remember what I told you at the end of our visit. Someday sooner than you think, you're going to have to remember how much he meant to you."

"Yeah," I nodded and looked around, noting the look of confusion on Maddie's face. "But today isn't that day and I'm not ready to remember."

He sighed but nodded, folding the paper up and put it in his breast pocket, "When you are ready, come see me." Lawyers started walking into the room, signaling the beginning of the session, "But don't wait too long, or I'll come looking for you." He said and then walked away back to his seat.

Maddie pulled me down the aisle to sit behind the prosecution desk as the bailiffs and court personnel walked in.

"Say the word and we'll leave." Maddie whispered, "The DA can call us later and tell us what happened."

I smiled tightly at her but looked away when the door on the far side of the courtroom opened and police officers walked in with a shackled Fox between the group of them.

Six.

Six police officers escorted him.

Like they were expecting a problem from him or the large crowd of rowdy bikers.

Fox's hazel eyes searched the crowd until they landed on me, and he took a deep breath, like he was breathing for the first time in months.

And I did the same, because it was exactly how it felt for me, too.

His hair was a little shaggier than the time I saw him at visitation and there was a healing scar on his forehead that hadn't been there before.

Maddie's hand tightened around mine as I watched the guards shackle him to the chair and table like they had in the visitation room. Instead of paying attention to them, he looked over his shoulder at me the whole time. Like he was trying to say something with his eyes.

It looked a hell of a lot like longing and pain.

"All rise." The bailiff said and everyone stood up, including Fox and his weighted chains.

I listened on autopilot as the judge and her staff went through the normal court stuff until she told Fox to stand again.

This was it.

Numbers flashed in front of my eyes as I imagined what his sentence would be. When I called the DA's office last week, they told me they were requesting twenty-five years for the charges he admitted to.

First degree murder.

But they weren't sure he'd serve that if he kept his nose clean.

Twelve and a half was what the junior lawyer had told me.

Twelve and half years for killing someone else.

I was so fucking torn about how that made me feel. If it was anyone else in the entire world, I'd be outraged that someone could cut someone's life short by sixty plus years and destroy a family, and only see the inside of a jail cell for twelve years.

But then I put Fox's face on the man standing there facing the sentence and twelve and half years felt like an eternity.

Our daughter would be almost a teenager before he was free.

He'd miss it all.

I hated that I even thought of it like that. But I had to play both sides of the story out, because my daughter deserved a mother and father in her life.

The judge began, "Mr. St. Claire, I've reviewed the case thoroughly and I have to say, I'm feeling pressure from the DA to go hard on you here." She took her glasses off and laid her elbows on her desk and looked him square in the eye. I knew he was holding her stare, because he was a proud and honorable man, even if he was a murderer. "I've considered every side of this case when making my decision. But the fact of the matter is, that you're a thug." She said, and I saw the expression on her face change like a lightbulb had been turned on. "You're the scum of this town, with your motorcycle gang doing all sorts of illegal activities and your rap sheet is a mile long of small-time crime. At least until now. Now it has an even darker smear over it, and I'm not willing to let you add to it after today. I'm not willing to let you darken someone else's life with your presence in it."

"Oh my God." I whispered in horror.

Twenty-five.

She was going to give him the full twenty-five. I felt sick.

"So, to protect the people of not only this town, but any other town you might have dared to grace with your evilness, I'm using every ounce of my authority to make an example out of you. Mr. St. Claire, I hereby sentence you to life behind bars, without the possibility of parole."

Gasps filled the room, mine and Maddie's mixed with those of Fox's friends and allies. The judge pounded her gavel down on her desk over and over as outbursts started flying from the biker's mouths.

Things like, "Fucking uncalled for," and "You psychotic cunt," flew her way as chaos started building.

"Bailiffs," The judge slammed her gavel down again, "Clear the courtroom, take Mr. St. Claire back to his cell."

I stood up on shaking legs, clinging to the pew back in front of me as the guards started pulling Fox away. He turned to me, and the calm look on his face chilled me to the core.

"I love you." He shouted over the noise. "Don't you forget that!"

"Oh my God," Maddie cried next to me, holding my weight up with an arm around my waist. "I didn't want him to go away for life." She whispered. "That's not fair to you."

"Shh." I hushed her in complete shock, tears streamed down my face. "Let's get out of here."

We turned and walked away from the chaos as the bikers started picking up seats and throwing them towards the bench, proving just how uncivilized they could be when provoked.

And we ran away in the fury of it.

Chapter 22 – Delilah

Past

"Maddie." I groaned, clutching my stomach as I tried to get out of the tub. "Maddie!" I yelled louder as pain and fear burned through my stomach.

"What?" She asked, pushing the door open, "Oh shit." She grabbed my towel off the back of the door and wrapped it around me, "What's wrong?"

"Ughhhhh." I groaned in pain and grabbed a handful of her shirt to hold myself up. "Contractions."

"Do you think it's time? Are you in labor?" She held my weight up and helped me down the hall to my bedroom.

"Yep." I cried as the contraction finally loosened up enough so I could talk.

"Okay." She sat me down on the edge of my bed. "Okay, don't panic. We planned for this. We're prepared." She pushed her hair out of her face and circled around, looking at my room. "Hospital bags, purses, and snacks. The car seat is in the car." She looked back at me with an excited grin on her face. "Holy shit, D."

"I know." I said and started getting dressed in a flowy dress and sandals, the only thing that fit my swollen body at forty weeks pregnant. "But we need to move fast because these hurt like holy hell."

"Okay," She said again and ran from my room. After I finished dressing and started downstairs, she came back in through the front door, having loaded the bags into my car. "Ready?" She asked gleefully.

"Not in the least." I groaned and froze as another contraction started lighting up my spine. "Fuck these hurt."

"Deep breath, babe." She pulled me forward to rest my weight against her chest as she squeezed my hips. She went to every Lamaze class with me and was prepared to be my birth partner in Fox's absence. And thank god too, because if she didn't do it, I'd be alone.

She held me and swayed with me as the contraction worked its way through my body and then as soon as it was done, we went outside and got in my car. I watched as she checked her mirrors no less than four times before pulling out of the driveway, and she drove ridiculously slow as I hid my smile from her. She was like a brand-new dad trying to bring the baby home safely and I hadn't even had her yet.

Sadness swept through my chest as I thought about how Fox was missing this moment. I had avoided Colt and his cronies for months now, and I didn't go visit Fox again after the sentencing. The way he told me he'd always love me felt like a final goodbye, even if a giant part of me didn't want it to be.

It wasn't like I could go visit him with a giant baby belly in front of me and pretend like he wasn't about to be a dad. I told myself over and over again how maybe after the baby was born, I'd go see him. Except, I couldn't come up with a good excuse to visit him when the reason he was in jail to begin with should have been more than enough for me to write him off completely.

Besides, he had been transferred to a state prison in southern California and then transferred again to another one a few weeks later.

All that information was available on the internet and sometimes, late at night when my resolve to be a rockstar single mom slipped a little bit, I would search his name on the department of corrections website and check up on him.

More times than I could count, I wrote a letter to him, only to stash it away in my underwear drawer in case someday I got brave enough to send any of them. Sometimes I'd start at the beginning and tell him about our daughter. Other times I'd write to him like we'd just talked the day before, sharing things about my day and my plans for the next.

In a way, it was therapeutic and a bit sad. It was mainly a way to pass the time. A few weeks after that day in court, I forced myself to acknowledge what everyone already knew. Fox's life was over; even a miracle couldn't change the fact he'd die in prison.

"Fuck." I groaned as another one hit and Maddie sped up a bit.

"Please don't have her in the car, I'm totally prepared to be an aunt, your birth partner, and your baby daddy for the immediate future, but I am so not prepared to deliver her myself. Okay?"

"I won't." I hissed, "This is my first labor, you know they take a long time."

"Yeah, okay, right." She nodded and focused on driving, thankfully the hospital entrance was up ahead and soon we were parking in the lot and making our way inside.

She was off the hook to deliver the baby.

"I can't do this!" I cried an hour later. Groaning, I leaned over the edge of the bed; it felt like my insides were splitting. "I change my mind."

My doctor smiled at me goodheartedly as she put on a pair of gloves. "I know it seems daunting, Delilah. The downside of being so far progressed means no epidural. I know that was part of your plan, but the upside is that it's almost over and I promise you when you start pushing in a minute, you'll feel relief from it all. Then your healthy baby girl will be here."

"Okay." I nodded in a daze, and Maddie loosened the tie on my gown as I got up onto the bed. When I walked into labor and delivery, I was already eight centimeters dilated and progressing fast. It had been a whirlwind of chaos as I got into a room and set up for delivery, and each time I looked over at Maddie, I was genuinely afraid that she was going to pass out from it all. I prayed the experience would serve as birth control for her teenage body for the next few years, at least.

"You got this, babe." She said as she ran the cold washcloth over my forehead. "I'm so proud of you."

"I can't." Another contraction hit, leaving almost no time to rest between them, I hissed. "I want Fox." I whispered, as tears filled my eyes. "I want him here so bad. He should be here for this. I need him to be here for this." I spoke the words I'd kept locked inside for months as my fears and grief ran over in the moment.

My sister's eyes filled with tears of her own as I broke down, "I'm sorry, D." She squeezed my hand and smoothed my hair out of my face, "I'd give anything for him to be here for you right now, I swear I would."

Sobs shook my body as the nurses prepared me to push, I felt like a tidal wave was cresting above me and I had no way to stop it or get out of its way. I just wanted off the ride for a moment to catch my breath and regroup, but there was no pause button on life. Lacking an anchor in the storm, I couldn't stay afloat and safe. I had no Fox anymore.

"Okay, Delilah," My doctor said, interrupting my pity party as she stood at the foot of the bed fully gowned and ready to go. "Your body is ready to push, this little girl is ready to come out and meet her mama. Are you with me?"

I took a deep breath and looked at her, letting her wise and experienced eyes guide me as I nodded. "Yes." I swallowed and squeezed Maddie's hand. "I'm ready."

"Good girl." She said, "Now, with the next contraction, I want you to push for me."

"She's perfect." I whispered into the dimly lit room as I stared down at my newborn daughter. "How is it possible for her to be so utterly perfect?"

"Because you're perfect." Maddie whispered from next to me on the bed. "You're incredible, Delilah." She ran the tip of her finger over her niece's forehead, "I haven't told you that in a while. But without you I'd be lost, and watching you hold it all together this last year," She shook her head and sniffled as emotions bubbled up in her voice. "I'm in awe of you and the absolutely incredible woman that you've become in the blink of an eye."

"Maddie." I whispered as tears filled my eyes again. "Thank you. For everything. Without you I wouldn't have made it through everything. So, thank you for having my back and standing at my side."

"Any time." She smiled and sniffled again, steeling her emotions, "Besides, someone has to be around to spoil this baby absolutely rotten." She cooed and my daughter stretched and made a cute baby noise in response, like she was on board with that idea. "Have you decided on a name?"

The one hang-up I'd had the whole time was picking out a name for the baby, like somehow if I got it wrong, it'd impact her for the rest of her life. Which was absurd and realistic all at the same moment. That was one of the things I talked to Fox about in my unsent letters. I asked him almost every time what he would want her to be named. But the response was silent because he never read them. He didn't even know he was a father. Which felt wrong, yet necessary.

What good would it do to torture him further with the loss of everything else by telling him he'd never know his own flesh and blood? Because I would never take my daughter into a state prison to meet him, even if it was what was best for him.

I had to think about what was best for her, because in the end, she couldn't do it for herself yet. It was my job.

"I have." I breathed as a smile crossed my face. "Blaine's middle name was Peter, and Mom's name was June, so I decided to name her Penelope June. To go along and honor them both."

I didn't bother to tell her that Fox's full name was Paxton Paul and that he also played a factor in choosing a name that started with P. That could be something for just me to hold on to when the nights were long and cold.

She smiled knowingly, "That's beautiful, Delilah." She kissed my cheek and then leaned down to kiss Penelope's forehead, "Hi, little Penny bug, we both love you so much already and you're going to be the absolute light of our lives, I promise you."

I wiped away a tear at the mix of happiness and sorrow and made a vow to myself at that moment. I'd never show Penelope the pain and turmoil inside of me as long as I lived. She would know nothing but love and happiness and comfort and joy. I'd shield her from heartbreak and agony with my dying breath for as long as I could. Because she was the absolute light of my life, the only thing to keep me going strong every day, and I'd honor that.

After today, I'd be everything she needed and more. I had to be.

Chapter 23 – Delilah

Present

I showered quickly, even though everything inside of me wanted to just sit on the warm stone bench and bask in the relaxing water. Past experience told me if I took too much time, Fox would come join me, and I wasn't ready for that.

Thus, I showered quickly and toweled off and put on the white tee and boxers he left for me on the counter. They were both giant and hung off me, but there was something soothing about wearing his clothes in his home, so I didn't fight it.

I toweled my hair dry and brushed it out with his brush before tying it up in a messy bun. There was no short supply of hair accouterments in Fox's home, and I loved that. There was also a bottle of extra strength ibuprofen sitting next to the pile of clothes and I eagerly took a few. I wasn't overly anxious to take any more of the prescription pain pills when I knew we needed to have difficult talks. I needed my wits about me. And Fox was always ready to anticipate my needs and be ready for them before I asked him to be.

When I couldn't prolong it anymore, I walked out of the bedroom to find him.

And man, the mouthwatering view I experienced when I did.

Fox stood with his back to me at the stove in the kitchen, flipping what smelled like delicious chicken in a pan. He had his hair down, and it looked like silk where it brushed his bare shoulders.

Those shoulders.

Drool.

He was so fucking wide and strong, and standing in a pair of gray sweatpants and nothing else, he was drool worthy.

Duly, I took the moment to admire his body and expansive tattoos that covered his back and arms.

His back had a giant dark tattoo of an ocean scene and something about it called to me, drawing me in. From my spot across the room, I could make out a swirling sea with giant waves crashing down on a rocky shore. On the shore stood a woman, or goddess maybe, and it looked like she was singing.

But as I tried to decipher it further, he shifted, reaching for something, and the spell the tattoo had on me was broken.

My patience snapped; the quiet scrutiny felt invasive, so I told myself I could study his art properly later. "Hey." I said from the living room as I walked closer, and he looked over his shoulder at me with a grin on his face.

"You look good in my clothes, baby." He bit his bottom lip as his eyes scanned me from head to toe. "Damn good."

"Thanks for lending them to me." I put my hands on the cool marble top of the island. "Is there something I can do to help?"

"Nah, I want you to sit down and relax while I cook for you." He said, turning off the burner as he moved to the island with a cutting board and an array of vegetables.

"What are we having?" I leaned over the countertop to look closer. He was chopping up scallions, mushrooms, and squash.

"I'll be honest with you." He smirked and winked at me as he slid the big knife through the mushrooms, "I don't cook too often; It's kind of depressing to do for one person, therefore I didn't have a full meal ready to go for us on short notice. I just kind of tossed stuff together and we'll have to pretend they all taste good together."

"Well, thank you for your honesty." I smirked, "Now that I know, I'll make sure to keep my critiquing gentle."

He chuckled and moved onto the scallions. "Tell me about your life." He watched the motion of the knife with laser sharp precision. "What brought you to Belden?"

"The hospital here offered a giant sign-on bonus for fresh graduates," I shrugged my shoulders. "And it was as far away from Rawlins County as I could get on my gas money."

He paused and looked up at me as his jaw clenched tightly. "Why didn't you take the money that Colt set up for you?"

"Because I didn't want anything from you." I answered honestly.

"You'd rather suffer and struggle working twenty hours a day?" The anger was impossible to miss in his tone and I sighed, because not very often did he aim it my way.

"I wanted to prove to myself that I could do it on my own." I played with a hangnail on my thumb, refusing to meet his eyes because I knew I'd see the disappointment there. "Taking money from you felt wrong, like it was you trying to compensate for stealing my brother from me." I sighed, "Which obviously I didn't know the truth back then."

"Would you have taken the money if you knew I was innocent?"

"No." I answered quickly, "Maybe, I don't know. I think first I need to know why you're innocent, yet willingly went to jail."

He nodded but remained quiet as he turned and tossed the veggies in a pan next to the chicken. "I know." He sighed but didn't offer up anything else.

"Why did *you* choose Belden?" I asked, trying to change the subject and get back to the present time information I sought so we could leave the heavy stuff until after dinner.

He shrugged his shoulders, "I met Houston in prison. We got along well enough, and he told me about the troubles he was having with his crew here, apparently there was a civil war going on between members, dividing them up and making things sketchy. He said he needed someone to help straighten things out, someone new and from the outside so there wouldn't be any bias bullshit." He turned and looked at me, "When I couldn't find you and had no leads to follow, I figured I'd come out here for a while and help him out. Distract myself and bide my time until I could find you."

"You were still looking for me?" I questioned.

He nodded, "I paid a private investigator thousands of dollars to find you when I got out of prison. When I moved here and paid another one even more. It turned out you were hiding in plain sight the whole time. Right under my nose."

"I wasn't hiding from you." I said gently.

"It wasn't like you wrote to me with your forwarding address, either." He countered and flipped the veggies over.

"I thought you were never getting out." Shaking my head. "I wanted a fresh start away from all the death and heartache that town represented for me."

"I know." Fox nodded and then wiped his hands on a towel and tossed it over his shoulder. He turned and stalked towards me with the agile gentleness I recognized as the stalk of a predator. He had perfected it long before we met, and it made my knees weak every time he aimed it my way. "I believe we both ended up here for a reason. Don't you?"

"Maybe." I admitted in a whisper. I licked my lips as he rounded the island and stopped right in front of me. "Yes." I corrected myself. "I do, I just—so much happened since the day up on the cliff when you ended things." Shrugging my shoulders, the secrets felt impossible to get past, "I don't know how to heal this."

"We start right here." He slid his hands around the back of my neck and linked them together, tilting my head back to look up at him. I placed my hands flat on his lower abs and leaned into him. "Just like this, relearning each other and talking about everything that happened and we'll heal those wounds and the distance between us together. I just need you to tell me it's what you want." He closed his eyes and took a calming breath, "Because I won't force myself on you like this if you don't want me, D. I need you to want this and want me as bad as I do you. Tell me this means you're still mine and we can go from there."

"There's only you." I leaned against him further, "I've only ever wanted you. I want this."

"Thank fuck." He groaned and lowered his lips to mine, kissing me deeply before picking me up and putting my ass on the island. I spread my legs on instinct, and he walked straight between them, pressing his hard front to mine and I wrapped my ankles around his ass. He growled into my mouth as I dug my nails into his back, pulling him even closer.

"Your food is going to burn." I whispered, and bit his lip.

"Fuck it, we'll order in." He bit mine back and I moaned for him. "Again." He demanded and spread my legs even wider, pushing his erection against my clit. Taking what he wanted. I moaned and let my head fall backward as he buried his teeth into my neck and rocked against me, bringing us both pleasure and torment together. "I missed the way you moan for me." He growled.

I giggled and sagged against him. "I missed the things you did to me to make me moan." I licked my lips and pulled my head back. "But if you don't feed me soon, I might go rabid and start eating things you put close to my face." I smirked as he chuckled.

"Fair enough." He pulled back and stared at me as he reached down and palmed his erection growing inside of his sweats. He stroked it once and twice and then a third time as I watched and then rubbed his hand up his washboard abs in such a sexy, manly way. "Sit in a chair or I'll eat your sweet pussy for my meal."

"Yes, Sir." I swallowed audibly and slid from the counter onto a barstool as he plated our dinners. Grilled chicken breasts, smothered in a cheese sauce with roasted veggies. "This smells delicious." I said as I cut into a piece.

"Fingers crossed." He watched me closely as I took a bite. I moaned as the flavors hit my taste buds and closed my eyes, savoring the taste. "Good?" He asked.

"So good." I smiled at him, "Thank you for cooking for me."

"You're welcome." He smiled proudly and then dug into his meal. We ate in silence for a while, stealing glances at each other and occasionally touching. And it felt—effortless.

Right, even.

We were almost done eating when his facial expression darkened a bit, and I knew he was thinking about our time apart and what led up to it. I stayed quiet while he worked out what he wanted to say. "I never wanted to leave you." He said finally, putting his fork down on his plate. "I wrestled with my decision over and over again, trying to come up with some other way to achieve what I needed to achieve, but there wasn't one." He looked at me. "But I want you to know, I didn't mean a single thing I said to you up on that cliff that day. It was all just part of the plan. There was no way around it."

"What plan?" I pushed my plate away and washed down the delicious dinner with some water before turning to face him. "What happened? Start at the beginning."

He nodded and pushed his own plate away. "I never saw Blaine again after he left the club looking for a fight that night." He clenched his jaw, "I wanted to follow him and make him see reason and calm him down. But I knew you were out there, upset and alone, and my need to comfort you won out." I stayed silent and let him continue. "But when I went to leave to meet you at your place, a fight went down with some of our guys at a bar across county lines. The orders were given, and we were all to show up there. If you didn't obey, you faced a beat down for leaving our men to defend themselves."

"That's why you didn't show up when you said you would." I whispered.

He nodded, "I was an hour away, fighting someone else's fight while you and Blaine, both needed me. It tore me to fucking shreds. I had just gotten back to the club when you called me." He clenched his jaw again and his hands tightened into fists on the countertop. "I raced right over to you, but it was too late. Blaine was gone."

"What happened between then and the cliff?" I shook my head, remembering the pain in my heart that day.

"I found out who really killed Blaine."

"Jason Harter." I replied, and he looked over at me. He turned on his stool and put his hands on my thighs, leaning forward to look directly at me.

"Do you know who Jason Harter was?"

I shook my head, "No."

"JJ." He said firmly as my blood ran cold inside of my veins. "Jason Harter Jr."

JJ was the low life neighbor that constantly made my life a living hell.

"No." I whispered in shock, backing up a bit as a haunted feeling came over me. "JJ killed Blaine?"

Fox nodded solemnly, "We beat him up that first night I slept in your room. When Blaine found out that he had been harassing you, we went looking for him and beat him until he pissed himself and left him there with the warning that if he ever even looked your way again, we'd kill him."

"But he didn't listen," I said, putting my hands on top of his on my legs. "He never stopped."

"I didn't know that; neither did Blaine because you kept it to yourself. But JJ knew he was living on borrowed time. That night Blaine found out about us, he was at the Corner Stop fueling up when JJ and his crew caught him there. Alone."

"Oh, my god." I closed my eyes and sagged on the stool. Fox reached forward and put his hand around the back of my neck to keep me from toppling over. "JJ knew the Hawks were across county lines and took the opportunity to strike. They fought with fists and then, out of nowhere, JJ pulled a knife and stabbed him."

"And left him there." Fox nodded sadly as I cried.

"I should have ignored the order to ride out to the fight. I should have been there for him and you to make it work."

"You didn't know." I whispered, grabbing his arm and clinging to him. "You couldn't have known some low life like JJ was going to act like a big man and do that. Up until that point, it had all been amateur shit he pulled. Murder was out of his scope. Even I know that Fox."

"Either way, your brother died alone, and I wasn't with you when you found out about it. I'll never forgive myself for either of those events."

"What happened after that? Why did you admit to killing him?"

"One of JJ's guys recorded the whole thing. He came to the clubhouse a couple of days after it all, trying to barter the video and information for a spot with the Hawks."

"Jesus fuck." I cursed, hating that there were people out there like that.

"By the time we got the video, JJ had already gotten himself locked up for aggravated armed robbery; he was locked down facing hard time in state prison. He was a three-strike idiot already, he wasn't going to see daylight for a long time. Apparently, the night of Blaine's murder, he went on a whole adrenaline-high power trip and fucked with more people he didn't have any business facing off against. But that meant he was untouchable to us."

"Untouchable?"

"To retaliate against. To get real fucking justice for Blaine."

"An eye for an eye." I whispered as pieces clicked into place. "You went to jail to get to him." My sister's words whirled through my head.

"He was killed in prison, babe. He went to jail on a robbery charge after he killed Blaine. And he was… murdered behind bars. The file said it was a gang retaliation or something."

"Delilah, look at me." Fox said firmly as horrors played out in my head.

"You killed him, didn't you?" I asked, sliding off my stool to pace around his kitchen, "You killed JJ to get justice for Blaine." I pinched my temple as my head started to hurt from the mind fuck of it all. "You lied to me and pushed me away because you knew you were going to go to jail to murder that son of a bitch. And you didn't tell me!" I yelled. "Why didn't you tell me the truth the whole time?"

"I didn't want that darkness on your soul, D, not until I had justice for Blaine." He tried to reason. "I thought keeping it to myself would make life easier on you."

"Easier!" I screamed through my clenched teeth. "You have no idea how fucking hard my life has been since that moment, Fox! I thought you were gone forever! I left California with a chip on my shoulder and the weight of the world pushing me down into the fucking dirt!"

"I'm sorry." He hissed and scrubbed his hand over his face. "I promise you; I thought I was doing what was best. To keep my promise to Blaine, I needed to ensure the police didn't interrogate the truth from you first. I needed time to get close to JJ behind bars. He was a snitch and a little crybaby, so he was in protective custody. I had to work the guards and the system to get to him." He grabbed me as I paced by him and pulled me to a stop between his spread thighs. "But I promise you, I made him fucking suffer for what he did to Blaine. I left him to die alone the same way he did your brother. I thought you'd take the money I left for you, and you'd be fine for the time I was locked down. I didn't think you'd bolt and take off to fight life on your own. Or that I wouldn't be able to find you after. I knocked six teeth out of Colt's head when I got out and found out you were gone and that he didn't have a fucking clue where you went, baby."

I leaned forward and buried my face in his neck, letting him wrap his strong arms around me and hold me as I cried. I cried for all the things Blaine was cheated out of, and for all the pain that Maddie and I had to endure without it. I cried for Fox and the sacrifices he made to avenge my brother and keep his loyalty to me.

But most of all, I cried for my baby girl who went the first four years of her life without her dad because I thought he was a monster.

When he had been the knight in shining armor the whole time.

Even if his armor smelled like leather and his horse was a hog.

"I'm here now." He whispered. "I'm never leaving you again, baby, I promise."

I opened my mouth to tell him my part of the secrets we had kept from each other, but my phone went off in my purse on the bench by the door. Not a single part of me wanted to leave Fox's embrace, but I also couldn't deny the fact that it could be my daughter calling, either. So, I walked over to get it and sure enough, Maddie's name was on the screen and I turned to Fox. "I need to take this. Can I have a minute somewhere?"

He scowled a bit, but then nodded, running his hand through his hair to push it off his face. "You can use the patio or wherever you want, D. This place is yours now too."

I nodded, biting my tongue to retort that and pressed answer before it went to voicemail. "Hang on." I said in place of greeting and walked past him to the patio door and let myself out onto the giant screened in area, closing the door behind me. Loungers laid out across the space with hanging hammock chairs and a fire pit. Beyond that, a yard of lush green grass laid out like any kid's biggest dream come true. "Hi, sorry about that."

"It's okay, where are you?" My sister asked curiously.

"Uh—." I paused, chewing on the inside of my cheek, "Are you sitting down?"

"Yep, spill the tea." She ordered.

"Fox's house."

She gasped dramatically, "Tell me everything."

"I—." I paused again and sighed, "It's a long story about how I got here."

"Then tell me something else."

"He lied all those years ago to protect us." I paced around the place, "There's a lot I don't want to say on the phone because who the fuck knows who listens in on calls these days."

"But he was innocent of Blaine's murder?" She asked, to be sure.

"One hundred percent." I answered with conviction. "He says he still loves me." I whispered, "Says he wants to pick up where we left off and, my God Maddie, I'm so tempted to fall into the flame like a moth."

"So, you told him about Penny? And he's not mad?" She asked, and I winced.

"No, actually I haven't told him yet."

"Delilah!" She snapped, and I groaned.

"I know. I was getting ready to when you called and interrupted me."

"Well fuck," She hissed, "Hang the phone up and go do it!"

"Let me talk to P." I ignored her. "How is she? Is she loving it?"

"She hasn't stopped smiling since we pulled into the driveway." Maddie said and I could hear the elation in her voice. "She's so happy and is having so much fun. I think this was the perfect way to make everything work, it sounds like things are working out there. And she's having the best time. It's a win-win."

"Let me talk to her and then I'll go tell him. I promise."

"Penny!" Maddie yelled, "Mama is on the phone."

I smiled as I heard my little girl cheering as she ran to Maddie. She had no idea how close she was to getting her happily ever after.

"Mama!" She sang as she took the phone over. "I rode a horse today!" She almost screamed into my ear.

"You did?" I asked eagerly, "Did you wear a helmet?"

She groaned, and I heard Maddie snicker in the background, "Yes, Mama," Penelope groaned.

"Good." I smiled, "Are you having fun? Do you miss me?" I asked slyly and she giggled.

"Yes! Are you going to work tonight?"

"Not tonight, baby, I'm staying home on the couch curled up with a blanket and one of my boring movies. Then I can fall asleep without you poking me the whole time. And then I can sleep alone in my bed without you hogging the blankets all night."

"You're so boring." She giggled again. I heard Aunt Suzie call her from somewhere off in the distance and she yelled out, blaring in my ear, "Coming! Mama, I have to go help mop a stall or something like that."

"Ooh," I laughed, "You have fun with that one, you'll have to let me know tomorrow if you're as excited about that task as you are now."

I could almost hear her pretty hazel eyes roll, "Mom." She groaned, "I have to go. I'm important things to do."

I didn't correct her grammar because I loved the sass behind it, and I missed her already. "You go have the time of your life. I love you. I can't wait to see you."

"Love you, Mama." She said and hung up.

I held the phone to my chest and took a deep breath, feeling lighter from just speaking to my baby girl and knowing that she was safe and having fun.

When I turned around to go back into the house and tell Fox the truth though, I found him standing in the doorway to the house waiting for me.

His hazel eyes were nearly black with anger, and his face was pinched tight. "Who the fuck was that?"

Chapter 24 – Delilah

Present

I tripped over my feet as I took a step backward, away from the menace in Fox's voice and body language as he stood in the doorway.

"I asked you a fucking question, D!" He snapped, "Who was on the phone?"

"Were you spying on me?" I countered angrily, but it wasn't really anger that I was feeling. It was fear. And guilt.

He glared at me, "I came out to make sure you were okay, and because I can't fucking stand to be apart from you. Then I hear you talking to some fucker about spending your night alone in bed without him hogging the blankets. Then you hang up the phone and tell him you love him!" He bellowed, taking another step towards me. "Love him?"

"Him?" I shook my head as I tried to remember what I said to Penny and Maddie, "Wait." I walked toward him, but he held his hand up and backed away.

"I'm so fucking pissed right now. Just give me some space."

"Let's go inside and I'll tell you everything." I tried again gently, because as I replayed my conversation over in my head, I could understand why hearing just my side of it looked bad.

Really bad. Fox had never been good at sharing me with others, and it didn't seem like five years apart helped with that at all.

He growled but turned and stormed back inside and I followed him, tossing my phone down on the counter as he started pacing in front of the fireplace. "Just spit it out." He ordered, "Tell me now if there's someone else." He stopped with his hands fisted on his hips and glared at me. "Whoever it is, it's fucking over between you two. But tell me who it is."

"Please, sit down." I asked softly, but he growled again and started pacing again as I sighed and tried to find the right words. I sat down on the couch and patted the cushion next to me, but he just balked at that.

"Delilah!" He snapped as his anger mounted.

"It wasn't a man." I laced my fingers together in my lap and squeezed tight to ground myself as I fought through this part. "It was Maddie."

"Maddie?" He snapped with a glare, "Do you think I'm stupid?"

"Yes I do, if you keep cutting me off while simultaneously demanding answers." I deadpanned, and he clenched his jaw shut and scowled even more. "She's at my Aunt Suzie's in Kansas for a week. She left yesterday and was calling to check in with me."

"Why?" He barked, "Why was that so important that you let her call interrupt us and our five year long overdue conversation?"

I bit my bottom lip as tears burned the back of my eyes, "Because she has my daughter with her. And I'll drop everything in this world when my little girl calls. Even our important conversations."

He froze in place and stared at me, like the words weren't computing inside of his brain. His face relaxed from anger into utter shock and his fists dropped from his sides. "Daughter?" He whispered the words as tears ran down my cheeks. "You have a daughter?"

Shivers wracked my body as he said the words for the first time, and I nodded in response.

"Wow." He whispered and looked off over my head where I sat on the couch alone. "Wow." He repeated, "Okay." He put his hands back on his hips and squared his shoulders. "Is her father in your life?" He asked and I raised an eyebrow at him in silent surprise. He walked over to the couch and threw himself down into the seat next to me and took my hand in his. "I can deal with this, D. But I just need to make sure you aren't hung up on your daughter's father still. I can't compete with someone that has shared such a momentous life event with you, if you love him."

"I do love him." I whispered and pain darkened his face when he processed my words. "Because she's yours, Fox."

Time froze between us as his face contorted in confusion again, and I reached up to push his hair back over his ear. "What?" He whispered, and his voice cracked a little.

"I was pregnant when you left me. I found out the day they told me you killed Blaine; the day the detectives arrived at my door and read me your signed confession, reading every brutal word you wrote. That's when I learned the truth. I called you right before they showed up and left you a voicemail, asking you to call me back because I had something to talk to you about. But you were already in jail."

"No." His massive body trembled. "No." He shook his head.

I held my breath as he fought to contain his reaction, and I told myself to give him grace and forgiveness for anything mean or off-putting that came out of his mouth, given the magnitude of the news.

"Why didn't you tell me?" His eyes darted back and forth between mine, "I wouldn't have—. I never would have gone away!"

"I didn't know until you already did it. And by then, you were my brother's murderer in my head." My shoulders slumped forward. "What good would it have done for her to have a dad serving a life sentence?"

"I have a daughter?" He agonized. "*We* have a daughter?"

I nodded and gave him a cautious smile, gripping his hand in mine. "When I told you that so much had happened since that day on the cliff, I didn't mean just on your end."

"I'm so sorry." He fell to his knees on the floor and buried his head in my lap as he wrapped his arms around my waist and pulled me in tight. "I left you when you needed me. I abandoned you."

"Shh," I tried to soothe him as I ran my fingers through his silken hair, "You didn't know. You would have done the right thing if you knew. But I thought you were a killer."

"I am a killer." He countered and looked up at me. "I'm no good."

"Stop it." I covered his mouth with my hand as anger filled my entire body. "Don't you dare fall into that self-loathing pit right now, Paxton St. Claire." I used his full name, and his body tensed when I did. "You are honorable, loyal, protective, and loving, a girl like Penny couldn't do any better where her dad is concerned."

"Penny?"

I sighed and tilted my head sadly. The weight of the unspoken hung heavy; he didn't know her name, making the absence of Blaine feel like a physical blow, compounded by everything else JJ had stolen.

"Penelope June." I smiled gently at him as a mystified look crossed his face. "She looks just like you. It nearly broke my heart every day to see so much of you in her, but deep down I was still madly in love with you, and it brought me so much pride to see the resemblance, too." I chuckled, "It's been a weird couple of years."

"How old is she?" He slid down onto his ass and pulled me with him until we both sat on the floor. He held onto me, and I couldn't tell if he was holding me, or if I was holding him. Probably a bit of both.

"Four."

"Tell me everything." He demanded, "I want to know all about her and her life and how her birth went and—." He swallowed audibly, "I missed all the important stuff."

I shook my head and climbed into his lap, forcing him to look me in the eye. "If I could go back with what I know now, I would have told you immediately. I would have brought her to see you and I would have let you experience every milestone along the way. But I can't, baby." I swiped angrily at my tears that finally spilled over. "I'm sorry I can't go back and make it right. But she's perfect. She's still too young to truly understand that mommies need daddies to have babies, and that there was something missing from her life. She's so happy and full of joy and smart." I sighed, "She's so fucking smart, Fox." I laid my forehead against his. "You told me once upon a time, that you wanted a wife, a couple of kids, and a house to come home to every night. And you can have that; with us."

"I love you." He breathed. "I love you with every fucking thing inside of me, Delilah. And Penny." His chest fell as emotions took over. "I love her so fucking much, and I don't even know what she looks like."

I climbed out of his arms, forcing him to let go of me as he tried to hold me tight and grabbed my phone off the table. He opened his arms back up the second I was within reach and pulled me back down into his lap like he couldn't stand the thought of not touching me.

"Here." I said and pulled open the folder of pictures I had on my phone of her over the years. "I have thousands of pictures and videos of her life. Every milestone and everything you were robbed of, they're all right here." I opened the most recent picture of her and smiled at it before turning my phone around so he could see.

It was a picture of her standing in the bright sunshine next to the side of my car before school one morning. She wore a baby blue tee shirt and a pair of white denim shorts and white sandals with her dark hair tied up in cute little braids. Her smile was megawatt bright, and I could feel her love through the screen. I hoped that Fox's affection for her was as instant as mine was the first time I laid eyes on her in the delivery room.

"My god." He croaked and zoomed in on the picture to get close to her face. Her hazel eyes glowed in the sunshine and the smattering of freckles that adorned her nose popped out brightly. "She's breathtaking, Delilah." He looked at me and slid his hand against my cheek. "You did this." He shook my phone gently, indicating the little girl on the screen. "You made her and birthed her into this world and raised her without my help. You're incredible."

I buried my face in his neck as he clung to me, and I let the torment of emotions I'd locked away over the last few years free into the safety of his arms. In five minutes, he had managed to validate all my hard work and loneliness. He tossed my phone to the couch and held me as I sobbed and sobbed in relief at having him now, but also from the grief I still felt from before.

He ran his big hand over my neck and back, rocking me gently while I forced myself to calm down and feel joy and happiness.

"When is she coming back?" He asked after a while. "I need to meet her, D. But I don't know how to walk up to her for the first time and not scare the ever-loving shit out of her with my love and affection as a total stranger. Look at me for fuck's sake, I'm probably a walking monster in her eyes."

"She's seen pictures of you." I smiled, "I don't have many, but she found them sometime last year and asked me who you were."

"What did you tell her?" He whispered like he was expecting bad news.

"I told her you were the man I loved." I smiled at the memory. "She asked if you were my Prince Charming. She's big into fairy tales and princesses right now."

"I'm the villain." He said darkly.

"Fox." "I don't want you to call me that anymore." His brow furrowed. "Fox is the name I got for being sly and deceptive." He asserted. "That's not what I want our daughter thinking my name is."

"Okay." I swallowed and took his feelings to heart. "Tell me what you want me to address you as."

"Paxton, or Pax." He looked back up at me. "You're the only one in the world that I've let call me that without knocking them the fuck out for it. But I don't want her to know me as Fox. Because he's dead. From this moment forward, I'm a different man."

"Baby, she won't care if you're not perfect. That's the thing about kids." I smoothed my hand over his brow. "She won't see any of your flaws if you love her openly and honestly."

"But I know I'm not perfect. And I'm un-fucking-worthy of both of you, so I want to do the best I can with what I can control. Okay?"

"Okay," I nodded and conceded.

He sighed and stood up off the ground, gentle with me as he held me tight. "Show me more." He said, laying down on the couch with me nestled against this chest. He grabbed a blanket off the ottoman and covered us up. "I want to see everything."

"Okay, baby." I smiled against his bare chest and opened the folder again. I scrolled down to the bottom, where a few pictures of my baby bump were. "This was the first picture I ever took of my bump—."

Chapter 25 – Delilah

Present

I woke up with the worst kink in my neck and tried to roll over to rest my head the other way, but a brick wall laid against my back. Fox.

Or rather, Paxton.

I smiled to myself when I recognized his now familiar body heat pressed against me from head to toe on the oversized couch.

We had laid there until late, looking through all the pictures of our daughter and watching all the videos I had of her. That trip down memory lane was beautiful because remembering the loneliness and grief I felt when those pictures were first taken gave way to love and excitement.

We were going to be a family. I wasn't sure how I was going to introduce Fox to Penny or tell her he was her dad, but I knew after some initial uncomfortableness, it was going to work out.

Fox stirred behind me, flexing his hips and pushing his erection into my ass like he had when we first got into bed for a nap. Only this time he had sweats on, thankfully. My core tingled as I felt him grow even longer and harder between us. It had been so long since I'd felt him inside of me, and feeling him this close with the weight of our past heartbreaks lifted, damn.

I ached for him.

Physically and emotionally ached for him to be inside of me again.

"Fox." I whispered, sliding my hand down his arm to where his hand was, of course, wedged against my breasts, this time on the outside of my shirt. "Are you awake?"

He didn't answer me, so I stared at the pattern on the comfy couch underneath my head as I contemplated what to do. I was needy, and desperate for pleasure.

Sad to say, I was too uncertain to wake him up and ask him to fuck me.

It had been five years, after all, and I was a totally different woman today than I was back then. But still, I had needs.

My heart pounded in my chest, a frantic drumbeat against my ribs, as I continued to lie there, paralyzed by indecision. Finally, I decided to slip from the couch and go to the bathroom. Maybe some distance away from Fox's sexy body and presence would ease some of the carnal desire coursing through my veins. And if it didn't, at least I'd be in the bathroom, and I could silently bring myself to orgasm to hold myself over for a while.

I gently tried to slide his hand off me so I could get off the couch, but the second I moved it, he moved it back even tighter, slightly grumbling in his sleep.

Fuck.

My skin tingled where he touched me, and I licked my lips, the nearness of his body making me tremble with a heat that felt like it could set me ablaze. I kicked my legs over the edge of the couch and tried to slide out that way, but once again, he tightened his hold on me and I was in a worse position than when I started.

I was desperate.

And terrified.

I could feel my arousal dampening the boxers he lent me, and my nipples were hard rocks against his tee that I wore, so I tried a different approach.

I slid one hand down to the waistband of the boxers I wore and pushed them down to reach my pussy. When I got to where I needed it, I froze. Waiting for him to wake up and embarrass me. When he didn't move, I slid my fingers through the wetness that was growing by the second and rolled my clit under my two fingers in a slow circle, just how I liked.

I bit my bottom lip to silence the moan that burned in my throat as pleasure shot through my body. I tried to keep my breathing even as I pushed down lower and slid a finger inside of myself and rubbed my clit with my palm. My hips flexed forward of their own accord, seeking the pressure on my clit that I craved, and I nearly squeaked with fear when he pushed his knee forward in between mine.

I thought for sure I was caught, but as soon as his thigh opened mine, he settled again like he was simply getting comfortable. The new position gave me easier access to my pussy, so I pushed on, adding a second finger inside of me and using the wetness to create a silky-smooth friction against my clit.

I was close.

So, fucking close I could taste it, and I knew the orgasm would be a big one. Having him so close to me after all this time, seeing him naked, kissing him and touching his body as my own again, had left me desperate for hours. I'd essentially edged myself all day, and I was eager to fall over to the other side of bliss.

I just needed one last stimulation to push myself over. Bending my other arm across my chest, on top of his, I found my hard nipple through the fabric of the shirt. Zings of pleasure burned straight through my body as I pinched it and pulled on it, imagining Fox's mouth on it instead of my fingers and moaned, unable to keep it inside any longer.

Suddenly, Fox moved behind me with lightning speed and flipped me onto my back as he towered over me with one thigh pushed between mine. He grabbed my wrist, pulling my fingers from my shorts, and pinned it to my chest as he stared down at me with a wild look in his eyes.

"Did you think I'd let you come on your own fingers while I laid behind you like some simp?" He growled in a sleepy, gravelly voice.

"Fox." I panted and rolled my hips forward, pushing against his thick thigh nestled against my crotch. "I'm so horny."

"And you thought you'd take care of it by yourself instead of letting me do it for you?" He asked and picked my hand up from between my breasts, bringing it to his face.

I watched in horror and absolute rapture as he sucked my fingers into his mouth and licked them clean of my arousal, moaning and letting his eyes close as he savored the taste.

"I've missed the way you taste when you come on my tongue." He pushed his thigh forward and I could feel the solid length of his cock against my hip. "Do you have any idea how hard it was to lie there, still as stone with this hard-on while you finger fucked yourself?"

"I'm sorry." I panted because I felt like I'd just been caught with my hand in the proverbial cookie jar.

"Your orgasms are mine." He clenched his jaw, nipping the pad of my middle finger with his perfect teeth, and then pinned it to my side. "I've missed out on too many. There was once a time I thought I'd be the only man to ever get your pleasures, but then our lives were torn apart, and we spent five years alone. But I promise you this right here and now, D," He stared down at me, "Your pleasures are mine. Every single last one of them is mine. You want to ride a dildo instead of my cock sometime? Spread your legs and lay back, baby, I'll fuck your pussy with whatever toy you want. You want a vibrator on your clit? Show me how you like it, and I'll make you come for hours. You want something in your ass while my cock fucks your pussy? Beg me for it and I'll push it deep for you until you cream on both of them. Want to come on my tongue? Climb on top sweetheart, and make my face your seat cushion until your legs give out. But the common denominator in all of those situations remains the same. Me."

"Fox!" I whined, using my free hand to push between us and rub my clit desperately, "I need to come."

"Tell me what you want."

"You." I panted. "I want you."

"Hold on tight, because I have five years' worth of come to empty out of my balls, and that pussy is about to get used. I won't stop once I start, I can't. I'm going to wipe away the memory of any man you've let inside of you since I fucked up until only I exist again."

"There's been no one." I cried, thrashing as he took my hand away and pulled the boxers I was wearing down and tossed them to the floor. "I haven't touched another man."

He paused, "No other man has touched your body in the five years we've been apart?" He asked very carefully.

I shook my head, "You were my first and my true love. No one else could compare." I admitted, embarrassed.

I watched the look on Fox's face turn from shock to utter primal instinct as he lowered himself between my thighs. "Then get ready to come on my face baby, because I'm going to reward you for your loyalty with every single inch of my body."

"Yes!" I cried and let my thighs fall wider around his massive shoulders, "Please baby, fucking let me come. I need it so bad."

He pushed the shirt I was wearing up until my breasts were free and he growled deep inside of his chest. "Your tits are massive compared to what they were before, and I was positively insane for them even then." He grabbed them both in his hands and pinched my nipples, making my back bow off the couch as I silently begged for more. "I'm going to fuck my cock between these and come all over your face sometime. I'm going to coat your tongue with come and make you lick me clean."

"Cock. Pussy. Now." I demanded, dragging my nails up his neck as I tried to pull him up.

"How are your ribs?" He asked, and as he kissed his way down my stomach, he paused to gently kiss the purple bruise on my side and then the faded stretch marks around my belly button.

"Fine." I gasped and mewed when he lifted my knees towards my breasts to open my pussy for him.

"Don't lie to me." He demanded and paused inches above my clit as he stared at me.

"If you don't put your mouth on my pussy, I'm walking out your front door and telling your daughter you were hit by a bus five years ago." I challenged and a fire lit behind his eyes. He lifted the side of his upper lip in a snarl and then blew on my clit, lowering his lips until he almost touched it, but stopped.

"Fox!" I screamed in frustration, burying my fingers in his hair and pulling his head down until he opened his mouth and twirled his tongue around my aching clit. "Fuck yes." As he groaned and sucked it into his mouth, I moaned, throwing my head back. In a desperate plea for more, I gripped his hair with my fingers and arched my hips towards his face. I needed to feel him inside of my soul again after so long, and I couldn't take his light teasing. "More." I panted, curling up to stare at him as he pushed two fingers inside of me and pumped them. "No." I shook my head crazily, "I need you. Your cock. I need you to fuck me. For the love of God, please."

He growled and pulled my hands from his head, pinning them against my chest with one big hand. "This is the first pussy I've tasted in five years, Delilah." He sucked my clit into his mouth and moaned, "Don't rush me while I eat my favorite meal."

"What?" I gasped, fighting against his hold. "What do you mean?"

He hummed against my clit and the vibration sent me over the edge, tipping me into a blinding orgasm that made my back bow, and an animalist scream rip from my lips as he pinned me down and pushed me through it. "That's my good girl." He responded as he climbed up my limp body as I panted for breath.

When he laid between my legs, he stroked his hard cock against me through his sweats and pinned my wrists up over my head until I stared at him. "I haven't touched another woman since the first time I fell asleep in your bedroom, D. Not a single other person has had my pleasure since I realized how perfect you were for me. So, believe me when I tell you I understand how crazed you are for me right now, because I'm right there with you, baby."

"I can't believe—." I shook my head as tears burned once again, "Why would you wait for me, when you didn't even know that you'd find me?"

"Because you're my entire world." He replied firmly, "You're my heart, and my home; my future and my past. No one else compared to you when I knew what my soulmate felt like in my arms. I couldn't bring myself to do it."

"I love you." I whispered in awe. "I don't deserve you and the sacrifices you've made for me."

"You deserved so much more than what I could give you back then, so I'm going to spend the rest of my life earning your love and commitment the same way you've earned mine by bringing our daughter into the world on your own and providing for her in my absence." He flexed his hips again, "But first, I'm going to make up for lost time and finally sink into your body again." He smirked before standing up and pulling me to my feet and ushering me toward the bedroom. I skipped quickly towards the doorway as he spanked my ass and pulled me back to the front of him and I moaned as the fire that had lowered to a smolder inside of my belly roared back to life. "If your ribs weren't busted, I'd rut into you right here against the wall like a man possessed." He growled in my ear before dipping his fingers between my legs as I tried to stay upright.

"Do it. I don't care about the pain, I want your pleasure." I begged, my hips swaying rhythmically on his strong fingers, desperate for the pleasure we'd both denied ourselves for too long; the scent of his skin filled my senses.

When we got into his bedroom, he threw me down on the bed and I bounced and giggled as I scrambled up towards the pillows. My heart was racing, and my body was on fire with the need to match the fire burning in his green eyes as he pushed his sweatpants down and crept towards me on his knees. "Come here." He growled, catching my ankle and pulling me down towards him, drawing a girly squeal from my lips before he silenced it with his. "Taste your pussy on my tongue." He uttered before pushing it past my lips, and I eagerly stroked it with mine, moaning at every sensation he was making me feel.

I wrapped my legs around his waist and humped him shamelessly as he kissed me to within an inch of my life. "Take me." I pleaded. "Make me yours again."

"You've always been mine, minx." He taunted.

"Prove it." I dared recklessly. "Make it hurt and show me exactly what I've missed."

"Careful." He grunted. But at the same time he lined up with my soaked entrance and pushed deep, in his signature brute way. "Fuck." He hissed and bit my shoulder as I clung to him, dragging my nails down his neck and back as my body revolted against the invasion.

Too long I'd gone empty without him. Feeling him slide inside of me was like breathing fresh air for the first time in decades. I ached for more.

"Are you on birth control?" He questioned as he rolled his hips against my clit before pulling out and slamming back in, pushing the air from my lungs. "Delilah, answer me."

"No." I gasped and moaned when he rolled his hips again.

"Make me pull out, then." He bit my neck and licked it to soothe the delicious pain. "Make me be responsible because I want nothing more than to come inside of you and knock you up again."

"Fox." I panted, shaking my head back and forth as his words pushed at the taboo part of my brain that thrived on his dirty talk.

"Tell me to pull out and be responsible." He ordered and slammed into me again, "Because I'm not capable of making that decision for you. Not when I haven't had this in so long. You drive me absolutely feral with the need to breed you."

"I'm coming." I shivered from head to toe as he widened his knees and grabbed my hip, pinning me down to fuck me into the bed even harder. "Harder."

"Take that cock like a good girl." He hissed, and I screamed against his shoulder as he took me even higher into bliss. "Tell me to pull out."

"No." I tightened my arms and legs around him as his thrusts went crazed and uncoordinated. "I want you to come inside of me."

"Delilah!" He bellowed, throwing his head back and baring his teeth in a snarl as he exploded deep inside of me. "Take it, baby." He shook and opened his eyes to stare at me, "Take every fucking drop."

"Yes." I moaned, reveling in the feel of him jerking inside of me and the wetness that he left in his wake as he slowly pulled out. I groaned as he pushed my knees wide and stared down at my exposed pussy.

"What a pretty, pretty pussy, baby." He ran his fingertips around the edges of my hole and pushed them into me. "Every fucking drop. Not one wasted."

"God, you're so sexy." After dragging my nails along his washboard abs, I seized his still hard cock and clenched my fist around it, utilizing the wetness to stroke him. I leaned up to reach him, stroking him from root to tip as his eyes rolled and his nostrils flared before he fell forward on straight arms, holding himself upright above me as he let me tease him. I was hardly ever bold enough to take control of him when we were together before because I was young and inexperienced. But now I was older and while I was still inexperienced, I had longed for him for years and I was ready to take what I wanted. "Mine." I declared in a whisper against his lips before kissing him and letting him push his tongue into my mouth and moan as his cock throbbed.

"Roll over." Fox hissed with a clenched jaw and then pulled his cock from my hand and flipped me over until I laid on my stomach. He pushed my legs together as I looked over my shoulder at him in amusement. He lifted my hips and shoved two pillows under them, popping my ass up into the air before kissing his way down my spine with sharp teeth nips until he palmed both of my ass cheeks. "Your ass was made for worshiping." He kissed each cheek before spreading them and lowering his mouth to run his tongue up from my pussy to my asshole.

And then it was my turn to shiver and moan. "Holy fuck." I popped my ass as far as my sore side would allow and used my elbows to brace myself as he twirled his tongue over my ass teasingly.

He chuckled and then slapped my cheek again, drawing another moan from me. "Let me hear you, pretty girl." He slapped me again, and I gave him what he wanted eagerly. "Good girl."

"Are you planning on fucking me with that?" I asked over my shoulder, staring at his rock-hard cock again. "You told me he missed me."

He crawled up until he straddled my upper thighs and pulled my cheeks apart before spitting down on my exposed holes. "Oh, I'm going to fuck you baby." He pushed the head of his cock down to line it up with my pussy and pushed in. The silky lubrication of our orgasms made the invasion less obtrusive, and I moaned as he bottomed out in one thrust. He held himself up with his fists on the bed next to my head like he was doing a push up and thrusted in and out. "Does this hurt you?" He asked as my body rocked back and forth with each thrust.

"You didn't ask me that ten minutes ago when you were slamming into me." I teased, and he spanked my ass again.

"Because I couldn't have stopped if I wanted to ten minutes ago, but I'm a little more levelheaded now." He wrapped his hand around the front of my throat and turned my head to kiss my lips. "Tell me."

"No, it doesn't hurt." I lied because in truth it did, but it wasn't unmanageable. And I wanted the pain and pleasure he was eagerly giving to me.

"Good." He bottomed out and swirled his cock around, "Because I'm far from done with you."

"Prove it, big guy."

His hand tightened around my throat, and I groaned at how good it felt to be dominated by him like that. "You're going to milk my cock, baby girl. I'm going to fill you up until my come drips out of this pussy the rest of the night. And then I'm going to do it again and again until we make our sweet little Penny a sibling."

"Fuck." I knew breeding kink was a thing thanks to the insane amount of spicy romance books my sister read, but I hadn't realized I was into it until Fox talked like that. "Yes, Sir." I moaned and smirked to myself when he cursed and growled back at that.

My guy's alpha side knew no boundaries, and I eagerly fed it with my need for him.

I turned my head and noticed that his dresser along the other side of the wall had a giant mirror on it and I could see us both clear as day in the reflection. Watching Fox's muscles roll and bunch under his skin as he rolled his hips to give me his dick was so hot. "Fox, look." I nodded to the mirror, and he turned his head and stared at me through the glass with a wicked smirk on his lips. He slowed down the roll of his hips as we both watched in rapture as he fucked me sensually and within minutes, I was clawing at the blankets in ecstasy. "So good, baby." I dug my nails into his arm next to my head as my orgasm ripped through me and he grunted as I drew blood, but his thrusts never faltered. He went harder, fucking deeper into me with the same delicious roll of his hips, and I watched his face as his orgasm crested. His head hung forward until he pressed his forehead against the back of my skull, as his entire body shook and shivered as he filled me up once again.

I knew I couldn't get pregnant from our sex today, because of where I was in my cycle, but seeing and hearing him be so primal and animalistic towards me and our future did something to the girly parts inside of me.

"Delilah Faith Beckett, you're going to be the absolute end of me." He said against the back of my head before pulling out and collapsing next to me on the bed.

"Well, it was a good ride while it lasted, old man." I patted his abs as they worked to suck air into his lungs, and then giggled when he scoffed at me.

Chapter 26 – Delilah

Present

"What was her first word?" Fox asked me a couple of hours later as we lay wrapped around each other in bed.

It was late, and we should have been sleeping, but with the long nap we took at midday and the dozing we did on the couch after that, it was almost like neither of us was eager to miss out on any more time.

I laid on my back with Fox's head resting over my lower stomach sideways across the bed. He was naked. I was naked. And yet I'd never felt more comfortable with him before.

"Maddie." I said and snickered when he looked at me with a scowl. "Well, her version of it. She called her de-de for the first few years. She just grew out of it not too long ago, but if she's tired or sick, she calls her that still. Like a comfort item."

"What does she call you?"

"Mama." I smiled and ran my fingers through his hair. "God, I miss her."

"Have you ever been away from her before?"

I shook my head, "Never. I work too much to take any time off to go anywhere so other than the nights I worked at the ER, I've never been away from her overnight like this."

"How are you doing with it?" He turned and laid on his side, adjusting the pillow he was using to cushion the weight off my ribs.

"Well I'd be much worse off if you weren't with me," I admitted honestly, "When she left, I thought I'd be at home all alone and miserable missing her."

"Did Maddie take her away because of me?" He took a deep breath, but I could sense his fear of my answer.

"Yes. But not because we were afraid of you." I slid my fingers through his hair again and his eyelids closed. "We already knew that you didn't kill Blaine, even if we didn't know the why behind the lie. But Maddie wanted me to tell you about Penny without you showing up and finding out about her on your own. She was afraid you'd show up, see Penny, and get angry."

"I would have." He admitted, "I appreciate you telling me. Even though I know it wasn't easy for you to do so. And I know I didn't make it easy on you accusing you of having another man, either."

I smirked and rolled my eyes, "That's an understatement."

"I won't ever apologize for being protective of you." He replied without remorse. "I've never wavered in my commitment to you and I've never pretended to be anything but obsessed with you."

Turning: I turned in bed, rolling onto my side so that we were face to face, but upside down. "I wouldn't feel as passionately about you if you didn't make me feel so important to you." I admitted. "We just have to be careful with Penny though, I don't want her to be afraid of what you might do to someone else if you go all alpha around her. I want her to get to know you, to learn your heart before she sees the strong and dominant side of you."

"I want that too, baby. Don't worry, I'll be on my best behavior."

"Good boy." I joked as he grinned and rolled onto his stomach to stretch.

The tattoo scene on his back that I'd been admiring earlier came back into view and I leaned up onto my elbow to look at it closer, before climbing up onto my knees to get an even better look at the whole thing.

The woman standing on the beach had her arms out, and her head tilted back like she was singing a song towards the sea. She wore a long flowing gown with a slit up the side that revealed a long bare leg underneath. She was barefoot and had a crown of flowers twisted into her long hair. I'd be lying if I said she didn't look suspiciously like me.

Out in the middle of the waves was a man, with the likeness of Fox with his long dark hair and smoldering eyes. He was surrounded by angry waves but where he stood the water was calm and peaceful, like the storm that brewed behind him couldn't touch him. The sky was dark, and lightning streaked across the sky mixed with the rain. A motorcycle sat parked at the top of one side of the cliffs, next to a checkered picnic blanket laid out overlooking the scene below.

"Tell me about this." I whispered, trying to make sense of it.

He looked over his shoulder at me, but I turned his head back down so the skin of his back was flat and uninterrupted. There were so many details to it that my eyes jumped from piece to piece, finding likeness to things that had occurred in our life.

"What do you think it is?" He asked.

"Us."

"Correct." He slid his arms up underneath the pillow he was lying on and let me continue to stare. "Do you remember what you told me that day when I asked you to tell me something important?"

"The day you told me you loved me and wanted a family?" I whispered and traced my fingers over the other edge of the cliffs over his right shoulder. On top was a grassy knoll with a picnic table, and we sat on top of it. Me with my legs crossed under me and him leaned back with his legs stretched out. Takeout wrappers laid on the table around us. We were staring at each other with smiles on our faces and flashbacks burned in my brain of that afternoon.

"You told me you wanted to matter to someone someday." He said quietly, "You didn't want to die without affecting someone so deeply that they could look back on the moment they met you and remember it as the moment their life was changed for the better."

"Fox." I whispered in awe.

"You changed my life, D." He rolled over and sat up until his face was right in front of mine, "The moment you looked at me across your kitchen table the first night that Blaine brought me over after a job, my life was changed." He reached up and cradled the side of my face with his hand as he swallowed. "Without you, I never would have felt what it meant to love someone more than myself. I never felt anything towards anyone else until your perfect innocent face looked up from your textbooks when I walked in and then it was like this bolt of electricity shot right out of your eyes, directly into my soul. And I was never the same." He leaned forward and pressed his lips to mine as tears spilled over my cheeks. "When Blaine died, I told you to hold on to me and I'd hold you down and keep you afloat at the same time. I told you to grab onto me and let me hold you steady while the world swirled and tormented around us, I'd be your anchor. But I was wrong, because it was you that kept me steady and sane when I had nothing else to focus on." He cursed and laid his forehead against mine. "When I laid in my bunk in prison, listening to the tormenting screams and cries going on all around, I imagined you, like a goddess on the shore, drawing me in and grounding me as the ocean tried to take me under. Without you and your love burning deep inside of me, I never would have survived inside that place."

I clawed at him and pulled myself into his lap to feed my desperate need to feel him wrap around me. He held me as I cried and clung to him, "I missed you so much. I laid in bed alone at night with so much fear and heartbreak in my soul, and I longed for you. I ached for you, even though my brain told me to give it up, that we were never going to get our happily ever after."

"But we did." He said against my lips. "Look at us now, baby. We're here. Together." He put his hand over my heart, "And even without knowing what the other one was doing, we stayed true to each other. That, above all else, should prove to you that there isn't anyone else out there for us. If not that, then our miracle daughter, conceived at exactly the right moment to link us together forever, proves we're exactly where we're supposed to be.

"I love you so much," I cried and buried my face in his neck as my love for him soared even higher. "When did you get it done?" I asked after a long time of breathing him in and letting his scent soothe me.

"As soon as I got out of prison."

"But you didn't know if you'd ever see me again. Why would you dedicate your entire back to us?"

"I dedicated my entire life to you, Delilah." He affirmed, "My back was just the beginning of showing my dedication to you and us."

Shaking my head, I laid it back down in his neck as he laid down and pulled the blankets up over us. "I want our happily ever after, Fox." I whispered, "I want us and Penny and another baby or two. I want Maddie to be close to us all, and I want us to just be happy and safe."

"We'll have it. I promise you." He ran his hand up my back in slow, relaxing strokes and I sighed into his neck. "I love you, Delilah, with every single part of me."

Chapter 27 – Fox

Past

The screams were the worst.

That, and the food.

I laid in my bunk with my hands tucked under my head and stared up at the metal rungs of the bunk above me as sleep evaded me once again.

Someone down the line was losing his fucking mind, screaming and crying, and I just wanted it all to stop.

I just wanted it to be quiet for a fucking minute so I could think straight. For three years I'd been locked down, and it hadn't been quiet for one fucking minute the entire time.

Even when I spent time in the hole, locked into a six by ten cement box for three months straight, it wasn't quiet.

The screams were worse in the hole.

But I couldn't lose my focus, not when I was so close to finishing the job.

JJ was here. In this cell block.

I was so fucking close to him I could smell his fear. It took years of transfers and working the guards to end up here, locked behind bars with the animal that killed Blaine. My late-night transfer meant he didn't know I was here yet. Soon enough, he'd know I was near.

The boss guard on the block was an old friend of Colt's from his Army days. Apparently Colt had saved his life more than once and had called in the favor.

A favor to get me close to the piece of shit coward that killed Blaine, then turn a blind eye when I made my move on him.

Three fucking years I waited for the chance, and I was going to make it count.

In the idle time as I waited, I lost myself to the memory of Delilah and all that I was missing out on with her while I carried out my revenge. Times when it was dark, and I was still, when I couldn't distract myself with anything else, her memory would torment me.

God, I missed her.

I missed her smell and the way she looked up at me with so much love and trust. Her big doe eyes were always so easy to read, and I loved when she looked at me like that. I missed the way she laughed at my stupid jokes and made me smile like I hadn't done in years. The way she held onto me when we rode my bike and the girly squeals, she let free when I opened up the throttle and sped off. How she loved me in her wholesome and authentic way. I missed the way she looked when I had her in bed, with her hair fanned out on my pillow and her trusting eyes wide as I brought her to ecstasy and back over and over again. Most of all, I missed the way she made me feel alive, like I finally had a purpose and a direction in my life.

Regretfully every time I looked back on the good, I remembered the pain on her face that day on the cliff when I told her I changed my mind.

When I lied and told her I didn't want to settle down with one woman after all.

The look of betrayal in her eyes haunted me every time I closed mine, because with that betrayal there was grief and regret thinking that her brother had been right about me. I never knew he said those things to her about me, or I would have picked a different tactic to create space between us. I wouldn't have probed an already festering wound.

But I'd make it right. I'd see the plan out and finish it, and then I'd win her back. I'd make her see how much I loved her and tell her everything.

Her actions in the meantime didn't matter to me; I knew she was living her life out in the free world. I knew men were throwing themselves at her, and I knew she'd eventually give herself to one of them. And as much as that hurt to think about, I made myself imagine her happy and thriving as torment for the pain I put her through.

She didn't know the truth behind my deception; she thought I was a monster, so I wouldn't take anything she did while I was locked down to heart. I'd forgive her for anything.

I just wanted her back when I was free.

And I was going to get her back.

No matter what.

I ran every worst-case scenario through my head and had a plan for it. If she didn't believe me, I'd prove my innocence. If she didn't love me, I'd make her. If she wouldn't give me a chance to prove it all, I'd take her. I'd steal her away and force her to remember everything we had.

It'd all work out in the long run.

It had to, because we were meant to be.

I just had to finish this first, and then she was mine.

"St. Claire." The guard in my pocket stood at my bars, "Rec time."

Go time.

I stood up out of my bunk and walked forward as my bars popped open and then out onto the catwalk with the man and his partner. I was big, and I saw the uncertainty in both of their eyes as I stood between them and started walking down to the rec yard. Three years locked inside with nothing to do but work out and prepare my body for the fight I was here to have left me fucking primed.

The block was big and only parts of the cells were let out at a time to control the crowd, leaving most of the inmates behind their bars watching. More doors popped as we walked down and men who rarely ever had yard time together walked out onto the steel balcony behind me.

My men.

Men bought and paid for with club money and debts they owed.

Men that were going to make sure I got what I fucking wanted.

The last cell at the end of the line popped and the only other man in the entire place that I trusted stepped out as I approached.

"Houston." I nodded to him as he took his place next to me.

"Great day to get some sunshine, wouldn't you say?"

"Fucking perfect day." I grinned and cracked my neck.

When we got downstairs, we went down the dark hallway to the heavy steel door leading to the rec yard and I looked out of the small window and saw my prize on the other side.

JJ.

He stood with a group of his weak ass cronies that he'd paired up with behind bars, shooting a half-deflated basketball into a hoop. He laughed and smirked as he played, like he didn't have a care in the fucking world.

"Open the fucking door." I ordered the guard.

He stared at me as he spoke into his radio. "Marv, open rec door four and then go to lunch."

His radio squawked to life as his guard replied, "Roger that, boss."

The heavy door groaned as it popped open and slid on its tracks, letting in the hot California air. "Ten minutes tops, St. Claire." The guard reminded me.

"Go time." Houston whistled, and we walked out onto the court.

The men playing ball stopped when the door buzzed, signaling its opening, and watched as the six of us walked out. I stared at JJ's face as his eyes jumped from man to man in confusion before they landed on me.

Fear.

My favorite.

He swallowed and took a couple of steps back, putting his boys between me and him as mine circled around the group.

"Hey, Fox." JJ said, with feigned friendliness. "I didn't know you were locked down here."

The steel door groaned shut behind me and I watched his eyes snap to it.

"Long time no see, JJ." I said and started unbuttoning my uniform shirt. "Three years, give or take."

"Yeah," He licked his lips and took another step back. "What you here for?"

"Murder." I answered instantly. "Serving a life sentence."

His eyebrows rose in surprise. His cronies moved to the wall behind them, catching on that I was here for him and choose self-preservation by getting the fuck out of my way.

"That's rough man." JJ shrugged, looking around at my men as his slinked away.

"Yeah, but it's alright, I'll be out of here soon." I took my shirt off and handed it to Houston, "See, I didn't kill the man I'm here for." I brought my hands together in front of me and cracked my knuckles. "You remember Blaine Beckett, right?"

His face paled, and he took another step back. "Listen man," He put his hand up, but I didn't give him the chance to say anything else.

"No, you listen." I snapped and took a menacing step forward, "You murdered him, and you got away with it. But the only reason I let you was because I needed a charge to ride for to get to you."

"We can work something out," He yelled, "Blaine attacked me, it was self-defense."

I lunged, grabbing the front of his shirt and slammed my fist into his face. His friends backed away completely, falling behind the line of my men who stood guard. No one was going to interrupt this.

I waited too fucking long to serve this justice.

JJ yelled as his nose broke under my fist, blood poured out of his face as I slammed his head against the concrete wall. "You jumped him and pulled a knife in a fistfight." I hissed, bouncing my forehead off his, head butting him and splitting his forehead wide open. "You're a fucking coward, and a cheat."

"No!" He screamed, "Help!"

I slammed my fist into his face again, shoving him to the ground and kicked him over and over in the sides until he was gasping and crying, clawing his way to get away from me.

"You don't deserve to breathe air for another fucking minute. You've already had three years longer than you deserve."

"Please." He cried, sputtering as he choked on blood as it poured all over his face. "Please, man, I'm sorry."

"You're a bitch." I wrapped my hand around his throat and squeezed, watching as the blood pooled in his face as he struggled to breathe. "You harassed D for years, and then you killed her brother for beating your ass for it."

He swung his fists and kicked from under me as I picked him up by his neck and slammed him against the wall.

"Stand up like a man while I give you exactly what you gave Blaine." I held my hand out to Houston, and he laid a three-inch shank into it. I squeezed my fist tight around the sharp metal, enjoying the weight of it in my hand. "Four in the back." I hissed in his face as he cried like a bitch, "Five in the front." Leaning close, I whispered in his ear, "This death is too easy compared to what you deserve." I pulled him off the wall as he clawed at me, striking me in the sides, but I didn't feel a thing, "If we were on the streets I'd hold you somewhere, torturing you for weeks for what you did to him. But this will have to do, because I'm going to make sure you pay your debt in full."

I pushed the shank into his back beneath his shoulder blade and watched his eyes round as I pulled it out and did it again, lower, hitting important things like kidneys and shit that would bleed slowly. I wanted him to be alive for all nine.

He cried and spit fell from his mouth as I gave him the third and the fourth before shoving him to the ground, just like he had done to Blaine.

I lowered myself to my knee at his side and grabbed a handful of his hair, pulling his head up to look at the blood covered shank. "Watch these next five, coward." I plunged it into his gut, and he screamed before I did it again and again. Rage and endorphins raced through my blood as I wore his. His skin was pale, and his eyes rolled as I had two left, so I quickened my pace and landed the last two directly in his chest, ruining the chance for any miracle life-saving measures. "This is for Blaine, you bitch." I hissed as blood poured out of his nose and mouth as his eyes closed and he went limp in my arms.

Houston walked over to me and spit on JJ and then pulled the shank from my hand, wiping the blood off it onto JJ's pants before putting it back in his waistband. "Let's move." He smacked his hand on my shoulder, pulling me up.

We were on a time schedule and as much as I wanted to stand over the piece of shit's body to make sure he was truly dead and gone, I knew the stab wounds were placed strategically enough to ensure his death.

I turned and faced the four men JJ ran with behind bars. "Remember, my face when you think about opening your mouth." My threat was clear, "I waited three fucking years to get to him, I'll get to you even faster."

They all either looked away in fear or nodded quickly to me. They were low dogs in the food chain here, and there were enough bosses standing on my side they knew they didn't have a chance.

Houston slammed his fist down on the door three times and it popped open as the boss guard stood waiting on the other side. "All set, Fox?"

I smirked at him and took the bottle of water he held out to rinse the blood off my hands and chest. "All fucking set." I confirmed with a shake of my head. "Your assistance is appreciated," I wiped my hand off on the towel he handed me next and then held it out for him. He paused for a second before he shook it. "Your debt has been paid."

"Good." He looked around at my men and then at his own that stood behind him. "Let's get you the fuck out of here before this turns into a shit storm."

We followed him inside, leaving JJ and his men in the cement yard as we went down the hall in the other direction to the adjacent yard where we were put.

It was our alibi for the time of the murder.

I paced the space for only a couple of minutes in silence before the lockdown alarm sounded and I looked up at the sky and smiled.

"For you buddy." I said to the clouds and pointed, "And for Delilah."

Houston smirked at me and shook my hand, "You feel the relief you hoped you would?"

I nodded and clapped my hand on his back. "Sure fucking do."

"Good." We both laid down on the ground in lock down position as guards ran into the yard to secure us with their weapons drawn, "Remember, Belden Oklahoma when you get out and get bored," He said as a guard kneeled in the center of his back, "The Black Eagles could use a man like you."

"As soon as I find Delilah." I reminded him, "She's my priority."

"Whenever, man," He smirked again, "Something tells me my crew will still be fighting like a bunch of bitches when you get to us."

I didn't reply as the guard kneeled on my back and zip tied my hands together. I wasn't worried about being found out as JJ's killer. The pockets of the men around me were lined so deep and I had enough on every single one of them to ensure their silence. I just had to bide my time until Colt's men got the tape to the cops, and I got released.

Then I was going after Delilah.

She'd be mine again soon.

Chapter 28 – Fox

Present

Delilah sang a sweet tune to herself as she swung her hips back and forth at the kitchen island. She was making breakfast, French toast and bacon as I sat on the couch and watched hungrily.

Not just for the food I knew would taste delicious, either.

I was hungry for her. Starved really.

She wore one of my shirts and nothing else. I vowed to keep her here, just like that, for the rest of her life.

In my life. In my home.

Our home.

She was never going to struggle for anything ever again for as long as I lived, and neither would our daughter. I owed her that fucking much.

"Are you going to tell me how you afforded this place?" She called over her shoulder as she plated the toast and carried it to the table.

I got off the couch and joined her, setting my coffee cup down and taking my seat. But when she tried to sit down next to me, I pulled her onto my lap, straddling me, and kissed her neck.

She giggled and ran her fingers around the back of my neck, holding me to her. "God, you smell good." I sighed.

"You're avoiding the question, aren't you?"

"No." I pulled back and looked at her, "I'm never going to hide anything from you again, D."

"Good, because I can't stand it when you do. So, tell me."

I sighed and took another sip of my coffee. "I sued Rawlins County for framing me for Blaine's murder."

She froze and her cute little eyebrows lowered over her eyes. "But you admitted to it."

"True." I nodded, "But they wanted me for it, so I let them think they had me and in turn they did nothing by the book. They never read me my rights, they held me far longer than they legally could and then they persuaded me to confess, blackmailing and bribing me to give them what they wanted. So, when the proof came out that I, in fact, didn't do it, I sued them for wrongful arrest and conviction. They took three years from an innocent man for a crime they pinned on me. Regardless of whether or not it had been my plan all along. The county settled to keep it out of the public news. I took the money and ran."

"Wow."

"They had DNA evidence the entire time, it was their own fault for not running it to cover their asses."

"How much did you get?" She whispered like it was taboo to ask.

"Twelve million." I smirked when her mouth opened and her eyes went wide. "We're set for life; I told you that."

"Holy fuck, Fox." She shook her head and adjusted herself in my lap. "Wow."

I kissed the side of her lips and sat back in my chair further. "So, will you finally quit your jobs and let me take care of you?"

"I—." She opened and closed her mouth as she tried to come up with an answer, "I don't know."

Recognizing the honesty in the answer, I nodded and said, "We'll table it for now and revisit it later." I said and reached around her and grabbed a piece of bacon, holding it up to her lips. She raised an eyebrow at me, but leaned forward and took a bite.

"I can feed myself," She chewed, "And sit in a chair, I am a big girl."

"I know that." Sliding my hand up under the shirt she was wearing, I felt the smooth skin over her hips and to her waist as I took a bite, "You can also sit on my lap and let me feed you."

"You're not wrong." She smirked and turned slightly, grabbing a piece of French toast and holding it up to my lips, "You can also let me feed you, too."

I took the bite and licked my lips where syrup dripped on them and bit back a groan when she watched my lips with fascination. "Keep looking at me like you want to take a bite, and I'll fuck you right here on the table."

Her eyes flashed up to mine and a wicked smile crossed her face, "What if that was my plan all along?"

I growled and lifted her shirt off over her head, careful of her sore side, and tossed it on the floor. I leaned in and bit one of her nipples as she rocked in my lap with her head leaned back.

"Does my girl want Daddy's cock?" I asked and bit her nipple as she groaned loudly, digging her nails into my neck deep enough to draw blood.

"Why is that so fucking hot?" She whispered as she rocked forward again. "I shouldn't get turned on by things like that."

"Like what, baby girl?" I asked, grinding her on my cock. "Wanting to be Daddy's good girl?"

"Fox." She moaned. "You're Penelope's dad, not mine, it's–taboo."

"Say it." I ordered her, sucking on her other nipple. Delilah always was obsessed with dirty talk. There were times that I pushed her over the edge of an orgasm with words and light touches alone, and this morning was no different.

My girl had a daddy kink. I just knew it.

"Say what?"

"Tell me who you belong to."

"You." She panted and reached down to rub her clit with her fingertips, avoiding the word.

But I needed it, I needed to hear her say it like I needed to sink into her tight pussy again already.

"Get on your knees." I slid her off my lap onto the floor and she went down eagerly as I spread my legs around her shoulders. "Take Daddy's cock out."

She quickly reached up and pulled my erection out of my sweatpants and fisted me, licking her lips as she stared at me. "Now what?"

"Tell me who's cock that is."

"Yours, Daddy." She moaned and my cock throbbed in her hand.

"Good girl. Now lick me, nice and slow." I pushed my fingers into her hair and held on as she leaned forward and ran the flat of her tongue up my shaft. "That's it, baby." I praised her, "Get me nice and wet for that tight pussy."

"Fuck." She moaned and then dropped her lips to the crown of it and kissed it, spitting on it and rubbing it in with her fists.

She dropped down the shaft, licking my balls and I grunted, flexing my hips to give her more. "Off." I cursed, kicking my pants off so she could get to them better. "Fuck yes." I hissed, tightening my hand in her hair when she sucked one into her mouth and swirled her tongue around it. "That's my good girl."

"Mmh," She moaned, looking up at me from under her long lashes, "You taste so good, Paxton." She used my first name, and I groaned at how good it sounded on her lips with my cock in them.

"Suck me deep, just how I like." I ordered her and she spit on the top again before pushing it down her throat until it touched the back, and she gagged. "Fuck yes," I pushed up and went deeper before she pulled off and gasped.

"You love making me gag on your cock, don't you?" She asked seductively before dropping back down on it and gagging on it over and over.

"You know I do." I put my hand around her throat as she pushed my cock deep again and felt its thickness pushing her throat wide. It was such a turn on, and I was close to blowing down her throat.

My second favorite place to blow my load.

"I want you to come on my tongue." She purred and then twisted her fists around me until my eyes rolled. "And then I want you to eat my pussy right here on the table like it's your last meal."

"Careful." I growled. As much as she loved my dirty talk, she had never been overly vocal before, and it turned out it was as much a turn on for me as it was for her.

"Or what, Daddy?" Delilah purred again with a naughty smirk on her face before dropping down on my cock again. While she gagged and held it there, she gagged once more, teasing my balls, and I let out a roar as my climax filled her mouth. She sucked me down and then came up until just the head of my cock was in her mouth and stroked me, like she was sucking out of a straw, and I cursed a long line of words I didn't comprehend. With a satisfied smile, she sat back on her feet, opened her mouth to show me the load on her tongue, and then swallowed it down, letting out a moan.

"Fucking slut." I swore and picked her up by her hips and pushed the breakfast back on the table and laid her down on it. "You like being my dirty little come slut, don't you?" I growled and pinned her knees back as she smirked at me.

Minx.

"I like being anything you want me to be, Fox." She moaned and palmed her breasts.

"Then let me hear how good I make you feel while I eat this pussy for breakfast before I fuck it into lunch time."

She giggled and then moaned as I went to work, doing exactly that.

There was so much lost time to make up for. I knew that once our daughter was home from vacation, I wasn't going to get many opportunities like this to eat D's pussy out on the dining room table. So, I was going to use every chance I got.

Chapter 29 – Delilah

Present

It was Monday morning, and I had spent the last forty-eight hours naked, touching Fox. Reality weighed down on me the longer we stayed locked away inside of his lavish home.

Our home, as he kept referring to it.

And I didn't know how I felt about that. I needed to go home to my space and take a breath for a minute, but I didn't want to leave Fox behind to do it. I knew he wouldn't take that well.

"Don't you have any club stuff to do?" I asked when he washed the dishes from breakfast.

He looked at me where I sat next to him on the counter with a scowl. "Why?"

I shrugged, swinging my feet back and forth under me, "Because when you were a part of the Rust Hawks, you were always gone on club stuff. Yet you haven't left my side in almost three days." Short of a few hushed phone calls here and there, that was.

"Things aren't like they were before." He looked back down at the dishes, "I'm not some low man doing prospect work trying to make a name for myself anymore."

"How did you make the name for yourself?" I asked, almost afraid of what his answer would be.

He turned the water off and wiped his hands on a dish towel and stood between my knees. "I carried out an orchestrated murder in prison with so many moving parts to it, you would have gotten dizzy trying to unravel it."

"JJ." I whispered as a shiver ran down my spine. "Tell me about it."

"No," He shook his head and kissed my forehead, "You don't need that darkness on your soul."

When he backed up to go to the sink again, I grabbed a fistful of his shirt and anchored him to me. "Tell me anyway."

His eyes darkened and his jaw flexed as he tried to come up with an excuse to deny me what I wanted, but he couldn't. He knew I deserved to know.

He sighed and ran his warm hands up my thighs, "The lead guard on JJ's block was an old buddy of Colt's, who owed a favor or two to the President. Once we got him on board, I worked on men in the cell block. Bosses of different crews and gangs, inside and out. When they were on board, paid for and ready, I ordered my transfer to the block. I didn't want to get there before I had all my pieces in motion, because I knew if JJ saw me, he'd bolt to protective custody like a little bitch." He grunted in disdain.

"Then what?" I asked, unsure of where the desire to hear about the bloodshed came from.

"He was in a rec yard, playing ball when me, Houston, and the other bosses got to him. His boys quickly discovered he was on a short train ride to hell and abandoned him, leaving him a sniveling, begging, pleading coward for me to eliminate."

"Did you beat him?"

"Broke his face pretty good, then kicked him around a bit." I watched the pulse in his neck beat quicker the more he talked about it. "Then I told him I was going to give him an eye for an eye justice."

"You stabbed him."

"Four in the back, five in the front." He nodded, "Just like he did to Blaine."

My eyes closed as the movie rendition of Blaine's murder played in my head like it had done on repeat over the last five years. "You made him suffer, though, right?"

"For as long as I could. I didn't have nearly as much time with him as I wanted, but I made it fucking hurt. We walked out and the lockdown alarm rang within a few minutes after that, signaling his death. And Colt had the tape to the cops that night, starting the process for my release. Because I was in the cell block for less than twenty-four hours, the paperwork hadn't even been finalized, placing me there. As far as anyone knew, the man that killed your brother and the man falsely convicted of doing it were miles apart in different facilities."

"So, there's no chance that you'll get pinned for it?" I asked one of my biggest fears. I didn't want to start my life with him again and have him ripped away from me, identical to the last time.

"There's always that chance, baby, I won't lie and say that there isn't. But I've done my due diligence over the last two years, making that less and less likely."

"Do I want to know how?" I questioned, running my hands up his arms to his neck, holding myself to him.

"I got my road name Fox for being sneaky and having an insane ability to get into places I shouldn't be." He shrugged with a smirk, "I've padded my pockets with even more dirt on all the parties involved and popped in periodically to remind them who holds the cards."

"Do you still talk to Colt?"

Fox nodded, "Occasionally. He wasn't super excited for me to leave Rawlins, but he knew I was looking for you and he knew I had a debt to settle with Houston." He shrugged, "I'm not opposed to going back there someday, but I won't be in the game like I used to be."

"I don't want to go back." Firmly, I replied, "Rawlins holds too many bad memories for me." I shivered as panic at the idea built. "I don't want Penny growing up like I did."

"Okay." He put his hands on the sides of my face as I got worked up, "Hey, D," He held me firm when I tried to pull away, "Stop. We won't go back." He leaned in and kissed my forehead, and then I clung to him. "I'm never going to choose anyone over you and Penny, baby. My loyalty is to you two first and foremost."

"Promise?"

"On my last breath," He assured me.

"Okay." I sighed and leaned into him. "I'm sorry." Hugging him, I confessed, "I don't mind visiting, it's been years since I've seen my mom and Blaine. I just don't want to live there."

"I hear you." He ran his hands up and down my spine, soothing me, "Loud and clear, baby."

"Good." I feigned dominance, "Don't make me repeat myself." I chuckled before I could finish the impression.

"Hmm. You want to be a boss huh?" He asked, picking me up off the counter before walking us towards his bedroom. "Well then, let's see what you got, baby."

"Good boy." I giggled and then moaned when he slid his fingers against my naked pussy under the hem of the shirt I was wearing.

We rode across town on his motorcycle to my rental as the sun started sinking down over the horizon. I desperately needed my own clothes to wear, and I needed to check on my home. And figure out my car. And so many other things.

Fox had been hush-hush about the Taz situation, which led me to believe that he was still on the run. A part of me hoped he had just left town and never came back, but another part of me, a darker part of me, hoped he showed his ugly head one more time so Fox could bury him in the ground for what he did to me.

I didn't recognize that part of myself, but I remembered her from the night I found out Blaine was dead when I demanded Colt find the man that did it and make him pay. Perhaps there was a dark side to me after all.

Last night when Penelope called me, I had put her on speakerphone and Fox listened, hearing her voice for the first time and the awe that shined from his watery green eyes amazed me. He was smitten with her already and I couldn't wait to see them together for the first time. I desperately wanted them to live in one home and make up for lost time. I just had to do it right.

When we pulled into my driveway, I was surprised to see my car, which now had four new tires, parked in the back. Of course, Fox hadn't told me he'd fixed it, but I wasn't surprised by his actions. He had a knack for taking care of things on his own.

I slid off his bike and gave him a pointed eye roll as I looked at my car before leaning down and kissing him, "Thank you."

"Hmm." He hummed with a smirk and stood up off his bike, as I drooled, watching his long legs and strong shoulders move under the blue and white flannel and jeans he wore.

I shook my head when he stared at me knowingly and walked away before I got the urge to jump him right there on the front lawn. "Come on, Casanova." I called and walked up the back steps before unlocking the door and going inside. "It's nothing like your place, but it's home."

Fox looked around the small kitchen and into the living room as I stood off to the side to watch him meander around my space. He walked over to the wall where pictures of Penelope hung and stared at them, running his finger over the frame like he was looking into the eyes of the holy spirit or something.

"God, she's so beautiful." He murmured with a slight shake of his head, "Teenage years are going to be the death of me."

I snorted and ran my hand over his back as I walked past, "Honey, you should see the temper tantrums a four-year-old can throw. Maddie calls her a sass-hole some days."

He chuckled and followed me as I climbed the stairs. When we got to the top, I went to her room and opened the door, stepping to the side so he could see in.

"Holy purple." He smiled and walked in, turning around in the small space to take it all in.

"That's her favorite color, for the time being. Anything unicorns and rainbows are pretty much guaranteed to make her happy, too."

"I want this, D." He said with a sense of wonderment in his voice. "I want this feeling I have inside," he ran his hand over his heart, "and I want it all the time. In our home, together."

"We will." I assured him. "Believe me, I want nothing more than to live with you and be a happy family, but I have to figure out how to do all of that the right way."

He clenched his jaw, and his shoulders deflated a little. "Just tell me what you need, and I'll make it happen."

I smiled at him, "Well, I have Maddie to think about, for one." I looked around the room, "She goes to school full time and takes Penelope to school for me when I work, and I can't just abandon her now that I have you."

"I would never ask you to, Delilah, Maddie is important to me too." He looked around and then back to me. "There's a flex space over the garage at my place, I think the other owners used it as a game room or entertainment space. It has a small kitchenette and a full bath. She could live up there, make it her own studio apartment or something. I'll get a contractor there to update it and make it everything she wants.

She'd still be close so I could keep an eye on her, and she could focus on school without having to worry about Penny or work."

I swallowed as I envisioned how excited Maddie would be to have her own space like that, and how happy it would make me to have her close but not underfoot while I traversed this new relationship phase with Fox and P.

"I think that sounds great," I agreed, "I'll talk to her about it when I call them tonight."

"Good." He nodded like he was proud of his accomplishment and that I didn't fight him on it.

We did have the same end goal in mind, after all.

"I'm going to go pack some stuff for tonight." I patted his chest on my way by.

"Pack all your stuff."

"Fox," I smiled and shook my head.

"I'm not sleeping apart from you anymore," He followed me into my room, "And it's been a lot of years since you and I have shared a bed that small." He eyed my full-size mattress with doubt.

"How about we compromise, and I agree to stay until Friday night and then we can figure it out from there? Maddie and P will be home Friday night, and I don't want to just throw it all on them the second they walk through the door and expect Penny to be okay with staying at your place. Besides, we have to get a moving truck and get everything over there at some point," I sighed at the overwhelming feeling of it all.

"Stop." He instructed me as he spun me around to face him, "Take a deep breath." He stared at me hard until I did as he said, and took a deep breath, letting the calmness he exuded settle me. "I'm buying her all new stuff for our house," He eyed the mismatched stuff I'd managed to pick up here and there over the years, "I want to give her everything we never had, baby."

I didn't let his opinion on her current belongings chap my ass, even though I wanted to. I didn't take it personal that what I'd provided for her over the years on my own wasn't up to par with what he could give her now. Frankly, because my goal the entire time had been to do exactly what he said he wanted to do; give her everything we never had. I couldn't fault him for it.

"Okay." I agreed, and he eyed me suspiciously like he had expected more of a fight from me on it. "I want her to have the new things too, Fox. But let's agree to let her have a say in it too. She'll be tickled pink to go to a furniture store and pick out some new things," I smirked, "with our guidance, of course. Or she'll come home with a king-sized bunk bed if I know her at all."

He snorted and rolled his eyes, "Whatever she wants, she gets."

"We'll figure it out. Together."

"Fair deal." He leaned down and kissed me, "Now pack your shit so we can go back home, I'm itching to get you out of these clothes and back into my bed."

I rolled my eyes dramatically like he had a second ago, "One track mind, Mr. St. Claire?"

"Very." He admitted and then spanked my ass as I went to my dresser to pack some clothes. "Very fucking much so."

Chapter 30 – Fox

Present

"Give me some good fucking news." I snapped at Houston and lit up a cigarette as I paced the parking lot of the clubhouse.

It was Tuesday and D was at her shift at the hospital. It was the first time we were apart since I took her home with me on Saturday and my body itched for her like a drug. I didn't want her to work at all, but I knew she needed to keep her hands busy. Especially with Penny not in town. Her ribs were hurting her less and less every day, so she wasn't going to stay at home with me any longer.

Logically, I had to give her some space, or I was going to smother her with my need to hold her close every single second of the day, in my attempt to make up for lost time.

So, I backed off and let her go to work with Tony and Hammer on watch while I checked in with Houston.

"He's hiding somewhere in East Tracks if I had to guess," The President said with a grimace, "But I haven't been able to chase him out yet."

"Well, we need to." I snapped, "My daughter is coming home Friday and I'm not going to chance that fucker getting anywhere near her or Delilah."

Houston smirked at me as I got more riled up, "How's it feel to be a dad?" He asked goodheartedly.

I told him on the phone a few days ago about Penelope and he could tell simply from my voice how fucked I was over the little girl already.

"Like I want to scream to the sky in excitement and puke in fear all at the same time." I admitted, and he grinned even bigger at me.

"I'm happy for you, man." He smacked my shoulder, "If I'd known that Delilah was here in Belden this whole time, I would have gotten you out here a lot sooner."

"I know." I shook my head and took a drag off the cigarette, "Fucking meant to be or something."

"Fate." He agreed and looked out over the pavement. "We'll find him, man; no fucking loner, piece of shit is going to come into my turf and fuck shit up now that I've finally got things in order, thanks to your mean ass."

"I ain't mean." I glared at him.

He snorted and turned away with a shrug, "Sure. And I ain't ugly."

I puffed my nicotine again and sighed. "I'm not going to be running club shit in the future for you, man." I said, grabbing his attention and dragging him back to the conversation. "I told D years ago the MC thing wasn't my long-term goal, and now that I have her and Penny to protect, I'm not dragging them back into this world. Look at how D's already suffered because of me in the last week alone." I shook my head as he watched me closely, "I can't put them in danger like that."

He mulled that over for a minute and then lit up his own cigarette. "I won't lie and say it's easy to watch you walk away. Fuck," He grunted, "Most men don't get a walk away option, and you've done it to two different clubs."

He was right, most members patched in for life. But I was a nomad, Colt let me walk away because I needed to find D, and he knew keeping me as an ally was better than turning me against him. When I agreed to come out and help Houston, I told him I wasn't a lifer, that it was temporary.

Then I went and bought a house a couple of months ago, I had no business owning, and it made no sense unless I planned to stick around. Now with D, Penelope and Maddie to think about, I needed to think about their wants and needs.

"But I get it." He added after a long pause, "And I'm grateful for your help while you were here. You're always welcome to stick around and be a member without being in the thick of it." He offered.

"I'll think on it." I agreed, "Delilah doesn't want to go back to Rawlins, and I don't know if she wants to stay here either." I shrugged, "I guess we'll have to wait and see."

He nodded in understanding, "I'm going to head over to a spot in East Tracks and rattle some cages. See if I can't spook out some info on Taz," He smirked at me knowingly as he walked to his bike, "Want to ride along?"

"You know I do." I grinned, because he knew me better than most. I was a bastard on a good day and the appeal of knocking some skulls together and riding my bike was my idea of having a fun time, even if I wanted to make better decisions for my daughter.

I'd start that tomorrow.

Or as soon as Taz was eliminated from the equation.

Chapter 31 – Delilah

Present

"Well, you look refreshed." Winnie smirked as I sat down at my desk a few hours into my shift. "Couldn't possibly have anything to do with that tall, dark and handsome Opie now, could it?"

I rolled my eyes even as my lips pulled up in a smirk, "You just never mind." I chided her as I tried to focus on charting my last med rounds.

"Ooh!" She gushed, rolling her chair closer, "Tell me, everything."

I laughed and shook my head, "No way."

"Yes way!" She whined, "I've worked alongside you for almost four years now, and not once have you ever looked so bright eyed and bushy tailed." Using one finger, she pushed my hair from my neck and asked, "Is that a hickey?" She giggled.

I slapped her hand away with a glare and tried to pretend to be serious, "Of course not, I'm an adult."

"An adult getting boned by a sexy biker that I'd give my left tit to ride."

"Oh, my god." I hissed at her bluntness. "You cannot say things like that about him."

"Why not? Are you territorial already?"

"It's not already." I droned, "It's still." I closed one of the charts and looked at her out of the corner of my eye. "Five years still."

"Five years!" She cried as I hushed her, "Wait!" She turned me in my chair with big, round eyes of excitement. "Is he Penny's dad?"

I groaned, "Yes."

"Oh, my god!" She jeered and I once again tried to get her to shut up.

"What are you ladies screeching about over here?" Oliver asked as he laid a chart down at the desk behind us and sat down.

"Nothing." I replied quickly, glaring at Winnie, but she simply rolled her eyes and blew me in.

"Delilah's baby daddy is in town and she's soaking up all the extracurricular activities she can, trying to turn back into a fun and happy twenty something year old."

Closing my eyes, I cringed as Oliver's eyes scanned the back of my head. "I didn't realize you had any contact with Penelope's father," he said.

"I didn't." I replied and then sighed, "It's complicated."

He tsked his teeth, and I cringed again as I continued to face forward, trying to avoid the conversation completely. The few times he asked me out, I was able to avoid any real reason why, but now that there was the conversation of Fox on the table, it was just awkward all around.

"Is he the one that broke your ribs?" He asked after a pause and the judgement and disdain was clear as day in his tone.

I whipped my head around to face him after looking around to see if anyone else heard the accusation he threw at me. "HIPAA." I snapped, putting him back into his role as my doctor for my injury and not as my friend who was good-heartedly gossiping about my personal life.

The only reason he knew about my ribs was because he treated me for them. Which meant he couldn't just throw that information around without recourse.

His boyish face darkened, "Mandated reporter." He clapped back.

"Whoa." Winnie cautioned, looking between us. "Let's just take a sec-."

"If he's putting his hands on you, then he's probably doing it to Penelope, too. I have no choice but to report it to the authorities. Even if you're too selfishly wrapped up in him to do it yourself."

"Fuck off." I snapped, feeling anger like never before as he crossed so many lines in one rude sentence. "He didn't touch me; it was a customer at Cherry's, and there were witnesses so don't even try to press on it. And don't ever speak my daughter's name again if you're going to throw around your pompous opinion at the same time." I stood up from my chair and pointed my finger at him, reveling in the pale color his face had taken in response to my outburst. "How dare you accuse me of allowing a man to hurt not only me but my daughter. Out of fucking line doesn't even begin to cover it." I clenched my fists and turned away towards the break room. I needed to get the fuck away from him before I told him exactly what I thought of him.

Because then I'd probably get fired.

But when I rounded to leave the nurse's station, Fox stood staring past me at the man that I used to enjoy working with, wearing a mask of pure unadulterated rage on his face. "Fox." I whispered, as panic burned in my spine.

I didn't know how much he heard, but it had to be enough to entice his anger. Especially given the warning he gave Oliver when he was here for stitches and the young doctor kept touching me.

"Do you make a habit of threatening to remove children from loving homes, Doc?" Fox sneered. "And think real fucking hard on that answer before you give it."

"Him?" Oliver glowered from behind me, and I recoiled from the wrath in Fox's glare. "Seriously?"

"Dr. Franklin, that's enough." Winnie said firmly, standing up and pointing at him. "Delilah's right, you're out of line."

He scoffed and stood up from his chair, "Unbelievable." He was red in the face and picked up his charts with agitation, muttering under his breath as he walked away. The man had no clue how close he was to losing the shape of his face to Fox's fists, and it showed in his arrogance.

I sighed and ran my hand over my forehead as I approached Fox. "I'm sorry."

He had his hands clenched so tightly his knuckles were white and I was afraid they'd dislocate from the pressure on them. "Don't apologize for him." He snapped at me, and I recoiled, finally drawing his eyes away from the retreating back of my boss. He sighed and his shoulders deflated, "I'm sorry."

Eyes from patients and coworkers alike watched us with fascination, so I walked past him towards an empty room, "Come here."

I paced the treatment room as Fox joined me and shut the door behind him. "I didn't mean to snap at you." He affirmed, and I turned towards him.

"I know." Slumping against the counter, I deflated. "I'm sorry you heard his comment; he was out of line."

Fox walked forward and put his hands on each side of my neck, cradling my head and holding my weight up as emotional fatigue weighed me down. "Yes, he was. But it wasn't your fault." He leaned forward and kissed my forehead, "I want to work on my reactions, because I can't do that around you and Penny. I won't."

"I know, baby." Running my hands up his stomach I took his emotions into consideration. He was a dominant alpha male and had been every day of his life. A few days ago, he vowed to dial it down to protect Penny's feelings, and he was actively trying. But it wasn't something he was going to have control of overnight; I knew that, and I appreciated that he was trying. He held me for a while just like that, as we let our presence calm each other. "What are you doing here?"

He snorted quietly, and I looked up at him, "I missed you, believe it or not."

"You did?" I smiled and leaned up on tippy toes and he closed the distance and covered my lips with his, "I would have thought you would be sick of me by now."

"Never. Going. To. Happen." He kissed me between each word and then longer until I was putty in his hands. "Quit this place and come home with me."

"Fox." I moaned with a sigh and sagged against him, "We talked about this."

"I know." He sighed and kissed me again, "But I'm not going to stop asking."

I snorted and laid my forehead against his chest, "That wasn't asking."

"Eh." He shrugged, "It wasn't a command either. *This* is a command." The corner of his lips pulled up as he reached around and grabbed two handfuls of my ass. "When you walk into our house tonight, you will strip yourself bare inside the front door and crawl to me naked."

My breath hitched and my eyes widened as his words turned my blood into lava. "And what will you do with me once I'm on my knees for you, Sir?" I purred, playing into the role he laid out for me. I really freaking loved this new side of our relationship.

"You'll have to wait and see. But I will tell you this; if you're a good girl I'll reward you, if you're a bad girl, I'll punish you."

"Do I get to know what the punishment is if you won't tell me what the reward is?" I begged, reaching out with the tip of my tongue to taste the side of his neck.

"Let's just say my come will flow all night long." He growled, sliding his fingers under my ass from behind me until they rubbed my pussy through my pants. "And your pussy won't be dripping with it." I moaned as he circled my clit and sagged into him, greedy for more. "But your asshole will be."

"Fuck." I groaned, and he smiled against my lips. "I don't want to wait."

"Then quit and get on my bike and I'll make you come from the vibrations alone before I even get you home and naked."

"Ugh," I sagged harder as he circled my clit with the perfect amount of pressure. "You're not fighting fair."

"I'm not fighting at all, baby." He kissed me and moved one hand around the front of me and down my pants until his bare skin rolled over my soaked and aching clit. "I'm loving you."

"Yes." I whispered and tilted my hips as he did everything I loved and more.

"I'm going to fuck you so good." He whispered in my ear, "You're going to be my good girl and crawl for me and I'm going to make you come so many times you won't walk straight when I'm done with you."

"Fox," I panted, "I'm coming." I gasped when he pushed two fingers in deep and palmed my clit as my orgasm took over. He kissed me deeply, pushing his tongue into my mouth and muffling my cries as I bucked on his hand as his arm held me up. "Yes, oh my God, yes." I cried.

He slowed down, bringing me down off the high with slow, leisurely strokes of his fingers and a gentle roll of my clit before pulling his hand from my pants. I sagged into the counter and watched in fascination as he brought his fingers to his mouth and licked them clean, closing his eyes like it was his favorite taste in the world. "To hold me over until tonight." He whispered and then stood up to his full height and took a step back.

"You're just going to leave?" I asked in surprise, nodding to his waist. "Like that." His cock was hard and visible down the side of his crotch where it grew down his pant leg.

"Hmm, give the old bitties something to talk about when I'm gone." He smirked and licked his lips one last time. "Remember your instructions, D. I really want to give you your reward."

"Yes Sir." I said and watched as he walked out the door, shutting it behind him and enclosing me in privacy for the moment. "Holy fuck water." I whispered and shook my head with a dreamy smile on my face. If there was any way to finish out my shift, it was on the high of an orgasm, that was for sure.

I went to the sink and washed my hands, splashing cold water on my face when the door opened behind me, and I looked over my shoulder to see Winnie standing in the room with eyes wide as saucers. "Um hello?" She droned, "You forgot to mention the man sported an anaconda in his pants!"

I giggled and shook my head. "We are not having this conversation, Winnie."

"The thing went to his knee, Delilah! I think he sent my patient here for the sniffles, into tachycardia." She gushed on dramatically and fanned herself.

"Let's get back out there." I pushed her towards the door with a permanent smile on my face.

"Promise me if you ever break up with that man that you tell me first so I can ride him like a pony in a horse show before anyone else swoops him up." She stage whispered as we walked back to the nurse's station before falling into a fit of giggles.

When we rounded the corner Oliver stood at the desk with another doctor doing a consultation and looked up at me, drying up any mirth I had in me. I couldn't read the look on his face, but it wasn't that of the approachable friendly man that he had been this morning.

I dropped his gaze and chose the high road, which meant spending the rest of my shift avoiding the man altogether.

He wasn't going to crush my high or darken my excitement about what laid waiting for me at home.

Fox's home.
Our home?
Home.

Chapter 32 – Fox

Present

Seven twenty-four PM.

The hum of the garage door motor sprang to life and with it, my excitement.

I sat on the couch in the living room in just a pair of jeans, undone, with a glass of whiskey and a cigar, laid back and relaxed. Waiting.

Anticipating.

I listened to the click of the door opening and closing in the kitchen and watched Delilah's messy bun come into view as she put her bags down on the kitchen table. Her eyes instantly found mine over the half wall, separating the two rooms and she bit her bottom lip as I inhaled on the cigar. The end burned bright orange before smoke clouded my sight of her.

I didn't speak, and neither did she.

The proverbial ball was in her court. Her decision to make.

Reward, or punishment. Though I'd be lying if I said I was going to be disappointed if she chose the latter.

I watched the slender column of her neck tighten as she swallowed before she disappeared out of sight behind the fridge. I listened intently, hearing her kick her sneakers off and then tried to discern the noise of her clothes hitting the floor. But she was silent.

On purpose, if I had to guess. She was baiting me, amping my suspense up as much as I had done to her earlier at her work.

Thankfully, I didn't have to wait hours for gratification, because moments later the top of her head came into view again. This time, around the bottom of the wall as she crawled to me around the corner.

"Good girl." I hissed, pouring back the rest of my whiskey as she took small and calculated steps forward with her hands and knees, watching me.

Her naked body was on display for me, and my cock thickened in my pants as the swell of her ass swayed back and forth with each foot of distance she closed between us. Her tits hung heavily underneath of her, and I ached to lay under her and suck on them. She was going to look sexy as hell nursing our next child with them.

One I planned on putting in her as soon as possible.

"You look so incredibly sexy on your hands and knees for me, darling." I praised her and her lips pulled up on the side. "How do you feel, crawling to me?"

"Embarrassed." She answered instantly. "Exposed." A blush rose across her chest, up her neck, mimicking the one that bloomed after her orgasms.

"You've never looked sexier to me." I contradicted and her eyes darkened. "The way your wide hips sway back and forth," I slowly shook my head and inhaled off my cigar again, "They were made to bring my babies into this world. Wide and supple, meant for me to grab onto and hold myself deep inside of you, filling you with my come. Designed to carry our babies until you deliver them for me, just like you did with Penelope." My cock twitched in my jeans as the primal side of me flared to life.

She fucking loved it, too. I could smell her arousal in the air as she neared my feet. She hesitated when she got close, looking up at me between my widely spread knees. I put my arm over the back of the couch and watched her keenly as I took another drag from the cigar, tilting my head back to blow the smoke out into the sky. "Does it please you to know that your body makes me positively feral?" I asked her after a moment.

"Yes." She moaned, biting her lip.

"Come here." I patted the inside of my thigh. "Kneel between my feet and put your cheek right here."

She scooted forward and rested her face against the inside of my knee and looked up at me from under her long, dark eyelashes. "Now what?" She whispered in apprehension.

"Now you look at me and tell me everything that has happened with the cunt doctor at work." Her nostrils flared, and I watched anger burn in her eyes as she went to lift her face from my leg. But I anticipated that and slid my hand around the back of her neck, pressing her back down before she even moved. "Reward versus punishment, Delilah," I reminded her. "Tell me what I want to know."

She swallowed and her neck vibrated under my hand as her little pink tongue swept out over her lips. The things I would do to taste that tongue.

"Nothing has happened with him." She said, pulling my stare from her lips. "I've never touched him; I told you I've never touched any other man but you."

"But he's tried, hasn't he?" I asked, sliding my hand around from the back of her neck to the front, wrapping it under her jaw and holding it over her airway. I didn't tighten it. I didn't need to, because arousal and excitement burned in her eyes from just the threat of it. "That's why he is so outraged by you being with me."

"Yes." She purred, "He wants me."

I watched the switch in her demeanor take place as she slid out of cautious and honest, and into bratty and daring. She knew what those words would do to me, she chose them specifically.

"He wants this mouth?" I slid my thumb up over her jaw to her bottom lip and pulled it down, baring her teeth before sliding the pad of it over her bottom pearly whites. She touched the tip of it with her tongue before sucking it with her plump lips. I pushed it in deeper, sliding it over the length of her tongue until I touched the back of her mouth, and she gagged, but never pulled back. Minx. "And your pussy?" I asked, sliding my thumb free of her lips, "Does he want to spread you open? Push his cock deep into your tight sinful body, baby?"

My cock hardened even more as my words turned me on, yet they were supposed to edge her.

"Yes." She purred again. "He's asked me out. As recently as the other week."

"And you told him what?" I provoked her, begging her to give me some warped, seductive lie so I could punish her. I ached to punish her for baiting me.

"I told him no," She licked her lips again and shifted on her legs. I knew she was dripping and swollen, begging to be filled. "I told him I belong to someone else."

"Me?" I questioned, liking the truth more than the bravado lie she was tempted to tell to get a rise out of me.

"Only you. Ever."

I slid my thumb back down, anchoring it under her jaw, and tilted her head up off my leg until she kneeled upright between my legs. I leaned forward, removing the cigar from my lips, and spoke against her lips. "Right answer, my good girl."

She smiled briefly and placed her dainty hands on my knees. "I want you." She mewed and let her eyes close as I tightened my hand around her throat.

"What do you want?" I quizzed her.

"You." She licked her lips again and swayed her hips, "Your cock. Anything. I'm so needy."

"My needy little girl."

"Yes." She panted instantly.

"Lay across my lap." I dropped my hand from her neck and leaned back, patting the pillow I already had laid out next to my hip, "Put your face here." She eyed the pillow and my lap cautiously, but hesitated. "Don't chicken out on me now, trouble." I raised an eyebrow at her, "Not when you're so close to your reward."

Her pupils dilated, and she scrambled up onto my lap, laying across it perfectly with her lush ass nestled right where I wanted it. She looked at me over her shoulder as she adjusted her face against the pillow, and I could see the fear and uncertainty behind the arousal. I thrived on it.

I ran my big palm up from the back of her knee to her ass cheek and over the roundness of it, groaning at how good it felt in my hand. Her hips shifted from left to right, and I felt her rub herself on the hard ridge of my cock underneath of her clit.

"Put your hands up on the arm of the couch above your head and hold on to it." I instructed her, taking another drag off my cigar before snubbing it out in the ashtray on the table behind the couch. "Don't let go of it, do you hear me?"

"Yes, Sir." She replied, and her slender fingers gripped the cushion above her.

I picked up a piece of ice out of my glass on the other side of me and watched her face as I slid it up over the lush globe of her ass. The muscle tensed at contact and then relaxed as a moan escaped her lips as I ran it over the luxurious flesh of her cheek. "I wanted you to disobey me tonight so I could spank you for punishment." I mused as I watched the trail of water cover her skin from one cheek to the other as I danced the ice around her ass.

"Mmh." She moaned, arching her hips and presenting her ass even higher for me. Which in turn, opened her pretty pink pussy just enough to see it through her thick thighs.

She wanted me to touch her there.

Naughty girl.

I slid my free hand up her spine into the bun on top of her head and tugged it, until she no longer looked at me and instead looked off the side of the couch, blinding her to what I had planned.

"Why did you obey me?"

"Because I wanted a reward."

"Did you think you wouldn't like my punishment?" I asked, "Are you saying you don't want my cock in your ass?"

"God." She gasped when I pushed the ice cube down between her cheeks to roam over the rosette of her virgin asshole.

"Answer me, D."

"No." She gasped, "Yes-." She moaned when I pushed the ice against it hard. "I don't know. I'm scared."

"You should be." Validating her fear. "I have a big cock." I pulled the ice away and pushed the pad of my finger against her wet hole, "And this ass is tight."

"Fuck, Fox." She moaned, clawing her nails into the cushion above her head.

I gave into the urge to see her ass cheeks ripple and spanked her, clapping my hand across the flesh creating a loud crack followed by her surprised gasp and throaty moan. "You like that don't you, baby girl?"

"Yes." She admitted, and I smiled knowingly.

I spanked her again, this time harder on the other cheek, and soothed my hand over the red print that blossomed instantly. She whimpered and moaned into the pillow as I smoothed my hand over her skin. She was rocking her hips back and forth on my erection, and if I didn't have bigger plans for her, I would have chastised her for it. But I wanted her on the edge of sanity, racing towards an orgasm with a one-track mind and she was just helping me get her there.

I took another piece of ice and drew it over her heated skin where my palm had landed and she wailed, begging for more. I opened the cap on the bottle of lube I had stashed and on the next swipe of ice, I pulled her cheeks apart and poured it directly onto her puckered flesh.

"Shit." She hissed as I rubbed my finger over her rosette and dipped another one down to her dripping pussy. "Yes," She bucked, "Right there."

"One with the other," I explained, pushing through the tight ring of muscles, "If you want your pussy stretched tonight, you get your ass stretched as well, baby."

"Please." She lifted her hips up off my lap, pushing back and taking me deeper into her virgin hole and pussy, greedily sucking me in. "I want it."

"Tell me how it feels." I massaged her back with my free hand as I started thrusting both fingers in and out of her holes. I'd fucked women in the ass before, but I never worked them up to it like this. They were just faceless cunts on the way to Delilah, so I never took the time to explore and experiment with them. And I had had no one since meeting her.

"Good." She panted, "Hot. I'm so hot. Like sweating hot."

"That's your fear," I massaged her neck as I added another finger to her pussy for a couple of strokes before pressing my last finger against her ass on the outward thrust, giving her time to prepare. "Take another one baby, let the fear go and give me your pleasure."

"Fuck!" She yelled into the pillow, but I fisted her hair bun and pulled her head back so I could hear what I did to her. "It burns."

"You can take it." I remained firm as I worked more lube into her loosened ass and pulled my fingers from her pussy, putting attention on her ass only. I didn't want her lost to the haze of pleasure of her pussy, I wanted her focused on this new experience. "Up on your knees, baby."

I pulled her back by her hair, and she moaned as she presented for me perfectly, face down, ass up.

"So good." She mewed.

"Reach back and spread your cheeks open, I want to watch your ass swallow and suck my fingers deep."

"Jesus fuck." She groaned, but reached back and pulled her lush cheeks apart. In this position, I had a clear view of what I was doing to her, and it had me keyed up and close to my own orgasm. "I'm going to come, Fox." She moaned, and I heard the beg on the edge of her whine.

"No." I ordered her, roughly pulling my fingers away from her body before pushing her back onto the cushions and climbing over her. "Not until I'm balls fucking deep in you."

"Fox!" She screamed in frustration as I pushed my jeans off and straddled her ass. Pouring more lube on her ass and my cock, I pushed deep into her pussy in one deep thrust, ignoring her need for time to acclimate. We were both too close for being slow right now. "Yes!"

I threw my head back and thrust hard and then pushed my fingers back into her ass, making her scream and buck back against me. "Take it." I growled and pushed her down into the couch so she couldn't move on or off of me as I savagely fucked her holes. "My good girl."

"I'm coming!" She screamed, and her head bounced back and forth as I slammed into her. "I'm coming so hard!"

Her words weren't lies either. Her pussy and her ass clamped down hard around me and I hissed as my balls tightened and burned as my orgasm exploded inside of me. "Fuck!" I roared and slammed into her a couple more times before coming to a halt buried deep, twitching and filling her body as her own aftershocks squeezed and pumped more out of me.

"You're filling me so full." She laid her forehead down against the pillow and gasped for breath, "It's going to drip out of me for days."

I smiled against the back of her head, removing my fingers from her ass and turning her so we were spooning on the large couch with my dick still buried balls deep inside of her. "No, it won't, because those swimmers are going straight into your womb."

She grunted and sighed, "I'm not due to ovulate for another few days, it'd be a miracle if it happened from this round."

I mulled that over in my brain and counted days out in my head, "What day?"

She shrugged her shoulders, "I don't know for sure, but my guess is Friday, maybe Saturday. Why?"

"Because that means I'm going to have to fuck you full before Penelope gets home, as I'm going to be hard pressed to leave her side once she does, even to put a baby inside of you." I slid my hand down to cradle her soft abdomen in my hand. "Tell me you want that."

"A baby?" She questioned, "Or you staying at P's side?"

"Both." I shrugged, "But a baby first, because I know you want me at both of your sides from now on."

"I do." She answered truthfully. "And yes, I want another baby with you, but I'd be lying if I said the idea didn't terrify me, though."

"Because I abandoned you last time." I replied, not asking. I already knew the answer.

"Because doing it alone was the hardest thing I've ever done before, Fox." She looked at me over her shoulder, "I'm terrified that I'll have to do it again, and I don't think I'll survive it a second time without you."

"I'm not going anywhere, baby." I kissed her temple and pulled her tighter against me, tucking my hand between her breasts against her heart, "Heaven doesn't want me and Hell's too scared of me. You're the only place I belong."

"Promise me." She looked back again, and I could hear the fear in her voice.

"I promise you. On my life." I kissed her, "I'm yours and Penelope's, for the rest of your life."

"Good." She sighed and turned around. "Because I'm far from done loving you."

"Same, baby," I sighed, letting my eyes fall closed as contentment overwhelmed me. "Same."

Chapter 33 – Delilah

Present

I groaned as my alarm blared from next to the bed. I blindly swiped my hand over it to silence it and then threw it back onto the table.

Fox wrapped his arms back around my waist and tucked me in against his body as I settled into the warmth of him again. "Ready to quit yet?" He pestered me with a voice thick with sleep and seduction.

"Yes." I answered truthfully and snickered when he jolted behind me in shock. "But not today." I burst his bubble, and he sagged back into bed.

"Think about it," He kissed my neck, "We could sleep in, and never set an alarm again." He sighed, "Fucking bliss."

"Except Penelope is an early riser and has to be at school by nine anyway, so." I droned.

"But nine am far more acceptable than," He leaned up to look over me at the clock. "Four forty-five."

"It wouldn't be so bad if you didn't keep me up until one am with your shenanigans."

"Please." He scoffed, "I distinctly remember you wrapping your pretty lips around my cock at half past midnight after I already tucked your sleepy ass into bed."

I smiled into the darkness because he was right. After my reward, he fed me, bathed me and tucked me into bed with such care and gentleness that I showed him my appreciation for it with a blowjob.

"Are you complaining?"

"Nope," he popped the 'p' enthusiastically, "but I'm also not the one that has to go work a twelve-hour shift."

"Ugh, don't remind me." I whined. He was right, I was ready to quit the monotonous job at the ER to spend time with him. I knew eventually I'd get bored with not having a job to go to, but for the time being, I just wanted to focus on getting to know Fox again. And I wanted to focus on nurturing the new relationship between him and Penelope, too. Which I couldn't do if I was at the hospital for twelve hours a day.

"I can't wait for P to come home." He said wistfully.

I rolled over in his arms and hitched my leg over his hip. His hair was down and rustled from sleep and I feathered my fingers through it soothingly. "I never thought I'd see the two of you together, and now it's only a couple of days away," I groaned, "so fucking close yet so far."

"I hope she likes me." He admitted quietly, "Or at least isn't afraid of me."

"She'll love you." I stated, "As soon as she sees how comfortable Maddie and I are around you, she'll relax and settle in, too."

"Hmm." He hummed, leaning in to kiss my lips. He deepened it and rolled over until he was between my spread thighs and rocked his quickly growing erection against me. The blaring of my second alarm broke us apart as we both groaned and then smiled at each other in the dim morning light. "I'll get the coffee going." He kissed the end of my nose and pulled himself out of my arms.

I rolled onto my side as he turned the bedside lamp on and walked across the room to the large walk-in closet in his naked tattooed glory and smiled. "Look at you all domesticated and sweet." I mused as he shot me a smirk over his shoulder, "You going soft on me, Paxton St. Claire?"

He growled his response, and I giggled, forcing my feet into the plush carpet next to the bed. Even so, the very last thing I wanted to do was leave our cocoon of happiness and go to work.

I'd done a good enough job the last few days, letting all the new excitement of having Fox back in my life distract me from the fact that Taz was still out there and a threat. And having Penelope coming home any day now only added to the fear.

But as soon as the stress and anxiety of the whole situation started growing in my chest, I took a deep breath and trusted Fox and his love for us. He would protect us.

He would keep his word.

The man served years in prison for a crime he didn't commit to keep his word the last time he gave it to me, so I was going to trust him again this time.

I just hoped we didn't lose another five years in the aftermath of it all.

"So." Winnie asked me a few hours later when she sat back down at her desk. "Oliver."

I groaned and rolled my eyes, "Is lucky Fox didn't rearrange his face."

"Clearly," She smirked, "He's off today but he'll be here tomorrow, what are you going to do?"

I shrugged my shoulders as I loaded up a saline syringe, "Hope he got an ice pick lobotomy on his way home from work yesterday and comes in fresh and relaxed and the normal good boy Oliver that he usually is."

"Not the jealous, jaded not-even-once a lover?" She joked.

"Exactly," I nodded, "What the heck was with that, anyway? He's asked me out a couple of times, but it wasn't like he was actually interested in me, he doesn't even know me. Hell, he stares at my sister with more interest when she visits than he does at me. So why the hell did he try to go all alpha over me being with someone?" I turned toward her and raised my eyebrows, "I know he doesn't know it, but Fox is the alpha-est of alphas and Oliver doesn't stand a chance in a head-to-head competition. If Fox wasn't trying to be more levelheaded and calmer for Penny's sake, he would have taken Oliver's head off right here. No question."

She shook her head, "I hope he gets his shit together before he comes back tomorrow."

"Me too." I turned back and finished preparing my meds for a patient. "But it doesn't matter in the long run anyway," I sighed, feeling her eyes come back to me, "I'm putting my notice in."

"What?" She gasped and then looked around, "No! You can't leave me."

I smiled at her gently, "I have to focus on my family, and I can't do that if I'm here with you all the time. I'm finally getting a chance at the happily ever after I got robbed of, and I'm not going to miss out on it this time."

She sagged in her chair with a dreamy smile on her face, "Well, when you put it that way." She grimaced, "Gosh though, I'm going to miss you. Are you going to keep working at Cherry's?"

I shuddered and laughed, "Fox put an end to that after I took a boot to the side in the parking lot." She shrugged and smirked, "I think I'm going to play housewife and mom for a while and figure out what to do after that."

"Good for you," She sighed, "God, okay. Get your shit together, Win." She stood up, "Even dark and desolate Delilah found her man, what's your excuse?"

"Hey!" I scoffed at her dig, and she winked at me. "Funny girl."

Chapter 34 – Fox

Present

"Hi," Her sweet honey voice filled the speakers through the Bluetooth as I pulled up outside of the hospital.

"Hi." I said, gripping my hand tighter around the steering wheel as my chest swelled with longing for her. It had only been twelve hours, but I was needy to see her again already. "I'm parked outside, so come out the front entrance when you get out."

"What?" She questioned, "Why?"

"Just do as you're told." I commanded her with a smirk.

There was a long pause, and I could hear people talking in the background before her voice dropped down quietly, "Will I get a reward if I am a good girl?"

"Fuck D," I groaned, "Yes. Yes, you will."

"Hmm." She mused, "See you in two minutes then. I'm clocking out now."

"See you then."

She hung up and I parked along the side loading area at the front door, taking a deep breath and looking at myself in the rearview mirror again. Today was about setting forth the changes I needed to make for her and my daughter, but I was nervous and anxious and needed her to be okay with them before I could feel the comfort in them that I was seeking.

I watched her walk out the front door and look around the parking lot for me and got out, walking around the front of the brand-new truck I'd picked up today. It took her a minute to spot me and when she did, she gasped and covered her mouth adorably as she walked closer.

"Oh my god!" She whispered when she reached me, staring up at me intently and not even noticing the giant brand-new truck behind me. "What did you do?"

I chuckled and ran my hand over my new short haircut. It was faded on the sides, down to the scalp at the bottom and long enough on top I could style it to look fashionable. Or so the barber at the shop told me so. "I figured it was time to upgrade my look from scary biker to…" I paused with a shrug.

"To corporate bad boy?" She smirked and bit her lip as she reached up to run her fingers over my bare scalp, above my neck.

"To dad."

She looked at me and sighed dreamily, "I love it."

"Promise?" I asked and my voice cut out as emotions I didn't realize I was feeling shined through, "Because I feel like I'm cutting myself open and bleeding out here, and I can't tell if it's all for nothing or not."

"I promise." She leaned up on her toes and pulled my head down to kiss me, and instead of giving me a quick peck, she deepened it and expressed her feelings through her touch. "It looks amazing baby, not that the long hair didn't." She dropped back to onto her heels, "The only other time I've seen you with short hair was in jail."

"I know." I ran my hand over the top of my head and sighed, "I didn't want it that short to remind either of us of that time. But I didn't want to look wild and out of control when I met Penelope."

"I think it's a great compromise." She smiled and laid her head against my chest, wrapping her arms around my waist. "And what is this?" She tapped her knuckles against the hood of the truck I leaned against, and I chuckled, kissing the top of her head.

"My new dad mobile." I smirked and turned us so we could look at it. "Like it?"

"It's massive."

"Like my dick." I joked, and she pinched my side and rolled her eyes. She pulled away from me to walk around the side and opened up the back door to look in the back seat.

"This thing has more room in the back seat alone than my entire car does. Penelope will be tickled pink to sit so high up in the air."

I sighed and relaxed muscles I didn't realize had been tight until she reassured me. "Good. That was my hope."

She closed the door and walked back to me. "Why didn't you just wait for me to get to your house to show me, though?" She reached into her purse and pulled her keys out.

"Uh- well," I smiled as she squinted her eyes at me in speculation, "I jacked your car from the lot this morning and got you a new one, too."

"You what?" She tilted her head like she hadn't heard me right. "What does that mean?"

"It means, I showed up, hot-wired your heap of junk, took it to the dealer and traded it in for a new, safer car for you and P."

She shook her head and closed her eyes, "One," she held her finger up, "how do you know how to hot wire a car?" And then she held her whole hand up, "Never mind, don't answer that. Two, who do you think you are just making decisions like that without talking it over with me?"

I could hear the anger in her voice, but I also knew she was working really hard at containing it and staying levelheaded. She had been on her own for so long, giving up control like this had to be hard, and I knew I wasn't going to get away with keeping her out of the loop very often, but I wanted to spoil and surprise her today with it.

"I know." I pulled her against my chest, and she stiffly leaned against me before I tipped her head back with my hands on both sides of her face. "I won't make decisions like this without you all the time, but I wanted to surprise you, and I wanted to make you feel taken care of for once, without stressing or worrying about it."

"Fox." She sighed again, and I saw the battle raging behind her perfect eyes.

"Wait to decide if you hate it or love it until we get home, and you see it." I kissed her forehead and steered her back towards the truck, opening the door and pinning her against the seat with my hard body pressed to her front. "But if you ever call it *my house* again, I'm spanking your perfect sweet ass until it's flaming red. Got it?" I reached down and grabbed onto her ass with both hands, shaking the supple flesh to accentuate my point. "It's our house, and the only way Penelope is going to feel comfortable with it, is if you lead her by example." I picked her up and put her into the front seat, "Don't make me have to repeat myself either."

I shut her door and reveled in the way her eyes rounded, and her lip stayed firmly planted between her teeth as my command hit its mark.

I was the boss here, and everything I did was with her best interest in mind.

I just had to remind her sometimes.

"Holy fuck, Fox." Delilah said, running her hand through her hair as she stood outside of the garage door, looking at her brand-new car. "It's a Range Rover." She deadpanned.

Her brand new pearly white Range Rover was parked in the first spot in the garage, and I was impressed with how much joy it brought me.

"I'm aware." I leaned my shoulder against the door frame and watched as she slowly walked around it. "It's top rated in safety and space, seating up to seven so multiple car seats can fit. It gets great gas mileage, and it's the best that money can buy here in Belden."

She looked over her shoulder as she neared the driver's door, but she wouldn't take the handle and open it. Almost like it wasn't hers to touch.

I wasn't having that.

I slid next to her and opened the door for her, stepping to the side and ushering her into her new car.

"It's too much." She said cautiously even as she slid onto the soft leather seats. "Like fifty grand too much."

"Psh." I scoffed, "I got a deal. Practically buy one get one with the truck."

She rolled her eyes and smirked at my attempt to make light of the situation. "Fox."

"Paxton." I corrected her, "Or Pax." And rested my forearms on the roof of the SUV as I ducked my head in until I was close to her. "Let me be the man you deserve, D."

"You are." She whispered back, looking up at me.

"Then give me this. It's what I want."

"Okay." She smiled tentatively and ran her hands over the steering wheel. "Can we go for a drive?" She smirked up at me and I hit the roof of the car.

"Go get dressed, baby, and we'll go out to dinner to celebrate."

"Yes!" She hissed and jumped from the front seat. "I love you." She jumped into my arms and wrapped her legs around my waist. "And I'm totally sucking your cock on the way home for my present."

She jumped down, and I smacked her ass as she ran into the house with a laugh.

I was a lucky fucking man.

Chapter 35 – Fox

Present

"You're breathtaking." I said, leaning back in the booth across from Delilah as I ran my hand over the condensation on my beer bottle as our waitress cleared our food plates.

Her cheeks pinked up and she pushed her hair behind her ear coyly. "How is it you can do," She looked around and leaned forward to whisper, "crazy wicked things to me, yet words like that can make me blush?"

"It's a gift, really." I shrugged and then smirked at her as she tilted her head back and laughed.

She was relaxed and happy and I was enjoying her simple presence across from me. What would our lives have looked like if we didn't miss out on regular things like dates like this? Would we take them for granted at this point in life if we had five years' worth of them under our belt already?

Or would they still give me those stupid butterflies that I didn't know existed until I met D?

"Thank you for this." She smiled dreamily with her bedroom eyes.

"For what?"

"My car. Dinner. This date." She shrugged, "Romance."

I took a pull off my beer and then leaned forward to rest my elbows on the table and spoke, "Everyday. For the rest of my life, Delilah." She swallowed and took a deep breath like the words overwhelmed her. "I love you."

"I love you, too." She smiled and shook her head. "Okay, I have to pee, and splash cold water on my face or I might give into my desire to mount you right here." She swallowed the rest of her beer, "Then if you're lucky, I'll let you take me home and touch my butt." She stage whispered before falling into a fit of girly giggles, loosened up by the beers we drank with dinner and sashayed her way to the bathroom.

I tracked her movement across the room, before turning my attention to the three other men in the room who watched her walk away.

Men that were unworthy of even watching her.

The door to the bar opened and I watched a few bikers, wearing Riders patches on their cuts walk in.

Taz's crew.

Go time.

I pulled up my message app and shot a text to D.

Stay in the bathroom. Riders are here. I'll get you when it's clear.

This was Black Eagle turf, and his crew knew we were hunting him down. The fucking balls to even step foot in here.

The bartender, a man on Houston's books looked from the crew of three to me and back before pulling his phone out and sending out a message.

No doubt to my club.

But I didn't need them.

I stood up and grabbed a couple of fifties, more than enough for our tab and caught our waitress as she passed. "My girl's in the bathroom," I nodded to the crew of Riders at the bar, completely oblivious to my presence, thanks to the lack of my bike in the parking lot. "Make sure she's safe while I chat with those boys." I handed her the cash, and she nodded knowingly.

"Sure thing, Fox."

I walked to the bar and eyes followed me, catching on to the impending drama as the crowded bar quieted. "You here to give me some news on your President?" I called, standing a few feet behind them.

The three of them turned quickly, eyeing me before looking around the bar for more Eagles.

The one I recognized as Taz's VP licked his lips with cautious eyes, "If I had news, I could be persuaded to share it."

I squinted my eyes at him and fought the urge to smash his face off the bar top for his stupidity. He pretended to be brave because I was alone, but we both knew he'd piss his pants if I wasn't.

Little did *he* know, he was going to piss himself before I was done with him regardless.

"Are you asking for a little incentive?" I chewed on a toothpick and then spit it out, "Because I could be persuaded to give it to you."

His eyes flashed with fear before his buddy nudged him, physically having his back like it would fucking help him.

"Let's have this conversation outside." The VP said, nodding to the door behind me.

"No need, you're going to tell me where your piece of shit President is and then you're going to walk back out that door, unscathed."

He smirked and his pathetic back up spit on the floor in front of my boot. I wasn't wearing my cut, but he knew who I was, but he clearly underestimated my reputation.

A mistake he wouldn't make again.

"Five seconds, VP." I warned, putting my hand in my pocket, "Then I'm going to wipe the floor with your ugly faces and feed you to my dogs for breakfast."

Dogs was a slang term for prospects in the club who needed to prove themselves for their position. They earned their patch with violence and loyalty.

"You're outnumbered, fuck wad." The smart mouth second sneered with a look of amusement in his eyes. "You're all alone and you ain't going to do shit to the three of us." He nodded to the door, "So get on out of here." He turned around to the bar again and smacked his hand on the top, "Get me a beer, old fuck!" He sneered at the barkeep.

The VP and the third shared a glance and decided to let their friend's false bravado lend them bravery.

Mistake.

I grabbed a pool stick from the hands of a man at the table beside me and swung it wide, cracking the wise ass on the back of the head and splitting his head wide open like a ripe melon, splintering the cue into shards as he dropped like dead weight.

And then it was on.

The VP rushed me, breaking a loose beer bottle for a weapon, and swung it at me, swiping for my face. I dodged it and the roundhouse kick from the third before grabbing the VP's arm and twisting it until loud cracks sounded through the silent room. His agonized howls followed after it as I caught the thirds right hook to my cheek and grabbed the back of his head and swung him around to slam his forehead off the bar top, clearing the errant bottles and glasses with his face.

I kicked the back of his knee, dislocating it before throwing him down on the ground where he landed with his head on the brass foot bar under the stools.

I lifted my boot and curb stomped him, splitting his face wide open in a classic American History X move, rendering him completely useless. I turned, feeling the rage and adrenaline rushing through my veins like the Hulk and picked the VP up, slamming his back against the bar and wrapping my hand around his throat, squeezing as he tried to fight me off with his one usable arm.

"I'm only going to ask you once." I hissed, "Tell me where he is, and I'll let you crawl out of here with your life." I looked down where his man laid with a new Joker look on his face, "Unlike your third here." I slammed him backwards again to rattle him more as his face purpled, "Where is Taz?"

He grunted and his lips worked as blood spilled from them. He tried to be brave, but it was useless. He was dead either way.

"Taycot." He gurgled as the lack of air and blood pooling in his throat closed off his windpipe. I released my hand from his neck enough for him to suck in a breath. "Taycot Garbage." He tried again, "Where they store their trucks."

Anger flooded my body at the information, because Stu Taycot was on Eagle payroll, and he was helping the piece of shit that attacked my girl.

The door opened behind me, and my men rushed in, finding the scene before pausing behind me as I threw the man to the floor at their feet.

Houston raised an amused brow at me with a smirk. "Guess you've got everything under control."

"Hmm." I grunted and straightened out my shirt, wiping blood off my boot onto the leg of one of the men. I looked to my right towards the bathroom and froze as I caught Delilah staring at me with horror in her eyes. Her face was white, and her hands were clutched together in front of her. "He knows where Taz is, I'll meet you at the club house in an hour." I glanced at Houston, and he gave me a nod of understanding as he picked up the VP and our others picked up the two less conscious ones.

I walked toward D cautiously and her eyes widened briefly before falling closed completely. I leaned down and whispered, "Outside, and then we can talk."

I went to put my hand on her back and lead her out the side door where her new car was parked, but she turned and bolted out ahead of me, keeping just out of reach.

I scrubbed my hand over my face and followed her, haunted by the look in her eyes back inside as she stared at me in fear.

She climbed into the passenger seat of her car and tucked her knees to her chest silently leaving me to drive. I got in the driver's seat and turned to her, but she wouldn't meet my gaze. "Please look at me."

"I can't." She whispered and then closed her eyes, laying her forehead on her knees. "You were-." She paused, "An entirely different person."

"I was exactly who I have been my entire life, D." I said sadly. "I told you I was the villain."

She lifted her head and finally looked at me. "I've never seen that side of you."

"That was on purpose." I admitted and reached out, praying that she didn't flinch away from my touch. She looked at my hand before staring into my eyes as I gently pushed her hair over her shoulder. "I'm sorry you saw that side of me."

"That's the side that killed JJ, isn't it?"

"Yes."

"And the side that runs with the MC's," She added, not quite asking.

"Yes."

She swallowed and then leaned her face into my touch and grabbed onto my wrist, anchoring herself to me. I sighed in relief and pulled her over the center console into my lap, desperate to close the distance she put between us. "I-." She licked her lips and stared at mine, "I can't explain the feelings inside of me right now."

"You don't have to explain them, D." I assured her, trying to be gentle with her when all I wanted to do was beg and plead for her to love me regardless of the monster that lived inside of me. "I'm sorry." I laid my forehead against her chest as she turned to face me and straddled my thighs.

"You're misunderstanding my reaction, Pax." She whispered, using my legal name like I asked her to. I pulled up and looked at her as she dragged her fingernails over the back of my neck. Her eyes were wide, and her face was flushed.

"You're repulsed and scared baby." I ran my thumbs over the apple of her cheeks, "It's okay, I get it."

"I'm-," She licked her lips, "turned on."

My eyes snapped up from her lips to her gaze in confusion, "What?"

She groaned and rocked her hips in my lap. "Seeing you like that," She hissed and dug her nails into my shoulders, "Watching you make those men fear you," She shook her head as my hands tightened around the back of her neck. "Turned me on so fucking much."

"I thought you were horrified." I was confused as fuck.

"I was horrified at how hot you looked breaking skulls open with hardly any effort at all, baby." She moaned, pressing herself down into my lap, "I don't think I've ever been this turned on towards you before." She bit her lip and her eye lids fluttered closed, "It's animalistic and primal and, Jesus, you're so hot."

She leaned forward and kissed me, pushing her tongue into my mouth and then sucking on mine seductively. "Delilah." I growled, tightening my hands around her waist as she rocked in my lap.

"Touch me baby." She moaned, taking my hands and pushing them under her shirt to grab her breasts over the lace of her bra, "Suck on them, or bite them, or fuck me," She groaned, "Something, please. I need you." She bit my bottom lip until it bled and moaned as she sucked the blood free of it, "I want you to make it hurt."

"Fuck." I grunted, popping open the door of the car and standing with her in my arms. It was dark out and we were parked along the side of the building where the employees parked, shrouded in darkness from the lack luster spotlight over the door. I opened the back seat door and threw her down on it. "Promise me this is what you want?" I demanded, even as I tore at her jeans and pulled them down her legs.

"Yes." She panted, kicking her sneakers off and then pushing her panties down until I held them in my hands. She rolled over and backed up, giving me her ass. "Fuck me so hard, I wear your handprints on my hips."

"You're incredible." I grunted, pulling my rock-hard cock out of my pants and spanking her ass. She moaned loudly, and I looked around outside of the car, we were alone, and my body shielded hers but I still wanted to make sure no one was peeping on our moment. "Back up and take my cock like a good girl."

"Yes!" She moaned, pushing back as I fed my erection into her wet pussy. "So good," She groaned and swayed her hips side to side to stretch herself out. "Deep baby, I need you so fucking deep."

I impaled her, drawing a scream from her lips as my balls touched her lower ones. "Take it." I grunted, reaching around to wrap my hand around her throat and hold her still as I started fucking her hard. "Good girl, such a good fucking girl for Daddy."

"Spank me." She begged, "Pull my hair and fucking ride me, Fox."

She slipped back to using my road name and I loved that when the word was tumbling from her lips, it was in ecstasy. Maybe I'd let her continue to call me that when I was balls deep inside of her like I was now.

I grabbed a fist full of her hair and tightened my hand around her throat, "Such a pretty little slut begging me for more." I dropped the hand from her throat and peppered her ass with my palm over and over again as I kept fucking her and then spit into my palm and rubbed it over her asshole. "I'm going to finger your ass to make you come and you're going to milk my cock dry with this tight pussy. Do you understand me?" I barked and pushed two fingers directly into her ass as she twerked on my cock.

"Yes, Daddy." She moaned and my fist tightened in her hair, pulling her head back until she was bent backwards staring at the roof of the car. I knew the position was probably giving her discomfort in her ribs, but she didn't seem to care. And I was too far gone to stop now. "Fuck that pussy and ass, daddy."

"Slut." I hissed, "Daddy's perfect little slut."

"I'm coming." She gasped but I already knew that thanks to the tight vice grip her ass and pussy had on my cock and fingers. When she was in the deepest part of her orgasm, I hooked my fingers and added a third, scissoring them and stretching her out real good as she screamed and begged for more.

"Milk me," I grunted as my balls tightened up so far, they were nearly inside of me, "Take that come deep baby." I moaned and stilled as my cock pumped jets of my DNA into her waiting womb, trying to let nature do what we were intended to do.

"Yes, yes, yes!" She mewed, sagging against the back seat when I finally released her hair and ran my hands up the length of her spine.

A laugh from inside the building brought me down from my high as reality slipped in through the haze of arousal. I put my cock away and helped her into her jeans, pocketing her panties for myself and then got in the front seat as she climbed through the middle into the passenger seat.

I turned the car on and cranked the A/C to cool down my over heated body as she smirked at me from her seat. "We are never speaking about the last half hour, ever again." She said, glaring at me with what I could only assume was her best mom face and stern voice.

"You mean the part where violence soaked your panties, or when Daddy's cock made you cream?" I grinned at her as she rolled her eyes and covered her face with her hands.

"All of it." Her muffled voice came out from behind her palms.

"Whatever you say," I put the car in drive, "slut."

"Fox." She hissed and then giggled as I pulled out of the parking lot toward the house.

"That's Daddy to you from now on."

Chapter 36 – Delilah

Present

"Are you sure there's nothing we can do to change your mind?" The head of HR sat at the conference table across from me with an easy smile on her face.

"I'm sorry, not at this time." I held firm in my decision to quit.

That morning, I gave my notice to my supervisor, leaving only today and tomorrow on my rotation at Belden Community Hospital. A couple of hours later, HR requested a meeting to convince me to stay.

I was terrified to walk away from the only stability I had managed to hold on to over the last five years. But I knew it was the right move in the end.

Watching Fox make all the changes that he had over the last few days since finding out he was a dad, proved to me that he wasn't taking this lightly. He was staying true to his word to put everything he had into being a dad, which meant I needed to meet his efforts with my own.

"Well," Julie with HR said as she rose from the table and I followed, "If you decide to get back into nursing in the future, we'd love to have you back. Just give me a call if you are looking and we'd be more than happy to get you right back into the rotation."

"I appreciate that," I shook her outstretched hand, "I've enjoyed my time here." She left me with some more pleasantries before I made my exit, returning to the ER for the remainder of my shift.

I texted Lori and officially quit Cherry's, to which she told me she already hired a new bar back after my run in with Taz. Apparently, she'd seen enough in her day behind that bar to know I wasn't coming back.

She was right.

So, I just had to get through today and tomorrow, and I was home free.

"D." Oliver called from the entrance of an exam room, "Can you help me for a sec?" He said and instead of waiting for my reply, he walked back in leaving the door ajar for me.

I sighed and pulled my proverbial big girl panties on and followed after him.

Two more days.

When I walked into the room, I was surprised to find it empty beside the once friendly doctor, though not completely shocked.

"What do you need?" I asked, standing in the open doorway.

"A minute of privacy with you." He said from his relaxed perch against the counter on the other side of the room. "To apologize."

I sighed and looked over my shoulder, locking eyes with Winnie, who watched him call me in here and then walked inside and closed the door behind me.

"I'd rather we just not talk about it at all, to be honest with you, Dr. Franklin." I said first, putting my opinion out in the open.

"I understand that." He nodded and then ran his hand down his face. "But I'm not the person I was the other day, and I need to apologize about that. Or I won't get any rest from the guilt and embarrassment." He gave me a small shrug, "Care to at least listen to help an old friend out?"

I smirked even though I didn't want to, "Two minutes at max." I answered and leaned against the closed door.

"Better than I deserve." He shrugged and then took a deep breath, "First, I was out of line for speaking about Penelope or your ability to parent and keep her safe. There was absolutely no need for me to say that, and I'm appalled that I did."

I swallowed and nodded, uncomfortable at how easy he was making this on me.

He continued, "And second, I let my personal feelings for you, which are obviously not returned, cloud my judgement and make me think I could give my personal opinion on your life when it was clearly not requested." He held my gaze. "I'm sorry for how that made you feel and I'm sorry for any trouble it started between you and Penelope's father."

"I appreciate that." I said sincerely and my shoulders relaxed. "I understand how it might have looked to you on the outside, but Fox is an incredible man. So, you don't have to worry about me or P. We're all good."

"Are you quitting because of me?" He asked sheepishly as he looked at the floor in front of my feet.

"No." I shook my head, "Fox and I need to focus on rebuilding our family and I can't do that with this work schedule."

"He can take care of you and P? What about Maddie?" He asked. I watched the gentle flush of his face as he asked about my sister, and something clicked in my head.

"Maddie's a big girl." I gazed at him closely, "She's almost done with college and then she'll be free to go anywhere she wants. With me not working crazy hours anymore, she'll be free to be a twenty one year old and date and have fun." I smirked as he followed my trail like a hungry puppy. "Maybe even go out on a date with a handsome eligible doctor who stares at her every time she visits her sister at the ER." I shrugged and then laughed as his eyes widened. "Stranger things have happened."

He chuckled and ran his hand over his face. "You see through everything, don't you?"

I shrugged and opened the door, ending the possibility of someone misinterpreting our private conversation. "It's my job as an older sister," He followed me out into the hallway, "and tending bar for years has left me pretty good at reading people."

"Hmm." He mused with a relaxed sigh, "Well, if she were to be interested."

I tipped my head back and laughed, "I'll feel her out and let you know."

"You know where to find me." He winked and walked toward the desk.

I turned and went into the linen closet to restock and smiled to myself, feeling lighter since clearing the air with him.

As I bundled my arms up with sheets to switch over rooms, my phone buzzed in my pocket and I looked at my watch, seeing a number I didn't recognize on it.

So, I did what any twenty-something year old did in that situation; ignored it.

A minute later, it rang again, showing the same number.

"What the hell?" I groaned, putting down my pile of sheets and pulling my phone out. "Hello?"

A familiar smoker's laugh echoed through the line and the hair on the back of my neck stood up. "Well, hey there, D, where the hell ya been?"

"Taz." I put my hand flat on the counter in front of me as my head swam with fear.

"Hmm," He groaned, "My voice on your lips sounds so good, baby."

"What do you want?" I hissed, standing upright as I tried to figure out how to call Fox at the same moment as I was speaking to Taz.

"I want what you took from me." He sneered back and I felt the anger in his voice through the phone.

"I didn't do anything to you. I already told you, the fight with the Eagles wasn't my fault. But you sealed your own death certificate when you attacked me at Cherry's. What the fuck did you expect to happen?"

"You stole my life; I'm on the run like a fucking coward!" He hissed and I swallowed, "You're going to make it right."

"How?" I snapped, "I don't owe you anything, Taz. And you know what? I'm not even going to entertain this conversation for another second."

"Oh, see that'd be a mistake, D." He crooned, "Because if you don't give me what I want, I'm going to take it out of this sweet little angel that looks like her daddy and has your firecracker sass."

My blood ran cold, and I froze solid. "What are you talking about?"

"I wonder what kind of noises Penelope will make when she feels my knife."

"Don't you dare." I whispered as blinding fury raced up my spine.

"You're not really in a great place to make demands, D." He said and then there was a rustling on the other end of the phone before silence.

"Mama?" Penelope's terrified voice carried through the line and my knees gave out. "Mama, are you there?"

"I'm here," I sobbed, covering my mouth as I sank to the floor. "I'm right here, baby."

"Mama, I'm scared."

Tears poured from my eyes as nausea burned in my throat, "Don't be scared, P. Mama's right here. I promise you, you're safe." More rustling and then I heard a hiss and Maddie cry out, "Maddie?" I yelled, "Maddie, talk to me, what's happening?" I pressed my phone so close to my ear, trying to make out the noises on the other end.

"Don't touch her!" My Aunt Suzie screamed, and Penelope cried as Maddie hissed again.

"Taz!" I screamed, "Taz! Don't touch them! Taz!"

I couldn't breathe as panic overtook me, dragging me under into darkness.

His sick laughter filled the phone again as I panted, "God, that sister of yours is a spitfire." He laughed again, and I cried harder. "You with me, D?" He asked when I was silently sobbing on my end, "Should I turn my interest to Penelope to get your attention?"

"What do you want?" I whispered as cold numbness filled my heart.

"I want money. Something I'm told your lover boy has plenty of. You're going to get it for me without letting him know what's going on."

"How am I supposed to get it to you?" I hissed, "I don't have it."

"You're going to use your fucking brain, D." He snapped as his anger surfaced again, "You're going to leave the hospital and go to Fox's house. There's a safe in his office. You're going to clear it out and bring it to me on the ranch. Then I'll let your sweet baby sister, your daughter, and the old bitch go."

"I can't-." I whispered, "I don't know the code." I didn't even know there was a safe in the house, until he told me. How was I supposed to get it open and get to Kansas without Fox knowing.

"You're going to figure it out, D. Or I'm going to rip open your sister and let your daughter watch before I start taking chunks out of her young skin. You have thirty minutes before I check back in, and when I do, you'd better have my fucking money and be on your way. Or I'm going to start carving."

"Please, Taz," I begged. The door to the linen closet opened and I whipped my head around as Oliver walked in with a concerned look on his face. I turned back around, "Please don't do this."

"Twenty-nine minutes, D." He ignored me, "And if you tell your fucking boyfriend, I'm going to take my time with both of them. I'm going to start with my dick first, and then I'll break out my knife." He laughed again as Maddie screamed at him in anger in the background. "Tick tock, baby." Without further delay, the line went dead.

"What's wrong?" Oliver asked as he kneeled down next to me on the ground, pulling my phone away from my ear to look at the unknown number on it. "Delilah," He snapped, "What's going on?"

"I can't-." I whispered and swiped at the tears on my face. "I have to go."

I stood up and my feet worked on autopilot as I pulled myself out of Oliver's arms and ran for the door. "Delilah," He called out after me as I ran blindly to the locker room and grabbed my keys and purse. "Let me help you." He tried again, but I shook my head as he tried to block my path.

"You can't." I whispered, as a sob broke through my lips, "I have to go."

"Where's Fox?" He asked, "What's going on?"

"Don't." I pointed my finger at him, "Don't get involved." I pushed past him and ran out of the side entrance to the employee parking lot as my brain ran into overdrive.

As I cleared the sidewalk, I saw the telltale bulk of Hammer and his smaller counterpart, Tony. They were hanging out on the curb under the shade of a tree a couple of rows over from where I parked, waiting for me.

They watched me every day while I worked so Fox could get stuff done.

Like find Taz.

But Fox never found the slimeball, and Taz had found my daughter and sister instead.

I ducked and ran behind the rows to my new SUV, checking over my shoulder as I got in the driver's seat and started up the engine. Neither of them noticed me as I pulled out of my spot without either of them turning my way. Sweat dripped down my spine and my stomach rolled so violently I rolled the window down in case I needed to vomit before I got to Fox's.

What if he was home?

How was I going to pull it off if he was home?

"Penny!" I cried, punching my fist off the steering wheel over and over again as fear tried to overtake me again.

I had to figure it out, though. I took a deep breath and forced myself to slow my heart rate and breathing down as I wiped the tears off my cheeks and pulled into the driveway of his home.

Our home.

Would he forgive me for this?

I opened the garage door and sagged with relief when I saw his motorcycle was gone from his bay as I pulled into mine. The car had barely stopped as I tore out of the seat and ran inside, towards the office Fox said he hardly ever used.

I looked around the room, trying to find the safe Taz told me would be there, but I couldn't see anything obvious.

"Fuck!" I screamed and started pulling paintings away from the walls and moving furniture in an attempt to find it.

I tore the room apart before a table on the wall rattled like something hit the back of it as I slid it down the wall.

"Yes." I hissed, shoving it even further, revealing a black solid steel safe door behind it.

I fell to my knees in front of it and stared at the electronic keypad as my brain shot random numbers through it like it'd somehow figure it out. "I don't fucking know what it is!" I screamed and hit the door in frustration as I panicked.

"Fucking focus, D." I chided myself and took a deep breath.

I put in Fox's birthdate, crying when it flashed red at me with a beep.

Denied.

I put mine in, hoping and praying, but it turned red again.

Denied.

"Please, please, please." I screamed, pulling my hair in agony.

I typed in the date of Blaine's murder, and it blinked red again.

Denied.

I stared at the ceiling and cried as I felt my daughter's life literally slipping through my fingers.

As a last ditch effort, I started punching in dates to important life events between Fox and I. On the third try, the date of the night he slept in my room for the first time, the keypad blinked green and the locking mechanism clicked.

"Yes!" I pulled the handle and opened it, rifling through the contents and finding an insane amount of stacks of hundred-dollar bills and other important documents. In the back of the safe, behind everything else, there was a pistol.

I picked it up and let the weight of it settle in my palm before pulling the slide back far enough to check to see if it was loaded.

Bingo. The brass round in the chamber both scared me and empowered me. "Please forgive me." I chanted as I cleared every dollar bill from the safe along with the gun and threw them in my oversized purse and ran from the house.

When I got in my car, my hands were shaking so uncontrollably as I sped off down the highway towards my aunt's ranch that when my phone rang through bluetooth, I screamed in fear.

The unknown number flashed across the screen again.

"I have it." I said, in place of answering.

"Good girl." Taz praised, and my skin crawled. "Very good girl. And I'm guessing your old man doesn't have a clue you've robbed him?"

"He doesn't know." I replied, as guilt burned in my chest. "I want to talk to Maddie." I demanded.

"That's not how this works."

"Let me talk to her, Taz, I've got your fucking money and I'm on my way. Now let me talk to my fucking sister!"

"No can-do Buckaroo." He joked and then whistled like he was at the end of a long workday, "I think I'm going to go play with her now as we speak."

"Don't you dare!" I screamed.

"Hurry up, D. Clock's ticking." The line died in my ear, beeping at the end of the call.

I screamed into the windshield in frustration as I put the pedal down, desperately trying to close the distance between me and my family.

I was an hour down the road when my phone rang again, and this time Fox's face lit up the screen on my dash.

Heaven help me.

I was supposed to be at work, which meant the only reason he was calling me was because he knew I wasn't.

I hit accept but stayed silent as I heard his breath through the speakers in the car. "Where are you?" His icy voice rang out loudly in place of a greeting.

"Fox."

"Answer me, D." He demanded and I could feel his anger climbing up my spine. But I couldn't give him what he wanted. "God damnit! Talk to me!"

"I can't."

"Why?" He snapped, "Who called you?"

"What?"

"The closet at work, Delilah, who the fuck called you when you were in the closet at work?"

"How did you—?"

"Oliver!" He snapped, "He came outside after you left and found Tony and Hammer, he told them someone called you and you were crying, begging them not to do something. Then you bolted."

"Fox." I sighed, as fresh tears poured down my face.

I didn't know what to do. I was at a loss, and fear paralyzed me.

"Talk to me, please!" He screamed, "I can't help you if you won't tell me what's going on!"

"He has them." I whispered, afraid that I'd made a giant mistake the second the words crossed my lips.

An eerie silence filled the space for a few seconds. "Has who?" He asked with a cold menace in his voice, which I'd never heard before.

"Penelope." I sobbed as my voice broke, "And Maddie and Aunt Suzie too."

"No." He whispered, and I imagined him shaking his head back and forth. "No, no, no."

"He hurt Maddie," I cried, "I don't know what he was doing to her, but I heard Penny screaming as he did it. He said he'd hurt her next if I didn't do what he said."

"What did he say?"

"He wants money." I choked on my fear and coughed, "Your money."

"Mine?" He questioned, "What did you do?"

"The safe, in your office, he knew about it. He told me to clean it out and meet him at the ranch."

"No," Fox barked, "Don't you fucking dare go there."

"He has Penelope, Fox!" I screamed in frustration. "She screamed for me, begging me to help her! What was I supposed to do?"

"Tell me!" He bellowed, "You were supposed to fucking tell me so I could stop him!"

"He told me if I did, he'd hurt her." I screamed again through my teeth as my heart broke. "I didn't know what else to do."

"Pull over, wherever you are, pull over. I'll meet you."

"I can't." I shook my head and tightened my hands around the steering wheel. "He only gave me barely enough time to get there. He said if I was late, he'd-." The words died on my tongue as nausea rolled again.

"He'd what?"

"He'd torture them."

He screamed and cursed into the phone as more tears fell down my face. "I'm coming."

"No!" I yelled, "You can't. He said he'd hurt them if I told you."

"He's not going to just go away once you give him the money, D! Think about it!" He roared.

"I know." I replied, chewing on my lip before whispering, "I took your gun."

"Oh, my God." He cursed again and then I heard him barking orders to men around him, rallying the troops to come after me.

"I'm going to save our daughter, Fox." I said finally, "I have to, I don't care what it costs me, I have to save her."

"Fuck!"

"I have to go." I said as the turnoff to my next route came into view. "I love you, but I have to keep going."

"I'm coming. I'll be there as soon as I can. The whole club is riding."

"It'll be too late."

"D!" He screamed again but I cut him off.

"I love you, Fox. If something happens to me, you love our little girl with every single thing that you have inside of you, and you tell her how much I loved her, too. Every day." And then I ended the call.

Heaven fucking help me, I had to get there in time to end this all before it was too late.

Chapter 37 – Delilah

Present

I pulled down my Aunt's long driveway to her private ranch as fear and dread tried to consume me. What would I find now that I arrived? What if he had killed them? Or tortured them?

How would they ever heal and forgive me?

I parked outside of the main barn and looked around, but the place seemed deserted, there were no workers or animals milling about. I slid the gun into the waistband of my pants with shaking hands and got out.

"Delilah." Taz called out, and I whipped my head towards the horse barn and saw his greasy face sticking out of the barn door. "Get in here."

I shouldered my heavy purse and followed his commands. As soon as I was close, he grabbed my arm and yanked me into the barn before slamming the door shut behind us and bolting it. "Where are they?" I hissed.

"Shut up." He shoved me forward and pushed me further into the barn with a long, scary-looking knife in his hand. The metal of the blade flashed in the overhead light and crimson blood stained the sharp edge.

"Penelope!" I yelled, "Maddie?"

"I said shut up!" He pushed me again, holding the knife up towards my face as I turned around to fight him. "Let's just get to the point here and then I'll be on my way, eh?" He shoved me again, and I walked through the stalls as curious horses stuck their heads out to see what the commotion was.

When we got to the end of the barn, the largest stall door was open, and I gasped when I saw Maddie and Suzie curled up in the corner with their hands and feet tied together and gags in their mouths.

Maddie's face was bleeding from a laceration on her forehead and her skin was pale. Her white shirt was crimson stained around her stomach. "Maddie!" I yelled and ran to her, sliding my hands over her face as she whimpered and cried into her gag. "I'm sorry." I whispered, looking over at Suzie and finding her mostly unscathed, though anger burned from her eyes towards the man behind me. "Where's P?" I asked, but they both shook their heads and dread poured down my spine like ice water. I turned back to Taz. "Where is my daughter?"

He smirked at me and flicked the knife over the tip of his finger as he stood in the doorway to the stall. "You'll find her when I'm good and gone."

"No." I snapped, standing up on my feet and facing him. "Tell me right now where she is."

"You don't get to make demands!" He screamed, his smirking face contorting with rage. "I'm in charge here, you fucking cunt! Now give me my money!"

I played this exchange in my head over and over again on my way here and I knew if I just gave it to him, it could go one of two ways. He'd either take it and run, or he'd go back on his word and kill us either way.

"Now, Delilah," He barked, taking a step forward, "Pretty little sister there doesn't have much longer with that gut wound I gave her."

I whipped my head back towards her and noticed how her eyes were half-mast and clouded.

Fuck.

I took my purse off my shoulder and dumped the money out onto the stall floor. "Take it." I snapped, "Just tell me where P is and take it and fucking go."

His eyes rounded at the cash that was laid out on the floor, and he eagerly fell to his knees and scooped it up, stuffing it into a bag he pulled out of his waistband while still holding the knife out like I was going to attack him. "This is going to set me up for quite a while, D." He smiled with enthusiasm, and I recoiled.

"Where's Penelope?" I asked again, growing more agitated the longer she was missing while he had what he wanted. "Just tell me where she is, Taz."

He stood up and hoisted the bag over his shoulder and smiled at me. I could read through that smile instantly.

He lied.

"I think I'm going to take the little girl with me for a while, make sure that no one ambushes me on the way out of here or follows me."

"No!" I roared and took a step forward as he took one backward. "That wasn't the deal, Taz."

"You're not in the position to give demands, D." He sneered again and then made a break for it, running out of the stall and slamming the door shut behind him and locking it. I threw myself against the door seconds after he slid it shut and tried desperately to reach the bolt through the bars. "Ha!" He laughed in my face and then ran from the barn.

Maddie and Suzie screamed through their gags as I struggled to reach the lock, finally giving up on it and jumping up to climb over the bars. My side screamed in pain as I scaled the tall wall, but I didn't stop. I had to get out and get him, he couldn't take my baby. He made it out the main door as I cleared the top of the stall and threw myself over, landing in a heap on the ground and taking a second to throw the lock open on the stall door as Aunt Suzie nodded to me, crawling across the floor.

I turned and ran from the barn, chasing Taz in the direction he was running, but when I got outside, I didn't see him anywhere.

I spun in circles as I panted and cried, trying to see him somewhere when my daughter's shrill scream filled the air.

"Penny!" I screamed back, turning and running in the direction it came from.

"Mama!" She screamed again, and I caught a glimpse of her as Taz ran from a shed with her over his shoulder.

I ran as fast as I could, closing the distance until I was close enough to see the fear in her eyes. "Taz, stop!" I shouted as he ran through the tree line, disappearing completely.

"Delilah!" Fox roared from the opposite direction; his truck and a dozen other trucks and bikes tore through the yard. But I didn't stop running.

"He has Penny!" And then I pointed to the barn, hoping someone would tear off and go back, "Maddie's hurt!" I hit the tree line before I could hear his response and covered my face as tree limbs cut my arms and legs, but I didn't stop.

"Penelope!" I screamed and listened to her response, so I knew where to run. "Penny, where are you?"

"Here, Mama!" She yelled back, and I turned a sharp right to follow her. "Hurry!"

"I'm coming!"

My face and arms bled from the sharp branches. Eventually, I hit a clearing and saw Taz trying to shove Penny into a truck he had parked waiting for him. She fought back against him and clung to the doorframe, giving me the precious time I needed to get closer to him.

I pulled the gun from my waistband as the noise crashed through the trees behind me and aimed it at the ground at Taz's feet. I didn't have enough skill with a gun to hit him without potentially hitting Penny, so I aimed at his ankles and fired a shot.

The bullet kicked up dust at his feet, making him flinch, yet he pressed on. He pushed Penny in, and I knew if he got in the truck, I'd lose her.

So, I aimed higher and fired again, this time hitting him in the thigh just as he slid into the driver's seat. He still didn't stop. As I cried out in fear, a blur passed me, racing toward the truck.

Fox.

Taz howled in pain and rounded to face me as Fox slammed into him, punching him in the face before Taz swung his knife back toward Fox's neck. Fox pulled Taz out of the truck and the fight was on.

"Fox!" I screamed in agony and fear, even as I ran around to the other side of the truck. As soon as I was around it, Penelope threw herself out of the passenger side and into my arms. "Oh my God," I sobbed, clutching her tight as she clung to my neck, bawling. I rounded the front of the truck as Houston and the other bikers cleared the tree line and surrounded the fighting men.

Houston walked over to me and held his hands up cautiously as I trembled, watching past his shoulder where Fox and Taz fought for the knife. "Give me the gun, D." Houston said, and I shook my head as confusion burned in my brain before I realized I still clutched the gun in my hand with a death grip. The metallic scent of blood filled my nostrils as my hands trembled; I'd just shot a man.

"Fox." I whispered as Houston covered my hand with his and tore the gun from my seized-up fingers.

"He's fine." Houston said as Taz wailed in pain from behind him. "Don't let her see it." He nodded to Penny, where she still clung to me. I held my hand over the back of her head and tried to soothe her as my eyes found Fox over the hood of the truck just in time to see him plunge Taz's knife into his neck and then tear it to the side, cutting open the man's entire throat.

Violent heaves of revulsion rolled through me as I cringed and buried my face in Penny's hair at the same moment that my legs gave out as the adrenaline wore off. I fell to my ass as the fear of it all overcame me and tears poured down my face. "Are you okay, baby?" I asked, pulling back and prying her face out of my neck to look her over. "Are you hurt?"

She shook her head as tears poured out of her, "I'm scared." She whispered, and I sighed and let her crawl back in against my neck.

"Where are they?" Fox bellowed from where he just killed Taz and Houston waved his hand over the hood to him.

Fox ran around and stared down at me with eyes wide with fear, hesitating a few feet away from me as he stared at his tiny daughter in my arms for the first time.

"She's okay." I stuttered, gasping for breath still. "She's okay." I repeated, like I was trying to convince myself at the same time.

He looked down and saw the blood he wore on the front of his shirt and his busted knuckles and grimaced, tearing the flannel off and wiping his hands off on it before tossing it aside.

His white tee shirt was clean of any crimson stains, and he raked his hand through his hair hesitantly.

"Let's give them a minute." Houston said to the other bikers as they backed up to give us space.

Fox was frozen stiff though, so I held my hand out for him, and he took it, falling to his knees at my side, bouncing his eyes back and forth between me and the back of Penny's head.

He lifted his hand and faltered an inch over her hair before gently running it over the brown locks that matched his perfectly. She jolted at his touch and then slowly pulled her face from my neck to look at the man kneeling at her side, staring at her in such wonder.

I watched the array of emotions cross his face as she pulled back further to look at him and I prayed she wouldn't fear him at the moment.

"Penny baby," I said gently, running my hand over her back, "This is—."

"Prince Charming." She said with such wonder in her voice and my heart completely fell into my stomach at the sweet memory of that day she saw his picture for the first time.

Fox's face relaxed as he sagged in relief and tried to give her a small smile. Tears pooled in his bright hazel eyes as he stared into his daughter's for the first time.

"You saved me." She whispered in awe, "You took him out of the truck so he couldn't hurt me. You're just like a brave knight."

"That's right, baby." I agreed excitedly, squeezing her even tighter as such joy flooded my heart. "He's not Prince Charming though, sweetie," I swallowed as Fox looked at me over her head, "He's your Dad." I said gently, leaning around to see the look on her face.

Her lips pulled into a big smile as she looked at me and then back to Fox. "Really?"

He nodded and swallowed, "Would that be okay with you? Would it be alright if I was your Dad?"

"Yes!" She nodded her head eagerly, "I've always wanted one."

I tipped my head back and laughed, with sweet relief and joy from her innocent opinion, and Fox chuckled.

Houston came around the truck and cleared his throat, uncomfortable at breaking up the moment, but nodded to Fox, "Cops and ambulance are here."

Fox nodded back and looked at me as reality burned through the shock of everything that had happened.

"Maddie." I gasped, standing up with Penny in my arms as Fox put his hands under my arms to help.

"Slow down," He commanded with his cool power and pushed my hair back off my face, "You're hurt." My face stung from the scrapes on it, but I didn't care.

I shook my head, "No, she is," I licked my lips and pushed Penelope's head back into my neck, covering her ear, "He stabbed her."

Houston interrupted again, "The Ken doll Doc is with her. She should be okay."

"The who?" I questioned in confusion.

"Oliver." Fox rolled his eyes before sighing, "He rode with us, refused to stay behind after he ratted you out."

"Jesus." I groaned at having him see this side of my life and Fox glared at me, so I clarified, "He has the hots for Maddie." I shook my head and took a step to walk out to the barn and check on my sister. "Long story, I'll tell you all about it someday."

But my legs were jelly, and fatigue had set in from the emotional roller coaster I'd been on for the last four hours.

"Jeeze, D." Fox hissed, catching me as I started falling.

Penny pulled back to look at me, "Are you okay, Mama?" She asked with her tiny little eyebrows pinched over her tired eyes.

Everything my daughter experienced today would follow her for the rest of her life, and that broke my heart. "Yeah, baby," I smiled to her, "Mama's just tired from running so hard to get you."

"Can Daddy carry me?" She asked, looking up at Fox. "So, Mama doesn't drop me."

The smile that broke over his face was something I'd never imagined seeing from him before in my life. Now that I had, I wanted to see it every second of every day. "I'd love to." He said, holding his hands out as she all but threw herself into his strong arms, tucking her face into his neck like she had mine.

So trusting.

So loving.

So natural, like she knew in her soul that he was hers.

Tears pooled in my eyes for the millionth time, and I shook my head as glee filled my heart. I'd remember the moment for the rest of my life, and it would sit in the top five best ones forever.

"Let's go get you checked out." Fox wrapped his arm around my waist and pulled me against his side, holding most of my weight up as we walked wide of the dead body spilling blood onto the barren ground beneath it, so Penny didn't see it and then through the trees back out to the clearing of the ranch.

Cop cars and ambulances lined the driveway, parked around a dozen abandoned vehicles that the Black Eagles rode in on.

My step faltered when the cops' eyes turned to us as we neared and the realization that Fox had just killed a man a couple hundred yards away dawned on me. "Don't worry." He said soothingly as he kissed the top of my head. "I'm not going to leave your side." I tilted my head back to look up at him as he stared down at me, with understanding in his eyes, "Never again."

"Promise me." I whispered, looking at my daughter in his arms as fear grew in my heart.

"I promise you." He kissed my forehead as an older cop walked forward with my Aunt Suzie at his side.

"Is she okay?" Suzie asked lovingly, at where Penny clung to Fox's neck still.

I nodded solemnly, "Physically, yes. How about you?"

Her jaw clenched and anger bloomed in her eyes, "I wish I had gotten my hands on that son of a bitch." She cursed, ignoring her normal rule to keep bad language away from kids, and given the circumstances, she was allowed.

"Easy, Suzie." The cop patted my Aunt's shoulder affectionately and her cheeks blushed even as her anger bristled.

Was there something romantic going on between them?

"I'm Sheriff Dodge." The cop introduced himself, holding his hand out for Fox to shake, who did so strongly. "Mind giving me a condensed version of what happened here today?"

"Is my sister okay?" I ignored his request and gave my own.

Suzie nodded, "The pretty boy said she'd be okay, though if he gives her any more attention, she might melt into a puddle." She shrugged, "The EMT's are getting her loaded up now to take her to the hospital."

The answer sufficed me for the time being, and Fox shifted Penny in his arms to run his free hand down the back of my neck. "Taz attacked D a week ago at her work, broke her ribs and then took off. He went into hiding and we couldn't find him. Until today when he called D, telling her he had the girls here and demanded that she show up with cash in exchange for their safety."

The cop eyed me and pursed his lips, "And I'm guessing you didn't call the cops."

I stiffened, "His orders were pretty clear."

He nodded and sighed, looking back at Fox. "So how did you all end up in the woods?"

I filled in my part, "When I got here, he had Maddie and Suzie in the barn, tied up. He said I'd get Penny back when I gave him the money. But then he locked us in the stall and said he was going to take her with him for insurance." I cringed, feeling Penny stiffen, "I took off after him as he ran into the woods to get away with her." I swallowed the bile down in my throat, "I couldn't let him get away or I'd never see her again, I knew that."

"What about the gunshots?" The Sheriff eyed me. "Heard those rolling onto the scene."

"I shot a warning at his feet as he fought to get her in his truck, and then another into his leg when he got her in and went to drive away."

"Is he?" He eyed Penny and shrugged, avoiding the word.

"Not from a gunshot wound." Fox answered for me. "Even with the hit to his leg, he had a knife to my daughter when I got to him. We fought, and he tried slashing me with it, but I got the upper hand and ended it."

"With the knife?" The sheriff asked for clarification.

"Yes."

The man looked around at the dozens of menacing bikers standing around, "And that's it?"

"Isn't that enough?" Suzie argued. "I know what you're thinking Tom," She hissed, "Not for one second is my niece or her boyfriend guilty of anything but self-defense. They had no choice but to save Penny. The same thing you'd do if it was one of your grandbabies that you dote on." She glared at him, and the Sheriff's scowl relaxed, and I knew she had him.

"I'd like to get to my sister now," I said, in a way to end the conversation. "I'm sure anything you have to follow up on can be done at the hospital."

He smirked and shook his head, "I see the family resemblance." He looked at Suzie and then nodded, backing up to let us pass. "I'll be in contact."

"Let's go," Fox said, steering us towards the ambulance parked outside of the barn with a nod to Houston. Bikes roared to life around us and the club members got on and left, avoiding any more interaction with the police now that the initial risk to Fox was gone.

EMT's rolled my sister out on a gurney towards the waiting ambulance as we neared, and I ran forward, taking her hand in mine as she opened her eyes and started crying. "I'm so sorry, D." She said, pulling the oxygen mask down to talk, "I tried to keep her safe."

"Shh," I smoothed my hand over her head, "She's fine." I moved, and she looked behind me as Fox walked up with Penny in his arms, who peeked out at her aunt lying on the stretcher.

"Thank God," My sister sank back with a sigh of relief and then I noticed Oliver holding her other hand on the other side of her.

"Thank you for taking care of her." I said to him with shame that he was needed at all.

"Don't even worry about it, Delilah," He nodded with a smirk, "I've already called ahead and got privileges, so I'll be with her in surgery too." He looked down at my sister, "I've got her."

I looked at the way my sister blushed before looking back over at me like she was looking for permission to let the man take care of her.

"No better hands than yours, Doc." I smiled reassuringly and patted Maddie on the shoulder. "We'll be there waiting when you get out."

"Please don't," She cringed and tried to sit up in the stretcher, "Take P home where she's comfortable and safe and I'll see you when I come home."

"Maddie-."

"No, D." She argued, "She needs to be home, with her mom and dad." She said pointedly and Fox's hand slid over the back of my neck again, "I'm fine."

"She's right," Suzie said, joining us, "Take P home and get some rest and I'll keep you updated."

"I'll have her transferred to Belden if she's going to be admitted for more than a day or two." Oliver added, giving his attention to Fox, "Take your family home man, take care of them."

"Planned on it, Doc." He replied and pulled me back so the EMT's could wheel her into the ambulance. "Let's get you two home."

"Our home?" I asked hopefully, because I wanted to take our daughter to the place where we were going to start our life together as soon as possible. I didn't want any reminders of what happened today haunting us in the future.

"No place I'd rather be, baby." He grinned and steered me toward my car.

Chapter 38 – Fox

Present

I stood in the doorway to the guest room in my home that had been empty for almost an entire year.

Yet now my daughter was sleeping peacefully in the center of the big king size bed surrounded by every spare pillow in the joint and covered up with sparkly unicorn blankets and rainbow-colored stuffed animals. Three different nightlights lit up the room with a kaleidoscope of rainbow lights and a sound machine hummed quietly from the nightstand.

I had never felt more fulfilled than I did in the moment.

"She's okay, Fox." Delilah whispered from behind me as she wrapped her arms around my stomach and laid her cheek against the center of my back.

"I'm not." I replied honestly, hating how it made me feel to admit.

"Come on," D pulled me out of the doorway and silently closed the door behind her and nudged me down the hallway.

I only went because I knew there was a camera monitor sitting on the kitchen counter with a perfect view of our daughter from the other room.

If not, there wasn't a chance in hell that I'd have left her side. I slept in a lot of shitty places over the years, and on the floor of my daughter's bedroom on a plush ass carpet wasn't a hardship to me at all.

But I also needed to see to Delilah's needs, too.

We stopped by their house on our way home from Kansas and packed a couple of bags of clothes and shit ton of kid's stuff for P to be able to make her new home as comfortable as possible.

"I can't explain to you what it feels like to be here, with her." She sighed and laid her head against my chest as I wrapped my arms around her. "I hate that I let my life darken hers more, but I'm happy to have this moment with both of you, nonetheless."

"I died a million deaths today, baby." I whispered, squeezing her tighter. "I don't know how to cope with this overwhelming sense of uncontrolled fear running through me right now. Like a million different things could go wrong at any second and she could be harmed by them. Both of you could."

She chuckled and rubbed her nose against my sternum, "Welcome to parenthood. And it never stops."

"Ugh," I groaned and ran my hand through her hair, catching snarls and pieces of tree still embedded in the locks. "Let's go take a bath." I suggested grabbing the monitor off the counter as I led her towards our room across the living room.

"I'm too tired." She yawned and leaned into me further, cringing slightly from the soreness in her body. We had been home for a few hours, and I watched the fatigue and stress of the day settle into her muscles, causing her to cringe and limp more and more as the night wore on.

"I'll take care of you." I kissed her temple and started the water in the bathtub as she sat down on the stool at the vanity. I poured lavender bubble bath in that I picked up the same day I bought her new car and added some salts to ease her soreness.

When I turned around, she was gazing up at me with her bottom lip tucked between her teeth.

Wicked girl.

I grabbed the back of my collar and pulled my shirt off over my head and tossed it into the hamper in the corner as I slowly walked over to her. "Do you have any idea how unbelievably sexy you are?" She asked, leaning back to look up at me as I stopped in front of her. "It's painful almost to look at you because the second I do my body turns to mush and an inferno burns in my belly, demanding that I convince you to fuck me somehow."

I chuckled and lowered myself to my knees at her feet, "It never takes any convincing for me to fuck you, and you know that."

She smirked and lifted her arms for me to pull her top off, gentle of her side and the scrapes on her forearms. A bruise bloomed on her shoulder, and I leaned forward, laying gentle kisses on it as I undid her bra and slid it off her arms. And even in the most tender of moments like the one we were sharing, my cock hardened in my jeans at how beautiful she was, regardless of her wounds.

"It just takes tits apparently," She smirked and sat up straighter to push them out. I palmed them both and ran my thumbs over her nipples before leaning down and kissing both gently.

"Apparently." I joked and pulled her to her feet in front of me so I could continue undressing her. I leaned in and kissed her feminine stomach and lingered, resting my forehead against her breasts and took a deep breath. "Think you're ovulating yet?" I asked, and then looked up at her.

She smirked and rolled her eyes, "Who knows," Before running her fingers through my hair, "We both know you're going to fill me up with come before we go to sleep just in case I am."

I snorted and kissed her stomach once more before kissing the enormous bruise that covered her entire hip from flinging herself over the top of the stall door eight feet onto the concrete floor, before standing and unbuttoning my own jeans. "Take me out, minx." If I didn't distract myself, I'd go to a dark place, seeing all the wounds and bruises to her body from today's events.

"Happily." She smiled and pushed my jeans and boxers down.

I wanted to distract us both and just take a minute to be calm and peaceful. When I stood naked before her, she kissed my chest over my sternum and let her fingertips trail down my abs to the sensitive skin right above my cock.

It bobbed and jerked at her gentle, teasing touch until I pulled her hands away and laced mine through them.

"You killed a man again today for me." She whispered, tilting her head back to look up at me. "With violence unmatched and unrestrained." I swallowed down the fear and uncertainty that her words bloomed in my chest and let her continue. "And as I think back on it, as I remember how you ripped him to pieces to protect our daughter," She hummed and cocked her head to the side, "I'm filled with nothing but need for you."

"D." I growled, tightening my fingers through hers.

"I ache to reward you, praise you, and worship you for it. I long to take your cock and milk you dry, while begging for another baby so I can watch you protect them like you do Penny." She moaned and rubbed her hardened nipples against my stomach. "It's animalistic, and primal and yet I've never wanted anything more than to scream to the sky how badly I burn for you."

"I'll make you scream for me, baby." I growled, bringing our joined hands to wrap around the length of my cock and stroked it together, "Get in the tub so I can loosen you up and make you limp before I push inside of you. I want you relaxed and nearly comatose before you come."

She smiled as I held her hand and steadied her as she sank into the steaming bath before following her in. I pulled her back against my chest and wrapped my legs around her, pulling them wide under the water.

"I almost lost you two today." I whispered and ran a washcloth over her arms and shoulders.

"I know." She sighed, leaning into my touch. "I'm sorry."

"Hmm." I hummed, because she didn't need me to acknowledge how she lied to me, stole from me and then ran away from me.

I tipped her head backward and poured a cup of water over it and then lathered it up with shampoo, gently massaging her scalp with my fingertips and working it through the shafts of her hair. "God, you're good at this."

"Perk of dating someone who had long hair." I smiled as she moaned when I got to her neck and let her head flop forward. "Lay back." I supported her neck, and she dunked her head in the water as I gently washed the shampoo out. When she sat back up, I started over with the conditioner, and her movements got looser and more exaggerated as my relaxation technique took hold.

"Will you ever grow it back out for me?" She asked when I was done and pulled her back into my arms to rest her head against my shoulder.

"My hair?" I asked, and she hummed, "I don't know."

"You liked it long though, right? You grew it out that way twice that I know of."

"Yeah, but I was a different person then," I ran my fingertips from her wrists to shoulders and back, "I'm a dad now, something about that doesn't mix for me."

"Hmm." She slid her fingertips up the back of my neck to the back of my head, turning hers into my jaw, "I miss having it to hold on to when you're in between my thighs."

"Trouble," I said, nipping her shoulder and running my hands flat down her stomach to the legs in question. "Spread them for me."

"Yes, Sir." She whispered and hooked her knees over mine, letting me hold her open as I lifted her to sit on my lap.

Her nipples popped above the top of the water, and I pinched one as my other hand soothingly circled her clit before dipping into her. "I want Penelope's last name to be St. Claire before we have another baby, because her sibling will have it from birth." It hurt knowing she gave Penelope her last name on her birth certificate, even if I understood it. The irrational part of my brain ached for my baby girl to have my name though.

"Yeah," She panted, tightening her hold on the back of my neck, "I agree."

"And I want your last name to be St. Claire at the same time."

"Paxton," She moaned and rocked against my hand.

"Say it." I purred into her ear as I used my palm on her clit and pinched her nipple. "Say yes."

"You didn't ask." She argued halfheartedly, making me smile.

I turned her quickly, pulling my fingers and lips from her body as she whined until I laid her across my lap, straddling my thighs with my cock pinned against her clit. Her hips flexed instinctively, and her head dropped against mine. "Delilah Faith Beckett," I gently spoke against her lips as I lifted her up until the crown of my cock nestled between her pussy lips, "Will you marry me and start our family off the right way?"

I pushed up into her body as she gasped and her eyes rolled in her head, "Yes." She wrapped her hands around the back of my neck and held on as I lowered her onto my cock completely, bringing her forehead mine, "God, yes. Yes. Yes. Yes." She moaned repeatedly.

"Good girl." I growled when she rose and pushed back down onto me, drawing the breath from my lungs with her tight pussy. "Now be a good girl and milk Daddy's cock so we can put another baby inside of you and give sweet Penny a baby sister or brother."

"Yes," She hissed almost deliriously, "Fuck me, Daddy."

Epilogue – Delilah

"Mama, are you alright?" Penelope asked me as she came in from the backyard, when she found me swaying with the fridge in the kitchen.

"Peachy, June bug." I said through gritted teeth. "Where's your Daddy?"

Her little head cocked to the side as she eyed me, walking around the sofa to take a closer look at me. "Outside, rinsing off the quads with Ollie," She stopped right next to me as my back seized up in another heinous contraction.

"Of course he is, darling." I smiled through the pain, "With his phone tucked somewhere safe from the water," I groaned, dropping the façade, "and my hundreds of phone calls." I cradled my stomach as pain erupted through my side as another contraction hit again already. I looked at the clock over the stove.

Two minutes in between.

Not good, considering how fast Penny's labor went.

"Baby, go get him."

"Is something wrong?" She asked, eyeing the way I held my stomach.

"Mmh, tell him your baby brother is on his way." I gritted out, and she squealed with excitement, jumping up and down before turning and running from the house.

"Daddy!" She screamed at the door on her way out.

"Hey, D!" Maddie called from the garage door leading up to her studio apartment, and I pressed my forehead against the fridge, holding my finger up to her as she rounded the corner. "Uh-oh."

She only needed one look at me to know what was going on, having been my birth partner for Penelope. "Yep." I popped the 'p' and then groaned as my water broke all over the floor underneath of my sundress.

Last time, my water broke a couple of minutes before I pushed, and fear burned in my gut as the pain ramped up almost instantly.

"No, no, no," I groaned, "Not again," I cried as I realized I was more than likely not going to get an epidural again.

"Shh, it's okay," Maddie said gently, pulling me away from the mess on the floor as I hummed through the pain. "How long apart are they?"

"Two minutes or less."

"Okay," She said, smiling excitedly, "We're doing this today then."

"I don't want to." I whined pathetically, I'd been excited for the arrival of our son for months now, but in that moment, fear and pain took the excitement away.

"I know." She ran her hands over my arms as I wrapped them over her shoulders and leaned on her, swaying again. "But there's no back button, you know that. So, we're going to get Fox," She trailed off and started patting her pockets for her phone.

"Penny just ran for him. I've been calling him for a half an hour, but he was out on those death traps with Ollie." I hissed, and she flinched at the anger in my voice aimed at her boyfriend.

Pretty boy Ken doll Doc had wooed my sister while she was under his care, showing up here for 'follow up' check ins after she was released until she gave in and let him take her out on a date. Now he was my husband's most unlikely best friend, and they hung out constantly.

It was so fucking weird.

"Delilah," My husband's voice boomed from the patio door as I was wracked with another contraction.

"Kitchen, Fox," Maddie called out as he, Penny, and Oliver, aka Ollie, ran inside.

"Baby," Fox's strong arms pulled me from my sister until I leaned on him like I had been with her.

"Back." I hissed, hating how close to tears I was in the moment, "My back."

"I got you," He put his big hands on my hips and squeezed, putting the perfect amount of pressure on them and I groaned in satisfaction and took a deep breath for the first time since the contractions really started. "I'm right here."

"I'm scared." I whispered, not wanting to frighten Penelope, even as tears tracked down my cheeks into his shirt. He smelled like sunshine and sweat, and I focused on the combination and groaned as he gave me such relief with his hands.

"I know sweetie, but I'm right here. Let's get you in the truck and we'll go to the hospital."

I shook my head and cried harder as I acknowledged what I'd been trying to avoid. "I don't think there's time."

"Talk it down to me, D." Oliver said, stepping forward as an emergency medicine doctor and I actually appreciated the clinical approach at the moment. Because I could focus on the facts and forget the fear if I looked at it that way.

"My water broke a few minutes ago, contractions are less than two minutes apart. Penny's labor was only two hours long, start to finish," I pulled up to look at the clock again, "And I've been having them for forty-five minutes now."

"Do you want me to check you, then we can decide if you can make the trip or not?"

"Fuck no." Fox snapped at his friend, and I felt his body bristle under me, but I bit down on his shoulder as another contraction burned straight up my back, letting his shirt muffle my scream of pain.

"Fox," Oliver tried gently.

"No, don't think I won't knock you on your ass just because we're friends, man," Fox hissed, "You're not touching her there."

"It doesn't matter," I snapped, and then grunted as my body started pushing on its own with my next breath, "He's coming! God, he's coming."

"Fuck." Fox hissed, and I could hear the fear in his voice. This was his first birth, even though it was baby number two for us.

"I'll get my med bag. Maddie, get towels and Fox, get her on the ground."

I trembled and screamed through my teeth as the pain turned blinding, like our son was trying to walk out through my belly button instead of through the birth canal. Everyone snapped into motion. Fox laid me down on the kitchen floor and held my head in the crook of his arm as Maddie ran around throwing towels down next to us. Seconds later, Penelope slid her unicorn pillow under my head before backing up in fear.

"I'm okay PJ." I tried to calm myself for her as tears welled up in her eyes, "This is sometimes how births happen, it's okay."

"Come here, darling," Fox pulled her down next to him at the top of my head and put my hand in hers, letting her be a part of it, which we had already discussed doing under normal circumstances. I just hadn't planned on it being on the kitchen floor, home birth style. "Are you excited to meet your brother?" He asked her, and she nodded eagerly.

Oliver kneeled down at my feet and risked a glance at Fox before gloving up and lifting the hem of my dress up and cutting off my underwear.

I groaned in mortification and then my body started pushing again, not even giving me the choice to participate or not.

"You're right, D, he's right there." Oliver said and Fox leaned down to see and cursed, paling a bit. "On the next one, I want you to go ahead and push for me. Push hard and we'll get him out in no time." Maddie slid down to her knees next to him with every towel in the house and smiled brightly at me with excitement coursing through her.

"This is all so exciting still." She smirked, and I flipped her off.

Fox leaned down to kiss my forehead, "I'm so proud of you baby." He said against my temple, smoothing back my hair.

"I love you." I replied and kissed him, forcing myself to take some calming breaths and bask in the moment with him. "You were the only thing I wanted during PJ's birth, and I'm so happy that you're here now. Thank you."

"I wouldn't be anywhere else, baby." He tightened his hold on my shoulders, and I tensed as another contraction started.

"Fox, lift her leg, Maddie, grab the other," Oliver instructed, and he looked at me over the swell of my belly. "Give me all you got, D."

"Yep." I groaned and tucked my chin to my chest and pushed with everything in me.

"Good job!" Maddie cheered and handed Oliver what he needed as he asked for it, "You're doing so good."

"His head is out," Oliver said, and Fox leaned over to look again, in complete shock of the whole situation.

"Jesus, baby." Fox said, smiling down at me in awe, "You're doing it."

I gasped for breath and smiled back to him as tears rolled down my cheeks.

"Again, D." Oliver instructed, and Fox lifted my shoulders back off the pillow, supporting me as I tried to catch my breath before bearing down again. "Good job, now wait." He said as he manipulated the shoulders out, "Hold on, D, relax. Don't push."

"Yep." I groaned, trying to hide my agony from Penny and Fox as my body rebelled against waiting. "I can't," I gasped, "I can't stop."

"Okay," Oliver nodded, "Ready, go for it, one last push and he'll be out."

"That's it baby, you can do it." Fox cheered, and I pushed one more time and our son was born, screaming and swinging his fists in anger the second he was free.

I cried in joy hearing his angry little voice as Oliver smiled brightly and laid my red-faced baby on my chest. I cried as he screamed, clearing his lungs and rooting around on my chest in anger. It was such a surreal moment; even having done it before, I was in awe of my body's capabilities. Fox cupped his giant hand over the babe's head, running his thumb over his wrinkled forehead and our son stopped crying instantly, opening his eyes and looking up at the big man leaning over him.

I knew in reality that our son couldn't see Fox yet, thanks to newborns terrible eyesight, but as I stared up at my husband's awe-struck face, I didn't have the heart to tell him. He was experiencing a moment that no one could put into words until you felt it firsthand, and I wasn't going to interrupt it.

I looked over my head and saw Penny staring down at the baby with a matching look of shock and wonder in her eyes. "Come here, sweetie." I held my hand out for her, and she scooted closer as Fox wrapped his arm around her and tucked her against his side. "Meet your little brother."

"He's so tiny." She whispered and Fox took her finger, holding it out for our son to grasp and smiled brightly when he squeezed onto it tightly, pulling her hand to his chest.

"He loves you so much already." Fox said, pleasingly. He looked at me over her head and I sighed, feeling contentment like no other fill my soul as he leaned down and kissed me thoughtfully as I cradled the babe. "I'm so proud of you, D. I've never loved you more than I do in this exact moment."

I beamed up at him and kissed him back.

"So, what's the name going to be?" Oliver asked to distract me as he continued caring for me in the middle of my kitchen floor like it was the most normal thing in the world.

"Blaine Paxton St. Claire," Fox said proudly, kissing Penelope's head as she giggled at the babe cooing loudly as he rooted around for milk.

Maddie's eyes glossed over as she sat back, giving us a moment, but I reached out and pulled her close, "Blaine would have been so proud to see your beautiful family grow, babe." She hummed affectionately. "And I'm honored to be a part of it all."

"We're honored to have you, Maddie. We never would have made it here to this point without your support and dedication to me and Penny." I reassured her, and she scoffed and brushed it off.

"I can't wait to spoil him rotten with PJ," She bopped Penny's nose with her finger and then stood up. "Okay, let's get you up off the floor and cleaned up."

"That'd be great." I chuckled, "I'm never going to look at this floor the same ever again."

"Me either," Oliver widened his eyes, and I smirked at him.

"Thanks for being here and helping out." Because truth be told, I enjoyed his friendship now that he was happily in love with my sister and without him here today, annoying me with the quads in the backyard, I would have had to talk Fox and Maddie through delivering little Paxton. And I was not ready for that anatomy lesson, so I was glad to skip it all together.

Epilogue – Fox

"**S**he's finally asleep." I yawned as I stumbled into our bedroom hours later. Penelope had been on such a high, and worried about missing a single second of the joys of big sisterhood, that getting her to sleep had been a two-hour event.

But the fatigue I'd felt moments ago melted away when I crawled into bed beside my beautiful wife, where she sat nursing my son.

My son.

Children.

Plural.

What a fucking mind trip to fall down into when I gave it the time of day.

But now was not that time because I was experiencing something I'd daydreamed of since the first time I'd imagined Delilah as a mom. She smiled sleepily at me as Paxton nursed eagerly from her breast. "He's a big boy." She smiled down at him, "He's going to be hard to keep fed until my milk comes in all the way."

"When do you think that will happen?" Breastfeeding was such a foreign concept for me, but I wanted to be supportive and helpful to anything she needed from me while she traversed such a challenging chapter in life.

"Should be in the next day or two." She giggled when Paxton pulled off and let out a whine before going back in for more. "Please let it be soon,"

"He's going to be big like me."

"No doubt," She smirked, "He's going to out eat you during his teenage years, we should probably buy some cows now."

I laughed and laid my head on the headboard next to her to stare down at our boy. "Thank you. Again."

She kissed my forehead, lingering there to breathe in deeply, "Thank you for giving me the gift of motherhood, Fox." She whispered. "Without you, I wouldn't have them."

"Same." I mused, "I love you, darling."

"Who would have thought six years ago when you snuck into my bedroom one night and sat in the chair next to my bed to watch over me while I slept that we'd be here. In this beautiful home, with two perfect babies and completely fulfilled. We have Maddie close by, and she's happy and thriving with a good man and our friends are good to us, if not a bit smelly," She joked about the guys from the club.

Even though I had taken a step back from the MC, I was still active. I ran day to day shit from afar and kept members in line, lending my skull splitting skills when needed.

But they were good to my family. Hammer and Tony, two misfits that never belonged anywhere before, had taken to D when they were on patrol, watching over her when Taz was on the run and they managed to worm their way into her heart. More times than a few I'd come home and one or both of them would be lounging around on my couch watching cartoons with P or getting their nails painted by her as they just soaked in her innocence and happiness.

In the MC world, a little sunshine in the middle of the dark night was exactly what we as dangerous men needed from time to time.

And I had a house full of it now.

My phone buzzed on the end table, and I opened it up, finding a message from the man that helped me pull off the biggest game of chance in my life.

"Who's that?" Delilah asked, never looking up from her task.

"Colt." I uttered. "He's looking to move to Belden."

"Really?" She questioned excitedly, "What on earth would make him want to leave Rawlins and come here?"

"I don't know." I closed the app and set my phone down on the end table. "My guess is the same thing that brought me here." I kissed her forehead, "Sunshine and happiness."

She smiled and leaned into my embrace, "We do seem to have a lot of that these days."

The End.

Other Books

Did you know Ally writes across so many other types of tropes and themes?

Check out some of her other books here.

Looking for Series and Duets?

The Line Walkers Series:
https://a.co/d/bx376wq
Beauty In the Ink Series:
https://a.co/d/6tc8M7M
Bailey Dunn & Co Duet:
https://a.co/d/i9gwqL2
Shadeport Crew Series:
https://a.co/d/dVzGcyo
Kings of Hawthorn Series:
https://a.co/d/h1AITKM

How about some spicy standalones?

<u>Sinister Vows:</u>
https://a.co/d/gbe35fF
<u>Guilty For You:</u>
<u>https://a.co/d/1ef3UPU</u>
<u>Secrets Within Us:</u>
https://a.co/d/cTZ04XQ